Collected Short Stories Featuring Doctor John Thorndyke Volume 2

Collected Short Stories Featuring Doctor John Thorndyke
Thirteen Criminal Investigations of an Edwardian Forensic Scientist

Volume 2

R. Austin Freeman

Collected Short Stories Featuring
Doctor John Thorndyke
Thirteen Criminal Investigations of an Edwardian Forensic Scientist
Volume 2
by R. Austin Freeman

FIRST EDITION IN THIS FORMAT

Leonaur is an imprint
of Oakpast Ltd

Copyright in this form © 2024 Oakpast Ltd

ISBN: 978-1-916535-92-3 (hardcover)
ISBN: 978-1-916535-93-0 (softcover)

http://www.leonaur.com

Publisher's Notes

The views expressed in this book are not necessarily those of the publisher.

Contents

A Fisher of Men	7
A Mystery of the Sand-Hills	29
The Trail of Behemoth	47
The Stranger's Latchkey	69
The Seal of Nebuchadnezzar	89
The Naturalist at Law	109
The Mysterious Visitor	133
The Man with the Nailed Shoes	151
The Case of the White Footprints	195
The Aluminium Dagger	225
The Mandarin's Pearl	249
The Blue Scarab	275
The Case of Oscar Brodski	297

A Fisher of Men

"The man," observed Thorndyke, "who would successfully practise the scientific detection of crime must take all knowledge for his province. There is no single fact which may not, in particular circumstances, acquire a high degree of evidential value; and in such circumstances success or failure is determined by the possession or non-possession of the knowledge wherewith to interpret the significance of that fact."

This *obiter dictum* was thrown off *apropos* of our investigation of the case rather magniloquently referred to in the press as "The Blue Diamond Mystery;" and more particularly of an incident which occurred in the office of our old friend, Superintendent Miller, at Scotland Yard. Thorndyke had called to verify the few facts which had been communicated to him, and having put away his notebook and picked up his green canvas-covered research-case, had risen to take his leave, when his glance fell on a couple of objects on a side-table—a leather handbag and a walking-stick, lashed together with string, to which was attached a descriptive label.

He regarded them for a few moments reflectively and then glanced at the superintendent.

"Derelicts?" he inquired, "or jetsam?"

"Jetsam," the superintendent replied, "literally jetsam—thrown overboard to lighten the ship."

Here Inspector Badger, who had been a party to the conference, looked up eagerly.

"Yes," he broke in. "Perhaps the doctor wouldn't mind having a look at them. It's quite a nice little problem, doctor, and entirely in your line."

"What is the problem?" asked Thorndyke.

"It's just this," said Badger. "Here is a bag. Now the question is, whose bag is it? What sort of person is the owner? Where did he come from and where has he gone to?"

Thorndyke chuckled. "That seems quite simple," said he. "A cursory inspection ought to dispose of trivial details like those. But how did you come by the bag?"

"The history of the derelicts," said Miller, "is this: About four o'clock this morning, a constable on duty in King's Road, Chelsea, saw a man walking on the opposite side of the road, carrying a handbag. There was nothing particularly suspicious in this, but still the constable thought he would cross and have a closer look at him. As he did so the man quickened his pace and, of course, the constable quickened his. Then the man broke into a run, and so did the constable, and a fine, stern chase started. Suddenly the man shot down a by-street, and as the constable turned the corner he saw his quarry turn into a sort of alley. Following him into this, and gaining on him perceptibly, he saw that the alley ended in a rather high wall.

"When the fugitive reached the wall he dropped his bag and stick and went over like a harlequin. The constable went over after him, but not like a harlequin—he wasn't dressed for the part. By the time he got over, into a large garden with a lot of fruit trees in it, my nabs had disappeared. He traced him by his footprints across the garden to another wall, and when he climbed over that he found himself in by-street. But there was no sign of our agile friend. The constable ran up and down the street to the next crossings, blowing his whistle, but of course it was no go. So he went back across the garden and secured the bag and stick, which were at once sent here for examination."

"And no arrest has been made?"

"Well," replied Miller with a faint grin, "a constable in Oakley Street who had heard the whistle arrested a man who was carrying a suspicious-looking object. But he turned out to be a cornet player coming home from the theatre."

"Good," said Thorndyke. "And now let us have a look at the bag, which I take it has already been examined?"

"Yes, we've been through it," replied Miller, "but everything has been put back as we found it."

Thorndyke picked up the bag and proceeded to make a systematic inspection of its exterior.

"A good bag," he commented; "quite an expensive one originally, though it has seen a good deal of service. You noticed the muddy marks on the bottom?"

"Yes," said Miller. "Those were probably made when he dropped the bag to jump over the wall."

"Possibly," said Thorndyke, "though they don't look like street mud. But we shall probably get more information from the contents." He opened the bag, and after a glance at its interior, spread out on the table a couple of sheets of foolscap from the stationery rack, on which he began methodically to deposit the contents of the bag, accompanying the process with a sort of running commentary on their obvious characteristics.

"Item one: a small leather dressing-wallet. Rather shabby, but originally of excellent quality. It contains two Swedish razors, a little Washita hone, a diminutive strop, a folding shaving-brush, which is slightly damp to the fingers and has a scent similar to that of the stick of shaving soap. You notice that the hone is distinctly concave in the middle and that the inscription on the razors, 'Arensburg, Eskilstuna, Sweden,' is partly ground away. Then there is a box containing a very dry cake of soap, a little manicure set, a well-worn toothbrush, a nail-brush, dental-brush, button-hook, corn-razor, a small clothes-brush and a pair of small hairbrushes. It seems to me, Badger, that this wallet suggests—mind, I only say 'suggests'—a pretty complete answer to one of your questions."

"I don't see how," said the inspector. "Tell me what it suggests to you."

"It suggests to me," replied Thorndyke, laying down the lens through which he had been inspecting the hair-brushes, "a middle-aged or elderly man with a shaven upper lip and a beard; a well-preserved, healthy man, neat, orderly, provident and careful as to his appearance; a man long habituated to travelling, and—though I don't insist on this, but the appearances suggest that he had been living for some time in a particular households and that at the time when he lost the bag, he was changing his residence."

"He was that," cackled the inspector, "if the constable's account of the way he went over that wall is to be trusted. But still, I don't see how you have arrived at all those facts."

"Not facts, Badger," Thorndyke corrected. "I said suggestions. And those suggestions may be quite misleading. There may be some factor, such as change of ownership of the wallet, which we have not allowed for. But, taking the appearances at their face value, that is what they suggest. There is the wallet itself, for instance—strong, durable, but shabby with years of wear. And observe that it is a travelling-wallet and would be subjected to wear only during travel. Then further, as to the time factor, there are the hone and the razors. It takes a good many years to wear a Washita hone hollow or to wear away the blade of a Swedish razor until the maker's mark is encroached on.

"The state of health, and to some extent the age, are suggested by the tooth brush and the dental-brush. He has lost some teeth, since he wears a plate, but not many; and he is free from pyorrhoea and alveolar absorption. You don't wear a toothbrush down like this on half a dozen rickety survivors. But a man whose teeth will bear hard brushing is probably well-preserved and healthy."

"You say that he shaves his upper lip but wears a beard," said the inspector. "How do you arrive at that?"

"It is fairly obvious," replied Thorndyke. "We see that he has razors and uses them, and we also see that he has a beard."

"Do we?" exclaimed Badger. "How do we?"

Thorndyke delicately picked a hair from one of the hairbrushes and held it up. "That is not a scalp hair," said he. "I should say that it came from the side of the chin."

Badger regarded the hair with evident disfavour. "Looks to me," he remarked, "as if a small tooth-comb might have been useful."

"It does," Thorndyke agreed, "but the appearance is deceptive. This is what is called a moniliform hair—like a string of beads. But the bead-like swellings are really parts of the hair. It is a diseased, or perhaps we should say an abnormal, condition." He handed me the hair together with his lens, through which I examined it and easily recognised the characteristic swellings.

"Yes," said I, "it is an early case of *tricliorrexis nodosa*."

"Good Lord!" murmured the inspector. "Sounds like a Russian nobleman. Is it a common complaint?"

"It is not a rare disease—if you can call it a disease," I replied, "but it is a rare condition, taking the population as a whole."

"It is rather a remarkable coincidence that it should happen to occur in this particular case," the superintendent observed.

"My dear Miller," exclaimed Thorndyke, "surely your experience must have impressed on you the astonishing frequency of the unusual and the utter failure of the mathematical laws of probability in practice. Believe me, Miller, the bread-and-butterfly was right. It is the exceptional that always happens."

Having discharged this paradox, he once more dived into the bag, and this time handed out a singular and rather unsavoury-looking parcel, the outer investment of which was formed by what looked like an excessively dirty towel, but which, as Thorndyke delicately unrolled it, was seen to be only half a towel which was supplemented by a still dirtier and excessively ragged coloured handkerchief. This, too, being opened out, disclosed an extremely soiled and rather frayed collar (which, like the other articles, bore no name or mark), and a mass of grass, evidently used as packing material.

The inspector picked up the collar and quoted reflectively, "He is a man, neat, orderly and careful as to his appearance," after which he dropped the collar and ostentatiously wiped his fingers.

Thorndyke smiled grimly but refrained from repartee as he carefully separated the grass from the contained objects, which turned out to be a small telescopic jemmy, a jointed auger, a screwdriver and a bunch of skeleton keys.

"One understands his unwillingness to encounter the constable with these rather significant objects in his possession," Thorndyke remarked. "They would have been difficult to explain away." He took up the heap of grass between his hands and gently compressed it to test its freshness. As he did so a tiny, cigar-shaped object dropped on the paper.

"What is that?" asked the superintendent. "It looks like a chrysalis."

"It isn't," said Thorndyke. "It is a shell, a species of *Clausilia*, I think." He picked up the little shell and closely examined its mouth through his lens. "Yes," he continued, "it is a *Clausilia*. Do you study our British *mollusca*, Badger?"

"No, I don't," the inspector replied with emphasis.

"Pity," murmured Thorndyke. "If you did, you would be interested to learn that the name of this little shell is *Clausilia biplicata*."

"I don't care what its beastly name is," said Badger. "I want to know whose bag this is; what the owner is like; and where he came from and where he has gone to. Can you tell us that?"

Thorndyke regarded the inspector with wooden gravity. "It is all very obvious," said he, "very obvious. But still, I think I should like to fill in a few details before making a definite statement. Yes, I think I will reserve my judgment until I have considered the matter a little further."

The inspector received this statement with a dubious grin. He was in somewhat of a dilemma. My colleague was addicted to a certain dry facetiousness, and was probably pulling the inspector's leg. But, on the other hand, I knew, and so did both the detectives, that it was perfectly conceivable that he had actually solved Badger's problem, impossible as it seemed, and was holding back his knowledge until he had seen whither it led.

"Shall we take a glance at the stick?" said he, picking it up as he spoke and running his eye over its not very distinctive features. It was a common ash stick, with a crooked handle polished and darkened by prolonged contact with an apparently ungloved hand, and it was smeared for about three inches from the tip with a yellowish mud. The iron shoe of the ferrule was completely worn away and the deficiency had been made good by driving a steel boot-stud into the exposed end.

"A thrifty gentleman, this," Thorndyke remarked, pointing to the stud as he measured the diameter of the ferrule with his pocket calliper-gauge. "Twenty-three thirty-seconds is the diameter," he added, looking gravely at the inspector. "You had better make a note of that, Badger."

The inspector smiled sourly as Thorndyke laid down the stick, and once more picking up the little green canvas case that contained his research outfit, prepared to depart.

"You will hear from us, Miller," he said, "if we pick up anything that will be useful to you. And now, Jervis, we must really take ourselves off."

As the tinkling hansom bore us down Whitehall towards Waterloo, I remarked, "Badger half suspects you of having withheld from him some valuable information in respect of that bag."

"He does," Thorndyke agreed with a mischievous smile; "and he doesn't in the least suspect me of having given him a most illuminating hint."

"But did you?" I asked, rapidly reviewing the conversation and deciding that the facts elicited from the dressing-wallet could hardly be described as hints.

"My learned friend," he replied, "is pleased to counterfeit obtuseness. It won't do, Jervis. I've known you too long."

I grinned with vexation. Evidently I had missed the point of a subtle demonstration, and I knew that it was useless to ask further questions; and for the remainder of our journey, in the cab I struggled vainly to recover the "illuminating hint" that the detectives—and I—had failed to note. Indeed, so preoccupied was I with this problem that I rather overlooked the fact that the jettisoned bag was really no concern of ours, and that we were actually engaged in the investigation of a crime of which, at present, I knew practically nothing. It was not until we had secured an empty compartment and the train had begun to move that this suddenly dawned on me; whereupon I dismissed the bag problem and applied to Thorndyke for details of the "Brentford Train Mystery."

"To call it a mystery," said he, "is a misuse of words. It appears to be a simple train robbery. The identity of the robber is unknown, but there is nothing very mysterious in that; and the crime otherwise is quite commonplace. The circumstances are these:

"Some time ago, Mr. Lionel Montague, of the firm, Lyons, Montague & Salaman, art dealers, bought from a Russian nobleman a very valuable diamond necklace and pendant. The peculiarity of this necklace was that the stones were all of a pale blue colour and pretty accurately matched, so that in addition to the aggregate value of the stones—which were all of large size and some very large—was the value of the piece as a whole due to this uniformity of colour. Mr. Montague gave £70,000 for it, and considered that he had made an excellent bargain.

"I should mention that Montague was the chief buyer for the firm, and that he spent most of his time travelling about the Continent in search of works of art and other objects suitable for the purposes of his firm, and that, naturally, he was an excellent judge of such things. Now, it seems that he was not satisfied with the settings of this necklace, and as soon as he had purchased it he handed it over to Messrs. Binks, of Old Bond Street, to have the settings replaced by others of better design. Yesterday morning he was notified by Binks that the resetting was completed, and in the afternoon he called to inspect the work and take the necklace away if it was satisfactory.

"The interview between Binks and Montague took place in a room behind the shop, but it appears that Montague came out into the shop to get a better light for his inspection and Mr. Binks states that as his customer stood facing the door, examining the new settings, he, Binks, noticed a man standing by the doorway furtively watching Mr. Montague."

"There is nothing very remarkable in that," said I. "If a man stands at a shop door with a necklace of blue diamonds in his hand, he is rather likely to attract attention."

"Yes," Thorndyke agreed. "But the significance of an antecedent is apt to be more appreciated after the consequences have developed. Binks is now very emphatic about the furtive watcher. However, to continue: Mr. Montague, being satisfied with the new settings, replaced the necklace in its case, put the latter into his bag—which he had brought with him from the inner room—and a minute or so later left the shop. That was about 5 p.m.; and he seems to have gone direct to the flat of his partner, Mr. Salaman, with whom he had been staying for a fortnight, at Queen's Gate. There he remained until about half-past eight, when he came out accompanied by Mr. Salaman. The latter carried a small suit-case, while Montague carried a handbag in which was the necklace. It is not known whether it contained anything else.

"From Queen's Gate the two men proceeded to Waterloo, walking part of the way and covering the remainder by omnibus."

"By omnibus!" I exclaimed, "with seventy thousand pounds of diamonds about them!"

"Yes, it sounds odd. But people who habitually handle portable property of great value seem to resemble those who habitually handle explosives. They gradually become unconscious of the risks. At any rate, that is how they went, and they arrived safely at Waterloo in time to catch the 9.15 train for Isleworth. Mr. Salaman saw his partner established in an empty first-class compartment and stayed with him, chatting, until the train started.

"Mr. Montague's destination was Isleworth, in which rather unlikely neighbourhood Mr. Jacob Lowenstein, late of Chicago, and now of Berkeley Square, has a sort of river-side villa with a motor boat-house attached. Lowenstein had secured the option of purchasing the blue diamond necklace, and Montague was taking it down to exhibit it and carry out the deal. He was proposing to stay a few days with Lowenstein, and then he was proceeding to Brussels on one of his periodic tours. But he never reached Isleworth. When the train stopped at Brentford, a porter noticed a suit-case on the luggage-rack of an apparently empty first-class compartment.

"He immediately entered to take possession of it, and was in the act of reaching up to the rack when his foot came in contact with something soft under the seat. Considerably startled, he stooped and peered under, when, to his horror, he perceived the body of a man, quite motionless and apparently dead. Instantly he darted out and rushed up the platform in a state of wild panic until he, fortunately, ran against the station master, with whom and another porter he returned to the compartment. When they drew the body out from under the seat it was found to be still breathing, and they proceeded at once to apply such restoratives as cold water and fresh air, pending the arrival of the police and the doctor, who had been sent for.

"In a few minutes the police arrived accompanied by the police surgeon, and the latter, after a brief examination, decided that the unconscious man was suffering from the effects of a large dose of chloroform, violently and unskilfully administered, and ordered him to be carefully removed to a local nursing home. Meanwhile, the police had been able, by inspecting the contents of his pockets, to identify him as Mr. Lionel Montague."

"The diamonds had vanished, of course?" said I.

"Yes. The handbag was not in the compartment, and later an empty handbag was picked up on the permanent way between Barnes and Chiswick, which seems to indicate the locality where the robbery took place."

"And what is our present objective?"

"We are going, on instructions from Mr. Salaman, to the nursing home to see what information we can pick up. If Montague has recovered sufficiently to give an account of the robbery, the police will have a description of the robber, and there may not be much for us to do. But you will have noticed that they do not seem to have any information at Scotland Yard at present, beyond what I have given you. So there is a chance yet that we may earn our fees."

Thorndyke's narrative of this somewhat commonplace crime, with the discussion which followed it, occupied us until the train stopped at Brentford Station. A few minutes later we halted in one of the quiet by-streets of this old-world town, at a soberly painted door on which was a brass plate inscribed "St. Agnes Nursing Home." Our arrival had apparently been observed, for the door was opened by a middle-aged lady in a nurse's uniform.

"Dr. Thorndyke?" she inquired; and as my colleague bowed assent she continued: "Mr. Salaman told me you would probably call. I am afraid I haven't very good news for you. The patient is still quite unconscious."

"That is rather remarkable," said Thorndyke.

"It is. Dr. Kingston, who is in charge of the case, is somewhat puzzled by this prolonged stupor. He is inclined to suspect a narcotic—possibly a large dose of morphine—in addition to the effects of the chloroform and the shock."

"He is probably right," said I; "and the marvel is that the man is alive at all after such outrageous treatment."

"Yes," Thorndyke agreed. "He must be pretty tough. Shall we be able to see him?"

"Oh, yes," the matron replied. "I am instructed to give you every assistance. Dr. Kingston would like to have your opinion on the case."

With this she conducted us to a pleasant room on the first floor, where, in a bed placed opposite a large window—left uncurtained—with the strong light falling full on his face, a man lay with closed eyes, breathing quietly and showing no sign of consciousness when we somewhat noisily entered the room. For some time Thorndyke stood by the bedside, looking down at the unconscious man, listening to the breathing and noting its frequency by his watch. Then he felt the pulse, and raising both eyelids, compared the two pupils.

"His condition doesn't appear alarming," was his conclusion. "The breathing is rather shallow, but it is quite regular, and the pulse is not bad though slow. The contracted pupils strongly suggest opium, or more probably morphine. But that could easily be settled by a chemical test. Do you notice the state of the face, Jervis?"

"You mean the chloroform burns? Yes, the handkerchief or pad must have been saturated. But I was also noticing that he corresponds quite remarkably with the description you were giving Badger of the owner of the dressing-wallet. He is about the age you mentioned—roughly about fifty—and he has the same old-fashioned treatment of the beard, the shaven upper lip and the monkey-fringe under the chin. It is rather an odd coincidence."

Thorndyke looked at me keenly. "The coincidence is closer than that, Jervis. Look at the beard itself."

He handed me his lens, and, stooping down, I brought it to bear on the patient's beard. And then I started back in astonishment; for by the bright light I could see plainly that a considerable proportion of the hairs were distinctly moniliform. This man's beard, too, was affected by an early stage of *trichorrexis nodosa!*

"Well!" I exclaimed, "this is really an amazing coincidence. I wonder if it is anything more."

"I wonder," said Thorndyke. "Are those Mr. Montague's things, Matron?"

"Yes," she replied, turning to the side table on which the patient's effects were neatly arranged. "Those are his clothes and the things which were taken from his pockets, and that is his bag. It was found on the line and sent on here a couple of hours ago. There is nothing in it."

Thorndyke looked over the various objects—keys, card-case, pocket-book, etc.—that had been turned out of the patient's pockets, and then picked up the bag, which he turned over curiously and then opened to inspect the interior. There was nothing distinctive about it. It was just a plain, imitation leather bag, fairly new, though rather the worse for its late vicissitudes, lined with coarse linen to which two large, wash-leather pockets had been roughly stitched. As he laid the bag down and picked up his own canvas case, he asked: "What time did Mr. Salaman come to see the patient?"

"He came here about ten o'clock this morning, and he was not able to stay more than half an hour as he had an appointment. But he said he would look in again this evening. You can't stay to see him, I suppose?"

"I'm afraid not," Thorndyke replied; "in fact we must be off now, for both Dr. Jervis and I have some other matters to attend to."

"Are you going straight back to the chambers, Jervis?" Thorndyke asked, as we walked down the main street towards the station.

"Yes," I replied in some surprise. "Aren't you?"

"No. I have a little expedition in view."

"Oh, have you?" I exclaimed, and as I spoke it began to dawn on me that I had overestimated the importance of my other business.

"Yes," said Thorndyke "the fact is that—ha! excuse me one moment, Jervis." He had halted abruptly outside a fishing-tackle shop and now, after a brief glance in through the window, entered with an air of business. I immediately bolted in after him, and was just in time to hear him demand a fishing-rod of a light and inexpensive character. When this had been supplied he asked for a line and one or two hooks; and I was a little surprised—and the vendor was positively scandalised—at his indifference to the quality or character of these appliances. I believe he would have accepted cod-line and a shark-hook if they had been offered.

"And now I want a float," said he.

The shopkeeper produced a tray containing a varied assortment of floats over which Thorndyke ran a critical eye, and finally reduced the shopman to stupefaction by selecting a gigantic, pot-bellied scarlet-and-green atrocity that looked like a juvenile telegraph buoy.

I could not let this outrage pass without comment. "You must excuse me, Thorndyke," I said, "if I venture to point out that the Greenland whale no longer frequents the upper reaches of the Thames."

"You mind your own business," he retorted, stolidly pocketing the telegraph buoy when he had paid for his purchases. "I like a float that you can see."

Here the shopman, recovering somewhat from the shock of surprise, remarked deferentially that it was a long time since a really large pike had been caught in the neighbourhood; whereupon Thorndyke finished him off by replying: "Yes, I've no doubt. They don't use the right sort of floats, you know. Now, when the pike see my float, they will just come tumbling over one another to get on the hook." With this he tucked the rod under his arm and strolled out, leaving the shopman breathing hard and staring harder.

"But what on earth," I asked, as we walked down the street (watched by the shopman who had come out on the pavement to see the last of us), "do you want with such an enormous float? Why, it will be visible a quarter of a mile away."

"Exactly," said Thorndyke. "And what more could a fisher of men require?"

This rejoinder gave me pause. Evidently Thorndyke had something in hand of more than common interest; and again it occurred to me that my own business engagements were of no special urgency. I was about to mention this fact when Thorndyke again halted—at an oilshop this time.

"I think I will step in here and get a little burnt umber," said he.

I followed him into the shop, and while the powder-colour was being weighed and made up into a little packet I reflected profoundly. Fishing-tackle and burnt umber had no obvious associations. I began to be mystified and correspondingly inquisitive.

"What do you want the burnt umber for?" I asked as soon as we were outside.

"To mix with plaster," he replied readily.

"But why do you want to colour the plaster? And what are you going to do with it?"

"Now, Jervis," he admonished with mock severity, "you are not doing yourself justice. An investigator of your experience shouldn't ask for explanations of the obvious."

"And why," I continued, "did you want to know if I was going straight back to the chambers?"

"Because I may want some assistance later. Probably Polton will be able to do all that I want, but I wished to know that you would both be within reach of a telegram."

"But," I exclaimed, "what nonsense it is to talk of sending a telegram to me when I'm here!"

"But I may not want any assistance, after all."

"Well," I said doggedly, "you are going to have it whether you want it or not. You've got something on and I'm going to be in it."

"I like your enthusiasm, Jervis," he chuckled; "but it is quite possible that I shall merely find a mare's nest."

"Very well," said I. "Then I'll help you to find it. I've had plenty of experience in that line, to say nothing of my natural gifts. So lead on."

He led on, with a resigned smile, to the station, where we were fortunate enough to find a train just ready to start. But our journey was not a long one, for at Chiswick Thorndyke got out of the train, and on leaving the station struck out eastward with a very evident air of business. As we entered the outskirts of Hammersmith he turned into a by-street which presently brought us out into Bridge Road. Here he turned sharply to the right and, at the same brisk pace, crossed Hammersmith Bridge and made his way to the towing path. As he now slowed down perceptibly, I ventured to inquire whether this was the spot on which he proposed to exhibit his super-float.

"This, I think, will be our fishing-ground," he replied; "but we will look over it carefully and select a suitable pitch."

He continued to advance at an easy pace, and I noticed that, according to his constant habit, he was studying the peculiarities of the various feet that had trodden the path within the last day or two, keeping, for this purpose on the right-hand side, where the shade of a few pollard willows overhanging an indistinct dry ditch had kept the ground soft. We had walked on for nearly half a mile when he halted and looked round.

"I think we had better turn back a little way," said he. "We seem to have overshot our mark."

I made no comment on this rather mysterious observation, and we retraced our steps for a couple of hundred yards, Thorndyke still walking on the side farthest from the river and still keeping his eyes fixed on the ground. Presently he again halted, and looking up and down the path, of which we were at the moment the only occupants, placed the canvas case on the ground and unfastened its clasps.

"This, I think, will be our pitch," said he.

"What are you going to do?" I asked.

"I am going to make one or two casts. And meanwhile you had better get the fishing-rod fixed together so as to divert the attention of any passers-by."

I proceeded to make ready the fishing-tackle, but at the same time kept a close watch on my colleague's proceedings. And very curious proceedings they were. First he dipped up a little water from the river in the rubber mixing bowl with which he mixed a bowlful of plaster, and into this he stirred a few pinches of burnt umber, whereby its dazzling white was changed to a muddy buff. Then, having looked up and down the path, he stooped and carefully poured the plaster into a couple of impressions of a walking-stick that were visible at the edge of the path and finished up by filling a deep impression of the same stick, at the margin of the ditch, where it had apparently been stuck in the soft, clayey ground.

As I watched this operation, a sudden suspicion flashed into my mind. Dropping the fishing-rod, I walked quickly along the path until I was able to pick up another impression of the stick. A very brief examination of it confirmed my suspicion. At the centre of the little shallow pit was a semicircular impression—clearly that of a half-worn boot-stud.

"Why!" I exclaimed, "this is the stick that we saw at Scotland Yard!"

"I should expect it to be and I believe it is," said Thorndyke. "But we shall be better able to judge from the casts. Pick up your rod. There are two men coming down the path."

He closed his "research-case" and drawing the fishing-line from his pocket, began meditatively to unwind it.

"I could wish," said I, "that our appearance was more in character with the part of the rustic angler; and for the Lord's sake keep the float out of sight, or we shall collect a crowd."

Thorndyke laughed softly. "The float," said he, "was intended for Polton. He would have loved it. And the crowd would have been rather an advantage—as you will appreciate when you come to use it."

The two men—builder's labourers, apparently—now passed us with a glance of faint interest at the fishing-tackle; and as they strolled by I appreciated the value of the burnt umber. If the casts had been made of the snow-white plaster they would have stared conspicuously from the ground and these men would almost certainly have stopped to examine them and see what we were doing. But the tinted plaster was practically invisible.

"You are a wonderful man, Thorndyke," I said, as I announced my discovery. "You foresee everything."

He bowed his acknowledgments, and having tenderly felt one of the casts and ascertained that the plaster had set hard, he lifted it with infinite care, exhibiting a perfect facsimile of the end of the stick, on which the worn boot-stud was plainly visible, even to the remains of the pattern. Any doubt that might have remained as to the identity of the stick was removed when Thorndyke produced his calliper-gauge.

"Twenty-three thirty-seconds was the diameter, I think," said he as he opened the jaws of the gauge and consulted his notes. He placed the cast between the jaws, and as they were gently slid into contact, the index marked twenty-three thirty-seconds.

"Good," said Thorndyke, picking up the other two casts and establishing their identity with the one which we had examined. "This completes the first act." Dropping one cast into his case and throwing the other two into the river, he continued: "Now we proceed to the next and hope for a like success. You notice that he stuck his stick into the ground. Why do you suppose he did that?"

"Presumably to leave his hands free."

"Yes. And now let us sit down here and consider why he wanted his hands free. Just look around and tell me what you see."

I gazed rather hopelessly at the very indistinctive surroundings and began a bald catalogue. "I see a shabby-looking pollard willow, an assortment of suburban vegetation, an obsolete tin saucepan—unserviceable—and a bald spot where somebody seems to have pulled up a small patch of turf."

"Yes," said Thorndyke. "You will also notice a certain amount of dry, powdered earth distributed rather evenly over the bottom of the ditch. And your patch of turf was cut round with a large knife before it was pulled up. Why do you suppose it was pulled up?"

I shook my head. "It's of no use making mere guesses."

"Perhaps not," said he, "though the suggestion is fairly obvious when considered with the other appearances. Between the roots of the willow you notice a patch of grass that looks denser than one would expect from its position. I wonder—"

As he spoke, he reached forward with his stick and prised vigorously at the edge of the patch, with the result that the clump of grass lifted bodily; and when I picked it up and tried it on the bald spot, the nicety with which it fitted left no doubt as to its origin.

"Ha!" I exclaimed, looking at the obviously disturbed earth between the roots of the willow, which the little patch of turf had covered; "the plot thickens. Something seems to have been either buried or dug up there; more probably buried."

"I hope and believe that my learned friend is correct," said Thorndyke, opening his case to abstract a large, powerful spatula.

"What do you expect to find there?" I asked.

"I have a faint hope of finding something wrapped in the half of a very dirty towel," was the reply.

"Then you had better find it quickly," said I, "for there is a man coming along the path from the Putney direction."

He looked round at the distant figure, and driving the spatula into the loose earth stirred it up vigorously.

"I can feel something," he said, digging away with powerful thrusts and scooping the earth out with his hands. Once more he looked round at the approaching stranger—who seemed now to have quickened his pace but was still four or five hundred yards distant. Then, thrusting his hands into the hole, he gave a smart pull. Slowly there came forth a package, about ten inches by six, enveloped in a portion of a peculiarly filthy towel and loosely secured with string. Thorndyke rapidly cast off the string and opened out the towel, disclosing a handsome morocco case with an engraved gold plate.

I pounced on the case and, pressing the catch, raised the lid; and though I had expected no less, it was with something like a shock of surprise that I looked on the glittering row and the dazzling cluster of steely-blue diamonds.

As I closed the casket and deposited it in the green canvas case, Thorndyke, after a single glance at the treasure and another along the path, crammed the towel into the hole and began to sweep the loose earth in on top of it. The approaching stranger was for the moment hidden from us by a bend of the path and a near clump of bushes, and Thorndyke was evidently working to hide all traces before he should appear. Having filled the hole, he carefully replaced the sod of turf and then, moving over to the little bare patch from whence the turf had been removed, he began swiftly to dig it up.

"There," said he, flinging on the path a worm which he had just disinterred, "that will explain our activities. You had better continue the excavation with your pocket knife, and then proceed to the capture of the leviathans. I must run up to the police station and you must keep possession of this pitch. Don't move away from here on any account until I come back or send somebody to relieve you. I will hand you over the float; you'll want that." With a malicious smile he dropped the gaudy monstrosity on the path, and having wiped the spatula and replaced it in the case, picked up the latter and moved away towards Putney.

At this moment the stranger reappeared, walking as if for a wager, and I began to peck up the earth with my pocket-knife.

As the man approached he slowed down by degrees until he came up at something like a saunter. He was followed at a little distance by Thorndyke, who had turned as if he had changed his mind, and now passed me with the remark that "Perhaps Hammersmith would be better." The stranger cast a suspicious glance at him and then turned his attention to me.

"Lookin' for worms?" he inquired, halting and surveying me inquisitively.

I replied by picking one up (with secret distaste) and holding it aloft, and he continued, looking wistfully at Thorndyke's retreating figure: "Your pal seems to have had enough."

"He hadn't got a rod," said I; "but he'll be back presently."

"Ah!" said he, looking steadily over my shoulder in the direction of the willow. "Well, you won't do any good here. The place where they rises is a quarter of a mile farther down—just round the bend there. That's a prime pitch. You just come along with me and I'll show you."

"I must stay here until my friend comes back," said I. "But I'll tell him what you say."

With this I seated myself stolidly on the bank and, having flung the baited hook into the stream, sat and glared fixedly at the preposterous float. My acquaintance fidgeted about me uneasily, endeavouring from time to time to lure me away to the "prime pitch" round the bend. And so the time dragged on until three-quarters of an hour had passed.

Suddenly I observed two taxicabs crossing the bridge, followed by three cyclists. A minute or two later Thorndyke reappeared, accompanied by two other men, and then the cyclists came into view, approaching at a rapid pace.

"Seems to be a regular procession," my friend remarked, viewing the new arrivals with evident uneasiness. As he spoke, one of the cyclists halted and dismounted to examine his tyre, while the other two approached and shot past us. Then they, too, halted and dismounted, and having deposited their machines in the ditch, they came back towards us. By this time I was able—with a good deal of surprise—to identify Thorndyke's two companions as Inspector Badger and Superintendent Miller. Perhaps my acquaintance also recognised them, or possibly the proceedings of the third cyclist—who had also laid down his machine and was approaching on foot—disturbed him. At any rate he glanced quickly from the one group to the other and, selecting the smaller one, sprang suddenly between the two cyclists and sped away along the path like a hare.

In a moment there was a wild stampede. The three cyclists, remounting their machines, pedalled furiously after the fugitive, followed by Badger and Miller on foot. Then the fugitive, the cyclists, and finally the two officers disappeared round the bend of the path.

"How did you know that he was the man?" I asked, when my colleague and I were left alone.

"I didn't, though I had pretty strong grounds for suspicion. But I merely brought the police to set a watch on the place and arrange an ambush. Their encircling movement was just an experimental bluff; they might have been chary of arresting the fellow if he hadn't taken fright and bolted. We have been fortunate all round, for, by a lucky chance, Badger and Miller were at Chiswick making inquiries and I was able to telephone to them to meet me at the bridge."

At this moment the procession reappeared, advancing briskly; and my late adviser marched at the centre securely handcuffed. As he was conducted past me he glared savagely and made some impolite references to a "blooming nark."

"You can take him in one of the taxis," said Miller, "and put your bicycles on top." Then, as the procession moved on towards the bridge he turned to Thorndyke. "I suppose he's the right man, doctor, but he hasn't got any of the stuff on him."

"Of course he hasn't," said Thorndyke.

"Well, do you know where it is?"

Thorndyke opened his case and taking out the casket, handed it to the superintendent. "I shall want a receipt for it," said he.

Miller opened the casket, and at the sight of the glittering jewels both the detectives uttered an exclamation of amazement, and the superintendent demanded: "Where did you get this, sir?

"I dug it up at the foot of that willow."

"But how did you know it was there?"

"I didn't," replied Thorndyke; "but I thought I might as well look, you know," and he bestowed a smile of exasperating blandness on the astonished officer.

The two detectives gazed at Thorndyke, then they looked at one another and then they looked at me; and Badger observed, with profound conviction, that it was a 'knock-out.'

"I believe the doctor keeps a tame clairvoyant," he added.

"And may I take it, sir," said Miller, "that you can establish a *prima facie* case against this man, so that we can get a remand until Mr. Montague is well enough to identify him?"

"You may," Thorndyke replied. "Let me know when and where he is to be charged and I will attend and give evidence."

On this Miller wrote out a receipt for the jewels and the two officers hurried off to their taxicab, leaving us, as Badger put it, "to our fishing."

As soon as they were out of sight, Thorndyke opened his case and mixed another bowlful of plaster. "We want two more casts," said he; "one of the right foot of the man who buried the jewels and one of the right foot of the prisoner. They are obviously identical, as you can see by the arrangement of the nails and the shape of the new patch on the sole. I shall put the casts in evidence and compare them with the prisoner's right boot."

I understood now why Thorndyke had walked away towards Putney and then returned in rear of the stranger. He had suspected the man and had wanted to get a look at his footprints. But there was a good deal in this case that I did not understand at all.

****

"There," said Thorndyke, as he deposited the casts, each with its pencilled identification, in his canvas case, "that is the end of the Blue Diamond Mystery."

"I beg your pardon," said I, "but it isn't. I want a full explanation. It is evident that from the house at Brentford you made a bee line to that willow. You knew then pretty exactly where the necklace was hidden. For all I know, you may have had that knowledge when we left Scotland Yard."

"As a matter of fact, I had," he replied. "I went to Brentford principally to verify the ownership of the wallet and the bag."

"But what was it that directed you with such certainty to the Hammersmith towing-path?"

It was then that he made the observation that I have quoted at the beginning of this narrative.

"In this case," he continued, "a curious fact, well known to naturalists, acquired vital evidential importance. It associated a bag, found in one locality, with another apparently unrelated locality. It was the link that joined up the two ends of a broken chain. I offered that fact to Inspector Badger, who, lacking the knowledge wherewith to interpret it, rejected it with scorn."

"I remember that you gave him the name of that little shell that dropped out of the handful of grass."

"Exactly," said Thorndyke. "That was the crucial fact. It told us where the handful of grass had been gathered."

"I can't imagine how," said I. "Surely you find shells all over the country?"

"That is, in general, quite true," he replied, "but *Clausilia biplicata* is one of the rare exceptions. There are four British species of these queer little univalves (which are so named from the little spring door with which the entrance of the shell is furnished): *Clausilia laminata, rolphii, rugosa* and *biplicata*. The first three species have what we may call a normal distribution, whereas the distribution of *biplicata* is abnormal. This seems to be a dying species. It is in process of becoming extinct in this island. But when a species of animal or plant becomes extinct, it does not fade away evenly over the whole of its habitat, but it disappears in patches, which gradually extend, leaving, as it were, islands of survival.

"This is what has happened to *Clausilia biplicata*. It has disappeared from this country with the exception of two localities; one of these is in Wiltshire, and the other is the right bank of the Thames at Hammersmith. And this latter locality is extraordinarily restricted. Walk down a few hundred yards towards Putney, and you have walked out of its domain; walk up a few hundred yards towards the bridge, and again you have walked out of its territory.

"Yet within that little area it is fairly plentiful. If you know where to look—it lives on the bark or at the roots of willow trees—you can usually find one or two specimens. Thus, you see, the presence of that shell associated the handful of grass with a certain willow tree, and that willow was either in Wiltshire or by the Hammersmith towing-path. But there was nothing otherwise to connect it with Wiltshire, whereas there was something to connect it with Hammersmith. Let us for a moment dismiss the shell and consider the other suggestions offered by the bag and stick.

"The bag, as you saw, contained traces of two very different persons. One was a middle-class man, probably middle-aged or elderly, cleanly, careful as to his appearance and of orderly habits; the other, uncleanly, slovenly and apparently a professional criminal. The bag itself seemed to appertain to the former person. It was an expensive bag and showed signs of years of careful use. This, and the circumstances in which it was found, led us to suspect that it was a stolen bag. Now, we knew that the contents of a bag had been stolen. We knew that an empty bag had been picked up on the line between Barnes and

Chiswick, and it was probable that the thief had left the train at the latter station. The empty bag had been assumed to be Mr. Montague's, whereas the probabilities—as for instance, the fact of its having been thrown out on the line—suggested that it was the thief's bag, and that Mr. Montague's had been taken away with its contents.

"The point, then, that we had to settle when we left Scotland Yard was whether this apparently stolen bag had any connection with the train robbery. But as soon as we saw Mr. Montague it was evident that he corresponded exactly with the owner of the dressing-wallet; and when we saw the bag that had been found on the line—a shoddy, imitation leather bag—it was practically certain that it was not his, while the roughly-stitched leather pockets, exactly suited to the dimensions of house-breaking tools, strongly suggested that it was a burglar's bag. But if this were so, then Mr. Montague's bag had been stolen, and the robber's effects stuffed into it.

"With this working hypothesis we were now able to take up the case from the other end. The Scotland Yard bag was Montague's bag. It had been taken from Chiswick to the Hammersmith towpath, where—judging from the clay smears on the bottom—it had been laid on the ground, presumably close to a willow tree. The use of the grass as packing suggested that something had been removed from the bag at this place—something that had wedged the tools together and prevented them from rattling; and there appeared to be half a towel missing. Clearly, the towpath was our next field of exploration.

"But, small as this area was geographically, it would have taken a long time to examine in detail. Here, however, the stick gave us invaluable aid. It had a perfectly distinctive tip, and it showed traces of having been stuck about three inches into earth similar to that on the bag. What we had thus to look for was a hole in the ground about three inches deep, and having at the bottom the impression of a half-worn boot-stud. This hole would probably be close to a willow.

"The search turned out even easier than I had hoped. Directly we reached the towpath I picked up the track of the stick, and not one track only, but a double track, showing that our friend had returned to the bridge. All that remained was to follow the track until it came to an end and there we were pretty certain to find the hole in the ground, as, in fact, we did."

"And why," I asked, "do you suppose he buried the stuff?"

"Probably as a precaution, in case he had been seen and described. This morning's papers will have told him that he had not been. Probably, also, he wanted to make arrangements with a fence and didn't want to have the booty about him."

There is little more to tell. When the case was heard on the following morning, Thorndyke's uncannily precise and detailed description of the course of events, coupled with the production of the stolen property, so unnerved the prisoner that he pleaded guilty forthwith.

As to Mr. Montague, he recovered completely in a few days, and a handsome pair of Georgian silver candlesticks may even to this day be seen on our mantelpiece testifying to his gratitude and appreciation of Thorndyke's brilliant conduct of the case.

A Mystery of the Sand-Hills

I have occasionally wondered how often Mystery and Romance present themselves to us ordinary men of affairs only to be passed by without recognition. More often, I suspect than most of us imagine. The uncanny tendency of my talented friend John Thorndyke to become involved in strange, mysterious and abnormal circumstances has almost become a joke against him. But yet, on reflection, I am disposed to think that his experiences have not differed essentially from those of other men, but that his extraordinary powers of observation and rapid inference have enabled him to detect abnormal elements in what, to ordinary men, appeared to be quite commonplace occurrences. Certainly this was so in the singular Roscoff case, in which, if I had been alone, I should assuredly have seen nothing to merit more than a passing attention.

It happened that on a certain summer morning—it was the fourteenth of August, to be exact—we were discussing this very subject as we walked across the golf-links from Sandwich towards the sea. I was spending a holiday in the old town with my wife, in order that she might paint the ancient streets, and we had induced Thorndyke to come down and stay with us for a few days. This was his last morning, and we had come forth betimes to stroll across the sand-hills to Shellness.

It was a solitary place in those days. When we came off the sand-hills on to the smooth, sandy beach, there was not a soul in sight, and our own footprints were the first to mark the firm strip of sand between high-water mark and the edge of the quiet surf.

We had walked a hundred yards or so when Thorndyke stopped and looked down at the dry sand above tide-marks and then along the wet beach.

"Would that be a shrimper?" he cogitated, referring to some impressions of bare feet in the sand. "If so, he couldn't have come from Pegwell, for the River Stour bars the way. But he came out of the sea and seems to have made straight for the sand-hills."

"Then he probably was a shrimper," said I, not deeply interested.

"Yet," said Thorndyke, "it was an odd time for a shrimper to be at work."

"What was an odd time?" I demanded. "When was he at work?"

"He came out of the sea at this place," Thorndyke replied, glancing at his watch, "at about half-past eleven last night, or from that to twelve."

"Good Lord, Thorndyke!" I exclaimed, "how on earth do you know that?"

"But it is obvious, Anstey," he replied. "It is now half-past nine, and it will be high-water at eleven, as we ascertained before we came out. Now, if you look at those footprints on the sand, you see that they stop short—or rather begin—about two-thirds of the distance from high-water mark to the edge of the surf. Since they are visible and distinct, they must have been made after last high-water. But since they do not extend to the water's edge, they must have been made when the tide was going out; and the place where they begin is the place where the edge of the surf was when the footprints were made. But the place is, as we see, about an hour below the high-water mark, Therefore, when the man came out of the sea, the tide had been going down for an hour, roughly. As it is high-water at eleven this morning, it was high-water at about ten-forty last night; and as the man came out of the sea about an hour after high-water, he must have come out at, or about, eleven-forty. Isn't that obvious?"

"Perfectly," I replied, laughing. "It is as simple as sucking eggs when you think it out. But how the deuce do you manage always to spot these obvious things at a glance? Most men would have just glanced at those footprints and passed them without a second thought."

"That", he replied, "is a mere matter of habit; the habit of trying to extract the significance of simple appearances. It has become almost automatic with me."

During our discussion we had been walking forward slowly, straying on to the edge of the sand-hills. Suddenly, in a hollow between the hills, my eye lighted upon a heap of clothes, apparently, to judge by their orderly disposal, those of a bather. Thorndyke also had observed them and we approached together and looked down on them curiously.

"Here is another problem for you," said I. "Find the bather. I don't see him anywhere."

"You won't find him here," said Thorndyke. "These clothes have been out all night. Do you see the little spider's web on the boots with a few dewdrops still clinging to it? There has been no dew forming for a good many hours. Let us have a look at the beach."

We strode out through the loose sand and stiff, reedy grass to the smooth beach, and here we could plainly see a line of prints of naked feet leading straight down to the sea, but ending abruptly about two-thirds of the way to the water's edge.

"This looks like our nocturnal shrimper," said I. "He seems to have gone into the sea here and come out at the other place. But if they are the same footprints, he must have forgotten to dress before he went home. It is a quaint affair."

"It is a most remarkable affair," Thorndyke agreed; "and if the footprints are not the same it will be still more inexplicable."

He produced from his pocket a small spring tape-measure with which he carefully took the lengths of two of the most distinct footprints and the length of the stride. Then we walked back along the beach to the other set of tracks, two of which he measured in the same manner.

"Apparently they are the same," he said, putting away his tape; "indeed, they could hardly be otherwise. But the mystery is, what has become of the man? He couldn't have gone away without his clothes, unless he is a lunatic, which his proceedings rather suggest. There is just the possibility that he went into the sea again and was drowned. Shall we walk along towards Shellness and see if we can find any further traces?"

We walked nearly half a mile along the beach, but the smooth surface of the sand was everywhere unbroken. At length we turned to retrace our steps; and at this moment I observed two men advancing across the sand-hills. By the time we had reached the mysterious heap of garments they were quite near, and, attracted no doubt by the intentness with which we were regarding the clothes, they altered their course to see what we were looking at. As they approached, I recognised one of them as a barrister named Hallet, a neighbour of mine in the Temple, whom I had already met in the town, and we exchanged greetings.

"What is the excitement?" he asked, looking at the heap of clothes and then glancing along the deserted beach; "and where is the owner of the togs? I don't see him anywhere."

"That is the problem," said I. "He seems to have disappeared."

"Gad!" exclaimed Hallett, "if he has gone home without his clothes, He'll create a sensation in the town! What?"

Here the other man, who carried a set of golf clubs, stooped over the clothes with a look of keen interest.

"I believe I recognise these things, Hallett; in fact, I am sure I do. That waistcoat, for instance. You must have noticed that waistcoat. I saw you playing with the chap a couple of days ago. Tall, clean-shaven, dark fellow. Temporary member, you know. What was his name? Pop-off, or something like that?"

"Roscoff," said Hallett. "Yes, by Jove, I believe you are right. And now I come to think of it, he mentioned to me that he sometimes came up here for a swim. He said he particularly liked a paddle by moonlight, and I told him he was a fool to run the risk of bathing in a lonely place like this, especially at night."

"Well, that is what he seems to have done," said Thorndyke, "for these clothes have certainly been here all night, as you can see by that spider's web."

"Then he has come to grief, poor beggar!" said Hallett; "probably got carried away by the current. There is a devil of a tide here on the flood."

He started to walk towards the beach, and the other man, dropping his clubs, followed.

"Yes," said Hallett, "that is what has happened. You can see his footprints plainly enough going down to the sea; but there are no tracks coming back."

"There are some tracks of bare feet coming out of the sea farther up the beach," said I, "which seem to be his."

Hallett shook his head. "They can't be his," he said, "for it is obvious that he never did come back. Probably they are the tracks of some shrimper. The question is, what are we to do! Better take his things to the dormy-house and then let the police know what has happened."

We went back and began to gather up the clothes, each of us taking one or two articles.

"You were right, Morris," said Hallett, as he picked up the shirt. "Here's his name, "P. Roscoff", and I see it is on the vest and the shorts, too. And I recognise the stick now not that that matters, as the clothes are marked."

On our way across the links to the dormy-house mutual introductions took place. Morris was a London solicitor, and both he and Hallett knew Thorndyke by name.

"The coroner will have an expert witness," Hallett remarked as we entered the house. "Rather a waste in a simple case like this. We had better put the things in here."

He opened the door of a small room furnished with a good-sized table and a set of lockers, into one of which he inserted a key.

"Before we lock them up," said Thorndyke, "I suggest that we make and sign a list of them and of the contents of the pockets to put with them."

"Very well," agreed Hallett. "You know the ropes in these cases. I'll write down the descriptions, if you will call them out."

Thorndyke looked over the collection and first enumerated the articles: a tweed jacket and trousers, light, knitted wool waistcoat, black and yellow stripes, blue cotton shirt, net vest and shorts, marked in ink "P. Roscoff", brown merino socks, brown shoes, tweed cap, and a walking-stick—a mottled Malacca cane with a horn crooked handle. When Hallett had written down this list, Thorndyke laid the clothes on the table and began to empty the pockets, one at a time, dictating the descriptions of the articles to Hallett while Morris took them from him and laid them on a sheet of newspaper. In the jacket pockets were a handkerchief, marked "P.R.;" a letter-case containing a few stamps, one or two hotel bills and local tradesmen's receipts, and some visiting cards inscribed "Mr. Peter Roscoff, Bell Hotel, Sandwich;" a leather cigarette-case, a 3B pencil fitted with a point-protector, and a fragment of what Thorndyke decided to be vine charcoal.

"That lot is not very illuminating," remarked Morris, peering into the pockets of the letter-case. "No letter or anything indicating his permanent address. However, that isn't our concern." He laid aside the letter-case, and picking up a pocket-knife that Thorndyke had just taken from the trousers pocket, examined it curiously. "Queer knife, that," he remarked, "steel blade—mighty sharp, too—nail file and an ivory blade. Silly arrangement, it seems. A paperknife is more convenient carried loose, and you don't want a handle to it."

"Perhaps it was meant for a fruit-knife," suggested Hallett, adding it to the list and glancing at a little heap of silver coins that Thorndyke had just laid down. "I wonder," he added, "what has made that money turn so black. Looks! as if he had been taking some medicine containing sulphur. What do you think, doctor?"

"It is quite a probable explanation," replied Thorndyke, "though we haven't the means of testing it. But you notice that this vesta-box from the other pocket is quite bright, which is rather against your theory."

He held out a little silver box bearing the engraved monogram "P.R.", the burnished surface of which contrasted strongly with the dull brownish-black of the coins. Hallett looked at it with an affirmative grunt, and having entered it in his list and added a bunch of keys and a watch from the waistcoat pocket, laid down his pen.

"That's the lot, is it?" said he, rising and beginning to gather up the clothes. "My word! Look at the sand on the table! Isn't it astonishing how saturated with sand one's clothes become after a day on the links here? When I undress at night, the bathroom floor is like the bottom of a bird-cage. Shall I put the things in the locker now?"

"I think", said Thorndyke, "that, as I may have to give evidence, I should like to look them over before you put them away."

Hallett grinned. "There's going to be some expert evidence after all," he said. "Well, fire away, and let me know when you have finished. I am going to smoke a cigarette outside."

With this, he and Morris sauntered out, and I thought it best to go with them, though I was a little curious as to my colleague's object in examining these derelicts. However, my curiosity was not entirely baulked, for my friends went no farther than the little garden that surrounded the house, and from the place where we stood I was able to look in through the window and observe Thorndyke's proceedings.

Very methodical they were. First he laid on the table a sheet of newspaper and on this deposited the jacket, which he examined carefully all over, picking some small object off the inside near the front, and giving special attention to a thick smear of paint which I had noticed on the left cuff. Then, with his spring tape he measured the sleeves and other principal dimensions. Finally, holding the jacket upside down, he beat it gently with his stick, causing a shower of sand to fall on the paper. He then laid the jacket aside, and, taking from his pocket one or two seed envelopes (which I believe he always carried), very carefully shot the sand from the paper into one of them and wrote a few words on it—presumably the source of the sand—and similarly disposing of the small object that he had picked off the surface.

This rather odd procedure was repeated with the other garments—a fresh sheet of newspaper being used for each and with the socks, shoes, and cap. The latter he examined minutely, especially as to the inside, from which he picked out two or three small objects, which I could not see, but assumed to be hairs. Even the walking-stick was inspected and measured, and the articles from the pockets scrutinized afresh, particularly the curious pocket-knife, the ivory blade of which he examined on both sides through his lens.

Hallett and Morris glanced in at him from time to time with indulgent smiles, and the former remarked:

"I like the hopeful enthusiasm of the real *pukka* expert, and the way he refuses to admit the existence of the ordinary and commonplace. I wonder what he has found out from those things. But here he is. Well, doctor, what's the verdict? Was it temporary insanity or misadventure?"

Thorndyke shook his head. "The inquiry is adjourned pending the production of fresh evidence," he replied, adding: "I have folded the clothes up and put all the effects together in a paper parcel, excepting the stick."

When Hallett had deposited the derelicts in the locker, he came out and looked across the links with an air of indecision.

"I suppose," said he, "we ought to notify the police. I'll do that. When do you think the body is likely to wash up, and where?"

"It is impossible to say," replied Thorndyke. "The set of the current is towards the Thames, but the body might wash up anywhere along the coast. A case is recorded of a bather drowned off Brighton whose body came up six weeks later at Walton-on-the-Naze. But that was quite exceptional. I shall send the coroner and the Chief Constable a note with my address, and I should think you had better do the same. And that is all that we can do, until we get the summons for the inquest, if there ever is one."

To this we all agreed; and as the morning was now spent we walked back together across the links to the town, where we encountered my wife returning homeward with her sketching kit. This Thorndyke and I took possession of and having parted from Hallett and Morris opposite the Barbican, we made our way to our lodgings in quest of lunch. Naturally, the events of the morning were related to my wife and discussed by us all, but I noted that Thorndyke made no reference to his inspection of the clothes, and accordingly I said nothing about the matter before my wife; and no opportunity of opening the subject occurred until the evening, when I accompanied him to the station. Then, as we paced the platform while waiting for his train, I put my question:

"By the way, did you extract any information from those garments? I saw you going through them very thoroughly."

"I got a suggestion from them," he replied, "but it is such an odd one that I hardly like to mention it. Taking the appearances at their face value, the suggestion was that the clothes were not all those of the same man. There seemed to be traces of two men, one of whom appeared to belong to this district, while the other would seem to have been associated with the eastern coast of Thanet between Ramsgate and Margate, and by preference, on the scale of probabilities, to Dumpton or Broadstairs."

"How on earth did you arrive at the localities?" I asked.

"Principally," he replied, "by the peculiarities of the sand which fell from the garments and which was not the same in all of them. You see, Anstey," he continued, "sand is analogous to dust. Both consist of minute fragments detached from larger masses; and just as, by examining microscopically the dust of a room, you can ascertain the colour and material of the carpets, curtains, furniture coverings, and other textiles, detached particles of which form the dust of that room, so, by examining sand, you can judge of the character of the cliffs, rocks, and other large masses that occur in the locality, fragments of which become ground off by the surf and incorporated in the sand of the beach. Some of the sand from these clothes is very characteristic and will probably be still more so when I examine it under the microscope."

"But", I objected, "isn't there a fallacy in that line of reasoning? Might not one man have worn the different garments at different times and in different places?"

"That is certainly a possibility that has to be borne in mind," he replied. "But here comes my train. We shall have to adjourn this discussion until you come back to the mill."

As a matter of fact, the discussion was never resumed, for, by the time that I came back to "the mill", the affair had faded from my mind, and the accumulations of grist monopolized my attention; and it is probable that it would have passed into complete oblivion but for the circumstance of its being revived in a very singular manner, which was as follows.

One afternoon about the middle of October my old friend, Mr. Brodribb, a well-known solicitor, called to give me some verbal instructions. When he had finished our business, he said:

"I've got a client waiting outside, whom I am taking up to introduce to Thorndyke. You'd better come along with us."

"What is the nature of your client's case?" I asked.

"Hanged if I know," chuckled Brodribb. "He won't say. That's why I am taking him to our friend. I've never seen Thorndyke stumped yet, but I think this case will put the lid on him. Are you coming?"

"I am, most emphatically," said I, "if your client doesn't object."

"He's not going to be asked," said Brodribb. "He'll think you are part of the show. Here he is."

In my outer office we found a gentlemanly, middle-aged man to whom Brodribb introduced me, and whom he hustled down the stairs and up King's Bench Walk to Thorndyke's chambers. There we found my colleague earnestly studying a will with the aid of a watchmaker's eye-glass, and Brodribb opened the proceedings without ceremony.

"I've brought a client of mine, Mr. Capes, to see you, Thorndyke. He has a little problem that he wants you to solve."

Thorndyke bowed to the client and then asked:

"What is the nature of the problem?"

"Ah!" said Brodribb, with a mischievous twinkle, "that's what you've got to find out. Mr. Capes is a somewhat reticent gentleman."

Thorndyke cast a quick look at the client and from him to the solicitor. It was not the first time that old Brodribb's high spirits had overflowed in the form of a "leg-pull", though Thorndyke had no more whole-hearted admirer than the shrewd, facetious old lawyer.

Mr. Capes smiled a deprecating smile. "It isn't quite so bad as that," he said. "But I really can't give you much information. It isn't mine to give. I am afraid of telling someone else's secrets, if I say very much."

"Of course you mustn't do that," said Thorndyke. "But, I suppose you can indicate in general terms the nature of your difficulty and the kind of help you want from us."

"I think I can," Mr. Capes replied. "At any rate, I will try. My difficulty is that a certain person with whom I wish to communicate has disappeared in what appears to me to be a rather remarkable manner. When I last heard from him, he was staying at a certain seaside resort and he stated in his letter that he was returning on the following day to his rooms in London. A few days later, I called at his rooms and found that he had not yet returned. But his luggage, which he had sent on independently, had arrived on the day which he had mentioned. So it is evident that he must have left his seaside lodgings. But from that day to this I have had no communication from him, and he has never returned to his rooms nor written to his landlady."

"About how long ago was this?" Thorndyke asked.

"It is just about two months since I heard from him."

"You don't wish to give the name of the seaside resort where he was staying."

"I think I had better not," answered Mr. Capes. "There are circumstances—they don't concern me, but they do concern him very much—which seem to make it necessary for me to say as little as possible."

"And there is nothing further that you can tell us?"

"I am afraid not, excepting that, if I could get into communication with him, I could tell him of something very much to his advantage and which might prevent him from doing something which it would be much better that he should not do."

Thorndyke cogitated profoundly while Brodribb watched him with undisguised enjoyment. Presently my colleague looked up and addressed our secretive client.

"Did you ever play the game of 'Clump', Mr. Capes? It is a somewhat legal form of game in which one player asks questions of the others, who are required to answer "yes" or "no" in the proper witness-box style."

"I know the game," said Capes, looking a little puzzled, "but—"

"Shall we try a round or two?" asked Thorndyke, with an unmoved countenance. "You don't wish to make any statements, but if I ask you certain specific questions, will you answer 'yes or no?'"

Mr. Capes reflected awhile. At length he said: "I am afraid I can't commit myself to a promise. Still, if you like to ask a question or two, I will answer them if I can."

"Very well," said Thorndyke, "then, as a start, supposing I suggest that the date of the letter that you received was the thirteenth of August? What do you say? Yes or no?"

Mr. Capes sat bolt upright and stared at Thorndyke open-mouthed.

"How on earth did you guess that?" he exclaimed in an astonished tone. "It's most extraordinary! But you are right. It was dated the thirteenth."

"Then," said Thorndyke, "as we have fixed the time we will have a try at the place. What do you say if I suggest that the seaside resort was in the neighbourhood of Broadstairs?"

Mr. Capes was positively thunderstruck. As he sat gazing at Thorndyke he looked like amazement personified.

"But," he exclaimed, "you can't be guessing! You know! You know that he was at Broadstairs. And yet, how could you? I haven't even hinted at who he is."

"I have a certain man in my mind," said Thorndyke, "who may have disappeared from Broadstairs. Shall I suggest a few personal characteristics?"

Mr. Capes nodded eagerly and Thorndyke continued:

"If I suggest, for instance, that he was an artist—a painter in oil"—Capes nodded again—"that he was somewhat fastidious as to his pigments?"

"Yes," said Capes. "Unnecessarily so in my opinion, and I am an artist myself. What else?"

"That he worked with his palette in his right hand and held his brush with his left?"

"Yes, yes," exclaimed Capes, half-rising from his chair; "and what was he like?"

"By gum," murmured Brodribb, "we haven't stumped him after all."

Evidently we had not, for he proceeded:

"As to his physical characteristics, I suggest that he was a shortish man—about five feet seven—rather stout, fair hair, slightly bald and wearing a rather large and ragged moustache."

Mr. Capes was astounded—and so was I, for that matter—and for some moments there was a silence, broken only by old Brodribb, who sat chuckling softly and rubbing his hands. At length Mr. Capes said:

"You have described him exactly, but I needn't tell you that. What I do not understand at all is how you knew that I was referring to this particular man, seeing that I mentioned no name. By the way, sir, may I ask when you saw him last?"

"I have no reason to suppose," replied Thorndyke, "that I have ever seen him at all;" an answer that reduced Mr. Capes to a state of stupefaction and brought our old friend Brodribb to the verge of apoplexy. "This man," Thorndyke continued, "is a purely hypothetical individual whom I have described from certain traces left by him. I have reason to believe that he left Broadstairs on the fourteenth of August and I have certain opinions as to what became of him thereafter. But a few more details would be useful, and I shall continue my interrogation. Now this man sent his luggage on separately. That suggests a possible intention of breaking his journey to London. What do you say?"

"I don't know," replied Capes, "but I think it probable."

"I suggest that he broke his journey for the purpose of holding an interview with some other person."

"I cannot say," answered Capes, "but if he did break his journey it would probably be for that purpose."

"And supposing that interview to have taken place, would it be likely to be an amicable interview?"

"I am afraid not. I suspect that my—er—acquaintance might have made certain proposals which would have been unacceptable, but which he might have been able to enforce. However, that is only surmise," Capes added hastily. "I really know nothing more than I have told you, except the missing man's name, and that I would rather not mention."

"It is not material," said Thorndyke, "at least, not at present. If it should become essential, I will let you know."

"M—yes," said Mr. Capes. "But you were saying that you had certain opinions as to what has become of this person."

"Yes," Thorndyke replied; "speculative opinions. But they will have to be verified. If they turn out to be correct—or incorrect either—I will let you know in the course of a few days. Has Mr. Brodribb your address?"

"He has; but you had better have it, too."

He produced his card, and, after an ineffectual effort to extract a statement from Thorndyke, took his departure.

The third act of this singular drama opened in the same setting as the first, for the following Sunday morning found my colleague and me following the path from Sandwich to the sea. But we were not alone this time. At our side marched Major Robertson, the eminent dog trainer, and behind him trotted one of his superlatively educated fox-hounds.

We came out on the shore at the same point as on the former occasion, and turning towards Shellness, walked along the smooth sand with a careful eye on the not very distinctive landmarks. At length Thorndyke halted.

"This is the place," said he. "I fixed it in my mind by that distant tree, which coincides with the chimney of that cottage on the marshes. The clothes lay in that hollow between the two big sand-hills."

We advanced to the spot, but, as a hollow is useless as a landmark, Thorndyke ascended the nearest sand-hill and stuck his stick in the summit and tied his handkerchief to the handle.

"That," he said, "will serve as a centre which we can keep in sight, and if we describe a series of gradually widening concentric circles round it, we shall cover the whole ground completely."

"How far do you propose to go?" asked the major.

"We must be guided by the appearance of the ground," replied Thorndyke. "But the circumstances suggest that if there is anything buried, it can't be very far from where the clothes were laid. And it is pretty certain to be in a hollow."

The major nodded; and when he had attached a long leash to the dog's collar, we started, at first skirting the base of the sand-hill, and then, guided by our own footmarks in the loose sand, gradually increasing the distance from the high mound, above which Thorndyke's handkerchief fluttered in the light breeze. Thus we continued, walking slowly, keeping close to the previously made circle of footprints and watching the dog; who certainly did a vast amount of sniffing, but appeared to let his mind run unduly on the subject of rabbits.

In this way half an hour was consumed, and I was beginning to wonder whether we were going after all to draw a blank, when the dog's demeanour underwent a sudden change. At the moment we were crossing a range of high sand-hills, covered with stiff, reedy grass and stunted gorse, and before us lay a deep hollow, naked of vegetation and presenting a bare, smooth surface of the characteristic greyish-yellow sand. On the side of the hill the dog checked, and, with upraised muzzle, began to sniff the air with a curiously suspicious expression, clearly unconnected with the rabbit question.

On this, the major unfastened the leash, and the dog, left to his own devices, put his nose to the ground and began rapidly to cast to and fro, zigzagging down the side of the hill and growing every moment more excited. In the same sinuous manner he proceeded across the hollow until he reached a spot near the middle; and here he came to a sudden stop and began to scratch up the sand with furious eagerness.

"It's a find, sure enough!" exclaimed the major, nearly as excited as his pupil; and, as he spoke, he ran down the hillside, followed by me and Thorndyke, who, as he reached the bottom, drew from his "poacher's pocket" a large fern-trowel in a leather sheath. It was not a very efficient digging implement, but it threw up the loose sand faster than the scratchings of the dog.

It was easy ground to excavate. Working at the spot that the dog had located, Thorndyke had soon hollowed out a small cavity some eighteen inches deep. Into the bottom of this he thrust the pointed blade of the big trowel. Then he paused and looked round at the major and me, who were craning eagerly over the little pit.

"There is something there," said he. "Feel the handle of the trowel."

I grasped the wooden handle, and, working it gently up and down, was aware of a definite but somewhat soft resistance. The major verified my observation, and then Thorndyke resumed his digging, widening the pit and working with increased caution. Ten minutes more careful excavation brought into view a recognisable shape—a shoulder and upper arm; and following the lines of this, further diggings disclosed the form of a head and shoulders plainly discernable though still shrouded in sand. Finally, with the point of the trowel and a borrowed handkerchief—mine—the adhering sand was cleared away; and then, from the bottom of the deep, funnel-shaped hole, there looked up at us, with a most weird and horrible effect, the discoloured face of a man.

In that face, the passing weeks had wrought inevitable changes, on which I need not dwell. But the features were easily recognisable, and I could see at once that the man corresponded completely with Thorndyke's description. The cheeks were full; the hair on the temples was of a pale, yellowish brown; a straggling, fair moustache covered the mouth; and, when the sand had been sufficiently cleared away, I could see a small, tonsure-like bald patch near the back of the crown. But I could see something more than this. On the left temple, just behind the eyebrow, was a ragged, shapeless wound such as might have been made by a hammer.

"That turns into certainty what we have already surmised," said Thorndyke, gently pressing the scalp around the wound. "It must have killed him instantly. The skull is smashed in like an egg-shell. And this is undoubtedly the weapon," he added, drawing out of the sand beside the body a big, hexagon-headed screw-bolt, "very prudently buried with the body. And that is all that really concerns us. We can leave the police to finish the disinterment; but you notice, Anstey, that the corpse is nude with the exception of the vest and probably the pants. The shirt has disappeared. Which is exactly what we should have expected."

Slowly, but with the feeling of something accomplished, we took our way back to the town, having collected Thorndyke's stick on the way. Presently, the major left us, to look up a friend at the clubhouse on the links. As soon as we were alone, I put in a demand for an elucidation.

"I see the general trend of your investigations," said I "but I can't imagine how they yielded so much detail; as to the personal appearance of this man, for instance."

"The evidence in this case," he replied, "was analogous to circumstantial evidence. It depended on the cumulative effect of a number of facts, each separately inconclusive, but all pointing to the same conclusion. Shall I run over the data in their order and in accordance with their connections?"

I gave an emphatic affirmative, and he continued:

"We begin, naturally, with the first fact, which is, of course, the most interesting and important; the fact which arrests attention, which shows that something has to be explained and possibly suggests a line of inquiry. You remember that I measured the footprints in the sand for comparison with the other footprints. Then I had the dimensions of the feet of the presumed bather. But as soon as I looked at the shoes which purported to be those of that bather, I felt a conviction that his feet would never go into them.

"Now, that was a very striking fact—if it really was a fact—and it came on top of another fact hardly less striking. The bather had gone into the sea; and at a considerable distance he had unquestionably come out again. There could be no possible doubt. In foot-measurement and length of stride the two sets of tracks were identical; and there were no other tracks. That man had come ashore and he had remained ashore. But yet he had not put on his clothes. He couldn't have gone away naked; but obviously he was not there. As a criminal lawyer, you must admit that there was *prima facie* evidence of something very abnormal and probably criminal.

"On our way to the dormy-house, I carried the stick in the same hand as my own and noted that it was very little shorter. Therefore it was a tall man's stick. Apparently, then, the stick did not belong to the shoes, but to the man who had made the footprints. Then, when we came to the dormy-house, another striking fact presented itself. You remember that Hallett commented on the quantity of sand that fell from the clothes on to the table. I am astonished that he did not notice the very peculiar character of that sand.

"It was perfectly unlike the sand which would fall from his own clothes. The sand on the sand-hills is dune sand—wind-borne sand, or, as the legal term has it, *æolian* sand; and it is perfectly characteristic. As it has been carried by the wind, it is necessarily fine. The grains are small; and as the action of the wind sorts them out, they are extremely uniform in size. Moreover, by being continually blown about and rubbed together, they become rounded by mutual attrition. And then dune sand is nearly pure sand, composed of grains of silica unmixed with other substances.

"Beach sand is quite different. Much of it is half-formed, freshly broken down silica and is often very coarse; and, as I pointed out at the time, it is mixed with all sorts of foreign substances derived from masses in the neighbourhood. This particular sand was loaded with black and white particles, of which the white were mostly chalk, and the black particles of coal. Now there is very little chalk in the Shellness sand, as there are no cliffs quite near, and chalk rapidly disappears from sand by reason of its softness; and there is no coal."

"Where does the coal come from?" I asked.

"Principally from the Goodwins," he replied. "It is derived from the cargoes of colliers whose wrecks are embedded in those sands, and from the bunkers of wrecked steamers. This coal sinks down through the seventy odd feet of sand and at last works out at the bottom, where it drifts slowly across the floor of the sea in a north-westerly direction until some easterly gale throws it up on the Thanet shore between Ramsgate and Foreness Point. Most of it comes up at Dumpton and Broadstairs, there you may see the poor people, in the winter, gathering coal pebbles to feed their fires.

"This sand, then, almost certainly came from the Thanet coast; but the missing man, Roscoff, had been staying in Sandwich, playing golf on the sand-hills. This was another striking discrepancy, and it made me decide to examine the clothes exhaustively, garment by garment. I did so; and this is what I found.

"The jacket, trousers, socks and shoes were those of a shortish, rather stout man, as shown by measurements, and the cap was his, since it was made of the same cloth as the jacket and trousers.

"The waistcoat, shirt, underclothes and stick were those of a tall man.

"The garments, socks and shoes of the short man were charged with Thanet beach sand, and contained no dune sand, excepting the cap, which might have fallen off on the sand-hills.

"The waistcoat was saturated with dune sand and contained no beach sand, and a little dune sand was obtained from the shirt and under-garments. That is to say, that the short man's clothes contained beach sand only, while the tall man's clothes contained only dune sand.

"The short man's clothes were all unmarked; the tall man's clothes were either marked or conspicuously recognisable, as the waistcoat and also the stick.

"The garments of the short man which had been left were those that could not have been worn by a tall man without attracting instant attention and the shoes could not have been put on at all; whereas the garments of the short man which had disappeared—the waistcoat, shirt and underclothes—were those that could have been worn by a tall man without attracting attention. The obvious suggestion was that the tall man had gone off in the short man's shirt and waistcoat but otherwise in his own clothes.

"And now as to the personal characteristics of the short man. From the cap I obtained five hairs. They were all blond, and two of them were of the peculiar, atrophic, "point of exclamation" type that grow at the margin of a bald area. Therefore he was a fair man and partially bald. On the inside of the jacket, clinging to the rough tweed, I found a single long, thin, fair moustache hair, which suggested a long, soft moustache. The edge of the left cuff was thickly marked with oil-paint-not a single smear, but an accumulation such as a painter picks up when he reaches with his brush hand across a loaded palette.

"The suggestion—not very conclusive—was that he was an oil-painter and left-handed. But there was strong confirmation. There was an artist's pencil—3B—and a stump of vine charcoal such as an oil-painter might carry. The silver coins in his pocket were blackened with sulphide as they would be if a piece of artist's soft, vulcanized rubber has been in the pocket with them. And there was the pocket-knife. It contained a sharp steel pencil-blade, a charcoal file and an ivory palette-blade; and that palette-blade had been used by a left-handed man."

"How did you arrive at that?" I asked.

"By the bevels worn at the edges," he replied. "An old palette-knife used by a right-handed man shows a bevel of wear on the under side of the left-hand edge and the upper side of the right-hand edge; in the case of a left handed man the wear shows on the under side of the right hand edge and the upper side of the left-hand edge. This being an ivory blade, showed the wear very distinctly and proved conclusively that the user was left-handed; and as an ivory palette-knife is used only by fastidiously careful painters for such pigments as the cadmiums, which might be discoloured by a steel blade, one was justified in assuming that he was somewhat fastidious as to his pigments."

As I listened to Thorndyke's exposition I was profoundly impressed. His conclusions, which had sounded like mere speculative guesses, were, I now realised, based upon an analysis of the evidence as careful and as impartial as the summing up of a judge. And these conclusions he had drawn instantaneously from the appearances of things that had been before my eyes all the time and from which I had learned nothing.

"What do you suppose is the meaning of the affair?" I asked presently. "What was the motive of the murder?"

"We can only guess," he replied. "But, interpreting Capes' hints, I should suspect that our artist friend was a blackmailer; that he had come over here to squeeze Roscoff—perhaps not for the first time—and that his victim lured him out on the sand-hills for a private talk and then took the only effective means of ridding himself of his persecutor. That is my view of the case; but, of course, it is only surmise."

Surmise as it was, however, it turned out to be literally correct. At the inquest Capes had to tell all that he knew, which was uncommonly little, though no one was able to add to it. The murdered man, Joseph Bertrand, had fastened on Roscoff and made a regular income by blackmailing him. That much Capes knew; and he knew that the victim had been in prison and that that was the secret. But who Roscoff was and what was his real name—for Roscoff was apparently a *nom de guerre*—he had no idea. So he could not help the police. The murderer had got clear away and there was no hint as to where to look for him; and so far as I know, nothing has ever been heard of him since.

The Trail of Behemoth

Or all the minor dissipations in which temperate men indulge there is none, I think, more alluring than the after-breakfast pipe. I had just lit mine and was standing before the fire with the unopened paper in my hand when my ear caught the sound of hurried footsteps ascending the stair. Now experience has made me somewhat of a connoisseur in footsteps. A good many are heard on our stair, heralding the advent of a great variety of clients, and I have learned to distinguish those which are premonitory of urgent cases. Such I judged the present ones to be, and my judgment was confirmed by a hasty, importunate tattoo on our small brass knocker, Regretfully taking the much-appreciated pipe from my mouth, I crossed the room and threw the door open.

"Good morning, Dr. Jervis," said our visitor, a barrister whom I knew slightly. "Is your colleague at home?"

"No, Mr. Bidwell," I replied. "I am sorry to say he is out of town. He won't be back until the day after tomorrow."

Mr. Bidwell was visibly disappointed.

"Ha! Pity!" he exclaimed; and then with quick tact he added. "But still, you are here. It comes to the same thing."

"I don't know about that," said I. "But, at any rate, I am at your service."

"Thank you," said he. "And in that case I will ask you to come round with me at once to Tanfield Court. A most shocking thing has happened. My old friend and neighbour, Giles Herrington has been—well, he is dead—died suddenly, and I think there can be no doubt that he was killed. Can you come now? I will give you the particulars as we go."

I scribbled a hasty note to say where I had gone, and having laid it on the table, got my hat and set forth with Mr. Bidwell.

"It has only just been discovered," said he, as we crossed King's Bench Walk. "The laundress who does his chambers and mine was battering at my door when I arrived—I don't live in the Temple, you know. She was as pale as a ghost and in an awful state of alarm and agitation. It seems that she had gone up to Herrington's chambers to get his breakfast ready as usual; but when she went into the sitting-room she found him lying dead on the floor. Thereupon she rushed down to my chambers—I am usually an early bird—and there I found her, as I said, battering at my door, although she has a key.

"Well, I went up with her to my friend's chambers—they are on the first floor, just over mine—and there, sure enough, was poor old Giles lying on the floor, cold and stiff. Evidently he had been lying there all night."

"Were there any marks of violence on the body?" I asked.

"I didn't notice any," he replied, "but I didn't look very closely. What I did notice was that the place was all in disorder—a chair overturned and things knocked off the table. It was pretty evident that there had been a struggle and that he had not met his death by fair means."

"And what do you want us to do?" I asked.

"Well," he replied, "I was Herrington's friend; about the only friend he had, for he was not an amiable or a sociable man; and I am the executor of his will.

"Appearances suggest very strongly that he has been murdered, and I take it upon myself to see that his murderer is brought to account. Our friendship seems to demand that. Of course, the police will go into the affair, and if it turns out to be all plain sailing, there will be nothing for you to do. But the murderer, if there is one, has got to be secured and convicted, and if the police can't manage it, I want you and Thorndyke to see the case through. This is the place."

He hurried in through the entry and up the stairs to the first-floor landing, where he rapped loudly at the closed "oak" of a set of chambers above which was painted the name of "Mr. Giles Herrington."

After an interval, during which Mr. Bidwell repeated the summons, the massive door opened and a familiar face looked out: the face of Inspector Badger of the Criminal Investigation Department. The expression that it bore was not one of welcome, and my experience of the inspector caused me to brace myself up for the inevitable contest.

"What is your business?" he inquired forbiddingly.

Mr. Bidwell took the question to himself and replied: "I am Mr. Herrington's executor, and in that capacity I have instructed Dr. Jervis and his colleague, Dr. Thorndyke, to watch the case on my behalf. I take it that you are a police officer?"

"I am," replied Badger, "and I can't admit any unauthorised persons to these chambers."

"We are not unauthorised persons," said Mr. Bidwell. "We are here on legitimate business. Do I understand that you refuse admission to the legal representatives of the deceased man?"

In the face of Mr. Bidwell's firm and masterful attitude, Badger began, as usual, to weaken. Eventually, having warned us to convey no information to anybody, he grudgingly opened the door and admitted us.

"I have only just arrived, myself," he said. "I happened to be in the porter's lodge on other business when the laundress came and gave the alarm."

As I stepped into the room and looked round, I saw at a glance the clear indications of a crime. The place was in the utmost disorder. The cloth had been dragged from the table, littering the floor with broken glass, books, a tobacco jar, and various other objects. A chair sprawled on its back, the fender was dislodged from its position, the hearth-rug was all awry; and in the midst of the wreckage, on the space of floor between the table and the fireplace, the body of a man was stretched in a not uneasy posture.

I stooped over him and looked him over searchingly; an elderly man, clean-shaved and slightly bald, with a grim, rather forbidding countenance, which was not, however, distorted or apparently unusual in expression. There were no obvious injuries, but the crumpled state of the collar caused me to look more closely at the throat and neck, and I then saw pretty plainly a number of slightly discoloured marks, such as would be made by fingers tightly grasping the throat. Evidently Badger had already observed them, for he remarked: "There's no need to ask you what he died of, doctor; I can see that for myself."

"The actual cause of death," said I, "is not quite evident. He doesn't appear to have died from suffocation, but those are very unmistakable marks on the throat."

"Uncommonly," agreed Badger; "and they are enough for my purpose without any medical hair-splittings. How long do you think he has been dead?"

"From nine to twelve hours," I replied, "but nearer nine, I should think."

The inspector looked at his watch.

"That makes it between nine o'clock and midnight, but nearer midnight," said he. "Well, we shall hear if the night porter has anything to tell us. I've sent word for him to come over, and the laundress, too. And here is one of 'em."

It was, in fact, both of them, for when the inspector opened the door, they were discovered conversing eagerly in whispers. "One at a time," said Badger. "I'll have the porter in first;" and having admitted the man, he unceremoniously shut the door on the woman. The night porter saluted me as he came in—we were old acquaintances—and then halted near the door, where he stood stiffly, with his eyes riveted on the corpse.

"Now," said Badger, "I want you to try to remember if you let in any strangers last night, and if so, what their business was."

"I remember quite well," the porter replied. "I let in three strangers while I was on duty. One was going to Mr. Bolter in Fig Tree Court, one was going to Sir Alfred Blain's chambers, and the third said he had an appointment with Mr. Herrington."

"Ha!" exclaimed Badger, rubbing his hands. "Now, what time did you let him in?"

"It was just after ten-fifteen."

"Can you tell us what he was like and how he was dressed?"

"Yes," was the reply. "He didn't know where Tanfield Court was, and I had to walk down and show him, so I was able to have a good look at him. He was a middle-sized man, rather thin, dark hair, small moustache, no beard, and he had a long, sharp nose with a bump on the bridge. He wore a soft felt hat, a loose light overcoat, and he carried a thickish rough stick."

"What class of man was he? Seem to be a gentleman?"

"He was quite a gentlemanly kind of man, so far as I could judge, but he looked a bit shabby as to his clothes."

"Did you let him out?"

"Yes. He came to the gate a few minutes before eleven."

"And did you notice anything unusual about him then?"

"I did," the porter replied impressively. "I noticed that his collar was all crumpled and his hat was dusty and dented. His face was a bit red, and he looked rather upset, as if he had been having a tussle with somebody. I looked at him particularly and wondered what had been happening, seeing that Mr. Herrington was a quiet, elderly gentleman, though he was certainly a bit peppery at times."

The inspector took down these particulars gleefully in a large notebook and asked: "Is that all you know of the affair?" And when the porter replied that it was, he said: "Then I will ask you to read this statement and sign your name below it."

The porter read through his statement and carefully signed his name at the foot. He was about to depart when Badger said: "Before you go, perhaps you had better help us to move the body into the bedroom. It isn't decent to leave it lying there."

Accordingly the four of us lifted the dead man and carried him into the bedroom, where we laid him on the undisturbed bed and covered him with a rug. Then the porter was dismissed, with instructions to send in Mrs. Runt.

The laundress's statement was substantially a repetition of what Mr. Bidwell had told me. She had let herself into the chambers in the usual way, had come suddenly on the dead body of the tenant, and had forthwith rushed downstairs to give the alarm. When she had concluded the inspector stood for a few moments looking thoughtfully at his notes.

"I suppose," he said presently, "you haven't looked round these chambers this morning? Can't say if there is anything unusual about them, or anything missing?"

The laundress shook her head.

"I was too upset," she said, with another furtive glance at the place where the corpse had lain; "but," she added, letting her eyes roam vaguely round the room, "there doesn't seem to be anything missing, so far as I can see—wait! Yes, there is. There's something gone from that nail on the wall; and it was there yesterday morning, because I remember dusting it."

"Ha!" exclaimed Badger. "Now what was it that was hanging on that nail?"

"Well," Mrs. Runt replied hesitatingly, "I really don't know what it was. Seemed like a sort of sword or dagger, but I never looked at it particularly, and I never took it off its nail. I used to dust it as it hung."

"Still," said Badger, "you can give us some sort of description of it, I suppose?"

"I don't know that I can," she replied. "It had a leather case, and the handle was covered with leather, I think, and it had a sort of loop, and it used to hang on that nail."

"Yes, you said that before," Badger commented sourly. "When you say it had a case, do you mean a sheath?"

"You can call it a sheath if you like," she retorted, evidently ruffled by the inspector's manner. "I call it a case."

"And how big was it? How long, for instance?"

Mrs. Runt held out her hands about a yard apart, looked at them critically, shortened the interval to a foot, extended it to two, and still varying the distance, looked vaguely at the inspector.

"I should say it was about that," she said.

"About what?" snorted Badger. "Do you mean a foot or two feet or a yard? Can't you give us some idea?"

"I can't say no clearer than what I have," she snapped. "I don't go round gentlemen's chambers measuring the things."

It seemed to me that Badger's questions were rather unnecessary, for the wall-paper below the nail gave the required information. A coloured patch on the faded ground furnished a pretty clear silhouette of a broad bladed sword or large dagger, about two feet six inches long, which had apparently hung from the nail by a loop or ring at the end of the handle. But it was not my business to point this out. I turned to Bidwell and asked:

"Can you tell us what the thing was?"

"I am afraid I can't," he replied. "I have very seldom been in these chambers. Herrington and I usually met in mine and went to the club. I have a dim recollection of something hanging on that nail, but I have not the least idea what it was or what it was like. But do you think it really matters? The thing was almost certainly a curio of some kind. It couldn't have been of any appreciable value. It is absurd, on the face of it, to suppose that this man came to Herrington's chambers, apparently by appointment, and murdered him for the sake of getting possession of an antique sword or dagger. Don't you think so?"

I did, and so, apparently, did the inspector, with the qualification that the thing seemed to have disappeared, and its disappearance ought to be accounted for; which was perfectly true, though I did not quite see how the "accounting for" was to be effected. However, as the laundress had told all that she knew, Badger gave her her dismissal and she retired to the landing, where I noticed that the night porter was still lurking. Mr. Bidwell also took his departure, and happening, a few moments later, to glance out of the window, I saw him walking slowly across the court, apparently conferring with the laundress and the porter.

As soon as we were alone, Badger assumed a friendly and confidential manner and proceeded to give advice.

"I gather that Mr. Bidwell wants you to investigate this case, but I don't fancy it is in your line at all. It is just a matter of tracing that stranger and getting hold of him. Then we shall have to find out what property there was on these premises. The laundress says that there is nothing missing, but of course no one supposes that the man came here to take the furniture. It is most probable that the motive was robbery of some kind. There's no sign of anything broken open; but then, there wouldn't be, as the keys were available."

Nevertheless he prowled round the room, examining every receptacle that had a lock and trying the drawers of the writing-table and of what looked like a file cabinet.

"You will have your work cut out," I remarked, "to trace that man. The porter's description was pretty vague."

"Yes," he replied; "there isn't much to go on. That's where you come in," he added with a grin, "with your microscopes and air-pumps and things. Now if Dr. Thorndyke was here he would just sweep a bit of dust from the floor and collect any stray oddments and have a good look at them through his magnifier, and then we should know all about it. Can't you do a bit in that line? There's plenty of dust on the floor. And here's a pin. Wonderful significant thing is a pin. And here's a wax vesta; now, that ought to tell you quite a lot. And here is the end of a leather boot-lace—at least, that is what it looks like. That must have come out of somebody's boot. Have a look at it, doctor, and see if you can tell me what kind of boot it came out of and whose boot it was."

He laid the fragment, and the match, and the pin on the table and grinned at me somewhat offensively. Inwardly I resented his impertinence—perhaps the more so since I realised that Thorndyke would probably not have been so completely gravelled as I undoubtedly was. But I considered it politic to take his clumsy irony in good part, and even to carry on his elephantine joke. Accordingly, I picked up the three "clues," one after the other, and examined them gravely, noting that the supposed boot-lace appeared to be composed of whalebone or vulcanite.

"Well, inspector," I said. "I can't give you the answer off-hand. There's no microscope here. But I will examine these objects at my leisure and let you have the information in due course."

With that I wrapped them with ostentatious care in a piece of note and bestowed them in my pocket, a proceeding which the inspector watched with a sour smile.

"I'm afraid you'll be too late," said he. "Our men will probably pick up the tracks while you are doing the microscope stunt. However, I mustn't stay here any longer. We can't do anything until we know what valuables there were on the premises; and I must have the body removed and examined by the police surgeon."

He moved towards the door, and as I had no further business in the rooms, I followed, and leaving him to lock up, I took my way back to our chambers.

When Thorndyke returned to town a couple of days later, I mentioned the case to him. But what Badger had said appeared to be true. It was a case of ascertaining the identity of the stranger who had visited the dead man on that fatal night, and this seemed to be a matter for the police rather than for us. So the case remained in abeyance until the evening following the inquest, when Mr. Bidwell called on us, accompanied by a Mr. Carston, whom he introduced as an old friend of his and of Herrington's family.

"I have called," he said, "to bring you a full report of the evidence at the inquest. I had a shorthand writer there, and this is a typed transcript of his notes. Nothing fresh transpired beyond what Dr. Jervis knows and has probably told you, but I thought you had better have all the information in writing."

"There is no clue as to who the suspicious visitor was, I suppose?" said Thorndyke.

"Not the slightest," replied Bidwell. "The porter's description is all they have to go on, and of course it would apply to hundreds of persons. But, in connection with that, there is a question on which I should like to take your opinion. Poor Herrington once mentioned to me that he was subjected to a good deal of annoyance by a certain person who from time to time applied to him for financial help. I gathered that some sort of claim was advanced, and that the demands for money were more or less of the nature of blackmail.

"Giles didn't say who the person was, but I got the impression that he was a relative. Now, my friend Carston, who attended the inquest with me, noticed that the porter's description of the stranger would apply fairly well to a nephew of Giles's, whom he knows slightly and who is a somewhat shady character; and the question that Carston and I have been debating is whether these facts ought to be communicated to the police. It is a serious matter to put a man under suspicion on such very slender data; and yet—"

"And yet," said Carston, "the facts certainly fit the circumstances. This fellow—his name is Godfrey Herrington—is a typical ne'er-do-weel. Nobody knows how he lives. He doesn't appear to do any work. And then there is the personality of the deceased. I didn't know Giles Herrington very well, but I knew his brother, Sir Gilbert, pretty intimately, and if Giles was at all like him, a catastrophe might easily have occurred."

"What was Sir Gilbert's special characteristic?" Thorndyke asked.

"Unamiability," was the reply. "He was a most cantankerous, overbearing man, and violent at times. I knew him when I was at the Colonial Office with him, and one of his official acts will show the sort of man he was. You may remember it, Bidwell—the Bekwè affair. There was some trouble in Bekwè, which is one of the minor kingdoms bordering on Ashanti, and Sir Gilbert was sent out as a special commissioner to settle it. And settle it he did with a vengeance. He took up an armed force, deposed the king of Bekwè, seized the royal stool, message stick, state sword, drums, and the other insignia of royalty, and brought them away with him. And what made it worse was that he treated these important things as mere loot kept some of them himself and gave away others as presents to his friends.

"It was an intolerably high-handed proceeding, and it caused a rare outcry. Even the Colonial Governor protested, and in the end the Secretary of State directed the Governor to reinstate the king and restore the stolen insignia, as these things went with the royal title and were necessary for the ceremonies of reinstatement or the accession of a new king."

"And were they restored?" asked Bidwell.

"Most of them were. But just about this time Gilbert died, and as the whereabouts of one or two of them were unknown, it was impossible to collect them then. I don't know if they have been found since."

Here Thorndyke led Mr. Carston back to the point from which he had digressed.

"You are suggesting that certain peculiarities of temper and temperament on the part of the deceased might have some bearing on the circumstances of his death."

"Yes," said Carston. "If Giles Herrington was at all like his brother—I don't know whether he was—" here he looked inquiringly at Bidwell, who nodded emphatically.

"I should say he was, undoubtedly," said he. "He was my friend, and I was greatly attached to him; but to others, I must admit, he must have appeared a decidedly morose, cantankerous, and irascible man."

"Very well," resumed Carston. "If you imagine this cadging, blackmailing wastrel calling on him and trying to squeeze him, and then you imagine Herrington refusing to be squeezed and becoming abusive and even violent, you have a fair set of antecedents for—for what, in fact, did happen."

"By the way," said Thorndyke, "what exactly did happen, according to the evidence?"

"The medical evidence," replied Bidwell, "showed that the immediate cause of death was heart failure. There were marks of fingers on the throat, as you know, and various other bruises. It was evident that deceased had been violently assaulted, but death was not directly due to the injuries."

"And the finding of the jury?" asked Thorndyke.

"Wilful murder, committed by some person unknown."

"It doesn't appear to me," said I, "that Mr. Carston's suggestion has much present bearing on the case. It is really a point for the defence. But we are concerned with the identity of the unknown man."

"I am inclined to agree with Dr. Jervis," said Bidwell. "We have got to catch the hare before we go into culinary details."

"My point is," said Carston, "that Herrington's peculiar temper suggests a set of circumstances that would render it probable that his visitor was his nephew Godfrey."

"There is some truth in that," Thorndyke agreed. "It is highly speculative, but a reasonable speculation cannot be disregarded when the known facts are so few. My feeling is that the police ought to be informed of the existence of this man and his possible relations with the deceased. As to whether he is or is not the suspected stranger, that could be settled at once if he were confronted with the night porter."

"Yes, that is true," said Bidwell "I think Carston and I had better call at Scotland Yard and give the Assistant Commissioner a hint on the subject. It will have to be a very guarded hint, of course."

"Was the question of motive raised?" Thorndyke asked. "As to robbery, for instance."

"There is no evidence of robbery," replied Bidwell. "I have been through all the receptacles in the chambers, and everything seems intact. The keys were in poor Giles's pocket and nothing seems to have been disturbed; indeed, it doesn't appear that there was any portable property of value on the premises."

"Well," said Thorndyke, "the first thing that has to be done is to establish the identity of the nocturnal visitor. That is the business of the police. And if you call and tell them what you have told us, they will, at least, have something to investigate. They should have no difficulty in proving either that he is or is not the man whom the porter let in at the gate; and until they have settled that question, there is no need for us to take any action."

"Exactly," said Bidwell, rising and taking up his hat. "If the police can complete the case, there is nothing for us to do. However, I will leave you the report of the inquest to look over at your leisure, and will keep you informed as to how the case progresses."

When our two friends had gone, Thorndyke sat for some time turning over the sheets of the report and glancing through the depositions of the witnesses. Presently he remarked: "If it turns out that this man, Godfrey Herrington, is not the man whom the porter let in, the police will be left in the air. Apart from Bidwell's purely speculative suggestion, there seems to be no clue whatever to the visitor's identity."

"Badger would like to hear you say that," said I. "He was very sarcastic respecting our methods of research," and here I gave him an account of my interview with the inspector, including the "clues" with which he had presented me.

"It was like his impudence," Thorndyke commented smilingly, "to pull the leg of my learned junior. Still, there was a germ of sense in what he said. A collection of dust from the floor of that room, in which two men had engaged in a violent struggle, would certainly yield traces of both of them."

"Mixed up with the traces of a good many others," I remarked.

"True," he admitted. "But that would not affect the value of a positive trace of a particular individual. Supposing, for instance, that Godfrey Herrington were known to have dyed hair; and suppose that one or more dyed male hairs were found in the dust from the floor of the room. That would establish a probability that he had been in that room, and also that he was the person who had struggled with the deceased."

"Yes, I see that," said I. "Perhaps I ought to have collected some of the dust. But it isn't too late now, as Bidwell has locked up the chambers, Meanwhile, let me present you with Badger's clues. They came off the floor."

I searched in my pocket and produced the paper packet, the existence of which I had forgotten, and having opened it, offered it to him with an ironical bow. He looked gravely at the little collection, and, disregarding the pin and the match, picked out the third object and examined it curiously.

"That is the alleged boot-lace end," he remarked. "It doesn't do much credit to Badger's powers of observation. It is as unlike leather as it could well be."

"Yes," I agreed, "it is obviously whalebone or vulcanite."

"It isn't vulcanite," said he, looking closely at the broken end and getting out his pocket lens for a more minute inspection.

"What do you suppose it is?" I asked, my curiosity stimulated by the evident interest with which he was examining the object.

"We needn't suppose," he replied. "I fancy that if we get Polton to make a cross section of it, the microscope will tell us what it is. I will take it up to him." As he went out and I heard him ascending to the laboratory where our assistant, Polton, was at work, I was conscious of a feeling of vexation and a sense of failure. It was always thus. I had treated this fragment with the same levity as had the inspector, just dropping it into my pocket and forgetting it. Probably the thing was of no interest or importance; but whether it was or not, Thorndyke would not be satisfied until he knew for certain what it was. And that habit of examining everything, of letting nothing pass without the closest scrutiny, was one of the great secrets of his success as an investigator.

When he came down again I reopened the subject.

It has occurred to me," I said, "that it might be as well for us to have a look at that room. My inspection was rather perfunctory, as Badger was there."

"I have just been thinking the same," he replied. "If Godfrey is not the man, and the police are left stranded, Bidwell will look to us to take up the inquiry, and by that time the room may have been disturbed. I think we will get the key from Bidwell tomorrow morning and make a thorough examination. And we may as well adopt Badger's excellent suggestion respecting the dust. I will instruct Polton to come over with us and bring a full-sized vacuum-cleaner, and we can go over what he collects at our leisure."

Agreeably to this arrangement, we presented ourselves on the following morning at Mr. Bidwell's chambers, accompanied by Polton, who, however, being acutely conscious of the vacuum-cleaner, which was thinly disguised in brown paper, sneaked up the stairs and got out of sight. Bidwell opened the door himself, and Thorndyke explained our intentions to him.

"Of course you can have the key," he said, "but I don't know that it is worth your while to go into the matter. There have been developments since I saw you last night. When Carston and I called at Scotland Yard we found that we were too late. Godfrey Herrington had come forward and made a voluntary statement."

"That was wise of him," said Thorndyke, "but he would have been wiser still to have notified the porter of what had happened and sent for a doctor. He claims that the death was a misadventure, of course?"

"Not at all," replied Bidwell. "He states that when be left, Giles was perfectly well; so well that he was able to kick him—Godfrey—down the stairs and pitch him out on to the pavement. It seems, according to his account, that he called to try to get some financial help from his uncle. He admits that he was rather importunate and persisted after Giles had definitely refused. Then Giles got suddenly into a rage, thrust him out of the chambers, ran him down the stairs, and threw him out into Tanfield Court. It is a perfectly coherent story, and quite probable up to a certain point, but it doesn't account for the bruises on Giles's body or the finger-marks on his throat."

"No," agreed Thorndyke; "either he is lying, or he is the victim of some very inexplicable circumstances. But I gather that you have no further interest in the case?"

Bidwell reflected.

"Well," he said, "I don't know about that. Of course I don't believe him, but it is just possible that he is telling the truth. My feeling is that, if he is guilty, I want him convicted; but if by any chance he is innocent—well, he is Giles's nephew, and I suppose it is my duty to see that he has a fair chance. Yes, I think I would like you to watch the case independently—with a perfectly open mind, neither for nor against. But I don't see that there is much that you can do."

"Neither do I," said Thorndyke. "But one can observe and note the visible facts, if there are any. Has anything been done to the rooms?"

"Nothing whatever," was the reply. "They are just as Dr. Jervis and I found them the morning after the catastrophe."

With this he handed Thorndyke the key and we ascended to the landing, where we found Polton on guard with the vacuum-cleaner, like a sentry armed with some new and unorthodox weapon.

The appearance of the room was unchanged. The half-dislodged table-cloth, the litter of broken glass on the floor, even the displaced fender and hearth-rug, were just as I had last seen them. Thorndyke looked about him critically and remarked "The appearances hardly support Godfrey's statement. There was clearly a prolonged and violent struggle, not a mere ejectment. And look at the table cloth. The uncovered part of the table is that nearest the door, and most of the things have fallen off at the end nearest the fireplace. Obviously, the body that dislodged the cloth was moving away from the door, not towards it, which again suggests something more than an unresisted ejectment."

He again looked round, and his glance fell on the nail and the coloured silhouette on the wall-paper.

"That, I presume," said he, "is where the mysterious sword or dagger hung. It is rather large for a dagger and somewhat wide for a sword, though barbaric swords are of all shapes and sizes."

He produced his spring tape and carefully measured the phantom shape on the wall. "Thirty-one inches long," he reported, "including the loop at the end of the handle, by which it hung; seven and a half inches at the top of the scabbard, tapering rather irregularly to three inches at the tip. A curious shape. I don't remember ever having seen a sword quite like it."

Meanwhile Polton, having picked up the broken glass and other objects, had uncovered the vacuum-cleaner and now started the motor—which was driven by an attached dry battery—and proceeded very systematically to trundle the machine along the floor. At every two or three sweeps he paused to empty the receiver, placing the grey, felt-like mass on a sheet of paper, with a pencilled note of the part of the room from whence it came. The size of these masses of felted dust, and the astonishing change in the colour of the carpet that marked the trail of the cleaner, suggested that Mrs. Runt's activities had been of a somewhat perfunctory character. Polton's dredgings apparently represented the accumulations of years.

"Wonderful lot of hairs in this old dust," Polton remarked as he deposited a fresh consignment on the paper, "especially in this lot. It came from under that looking-glass on the wall. Perhaps that clothes brush that hangs under the glass accounts for it."

"Yes," I agreed, "they will be hairs brushed off Mr. Herrington's collar and shoulders. But," I added, taking the brush from its nail and examining it, "Mrs. Runt seems to have used the glass, too. There are three long hairs still sticking to the brush."

As Thorndyke was still occupied in browsing inquisitively round the room, I proceeded to make a preliminary inspection of the heaps of dust, picking out the hairs and other recognisable objects with my pocket forceps, and putting them on a separate sheet of paper. Of the former, the bulk were pretty obviously those of the late tenant—white or dull black male hairs—but Mrs. Runt had contributed quite liberally, for I picked out of the various heaps over a dozen long hairs, the mousy brown colour of which seemed to identify them as hers. The remainder were mostly ordinary male hairs of various colours, eyebrow hairs and eyelashes, of no special interest, with one exception. This was a black hair which lay flat on the paper in a Close coil, like a tiny watch-spring.

"I wonder who this person was," said I, inspecting it through my lens.

"Probably some African or West Indian Law student," Thorndyke suggested. "There are always a good many about the Inns of Court."

He came round to examine my collection, and while he was viewing the negro hair with the aid of my lens, I renewed my investigation of the little dust-heaps. Presently I made a new discovery.

"Why," I exclaimed, "here is another of Badger's boot-laces—another piece of the same one, I think. By the way, did you ascertain what that boot-lace really was?"

"Yes," he replied. "Polton made a section of it and mounted it; and furthermore, he made a magnified photograph of it. I have the photograph in my pocket, so you can answer your own question."

He produced from his letter-case a half-plate print which he handed to me and which I examined curiously.

"It is a singular object," said I, "but I don't quite make it out. It looks rather like a bundle of hairs embedded in some transparent substance."

"That, in effect," he replied, "is what it is. It is an elephant's hair, probably from the tail. But, as you see, it is a compound hair; virtually a group of hairs agglutinated into a single stem. Most very large hairs are compound. A tiger's whiskers, for instance, are large, stiff hairs which, if cut across, are seen to be formed of several largish hairs fused together; and the colossal hair which grows on the nose of the rhinoceros—the so-called nasal horn—is made up of thousands of subordinate hairs."

"It is a remarkable-looking thing," I said, handing back the photograph; "very distinctive—if you happen to know what it is. But the mystery is how on earth it came here. There are no elephants in the Temple."

"I certainly haven't noticed any," he replied; "and, as you say, the presence of an elephant's hair in a room in the middle of London is a rather remarkable circumstance. And yet, perhaps, if we consider all the other circumstances, it may not be impossible to form a conjecture as to how it came here. I recommend the problem to my learned friend for consideration at his leisure and now, as we have seen all that there is to see—which is mighty little—we may as well leave Polton to finish the collection of data from the floor. We can take your little selection with us."

He folded the paper containing the hairs that I had picked out into a neat packet, which he slipped into his pocket; then, having handed the key of the outer door to Polton, for return to Mr. Bidwell, he went out and I followed. We descended the stairs slowly, both of us deeply reflective. As to the subject of his meditations I could form no opinion, but my own were occupied by the problem which he had suggested; and the more I reflected on it, the less capable of solution did it appear.

We had nearly reached the ground floor when I became aware of quick footsteps descending the stairs behind us. Near the entry our follower overtook us, and as we stood aside to let him pass, I had a brief vision of a shortish, dapper, smartly-dressed coloured man—apparently an African or West Indian—who carried a small suit-case and a set of golf-clubs.

"Now," said I, in a low tone, "I wonder if that gentleman is the late owner of that negro hair that I picked up. It seems intrinsically probable as he appears to live in this building, and would be a near neighbour of Herrington's." I halted at the entry and read out the only name painted on the door-post as appertaining to the second floor—Mr. Kwaku Essien, which, I decided, seemed to fit a gentleman of colour.

But Thorndyke was not listening. His long legs were already carrying him, with a deceptively leisurely air, across Tanfield Court in the wake of Mr. Essien, and at about the same pace. I put on a spurt and over took him, a little mystified by his sudden air of purpose and by the fact that he was not walking in the direction of our chambers. Still more mystified was I when it became clear that Thorndyke was following the African and keeping at a constant distance in rear of him; but I made no comment until, having pursued our quarry to the top of Middle Temple Lane, we saw him hail a taxi and drive off. Then I demanded an explanation.

"I wanted to see him fairly out of the precincts," was the reply, "because I have a particular desire to see what his chambers are like. I only hope his door has a practicable latch."

I stared at him in dismay.

"You surely don't contemplate breaking into his chambers!" I exclaimed.

"Certainly not," he replied, "if the latch won't yield to gentle persuasion I shall give it up. But don't let me involve you, Jervis. I admit that it is a slightly irregular proceeding."

"Irregular!" I repeated. "It is house-breaking, pure and simple I can only hope that you won't be able to get in."

The hope turned out to be a vain one, as I had secretly feared. When we had reconnoitred the stairs and established the encouraging fact that the third floor was untenanted, we inspected the door above which our victim's name was painted; and a glance at the yawning key of an old-fashioned draw-latch told me that the deed was as good as done.

"Now, Jervis," said Thorndyke, producing from his pocket the curious instrument that he described as a "smoker's companion"—it was an undeniable pick-lock, made by Polton under his direction—"you had better clear out and wait for me at our chambers."

"I shall do nothing of the kind," I replied. "I am an accessory before the fact already, so I may as well stay and see the crime committed."

"Then in that case," said he, "you had better keep a look-out from the landing window and call me if any one comes to the house. That will make us perfectly safe."

I accordingly took my station at the window, and Thorndyke, having knocked several times at the "oak" without eliciting any response, set to work with the smoker's companion. In less than a minute the latch clicked, the outer door opened, and Thorndyke, pushing the inner door open, entered, leaving both doors ajar. I was devoured by curiosity as to what his purpose was. Obviously it must be a very definite one to justify this most extraordinary proceeding.

But I dared not leave my post for a moment, seeing that we were really engaged in a very serious breach of the law and it was of vital importance that we should not be surprised in the act. I was therefore unable to observe my colleague's proceedings, and I waited impatiently to see if anything came of this unlawful entry.

I had waited thus some ten minutes, keeping a close watch on the pavement below, when I heard Thorndyke quickly cross the room and approach the door. A moment later he came out on the landing, bearing in his hand an object which, while it enlightened me as to the purpose of the raid, added to my mystification.

"That looks like the missing sword from Herrington's room!" I exclaimed, gazing at it in amazement.

"Yes," he replied. "I found it in a drawer in the bedroom. Only it isn't a sword."

"Then, what the deuce is it?" I demanded, for the thing looked like a broad-bladed sword in a soft leather scabbard of somewhat rude native workman ship.

By way of reply he slowly drew the object from its sheath, and as it came into sight, I uttered an exclamation of astonishment. To the inexpert eye it appeared an elongated body about nine inches in length covered with coarse, black leather, from either side of which sprang a multitude of what looked like thick, black wires. Above, it was furnished with a leather handle which was surmounted by a suspension loop of plaited leather.

"I take it," said I, "that this is an elephant's tail."

"Yes," he replied, "and a rather remarkable specimen. The hairs are of unusual length. Some of them, you see, are nearly eighteen inches long."

"And what are you going to do now?" I asked.

"I am going to put it back where I found it. Then I shall run down to Scotland Yard and advise Miller to get a search warrant. He is too discreet to ask inconvenient questions."

I must admit that it was a great relief to me when, a minute later, Thorndyke came out and shut the door; but I could not deny that the raid had been justified by the results. What had, presumably, been a mere surmise had been converted into a definite fact on which action could confidently be taken.

"I suppose," said I, as we walked down towards the Embankment *en route* for Scotland Yard, "I ought to have spotted this case."

"You had the means," Thorndyke replied. "At your first visit you learned that an object of some kind had disappeared from the wall. It seemed to be a trivial object of no value, and not likely to be connected with the crime. So you disregarded it. But it had disappeared. Its disappearance was not accounted for, and that disappearance seemed to coincide in time with the death of Herrington. It undoubtedly called for investigation. Then you found on the floor an object the nature of which was unknown to you. Obviously, you ought to have ascertained what it was."

"Yes, I ought," I admitted, "though I am not sure that I should have been much forrader even then. In fact, I am not so very much forrader even now. I don't see how you spotted this man Essien, and I don't understand why he took all this trouble and risk and even committed a murder to get possession of this trumpery curio. Of course I can make a vague guess. But I should like to hear how you ran the man and the thing to earth."

"Very well," said Thorndyke. "Let me retrace the train of discoveries and inferences in their order. First I learned that an object, supposed to be a barbaric sword of some kind, had disappeared about the time of the murder—if it was a murder. Then we heard from Carston that Sir Gilbert Herrington had appropriated the insignia and ceremonial objects belonging to the king of Bekwè; that some had subsequently been restored, but others had been given to friends as curios. As I listened to that story, the possibility occurred to me that this curio which had disappeared might be one of the missing ceremonial objects. It was not only possible: it was quite probable. For Giles Herrington was a very likely person to have received one of these gifts, and his morose temper made it unlikely that he would restore it.

"And then, since such an object would be of great value to somebody, and since it was actually stolen property, there would be good reasons why some interested person should take forcible possession of it. This, of course, was mere hypothesis of a rather shadowy kind. But when you produced an object which I at once suspected, and then proved, to be an elephant's hair, the hypothesis became a reasonable working theory. For, among the ceremonial objects which form what we may call the regalia of a West African king is the elephant's tail which is carried before him by a special officer as a symbol of his power and strength. An elephant's tail had pretty certainly been stolen from the king, and Carston said nothing about its having been restored.

"Well, when we went to Herrington's chambers just now, it was clear to me that the thing which had disappeared was certainly not a sword. The phantom shape on the wall did not show much, but it did show plainly that the object had hung from the nail by a large loop at the end of the handle. But the suspension loop of a sword or dagger is always on the scabbard, never on the hilt. But if the thing was not a sword, what was it? The elephant's hair that you found on the floor seemed to answer the question.

"Now, as we came in, I had noticed on the doorpost the West African name, Kwaku Essien. A man whose name is Kwaku is pretty certainly a negro. But if this was an elephant's tail, its lawful owner was a negro, and that owner wanted to recover it and was morally entitled to take possession of it. Here was another striking agreement. The chambers over Herrington's were occupied by a coloured nobleman. Finally, you found among the floor dust a negro's hair. Then a negro had actually been in this room. But from what we know of Herrington, that man was not there as an invited visitor. All the probabilities pointed to Mr. Essien. But the probabilities were not enough to act on. Then we had a stroke of sheer luck. We got the chance to explore Essien's chambers and seek the crucial fact. But here we are at Scotland Yard."

That night, at about eight o'clock, a familiar tattoo on our knocker announced the arrival of Mr. Superintendent Miller, not entirely unexpected as I guessed.

"Well," he said, as I let him in, "the coloured nobleman has come home. I've just had a message from the man who was detailed to watch the premises."

"Are you going to make the arrest now?" asked Thorndyke.

"Yes, and I should be glad if you could come across with me. You know more about the case than I do."

Thorndyke assented at once, and we set forth together. As we entered Tanfield Court we passed a man who was lurking in the shadow of an entry, and who silently indicated the lighted windows of the chambers for which we were bound. Ascending the stairs up which I had lately climbed with unlawful intent, we halted at Mr. Essien's door, on which the superintendent executed an elaborate flourish with his stick, there being no knocker. After a short interval we heard a bolt with drawn, the door opened a short distance, and in the interval a black face appeared looking out at us suspiciously.

"Who are you, and what do you want?" the owner of the face demanded gruffly.

"You are Mr. Kwaku Essien, I think?" said Miller, unostentatiously insinuating his foot into the door opening.

"Yes," was the reply. "But I don't know you. What is your business?"

"I am a police officer," Miller replied, edging his foot in a little farther, "and I hold a warrant to arrest you on the charge of having murdered Mr. Giles Herrington."

Before the superintendent had fairly finished his sentence, the dusky face vanished and the door slammed violently—on to the superintendent's massive foot. That foot was instantly reinforced by a shoulder and for a few moments there was a contest of forces, opposite but not equal. Suddenly the door flew open and the superintendent charged into the room. I had a momentary vision of a flying figure, closely pursued, darting through into an inner room, of the slamming of a second door—once more on an intercepting foot. And then—it all seemed to have happened in a few seconds—a dejected figure, sitting on the edge of a bed, clasping a pair of manacled hands and watching Miller as he drew the elephant's tail out of a drawer in the dressing-chest.

"This—er—article," said Miller, "belonged to Mr. Herrington, and was stolen from his premises on the night of the murder."

Essien shook his head emphatically.

"No," he replied. "You are wrong. I stole nothing, and I did not murder Mr. Herrington. Listen to me and I will tell you all about it."

Miller administered the usual caution and the prisoner continued: "This elephant-brush is one of many things stolen, years ago, from the king of Bekwè. Some of those things—most of them—have been restored, but this could not be traced for a long time. At last it became known to me that Mr. Herrington had it, and I wrote to him asking him to give it up and telling him who I was—I am the eldest living son of the king's sister, and therefore, according to our law, the heir to the kingdom. But he would not give it up or even sell it. Then, as I am a student of the Inn, I took these chambers above his, intending, when I had an opportunity, to go in and take possession of my uncle's property.

"The opportunity came that night that you have spoken of. I was coming up the stairs to my chambers when, as I passed his door, I heard loud voices inside as of people quarrelling. I had just reached my own door and opened it when I heard his door open, and then a great uproar and the sound of a struggle. I ran down a little way and looked over the banisters, and then I saw him thrusting a man across the landing and down the lower stairs. As they disappeared, I ran down, and finding his door ajar, I went in to recover my property. It took me a little time to find it, and I had just taken it from the nail and was going out with it when, at the door, I met Mr. Herrington coming in.

"He was very excited already, and when he saw me he seemed to go mad. I tried to get past him, but he seized me and dragged me back into the room, wrenching the thing out of my hand. He was very violent. I thought he wanted to kill me, and I had to struggle for my life. Suddenly he let go his hold of me, staggered back a few paces, and then fell on the floor. I stooped over him, thinking that he was taken ill, and wondering what I had better do. But soon I saw that he was not ill; he was dead. Then I was very frightened. I picked up the elephant brush and put it back into its case, and I went out very quietly, shut the door, and ran up to my rooms. That is what happened. There was no robbery and murder."

"Well," said Miller, as the prisoner and his escort disappeared towards the gate, "I suppose, in a technical sense, it is murder, but they are hardly likely to press the charge."

"I don't think it is even technically," said Thorndyke. "My feeling is that he will be acquitted if he is sent for trial. Meanwhile, I take it that my client, Godfrey Herrington, will be released from custody at once."

"Yes, doctor," replied Miller, "I will see to that now. He has had better luck than he deserved, I suspect, in having his case looked after by you. I don't fancy he would have got an acquittal if he had gone for trial."

Thorndyke's forecast was nearly correct, but there was no acquittal, since there was no trial. The case against Kwaku Essien never got farther than the Grand Jury.

The Stranger's Latchkey

The contrariety of human nature is a subject that has given a surprising amount of occupation to makers of proverbs and to those moral philosophers who make it their province to discover and expound the glaringly obvious; and especially have they been concerned to enlarge upon that form of perverseness which engenders dislike of things offered under compulsion, and arouses desire of them as soon as their attainment becomes difficult or impossible. They assure us that a man who has had a given thing within his reach and put it by, will, as soon as it is beyond his reach, find it the one thing necessary and desirable; even as the domestic cat which has turned disdainfully from the preferred saucer, may presently be seen with her head jammed hard in the milk-jug, or, secretly and with horrible relish, slaking her thirst at the scullery sink.

To this peculiarity of the human mind was due, no doubt, the fact that no sooner had I abandoned the clinical side of my profession in favour of the legal, and taken up my abode in the chambers of my friend Thorndyke, the famous medico-legal expert, to act as his assistant or junior, than my former mode of life—that of a *locum tenens,* or minder of other men's practices—which had, when I was following it, seemed intolerably irksome, now appeared to possess many desirable features; and I found myself occasionally hankering to sit once more by the bedside, to puzzle out the perplexing train of symptoms, and to wield that power—the greatest, after all, possessed by man—the power to banish suffering and ward off the approach of death itself.

Hence it was that on a certain morning of the long vacation I found myself installed at The Larches, Burling, in full charge of the practice of my old friend Dr. Hanshaw, who was taking a fishing holiday in Norway. I was not left desolate, however, for Mrs. Hanshaw remained at her post, and the roomy, old-fashioned house accommodated three visitors in addition. One of these was Dr. Hanshaw's sister, a Mrs. Haldean, the widow of a wealthy Manchester cotton factor; the second was her niece by marriage, Miss Lucy Haldean, a very handsome and charming girl of twenty-three; while the third was no less a person than Master Fred, the only child of Mrs. Haldean, and a strapping boy of six.

"It is quite like old times—and very pleasant old times, too—to see you sitting at our breakfast-table, Dr. Jervis." With these gracious words and a friendly smile, Mrs. Hanshaw handed me my tea-cup.

I bowed. "The highest pleasure of the altruist," I replied, "is in contemplating the good fortune of others."

Mrs. Haldean laughed. "Thank you," she said. "You are quite unchanged, I perceive. Still as suave and as—shall I say oleaginous?"

"No, please don't!" I exclaimed in a tone of alarm.

"Then I won't. But what does Dr. Thorndyke say to this backsliding on your part? How does he regard this relapse from medical jurisprudence to common general practice?"

"Thorndyke," said I, "is unmoved by any catastrophe; and he not only regards the 'Decline and Fall-off of the Medical Jurist' with philosophic calm, but he even favours the relapse, as you call it. He thinks it may be useful to me to study the application of medico-legal methods to general practice."

"That sounds rather unpleasant—for the patients, I mean," remarked Miss Haldean.

"Very," agreed her aunt. "Most cold-blooded. What sort of man is Dr. Thorndyke? I feel quite curious about him. Is he at all human, for instance?"

"He is entirely human," I replied; "the accepted tests of humanity being, as I understand, the habitual adoption of the erect posture in locomotion, and the relative position of the end of the thumb—"

"I don't mean that," interrupted Mrs. Haldean. "I mean human in things that matter."

"I think those things matter," I rejoined. "Consider, Mrs. Haldean, what would happen if my learned colleague were to be seen in wig and gown, walking towards the Law Courts in any posture other than the erect. It would be a public scandal."

"Don't talk to him, Mabel," said Mrs. Hanshaw; "he is incorrigible. What are you doing with yourself this morning, Lucy?"

Miss Haldean (who had hastily set down her cup to laugh at my imaginary picture of Dr. Thorndyke in the character of a quadruped) considered a moment.

"I think I shall sketch that group of birches at the edge of Bradham Wood," she said.

"Then, in that case," said I, "I can carry your traps for you, for I have to see a patient in Bradham."

"He is making the most of his time," remarked Mrs. Haldean maliciously to my hostess. "He knows that when Mr. Winter arrives he will retire into the extreme background."

Douglas Winter, whose arrival was expected in the course of the week, was Miss Haldean's *fiancé*. Their engagement had been somewhat protracted, and was likely to be more so, unless one of them received some unexpected accession of means; for Douglas was a subaltern in the Royal Engineers, living, with great difficulty, on his pay, while Lucy Haldean subsisted on an almost invisible allowance left her by an uncle.

I was about to reply to Mrs. Haldean when a patient was announced, and, as I had finished my breakfast, I made my excuses and left the table.

Half an hour later, when I started along the road to the village of Bradham, I had two companions. Master Freddy had joined the party, and he disputed with me the privilege of carrying the "traps," with the result that a compromise was effected, by which he carried the camp-stool, leaving me in possession of the easel, the bag, and a large bound sketching-block.

"Where are you going to work this morning?" I asked, when we had trudged on some distance.

"Just off the road to the left there, at the edge of the wood. Not very far from the house of the mysterious stranger." She glanced at me mischievously as she made this reply, and chuckled with delight when I rose at the bait.

"What house do you mean?" I inquired.

"Ha!" she exclaimed, "the investigator of mysteries is aroused. He saith, 'Ha! ha!' amidst the trumpets; he smelleth the battle afar off."

"Explain instantly," I commanded, "or I drop your sketch-block into the very next puddle."

"You terrify me," said she. "But I will explain, only there isn't any mystery except to the *bucolic* mind. The house is called Lavender Cottage, and it stands alone in the fields behind the wood. A fortnight ago it was let furnished to a stranger named Whitelock, who has taken it for the purpose of studying the botany of the district; and the only really mysterious thing about him is that no one has seen him. All arrangements with the house-agent were made by letter, and, as far as I can make out, none of the local trades-people supply him, so he must get his things from a distance—even his bread, which really is rather odd. Now say I am an inquisitive, gossiping country bumpkin."

"I was going to," I answered, "but it is no use now."

She relieved me of her sketching appliances with pretended indignation, and crossed into the meadow, leaving me to pursue my way alone; and when I presently looked back, she was setting up her easel and stool, gravely assisted by Freddy.

My "round," though not a long one, took up more time than I had anticipated, and it was already past the luncheon hour when I passed the place where I had left Miss Haldean. She was gone, as I had expected, and I hurried homewards, anxious to be as nearly punctual as possible. When I entered the dining-room, I found Mrs. Haldean and our hostess seated at the table, and both looked up at me expectantly.

"Have you seen Lucy?" the former inquired.

"No," I answered. "Hasn't she come back? I expected to find her here. She had left the wood when I passed just now."

Mrs. Haldean knitted her brows anxiously. "It is very strange," she said, "and very thoughtless of her. Freddy will be famished."

I hurried over my lunch, for two fresh messages had come in from outlying hamlets, effectually dispelling my visions of a quiet afternoon; and as the minutes passed without bringing any signs of the absentees, Mrs. Haldean became more and more restless and anxious. At length her suspense became unbearable; she rose suddenly, announcing her intention of cycling up the road to look for the defaulters, but as she was moving towards the door, it burst open, and Lucy Haldean staggered into the room.

Her appearance filled us with alarm. She was deadly pale, breathless, and wild-eyed; her dress was draggled and torn, and she trembled from head to foot.

"Good God, Lucy!" gasped Mrs. Haldean. "What has happened? And where is Freddy?" she added in a sterner tone.

"He is lost!" replied Miss Haldean in a faint voice, and with a catch in her breath. "He strayed away while I was painting. I have searched the wood through, and called to him, and looked in all the meadows. Oh! where can he have gone?" Her sketching "kit," with which she was loaded, slipped from her grasp and rattled on to the floor, and she buried her face in her hands and sobbed hysterically.

"And you have dared to come back without him?" exclaimed Mrs. Haldean.

"I was getting exhausted. I came back for help," was the faint reply.

"Of course she was exhausted," said Mrs. Hanshaw. "Come, Lucy: come, Mabel; don't make mountains out of molehills. The little man is safe enough. We shall find him presently, or he will come home by himself. Come and have some food, Lucy."

Miss Haldean shook her head. "I can't, Mrs. Hanshaw—really I can't," she said; and, seeing that she was in a state of utter exhaustion, I poured out a glass of wine and made her drink it.

Mrs. Haldean darted from the room, and returned immediately, putting on her hat. "You have got to come with me and show me where you lost him," she said.

"She can't do that, you know," I said rather brusquely. "She will have to lie down for the present. But I know the place, and will cycle up with you."

"Very well," replied Mrs. Haldean, "that will do. What time was it," she asked, turning to her niece, "when you lost the child? and which way—"

She paused abruptly, and I looked at her in surprise. She had suddenly turned ashen and ghastly; her face had set like a mask of stone, with parted lips and staring eyes that were fixed in horror on her niece.

There was a deathly silence for a few seconds. Then, in a terrible voice, she demanded: "What is that on your dress, Lucy?" And, after a pause, her voice rose into a shriek. "What have you done to my boy?"

I glanced in astonishment at the dazed and terrified girl, and then I saw what her aunt had seen—a good-sized blood-stain halfway down the front of her skirt, and another smaller one on her right sleeve. The girl herself looked down at the sinister patch of red and then up at her aunt. "It looks like—like blood," she stammered. "Yes, it is—I think—of course it is. He struck his nose—and it bled—"

"Come," interrupted Mrs. Haldean, "let us go," and she rushed from the room, leaving me to follow.

I lifted Miss Haldean, who was half fainting with fatigue and agitation, on to the sofa, and, whispering a few words of encouragement into her ear, turned to Mrs. Hanshaw.

"I can't stay with Mrs. Haldean," I said. "There are two visits to be made at Rebworth. Will you send the dogcart up the road with somebody to take my place?"

"Yes," she answered. "I will send Giles, or come myself if Lucy is fit to be left."

I ran to the stables for my bicycle, and as I pedalled out into the road I could see Mrs. Haldean already far ahead, driving her machine at frantic speed. I followed at a rapid pace, but it was not until we approached the commencement of the wood, when she slowed down somewhat, that I overtook her.

"This is the place," I said, as we reached the spot where I had parted from Miss Haldean. We dismounted and wheeled our bicycles through the gate, and laying them down beside the hedge, crossed the meadow and entered the wood.

It was a terrible experience, and one that I shall never forget—the white-faced, distracted woman, tramping in her flimsy house-shoes over the rough ground, bursting through the bushes, regardless of the thorny branches that dragged at skin and hair and dainty clothing, and sending forth from time to time a tremulous cry, so dreadfully pathetic in its mingling of terror and coaxing softness, that a lump rose in my throat, and I could barely keep my self-control.

"Freddy! Freddy-boy! Mummy's here, darling!" The wailing cry sounded through the leafy solitude; but no answer came save the whirr of wings or the chatter of startled birds. But even more shocking than that terrible cry—more disturbing and eloquent with dreadful suggestion—was the way in which she peered, furtively, but with fearful expectation, among the roots of the bushes, or halted to gaze upon every molehill and hummock, every depression or disturbance of the ground.

So we stumbled on for a while, with never a word spoken, until we came to a beaten track or footpath leading across the wood. Here I paused to examine the footprints, of which several were visible in the soft earth, though none seemed very recent; but, proceeding a little way down the track, I perceived, crossing it, a set of fresh imprints, which I recognised at once as Miss Haldean's. She was wearing, as I knew, a pair of brown golf-boots, with rubber pads in the leather soles, and the prints made by them were unmistakable.

"Miss Haldean crossed the path here," I said, pointing to the footprints.

"Don't speak of her before me!" exclaimed Mrs. Haldean; but she gazed eagerly at the footprints, nevertheless, and immediately plunged into the wood to follow the tracks.

"You are very unjust to your niece, Mrs. Haldean," I ventured to protest.

She halted, and faced me with an angry frown.

"You don't understand!" she exclaimed. "You don't know, perhaps, that if my poor child is really dead, Lucy Haldean will be a rich woman, and may marry tomorrow if she chooses?"

"I did not know that," I answered, "but if I had, I should have said the same."

"Of course you would," she retorted bitterly. "A pretty face can muddle any man's judgment."

She turned away abruptly to resume her pursuit, and I followed in silence. The trail which we were following zigzagged through the thickest part of the wood, but its devious windings eventually brought us out on to an open space on the farther side. Here we at once perceived traces of another kind. A litter of dirty rags, pieces of paper, scraps of stale bread, bones and feathers, with hoof-marks, wheel ruts, and the ashes of a large wood fire, pointed clearly to a gipsy encampment recently broken up. I laid my hand on the heap of ashes, and found it still warm, and on scattering it with my foot a layer of glowing cinders appeared at the bottom.

"These people have only been gone an hour or two," I said. "It would be well to have them followed without delay."

A gleam of hope shone on the drawn, white face as the bereaved mother caught eagerly at my suggestion.

"Yes," she exclaimed breathlessly; "she may have bribed them to take him away. Let us see which way they went."

We followed the wheel tracks down to the road, and found that they turned towards London. At the same time I perceived the dogcart in the distance, with Mrs. Hanshaw standing beside it; and, as the coachman observed me, he whipped up his horse and approached.

"I shall have to go," I said, "but Mrs. Hanshaw will help you to continue the search."

"And you will make inquiries about the gipsies, won't you?" she said.

I promised to do so, and as the dogcart now came up, I climbed to the seat, and drove off briskly up the London Road.

The extent of a country doctor's round is always an unknown quantity. On the present occasion I picked up three additional patients, and as one of them was a case of incipient pleurisy, which required to have the chest strapped, and another was a neglected dislocation of the shoulder, a great deal of time was taken up. Moreover, the gipsies, whom I ran to earth on Rebworth Common, delayed me considerably, though I had to leave the rural constable to carry out the actual search, and, as a result, the clock of Burling Church was striking six as I drove through the village on my way home.

I got down at the front gate, leaving the coachman to take the dogcart round, and walked up the drive; and my astonishment may be imagined when, on turning the corner, I came suddenly upon the inspector of the local police in earnest conversation with no less a person than John Thorndyke.

"What on earth has brought you here?" I exclaimed, my surprise getting the better of my manners.

"The ultimate motive-force," he replied, "was an impulsive lady named Mrs. Haldean. She telegraphed for me—in your name."

"She oughtn't to have done that," I said.

"Perhaps not. But the ethics of an agitated woman are not worth discussing, and she has done something much worse—she has applied to the local J.P. (a retired Major-General), and our gallant and unlearned friend has issued a warrant for the arrest of Lucy Haldean on the charge of murder."

"But there has been no murder!" I exclaimed.

"That," said Thorndyke, "is a legal subtlety that he does not appreciate. He has learned his law in the orderly-room, where the qualifications to practise are an irritable temper and a loud voice. However, the practical point is, inspector, that the warrant is irregular. You can't arrest people for hypothetical crimes."

The officer drew a deep breath of relief. He knew all about the irregularity, and now joyfully took refuge behind Thorndyke's great reputation.

When he had departed—with a brief note from my colleague to the General—Thorndyke slipped his arm through mine, and we strolled towards the house.

"This is a grim business, Jervis," said he. "That boy has got to be found for everybody's sake. Can you come with me when you have had some food?"

"Of course I can. I have been saving myself all the afternoon with a view to continuing the search."

"Good," said Thorndyke. "Then come in and feed."

A nondescript meal, half tea and half dinner, was already prepared, and Mrs. Hanshaw, grave but self-possessed, presided at the table.

"Mabel is still out with Giles, searching for the boy," she said. "You have heard what she has done!"

I nodded.

"It was dreadful of her," continued Mrs. Hanshaw, "but she is half mad, poor thing. You might run up and say a few kind words to poor Lucy while I make the tea."

I went up at once and knocked at Miss Haldean's door, and, being bidden to enter, found her lying on the sofa, red-eyed and pale, the very ghost of the merry, laughing girl who had gone out with me in the morning. I drew up a chair, and sat down by her side, and as I took the hand she held out to me, she said:

"It is good of you to come and see a miserable wretch like me. And Jane has been so sweet to me, Dr. Jervis; but Aunt Mabel thinks I have killed Freddy—you know she does—and it was really my fault that he was lost. I shall never forgive myself!"

She burst into a passion of sobbing, and I proceeded to chide her gently.

"You are a silly little woman," I said, "to take this nonsense to heart as you are doing. Your aunt is not responsible just now, as you must know; but when we bring the boy home she shall make you a handsome apology. I will see to that."

She pressed my hand gratefully, and as the bell now rang for tea, I bade her have courage and went downstairs.

"You need not trouble about the practice," said Mrs. Hanshaw, as I concluded my lightning repast, and Thorndyke went off to get our bicycles. "Dr. Symons has heard of our trouble, and has called to say that he will take anything that turns up; so we shall expect you when we see you."

"How do you like Thorndyke?" I asked.

"He is quite charming," she replied enthusiastically; "so tactful and kind, and so handsome, too. You didn't tell us that. But here he is. Goodbye, and good luck."

She pressed my hand, and I went out into the drive, where Thorndyke and the coachman were standing with three bicycles.

"I see you have brought your outfit," I said as we turned into the road; for Thorndyke's machine bore a large canvas-covered case strapped on to a strong bracket.

"Yes; there are many things that we may want on a quest of this kind. How did you find Miss Haldean?"

"Very miserable, poor girl. By the way, have you heard anything about her pecuniary interest in the child's death?"

"Yes," said Thorndyke. "It appears that the late Mr. Haldean used up all his brains on his business, and had none left for the making of his will—as often happens. He left almost the whole of his property—about eighty thousand pounds—to his son, the widow to have a life-interest in it. He also left to his late brother's daughter, Lucy, fifty pounds a year, and to his surviving brother Percy, who seems to have been a good-for-nothing, a hundred a year for life. But—and here is the utter folly of the thing—if the son should die, the property was to be equally divided between the brother and the niece, with the exception of five hundred a year for life to the widow. It was an insane arrangement."

"Quite," I agreed, "and a very dangerous one for Lucy Haldean, as things are at present."

"Very; especially if anything should have happened to the child."

"What are you going to do now?" I inquired, seeing that Thorndyke rode on as if with a definite purpose.

"There is a footpath through the wood," he replied. "I want to examine that. And there is a house behind the wood which I should like to see."

"The house of the mysterious stranger," I suggested.

"Precisely. Mysterious and solitary strangers invite inquiry."

We drew up at the entrance to the footpath, leaving Willett the coachman in charge of the three machines, and proceeded up the narrow track. As we went, Thorndyke looked back at the prints of our feet, and nodded approvingly.

"This soft loam," he remarked, "yields beautifully clear impressions, and yesterday's rain has made it perfect."

We had not gone far when we perceived a set of footprints which I recognised, as did Thorndyke also, for he remarked: "Miss Haldean—running, and alone." Presently we met them again, crossing in the opposite direction, together with the prints of small shoes with very high heels. "Mrs. Haldean on the track of her niece," was Thorndyke's comment; and a minute later we encountered them both again, accompanied by my own footprints.

"The boy does not seem to have crossed the path at all," I remarked as we walked on, keeping off the track itself to avoid confusing the footprints.

"We shall know when we have examined the whole length," replied Thorndyke, plodding on with his eyes on the ground. "Ha! here is something new," he added, stopping short and stooping down eagerly—"a man with a thick stick—a smallish man, rather lame. Notice the difference between the two feet, and the peculiar way in which he uses his stick. Yes, Jervis, there is a great deal to interest us in these footprints. Do you notice anything very suggestive about them?"

"Nothing but what you have mentioned," I replied. "What do you mean?"

"Well, first there is the very singular character of the prints themselves, which we will consider presently. You observe that this man came down the path, and at this point turned off into the wood; then he returned from the wood and went up the path again. The imposition of the prints makes that clear. But now look at the two sets of prints, and compare them. Do you notice any difference?"

"The returning footprints seem more distinct—better impressions."

"Yes; they are noticeably deeper. But there is something else." He produced a spring tape from his pocket, and took half a dozen measurements. "You see," he said, "the first set of footprints have a stride of twenty-one inches from heel to heel—a short stride; but he is a smallish man, and lame; the returning ones have a stride of only nineteen and a half inches; hence the returning footprints are deeper than the others, and the steps are shorter. What do you make of that?"

"It would suggest that he was carrying a burden when he returned," I replied.

"Yes; and a heavy one, to make that difference in the depth. I think I will get you to go and fetch Willett and the bicycles."

I strode off down the path to the entrance, and, taking possession of Thorndyke's machine, with its precious case of instruments, bade Willett follow with the other two.

When I returned, my colleague was standing with his hands behind him, gazing with intense preoccupation at the footprints. He looked up sharply as we approached, and called out to us to keep off the path if possible.

"Stay here with the machines, Willett," said he. "You and I, Jervis, must go and see where our friend went to when he left the path, and what was the burden that he picked up."

We struck off into the wood, where last year's dead leaves made the footprints almost indistinguishable, and followed the faint double track for a long distance between the dense clumps of bushes. Suddenly my eye caught, beside the double trail, a third row of tracks, smaller in size and closer together. Thorndyke had seen them, too, and already his measuring-tape was in his hand.

"Eleven and a half inches to the stride," said he. "That will be the boy, Jervis. But the light is getting weak. We must press on quickly, or we shall lose it."

Some fifty yards farther on, the man's tracks ceased abruptly, but the small ones continued alone; and we followed them as rapidly as we could in the fading light.

"There can be no reasonable doubt that these are the child's tracks," said Thorndyke; "but I should like to find a definite footprint to make the identification absolutely certain."

A few seconds later he halted with an exclamation, and stooped on one knee. A little heap of fresh earth from the surface-burrow of a mole had been thrown up over the dead leaves; and fairly planted on it was the clean and sharp impression of a diminutive foot, with a rubber heel showing a central star. Thorndyke drew from his pocket a tiny shoe, and pressed it on the soft earth beside the footprint; and when he raised it the second impression was identical with the first.

"The boy had two pairs of shoes exactly alike," he said, "so I borrowed one of the duplicate pair."

He turned, and began to retrace his steps rapidly, following our own fresh tracks, and stopping only once to point out the place where the unknown man had picked the child up. When we regained the path we proceeded without delay until we emerged from the wood within a hundred yards of the cottage.

"I see Mrs. Haldean has been here with Giles," remarked Thorndyke, as he pushed open the garden-gate. "I wonder if they saw anybody."

He advanced to the door, and having first rapped with his knuckles and then kicked at it vigorously, tried the handle.

"Locked," he observed, "but I see the key is in the lock, so we can get in if we want to. Let us try the back."

The back door was locked, too, but the key had been removed.

"He came out this way, evidently," said Thorndyke, "though he went in at the front, as I suppose you noticed. Let us see where he went."

The back garden was a small, fenced patch of ground, with an earth path leading down to the back gate. A little way beyond the gate was a small barn or outhouse.

"We are in luck," Thorndyke remarked, with a glance at the path. "Yesterday's rain has cleared away all old footprints, and prepared the surface for new ones. You see there are three sets of excellent impressions—two leading away from the house, and one set towards it. Now, you notice that both of the sets leading from the house are characterized by deep impressions and short steps, while the set leading to the house has lighter impressions and longer steps. The obvious inference is that he went down the path with a heavy burden, came back empty-handed, and went down again—and finally—with another heavy burden. You observe, too, that he walked with his stick on each occasion."

By this time we had reached the bottom of the garden. Opening the gate, we followed the tracks towards the outhouse, which stood beside a cart-track; but as we came round the corner we both stopped short and looked at one another. On the soft earth were the very distinct impressions of the tyres of a motor-car leading from the wide door of the outhouse. Finding that the door was unfastened, Thorndyke opened it, and looked in, to satisfy himself that the place was empty. Then he fell to studying the tracks.

"The course of events is pretty plain," he observed. "First the fellow brought down his luggage, started the engine, and got the car out—you can see where it stood, both by the little pool of oil, and by the widening and blurring of the wheel-tracks from the vibration of the free engine; then he went back and fetched the boy—carried him pick-a-back, I should say, judging by the depth of the toe-marks in the last set of footprints. That was a tactical mistake. He should have taken the boy straight into the shed."

He pointed as he spoke to one of the footprints beside the wheel-tracks, from the toe of which projected a small segment of the print of a little rubber heel.

We now made our way back to the house, where we found Willett pensively rapping at the front door with a cycle-spanner. Thorndyke took a last glance, with his hand in his pocket, at an open window above, and then, to the coachman's intense delight, brought forth what looked uncommonly like a small bunch of skeleton keys. One of these he inserted into the keyhole, and as he gave it a turn, the lock clicked, and the door stood open.

The little sitting-room, which we now entered, was furnished with the barest necessaries. Its centre was occupied by an oilcloth-covered table, on which I observed with surprise a dismembered "Bee" clock (the works of which had been taken apart with a tin-opener that lay beside them) and a box-wood bird-call. At these objects Thorndyke glanced and nodded, as though they fitted into some theory that he had formed; examined carefully the oilcloth around the litter of wheels and pinions, and then proceeded on a tour of inspection round the room, peering inquisitively into the kitchen and store-cupboard.

"Nothing very distinctive or personal here," he remarked. "Let us go upstairs."

There were three bedrooms on the upper floor, of which two were evidently disused, though the windows were wide open. The third bedroom showed manifest traces of occupation, though it was as bare as the others, for the water still stood in the wash-hand basin, and the bed was unmade. To the latter Thorndyke advanced, and, having turned back the bedclothes, examined the interior attentively, especially at the foot and the pillow. The latter was soiled—not to say grimy—though the rest of the bed-linen was quite clean.

"Hair-dye," remarked Thorndyke, noting my glance at it; then he turned and looked out of the open window. "Can you see the place where Miss Haldean was sitting to sketch?" he asked.

"Yes," I replied; "there is the place well in view, and you can see right up the road. I had no idea this house stood so high. From the three upper windows you can see all over the country excepting through the wood."

"Yes," Thorndyke rejoined, "and he has probably been in the habit of keeping watch up here with a telescope or a pair of field-glasses. Well, there is not much of interest in this room. He kept his effects in a cabin trunk which stood there under the window. He shaved this morning. He has a white beard, to judge by the stubble on the shaving-paper, and that is all. Wait, though. There is a key hanging on that nail. He must have overlooked that, for it evidently does not belong to this house. It is an ordinary town latchkey."

He took the key down, and having laid a sheet of notepaper, from his pocket, on the dressing-table, produced a pin, with which he began carefully to probe the interior of the key-barrel. Presently there came forth, with much coaxing, a large ball of grey fluff, which Thorndyke folded up in the paper with infinite care.

"I suppose we mustn't take away the key," he said, "but I think we will take a wax mould of it."

He hurried downstairs, and, unstrapping the case from his bicycle, brought it in and placed it on the table. As it was now getting dark, he detached the powerful acetylene lamp from his machine, and, having lighted it, proceeded to open the mysterious case. First he took from it a small insufflator, or powder-blower, with which he blew a cloud of light yellow powder over the table around the remains of the clock.

The powder settled on the table in an even coating, but when he blew at it smartly with his breath, it cleared off, leaving, however, a number of smeary impressions which stood out in strong yellow against the black oilcloth. To one of these impressions he pointed significantly. It was the print of a child's hand.

He next produced a small, portable microscope and some glass slides and cover-slips, and having opened the paper and tipped the ball of fluff from the key-barrel on to a slide, set to work with a pair of mounted needles to tease it out into its component parts. Then he turned the light of the lamp on to the microscope mirror and proceeded to examine the specimen.

"A curious and instructive assortment this, Jervis," he remarked, with his eye at the microscope: "woollen fibres—no cotton or linen; he is careful of his health to have woollen pockets—and two hairs; very curious ones, too. Just look at them, and observe the root bulbs."

I applied my eye to the microscope, and saw, among other things, two hairs—originally white, but encrusted with a black, opaque, glistening stain. The root bulbs, I noticed, were shrivelled and atrophied.

"But how on earth," I exclaimed, "did the hairs get into his pocket?"

"I think the hairs themselves answer that question," he replied, "when considered with the other curios. The stain is obviously lead sulphide; but what else do you see?"

"I see some particles of metal—a white metal apparently—and a number of fragments of woody fibre and starch granules, but I don't recognise the starch. It is not wheat-starch, nor rice, nor potato. Do you make out what it is?"

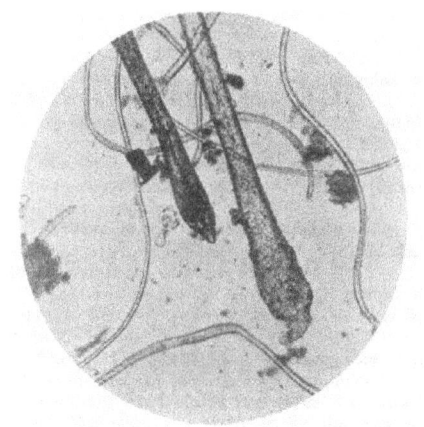

FLUFF FROM KEY-BARREL, MAGNIFIED 77 DIAMETERS

Thorndyke chuckled. "*Experientia* does it," said he. "You will have, Jervis, to study the minute properties of dust and dirt. Their evidential value is immense. Let us have another look at that starch; it is all alike, I suppose."

It was; and Thorndyke had just ascertained the fact when the door burst open and Mrs. Haldean entered the room, followed by Mrs. Hanshaw and the police inspector. The former lady regarded my colleague with a glance of extreme disfavour.

"We heard that you had come here, sir," said she, "and we supposed you were engaged in searching for my poor child. But it seems we were mistaken, since we find you here amusing yourselves fiddling with these nonsensical instruments."

"Perhaps, Mabel," said Mrs. Hanshaw stiffly, "it would be wiser, and infinitely more polite, to ask if Dr. Thorndyke has any news for us."

"That is undoubtedly so, madam," agreed the inspector, who had apparently suffered also from Mrs. Haldean's impulsiveness.

"Then perhaps," the latter lady suggested, "you will inform us if you have discovered anything."

"I will tell you." replied Thorndyke, "all that we know. The child was abducted by the man who occupied this house, and who appears to have watched him from an upper window, probably through a glass. This man lured the child into the wood by blowing this bird-call; he met him in the wood, and induced him—by some promises, no doubt—to come with him. He picked the child up and carried him—on his back, I think—up to the house, and brought him in through the front door, which he locked after him.

"He gave the boy this clock and the bird-call to amuse him while he went upstairs and packed his trunk. He took the trunk out through the back door and down the garden to the shed there, in which he had a motor-car. He got the car out and came back for the boy, whom he carried down to the car, locking the back door after him. Then he drove away."

"You know he has gone," cried Mrs. Haldean, "and yet you stay here playing with these ridiculous toys. Why are you not following him?"

"We have just finished ascertaining the facts," Thorndyke replied calmly, "and should by now be on the road if you had not come."

Here the inspector interposed anxiously. "Of course, sir, you can't give any description of the man. You have no clue to his identity, I suppose?"

"We have only his footprints," Thorndyke answered, "and this fluff which I raked out of the barrel of his latchkey, and have just been examining. From these data I conclude that he is a rather short and thin man, and somewhat lame. He walks with the aid of a thick stick, which has a knob, not a crook, at the top, and which he carries in his left hand. I think that his left leg has been amputated above the knee, and that he wears an artificial limb. He is elderly, he shaves his beard, has white hair dyed a greyish black, is partly bald, and probably combs a wisp of hair over the bald place; he takes snuff, and carries a leaden comb in his pocket."

As Thorndyke's description proceeded, the inspector's mouth gradually opened wider and wider, until he appeared the very type and symbol of astonishment. But its effect on Mrs. Haldean was much more remarkable. Rising from her chair, she leaned on the table and stared at Thorndyke with an expression of awe—even of terror; and as he finished she sank back into her chair, with her hands clasped, and turned to Mrs. Hanshaw.

"Jane!" she gasped, "it is Percy—my brother-in-law! He has described him exactly, even to his stick and his pocket-comb. But I thought he was in Chicago."

"If that is so," said Thorndyke, hastily repacking his case, "we had better start at once."

"We have the dogcart in the road," said Mrs. Hanshaw.

"Thank you," replied Thorndyke. "We will ride on our bicycles, and the inspector can borrow Willett's. We go out at the back by the cart-track, which joins the road farther on."

"Then we will follow in the dogcart," said Mrs. Haldean. "Come, Jane."

The two ladies departed down the path, while we made ready our bicycles and lit our lamps.

"With your permission, inspector," said Thorndyke, "we will take the key with us."

"It's hardly legal, sir," objected the officer. "We have no authority."

"It is quite illegal," answered Thorndyke; "but it is necessary; and necessity—like your military J.P.—knows no law."

The inspector grinned and went out, regarding me with a quivering eyelid as Thorndyke locked the door with his skeleton key. As we turned into the road, I saw the light of the dogcart behind us, and we pushed forward at a swift pace, picking up the trail easily on the soft, moist road.

"What beats me," said the inspector confidentially, as we rode along, "is how he knew the man was bald. Was it the footprints or the latchkey? And that comb, too, that was a regular knock-out."

These points were, by now, pretty clear to me. I had seen the hairs with their atrophied bulbs—such as one finds at the margin of a bald patch; and the comb was used, evidently, for the double purpose of keeping the bald patch covered and blackening the sulphur-charged hair. But the knobbed stick and the artificial limb puzzled me so completely that I presently overtook Thorndyke to demand an explanation.

"The stick," said he, "is perfectly simple. The ferrule of a knobbed stick wears evenly all round; that of a crooked stick wears on one side—the side opposite the crook. The impressions showed that the ferrule of this one was evenly convex; therefore it had no crook. The other matter is more complicated. To begin with, an artificial foot makes a very characteristic impression, owing to its purely passive elasticity, as I will show you tomorrow. But an artificial leg fitted below the knee is quite secure, whereas one fitted above the knee—that is, with an artificial knee-joint worked by a spring—is much less reliable.

"Now, this man had an artificial foot, and he evidently distrusted his knee-joint, as is shown by his steadying it with his stick on the same side. If he had merely had a weak leg, he would have used the stick with his right hand—with the natural swing of the arm, in fact—unless he had been very lame, which he evidently was not. Still, it was only a question of probability, though the probability was very great. Of course, you understand that those particles of woody fibre and starch granules were disintegrated snuff-grains."

This explanation, like the others, was quite simple when one had heard it, though it gave me material for much thought as we pedalled on along the dark road, with Thorndyke's light flickering in front, and the dogcart pattering in our wake. But there was ample time for reflection; for our pace rather precluded conversation, and we rode on, mile after mile, until my legs ached with fatigue.

On and on we went through village after village, now losing the trail in some frequented street, but picking it up again unfailingly as we emerged on to the country road, until at last, in the paved High Street of the little town of Horsefield, we lost it for good. We rode on through the town out on to the country road; but although there were several tracks of motors, Thorndyke shook his head at them all. "I have been studying those tyres until I know them by heart," he said. "No; either he is in the town, or he has left it by a side road."

There was nothing for it but to put up the horse and the machines at the hotel, while we walked round to reconnoitre; and this we did, tramping up one street and down another, with eyes bent on the ground, fruitlessly searching for a trace of the missing car.

Suddenly, at the door of a blacksmith's shop, Thorndyke halted. The shop had been kept open late for the shoeing of a carriage horse, which was just being led away, and the smith had come to the door for a breath of air. Thorndyke accosted him genially.

"Good-evening. You are just the man I wanted to see. I have mislaid the address of a friend of mine, who, I think, called on you this afternoon—a lame gentleman who walks with a stick. I expect he wanted you to pick a lock or make him a key."

"Oh, I remember him!" said the man. "Yes, he had lost his latchkey, and wanted the lock picked before he could get into his house. Had to leave his motorcar outside while he came here. But I took some keys round with me, and fitted one to his latch."

He then directed us to a house at the end of a street close by, and, having thanked him, we went off in high spirits.

"How did you know he had been there?" I asked.

"I didn't; but there was the mark of a stick and part of a left foot on the soft earth inside the doorway, and the thing was inherently probable, so I risked a false shot."

The house stood alone at the far end of a straggling street, and was enclosed by a high wall, in which, on the side facing the street, was a door and a wide carriage-gate. Advancing to the former, Thorndyke took from his pocket the purloined key, and tried it in the lock. It fitted perfectly, and when he had turned it and pushed open the door, we entered a small courtyard. Crossing this, we came to the front door of the house, the latch of which fortunately fitted the same key; and this having been opened by Thorndyke, we trooped into the hall. Immediately we heard the sound of an opening door above, and a reedy, nasal voice sang out:

"Hello, there! Who's that below?"

The voice was followed by the appearance of a head projecting over the baluster rail.

"You are Mr. Percy Haldean, I think," said the inspector. At the mention of this name, the head was withdrawn, and a quick tread was heard, accompanied by the tapping of a stick on the floor. We started to ascend the stairs, the inspector leading, as the authorized official; but we had only gone up a few steps, when a fierce, wiry little man danced out on to the landing, with a thick stick in one hand and a very large revolver in the other.

"Move another step, either of you," he shouted, pointing the weapon at the inspector, "and I let fly; and mind you, when I shoot I hit."

He looked as if he meant it, and we accordingly halted with remarkable suddenness, while the inspector proceeded to parley.

"Now, what's the good of this, Mr. Haldean?" said he. "The game's up, and you know it."

"You clear out of my house, and clear out sharp," was the inhospitable rejoinder, "or you'll give me the trouble of burying you in the garden."

I looked round to consult with Thorndyke, when, to my amazement, I found that he had vanished—apparently through the open hall-door. I was admiring his discretion when the inspector endeavoured to reopen negotiations, but was cut short abruptly.

"I am going to count fifty," said Mr. Haldean, "and if you aren't gone then, I shall shoot."

He began to count deliberately, and the inspector looked round at me in complete bewilderment. The flight of stairs was a long one, and well lighted by gas, so that to rush it was an impossibility. Suddenly my heart gave a bound and I held my breath, for out of an open door behind our quarry, a figure emerged slowly and noiselessly on to the landing. It was Thorndyke, shoeless, and in his shirt-sleeves.

Slowly and with cat-like stealthiness, he crept across the landing until he was within a yard of the unconscious fugitive, and still the nasal voice droned on, monotonously counting out the allotted seconds.

"Forty-one, forty-two, forty-three—"

There was a lightning-like movement—a shout—a flash—a bang—a shower of falling plaster, and then the revolver came clattering down the stairs. The inspector and I rushed up, and in a moment the sharp click of the handcuffs told Mr. Percy Haldean that the game was really up.

Five minutes later Freddy-boy, half asleep, but wholly cheerful, was borne on Thorndyke's shoulders into the private sitting-room of the Black Horse Hotel. A shriek of joy saluted his entrance, and a shower of maternal kisses brought him to the verge of suffocation. Finally, the impulsive Mrs. Haldean, turning suddenly to Thorndyke, seized both his hands, and for a moment I hoped that she was going to kiss him, too. But he was spared, and I have not yet recovered from the disappointment.

The Seal of Nebuchadnezzar

"I suppose, Thorndyke," said I, "footprints yield quite a lot of information if you think about them enough?"

The question was called forth by the circumstance of my friend halting and stooping to examine the little pit made in the loamy soil of the path by the walking stick of some unknown wayfarer. Ever since we had entered this path—to which we had been directed by the station-master of Pinwell Junction as a short cut to our destination—I had noticed my friend scanning its surface, marked with numerous footprints, as if he were mentally reconstructing the personalities of the various travellers who had trodden it before us. This I knew to be a habit of his, almost unconsciously pursued; and the present conditions certainly favoured it, for here, as the path traversed a small wood, the slightly moist, plastic surface took impressions with the sharpness of moulding wax.

"Yes," he answered, "but you must do more than think. You need to train your eyes to observe in conspicuous characteristics."

"Such as these, for instance," said. I, with a grin, pointing to a blatant print of a Cox's "Invicta" rubber sole with its prancing-horse trade-mark.

Thorndyke smiled. "A man," said he, "who wears a sole like that is a mere advertising agent. He who runs may read those characteristics, but as there are thousands of persons wearing 'Invicta' soles, the observation merely identifies the wearer as a member of a large genus. It has to be carried a good deal further to identify him as an individual; otherwise, a standardised sole is apt to be rather misleading than helpful. Its gross distinctiveness tends to divert the novice's attention from the more specific characteristics which he would seek in a plain footprint like that of this man's companion."

"Why companion?" I asked. "The two men were walking the same way, but what evidence is there that they were companions?"

"A good deal, if you follow the series of tracks, as I have been doing. In the first place, there is the stride. Both men were rather tall, as shown by the size of their feet, but both have a distinctly short stride. Now the leather-soled man's short stride is accounted for by the way in which he put down his stick. He held it stiffly, leaning upon it to some extent and helping himself with it. There is one impression of the stick to every two paces; every impression of his left foot has a stick impression opposite to it. The suggestion is that he was old, weak or infirm. But the rubber-soled man walked with his stick in the ordinary way—one stick impression to every four paces. His abnormally short stride is not to be accounted for excepting by the assumption that he stepped short to keep pace with the other man.

"Then the two sets of footprints are usually separate. Neither man has trodden nor set his stick on the other man's tracks, excepting in those places where the path is too narrow for them to walk abreast, and there, in the one case I noticed the rubber soles treading on the prints of the leather soles, whereas at this spot the prints of the leather soles are imposed on those of the rubber soles. That, of course, is conclusive evidence that the two men were here at the same time."

"Yes," I agreed, "that settles the question without troubling about the stride. But after all, Thorndyke, this is a matter of reasoning, as I said; of thinking about the footprints and their meaning. No special acuteness of observation or training of vision comes into it. The mere facts are obvious enough; it is their interpretation that yields the knowledge."

"That is true so far," said he, "but we haven't exhausted our material. Look carefully at the impressions of the two sticks and tell me if you see anything remarkable in either of them?"

I stooped and examined the little pits that the two sticks had made in the path, and, to tell the truth, found them extremely unilluminating.

"They seem very much alike," I said. "The rubber-soled man's stick is rather larger than the other and the leather-soled man's stick has made deeper holes—probably because it was smaller and he was leaning on it more heavily."

Thorndyke shook his head. "You've missed the point, Anstey, and you've missed it because you have failed to observe the visible facts. It is quite a neat point, too, and might in certain circumstances be a very important one."

"Indeed," said I. "What is the point?"

"That," said he, "I shall leave you to infer from the visible facts, which are these: first, the impressions of the smaller stick are on the right-hand side of the man who made them, and second, that each impression is shallowest towards the front and the right-hand side."

I examined the impressions carefully and verified Thorndyke's statement.

"Well," I said, "what about it? What does it prove?"

Thorndyke smiled in his exasperating fashion. "The proof," said he, "is arrived at by reasoning from the facts. My learned friend has the facts. If he will consider them, the conclusion will emerge."

"But," said I, "I don't see your drift. The impression is shallower on one side, I suppose, because the ferrule of the stick was worn away on that side. But I repeat, what about it? Do you expect me to infer why the fool that it belonged to wore his stick away all at one side?"

"Now, don't get irritable, Anstey," said he. "Preserve a philosophic calm. I assure you that this is quite an interesting problem."

"So it may be," I replied. "But I'm hanged if I can imagine why he wore his stick down in that way. However, it doesn't really matter. It isn't my stick—and by Jingo, here is old Brodribb—caught us in the act of wasting our time on academic chin-wags and delaying his business. The debate is adjourned."

Our discussion had brought us to the opening of the wood, which now framed the figure of the solicitor. As he caught sight of us, he hurried forward, holding out his hand.

"Good men and true!" he exclaimed. "I thought you would probably come this way, and it is very good of you to have come at all, especially as it is a mere formality."

"What is?" asked Thorndyke. "Your telegram spoke of an 'alleged suicide.' I take it that there is some ground for inquiry?"

"I don't know that there is," replied Brodribb. "But the deceased was insured for three thousand pounds, which will be lost to the estate if the suicide is confirmed. So I put it to my fellow that it was worth an expert's fee to make sure whether or not things are what they seem. A verdict of death by misadventure will save us three thousand pounds. *Verbum sap.*" As he concluded, the old lawyer winked with exaggerated cunning and stuck his elbow into my ribs.

Thorndyke ignored the facetious suggestion of bribery and corruption and inquired dryly: "What are the circumstances of the case?"

"I'd better give you a sketch of them before we get to the house," replied Brodribb. "The dead man is Martin Rowlands, the brother of my neighbour in New Square, Tom Rowlands. Poor old Tom found the telegram waiting when he got to his office this morning and immediately rushed into my office with it and begged me to come down here with him. So I came. Couldn't refuse a brother solicitor. He's waiting at the house now.

"The circumstances are these. Last evening, when he had finished dinner, Rowlands went out for a walk. That is his usual habit in the summer months—it is light until nearly half-past nine nowadays. Well, that is the last time he was seen alive by the servants. No one saw him come in. But there was nothing unusual in that, for he had a private entrance to the annexe in which his library, museum and workrooms were situated, and when he returned from his walk, he usually entered the house that way and went straight to his study or workroom and spent the evening there. So the servants very seldom saw him after dinner.

"Last night he evidently followed his usual custom. But, this morning, when the housemaid went to his bedroom with his morning tea, she was astonished to find the room empty and the bed undisturbed. She at once reported to the housekeeper, and the pair made their way to the annexe. There they found the study door locked, and as there was no answer after repeated knockings, they went out into the grounds to reconnoitre. The study window was closed and fastened, but the workroom window was unbolted, so that they were able to open it from outside.

"Then the housemaid climbed in and went to the side door, which she opened and admitted the housekeeper. The two went to the workroom, and as the door which communicated with the study was open, they were able to enter the latter, and there they found Martin Rowlands, sitting in an arm-chair by the table, stone-dead, cold and stiff. On the table were a whisky decanter, a siphon of soda water, a box of cigars, an ash-bowl with the stump of a cigar in it, and a bottle of photographic tabloids of cyanide of potassium.

"The housekeeper immediately sent off for a doctor and dispatched a telegram to Tom Rowlands at his office. The doctor arrived about nine and decided that the deceased had been dead about twelve hours. The cause of death was apparently cyanide poisoning, but, of course, that will be ascertained or disproved by the post-mortem. Those are all the known facts at present. The doctor helped the servants to place the body on a sofa, but as it is as stiff as a frozen sheep, they might as well have left it where it was."

"Have the police been communicated with?" I asked.

"No," replied Brodribb. "There were no suspicious circumstances, so far as any of us could see, and I don't know that I should have felt justified in sending for you—though I always like to have Thorndyke's opinion in a case of sudden death—if it had not been for the insurance."

Thorndyke nodded. "It looks like a straightforward case of suicide," said he. "As to the state of deceased's affairs, his brother will be able to give us any necessary information, I suppose?"

"Yes," replied Brodribb. "As a matter of fact, I think Martin has been a bit worried just lately; but Tom will tell you about that. This is the place."

We turned in at a gateway that opened into the grounds of a substantial though unpretentious house, and as we approached the front door, it was opened by a fresh-coloured, white-haired man whom we both knew pretty well in our professional capacities. He greeted us cordially, and though he was evidently deeply shocked by the tragedy, struggled to maintain a calm, business-like manner.

"It is good of you to come down," said he; "but I am afraid we have troubled you rather unnecessarily. Still, Brodribb thought it best—*ex abundanti cautela*, you know—to have the circumstances reviewed by a competent authority. There is nothing abnormal in the affair excepting its having happened. My poor brother was the sanest of men, I should say, and we are not a suicidal family. I suppose you had better see the body first?"

As Thorndyke assented, he conducted us to the end of the hall and into the annexe, where we entered the study, the door of which was now open, though the key was still in the lock. The table still bore the things that Brodribb had described, but the chair was empty, and its late occupant lay on a sofa, covered with a large table-cloth. Thorndyke advanced to the sofa and gently drew away the cloth, revealing the body of a man, fully dressed, lying stiffly and awkwardly on its back with the feet raised and the stiffened limbs extended.

There was something strangely and horribly artificial in the aspect of the corpse, for, though it was lying down, it had the posture of a seated figure, and thus bore the semblance of a hideously realistic effigy which had been picked up from a chair and laid down. I stood looking at it from a little distance with a layman's distaste for the presence of a dead body, but still regarding it with attention and some curiosity. Presently my glance fell on the soles of the shoes—which were, indeed, exhibited plainly enough—and I noted, as an odd coincidence that they were "Invicta" rubber soles, like those which we had just been discussing in the wood; that it was even possible that those very footprints had been made by the feet of this grisly figure.

"I expect, Thorndyke," Brodribb said tactfully, "you would rather make your inspection alone. If you should want us, you will find us in the dining room," and with this he retired, taking Mr. Rowlands with him.

As soon as they were gone I drew Thorndyke's attention to the rubber soles.

"It is a queer thing," said I, "but we may have actually been discussing this poor fellow's own prints."

"As a matter of fact, we were," he replied, pointing to a drawing-pin that had been trodden on and had stuck into one of the rubber heels. "I noticed this at the time, and apparently you did not, which illustrates what I was saying about the tendency of these very distinctive types of sole to distract attention from those individual peculiarities which are the ones that really matter."

"Then," said I, "if they were his footprints, the man with the remarkable stick was with him. I wonder who he was. Some neighbour who was walking home from the station with him, I expect."

"Probably," said Thorndyke, "and as the prints were quite recent—they might even have been made last night—that person may be wanted as a witness at the inquest as the last person who saw deceased alive. That depends on the time the prints were made."

He walked back to the sofa and inspected the corpse very methodically, giving close attention to the mouth and hands. Then he made a general inspection of the room, examined the objects on the table and the floor under it, strayed into the adjoining workshop, where he peered into the deep laboratory sink, took an empty tumbler from a shelf, held it up to the light and inspected the shelf—where a damp ring showed that the tumbler had been put there to drain—and from the workshop wandered into a little lobby and from thence out at the side door, down the flagged path to the side gate and back again.

"It is all very negative," he remarked discontentedly, as we returned to the study, "except that bottle of tabloids, which is pretty positive evidence of premeditation. That looks like a fresh box of cigars. Two missing. One stump in the ash-tray and more ash than one cigar would account for. However, let us go into the dining and hear what

Rowlands has to tell us," and with this he walked out and crossed the hall and I followed him.

As we entered the dining the two men looked at us and Brodribb asked: "Well, what is the verdict?"

"At present," Thorndyke replied, "it is an open verdict. Nothing has come to light that disagrees with the obvious appearances. But I should like to hear more of the antecedents of the tragedy. You were saying that deceased had been somewhat worried lately. What does that amount to?"

"It amounts to nothing," said Rowlands "at least, I should have thought so, in the case of a level-headed man like my brother. Still as it is all there is, so far as I know, to account for what has happened, I had better give you the story. It seems trivial enough.

"Some short time ago, a Major Cohen, who had just come home from Mesopotamia, sold to a dealer named Lyon a small gold cylinder seal that he had picked up in the neighbourhood of Baghdad. The Lord knows how he came by it, but he had it and he showed it to Lyon, who bought it of him for a matter of twenty pounds. Cohen, of course, knew nothing about the thing, and Lyon didn't know much more, for although he is a dealer, he is no expert.

"But he is a very clever faker—or rather, I should say, restorer, for he does quite a legitimate trade. He was a jeweller and watch-jobber originally, a most ingenious workman, and his line is to buy up damaged antiques and restore them. Then he sells them to minor collectors, though quite honestly as restorations, so I oughtn't to call him a faker. But, as I said, he has no real knowledge of antiques, and all he saw in Cohen's seal was a gold cylinder seal, apparently ancient and genuine, and on that he bought it for about twice the value of the gold and thought no more about it.

"About a fortnight later, my brother Martin went to his shop in Petty France, Westminster, to get some repairs done, and Lyon, knowing that my brother was a collector of Babylonian antiquities, showed him the seal; and Martin, seeing at once that it was genuine and a thing of some interest and value, bought it straight-way for forty pounds without examining it at all minutely, as it was obviously worth that much in any case. But when he got home and took a rolled impression of it on moulding wax, he made a most astonishing discovery. The impression showed a mass of minute cuneiformic characters, and on deciphering these he learned with amazement and delight that this was none other than the seal of Nebuchadnezzar.

"Hardly able to believe in his good fortune, he hurried off to the British Museum and showed his treasure to the Keeper of the Babylonian Antiquities, who fully confirmed the identity of the seal and was naturally eager to acquire it for the Museum. Of course, Martin wouldn't sell it, but he allowed the keeper to take a record of its weight and measurements and to make an impression on clay to exhibit in the case of seal-rollings.

"Meanwhile, it seems that Cohen, before disposing of the seal, had amused himself by making a number of rolled impressions on clay. Some of these he took to Lyon, who bought them for a few shillings and put one of them in his shop window as a curio. There it was seen and recognised by an American Assyriologist, who went in and bought it and then began to question Lyon closely as to whence he had obtained it. The dealer made no secret of the matter, but gave Cohen's name and address, saying nothing, however, about the seal. In fact, he was unaware of the connection between the seal and the rollings as Cohen had sold him the latter as genuine clay tablets which he said he had found in Mesopotamia. But, of course, the expert saw that it was a recent rolling and that someone must have the seal.

"Accordingly, off he went to Cohen and questioned him closely, whereupon Cohen began to smell a rat. He admitted that he had had the seal, but refused to say what had become of it until the expert told him what it was and how much it was worth. This the expert did, very reluctantly and in strict confidence, and when Cohen learned that it was the seal of Nebuchadnezzar and that it was worth anything up to ten thousand pounds, he nearly fainted; and then he and the expert together bustled off to Lyon's shop.

"But now Lyon smelt a rat, too. He refused absolutely to disclose the whereabouts of the seal; and having, by now, guessed that the seal-rollings were those of the seal, he took one of them to the British Museum, and then, of course, the murder was out. And further to complicate the matter, the Assyriologist, Professor Bateman, seems to have talked freely to his American friends at his hotel, with the result that Lyon's shop was besieged by wealthy American collectors, all roaring for the seal and all perfectly regardless of cost.

"Finally, as they could get no change out of Lyon, they went to the British Museum, where they learned that my brother had the seal and got his address—or rather mine, for he had, fortunately for himself, given my office as his address. Then they proceeded to bombard him with letters, as also did Cohen and Lyon.

"It was an uncomfortable situation. Cohen was like a madman. He swore that Lyon had swindled him and he demanded to have the seal returned or the proper price paid. Lyon, for his part, went about like a roaring lion of Judah, making a similar demand; and the millionaire collectors offered wild sums for the seal. Poor Martin was very much worried about it. He was particularly unhappy about Cohen, who had actually found the seal and who was a disabled soldier—he had been wounded in both legs and was permanently lame. As to Lyon, he had no grievance, for he was a dealer and it was his business to know the value of his own stock; but still it was hard luck even on him. And then there were the collectors, pestering him daily with entreaties and extravagant offers. It was very worrying for him. They would probably have come down here to see him, but he kept his private address a close secret.

"I don't know what he meant to do about it. What he did was to arrange with me for the loan of my private office and have a field day, interviewing the whole lot of them—Lyon, the Professor and the assorted millionaires. That was three days ago, and the whole boiling of them turned up; and by the same token one of them was the kind of pestilent fool that walks off with the wrong hat or umbrella."

"Did he walk off with your hat?" asked Brodribb.

"No, but he took my stick; a nice old stick that belonged to my father."

"What sort of stick did he leave in its place?" Thorndyke asked.

"Well," replied Rowlands, "I must admit that there was some excuse, for the stick that he left was almost a facsimile of my own. I don't think I should have noticed it but for the feel. When I began to walk with it, I was aware of something unusual in the feel of it."

"Perhaps it was not quite the same length as yours," Thorndyke suggested.

"No, it wasn't that," said Rowlands. "The length was all right, but there was some more subtle difference. Possibly, as I am left-handed and carry my stick on the left side, it may in the course of years have acquired a left-handed bias, if such a thing is possible. I'll go and get the stick for you to see."

He went out of the room and returned in a few moments with an old-fashioned Malacca cane, the ivory handle of which was secured by a broad silver band. Thorndyke took it from him and looked it over with a degree of interest and attention that rather surprised me. For the loss of Rowlands' stick was a trivial incident and no concern of ours. Nevertheless, my colleague inspected it most methodically, handle, silver band and ferrule; especially the ferrule, which he examined as if it were quite a rare and curious object.

"You needn't worry about your stick, Tom," said Brodribb with a mischievous smile. "Thorndyke will get it back if you ask him nicely."

"It oughtn't to be very difficult," said Thorndyke, handing back the stick, "if you have a list of the visitors who called that day."

"Their names will be in the appointments book," said Rowlands. "I must look them up. Some of them I remember—Cohen, Lyon, Bateman and two or three of the collectors. But to return to our history. I don't know what passed at the interviews or what Martin intended to do, but I have no doubt he made some notes on the subject. I must search for them, for, of course, we shall have to dispose of the seal."

"By the way," said Thorndyke, "where is the seal?"

"Why, it is here in the safe," replied Rowlands; "and it oughtn't to be. It should have been taken to the bank."

"I suppose there is no doubt that it is in the safe?" said Thorndyke.

"No," replied Rowlands; "at least—" He stood up suddenly. "I haven't seen it," he said. "Perhaps we had better make sure."

He led the way quickly to the study, where he halted and stood looking at the shrouded corpse. "The key will be in his pocket," he said, almost in a whisper. Then, slowly and reluctantly, he approached the sofa, and gently drawing away the cover from the body, began to search the dead man's pockets.

"Here it is," he said at length, producing a bunch of keys and separating one, which he apparently knew. He crossed to the safe, and inserting the key, threw open the door.

"Ha!" he exclaimed with evident relief, "it is all right..Your question gave me quite a start. Is it necessary to open the packet?"

He held out a little sealed parcel on which was written "The Seal of Nebuchadnezzar," and looked inquiringly at Thorndyke.

"You spoke of making sure," the latter replied with a faint smile.

"Yes, I suppose it would be best," said Rowlands; and with that, he cut the thread with which it was fastened, broke the seal and opened the package, disclosing a small cardboard box in which lay a cylindrical object rolled up in a slip of paper.

Rowlands picked it out, and removing the paper, displayed a little cylinder of gold pitted all over with minute cuneiform characters. It was about an inch and a quarter long by half an inch thick and had a hole bored through its axis from end to end.

"This paper, I see," said Rowlands, "contains a copy of the keeper's description of the seal—its weight, dimensions and so on. We may as well take care of that."

He handed the little cylinder to Thorndyke, who held it delicately in his fingers and looked at it with a gravely reflective air. Indeed, small as it was, there was something very impressive in its appearance and in the thought that it had been handled by and probably worn on the person of the great king in those remote, almost mythical times, so familiar and yet so immeasurably far away. So I reflected as I watched Thorndyke inspecting the venerable little object in his queer, exact, scientific way, examining the minute characters through his lens, scrutinising the ends and even peering through the central hole.

"I notice," he said, glancing at the paper which Rowlands held, "that the keeper has given only one transverse diameter, apparently assuming that it is a true cylinder. But it isn't. The diameter varies. It is not quite circular in section and the sides are not perfectly parallel."

He produced his pocket calliper-gauge, and, closing the jaws on the cylinder, took the reading of the vernier. Then he turned the cylinder, on which the gauge became visibly out of contact.

"There is a difference of nearly two millimetres," he said when he had again closed the gauge and taken the reading.

"Ah, Thorndyke," said Brodribb, "that keeper hadn't got your mathematically exact eye; and, in fact, the precise measurements don't seem to matter much."

"On the other hand," retorted Thorndyke, "inexact measurements are of no use at all."

When we had all handled and inspected the seal, Rowlands repacked it and returned it to the safe, and we went back to the dining-room.

"Well, Thorndyke," said Brodribb, "how does the insurance question stand? What is our position?"

"I think," Thorndyke replied, "that we will leave the question open until the inquest has been held. You must insist on an expert analysis, and perhaps that may throw fresh light on the matter. And now we must be off to the station. I expect you have plenty to do."

"We have," said Brodribb, "so I won't offer to walk with you. You know the way."

Politely but firmly declining Rowlands' offer of material hospitality, Thorndyke took up his research-case, and having shaken hands with our hosts, we followed them to the door and took our departure.

"Not a very satisfactory case," I remarked as we set forth along the road, "but you can't make a bull's-eye every time."

"No," he agreed; "you can only observe and note the facts. Which reminds me that we have some data to collect in the wood. I shall take casts of those footprints in case they should turn out to be of importance. It is always a useful precaution, seeing that footprints are fugitive."

It seemed to me an excessive precaution, but I made no comment; and when we arrived at the footpath through the wood and he had selected the sharpest footprints, I watched him take out from his case the plaster-tin, water-bottle, spoon and little rubber bowl, and wondered what was in his mind. The "Invicta" footprints were obviously those of the dead man. But what if they were? And of what use were the casts of the other man's feet? The man was unknown, and as far as I could see, there was nothing suspicious in his presence here.

But when Thorndyke had poured the liquid plaster into the two pairs of footprints, he went on to a still more incomprehensible proceeding. Mixing some fresh plaster, he filled up with it two adjoining impressions of the strange man's stick. Then, taking a reel of thread from the case, he cut off about two yards, and stretching it taut, held it exactly across the middle of the two holes, until the plaster set and fixed it in position. After waiting for the plaster to set hard, and having, meanwhile, taken up and packed the casts of the footprints, he gently raised, first the one and then the other cast; each of which was a snowy-white facsimile of the tip of the stick which had made the impression the two casts, being joined by a length of thread which gave the exact distance apart of the two impressions.

"I suppose," said I, as he made a pencil mark on one of the casts, "the thread is to show the length of the stride?"

"No," he answered. "It is to show the exact direction in which the man was walking and to mark the front and back of the stick."

I could make nothing of this. It was highly ingenious, but what on earth was the use of it? What could it possibly prove?

I put a few tentative questions, but could get no explanation beyond the obvious truth that it was of no use to postpone the collection of evidence until after the event. What event he was referring to, I did not gather; nor was I any further enlightened when, on arriving at Victoria, he hailed a taxicab and directed the driver to set him down at Scotland Yard.

"You had better not wait," he said, as he got out. "I have some business to talk over with Miller or the Assistant Commissioner and may be detained some time. But I shall be at home all the evening."

Taking this as an invitation to drop in at his chambers, I did so after dinner and made another ineffectual attempt to pump him.

"I am sorry to be so evasive," said he, "but this case is so extremely speculative that I cannot come to any definite conclusion until I have more data. I may have been theorising in the air. But I am going forth tomorrow morning at half-past eight in the hope of putting some of my inferences to the test. If my learned friend would care to lend his distinguished support to the expedition, his society would be appreciated. But it will be a case of passive observation and quite possibly nothing will happen."

"Well, I will come and look on," said I. "Passive observation is my speciality;" and with this I took my departure, rather more mystified than ever.

Punctually, next morning at half-past eight, I arrived at the entry of Thorndyke's chambers. A taxicab was already waiting at the kerb, and, as I stepped on the threshold, my colleague appeared on the stairs. Together we entered the cab which at once moved off, and proceeding down Middle Temple Lane to the Embankment, headed westward. Our first stopping-place was New Scotland Yard, but there Thorndyke remained only a minute or two. Our further progress was in the direction of Westminster, and in a few minutes we drew up at the corner of Petty France, where we alighted and paid off the taxi.

Sauntering slowly westward and passing a large, covered car that was drawn up by the pavement, we presently encountered no less a person than Mr. Superintendent Miller, dressed in the height of fashion and smoking a cigar. The meeting was not, apparently, unexpected, for Miller began, without preamble: "It's all right, so far, doctor, unless we are too late. It will be an awful suck-in if we are. Two plainclothes men have been here ever since you called yesterday evening, and nothing has happened yet."

"You mustn't treat it as a certainty, Miller," said Thorndyke. "We are only acting on reasonable probabilities. But it may be a false shot, after all."

Miller smiled indulgently. "I know, sir. I've heard you say that sort of thing before. At any rate, he's there at present; I saw him just now through the shop window—and, by gum! here he is!"

I followed the superintendent's glance and saw a tallish, elderly man advancing on the opposite side of the street. He walked stiffly with the aid of a stick and with a pronounced stoop as if suffering from some weakness of the back, and he carried in his free hand a small wooden case suspended by a rug-strap. But what instantly attracted my attention was his walking-stick, which appeared, so far as I could remember, to be an exact replica of the one that Tom Rowlands had shown us.

We continued to walk westward, allowing Mr. Lyon—as I assumed him to be—to pass us. Then we turned back and followed at a little distance; and I noticed that two tall, military-looking men whom we had met kept close behind us. At the corner of Petty France Mr. Lyon hailed a taxicab; and Miller quickened his pace and bore down on the big covered car.

"Jump in," he said, opening the door as Lyon entered the cab. "We mustn't lose sight of him," and with this he fairly shoved Thorndyke and me into the car, and having spoken a word to the driver, stepped in himself and was followed by the two plain-clothes men. The car started forward, and having made a spurt which brought it within a few yards of the taxi, slowed down to the pace of the latter and followed it through the increasing traffic until we turned into Whitehall, where our driver allowed the taxi to draw ahead somewhat.

At Charing Cross, however, we closed up and kept immediately behind our quarry in the dense traffic of the Strand; and when it turned to cross opposite the Acropolis Hotel, we still followed and swept past it in the hotel courtyard so that we reached the main entrance first. By the time that Mr. Lyon had paid his fare we had already entered and were waiting in the hall of the hotel.

As he followed us in, he paused and looked about him until his glance fell on a stoutish, clean-shaved man who was sitting in a wicker chair, who, on catching his eye, rose and advanced towards him. At this moment Superintendent Miller touched him on the shoulder, causing him to spin round with an expression of very distinct alarm.

"Mr. Maurice Lyon, I think," said Miller. "I am a detective officer." He paused and looked hard at the dealer, who had turned deathly pale. Then he continued: "You are carrying a walking-stick which I believe is not your property."

Lyon gave a gasp of relief. "You are quite right," said he. "But I don't know whose property it is. If you do, I shall be pleased to return it in exchange for my own, which I left by mistake."

He held it out in an irresolute fashion, and Miller took it from him and handed it to Thorndyke.

"Is that the stick?" he asked.

Thorndyke looked the stick over quickly, and then, inverting it, made a minute examination of the ferrule, finishing up by taking its dimensions in two diameters and comparing the results with some written notes.

Mr. Lyon fidgeted impatiently. "There's no need for all this fuss," said he. "I have told you that the stick is not mine."

"Quite so," said Miller, "but we must have a few words privately about that stick."

Here he turned to an hotel official, who had just arrived under the guidance of one of the plain-clothes men, and who suggested rather anxiously that our business would be better transacted in a private room at the back of the building than in the public hall. He was just moving off to show us the way when the clean-shaved stranger edged up to Lyon and extended his hand towards the wooden case.

"Shall I take this?" he asked suavely.

"Not just now, sir," said Miller, firmly fending him off. "Mr. Lyon will talk to you presently."

"But that case is my property," the other objected truculently; "and who are you, anyway?"

"I am a police officer," replied Miller. "But if that is your property, you had better come with us and keep an eye on it."

I have never seen a man look more uncomfortable than did the owner of that case—with the exception of Mr. Lyon; whose complexion had once more taken on a tallowy whiteness. But as the manager led the way to the back of the hall the two men followed silently, shepherded by the superintendent and the rest of our party, until we reached a small, marble-floored lobby or ante-room, when our conductor shut us in and retired.

"Now," said Miller, "I want to know what is in that case."

"I can tell you," said the stranger. "It is a piece of sculpture, and it belongs to me."

Miller nodded. "Let us have a look at it," said he.

There being no table, Lyon sat down on a chair, and resting the case on his knees, unfastened the straps with trembling fingers on which a drop of sweat fell now and again from his forehead. When the case was free, he opened the lid and displayed the head of a small plaster bust, a miniature copy of Donatello's "St. Cecilia," the shoulders of which were wedged in with balls of paper. These Lyon picked out clumsily, and when he had removed the last of them, he lifted out the bust with infinite care and held it out for Miller's inspection. The officer took it from him tenderly—after an eager glance into the empty case—and holding it with both hands, looked at it rather blankly.

"Feels rather damp," he remarked with a some what nonplussed air; and then he cast an obviously inquiring glance at Thorndyke, who took the bust from him, and holding it poised in the palm of his hand, appeared to be estimating its weight. Glancing past him at Lyon, I noticed with astonishment that the dealer was watching him with a ghastly stare of manifest terror, while the stranger was hardly less disturbed.

"For God's sake, man, be careful!" the latter exclaimed, starting forward. "You'll drop it!"

The prediction was hardly uttered before it was verified. Drop it he did; and in a perfectly deliberate, purposeful manner, so that the bust fell on its back on the marble floor and was instantly shattered into a hundred fragments. It was an amazing affair. But what followed was still more amazing. For, as the snowy fragments scattered to right and left, from one of them a little yellow metal cylinder detached itself and rolled slowly along the floor. The stranger darted forward and stooped to seize it; but Miller stooped, too, and I judged that the superintendent's cranium was the harder, for he rose, rubbing his head with one hand and with the other holding out the cylinder to Thorndyke.

"Can you tell us what this is, doctor?" he asked.

"Yes," was the reply. "It is the seal of Nebuchadnezzar, and it is the property of the executors of the late Martin Rowlands, who was murdered the night before last."

As he finished speaking, Lyon slithered from his chair and lay upon the floor insensible, while the stranger made a sudden burst for the door, where he was instantly folded in the embrace of a massive plainclothes man, who held him immovable while his colleague clicked on the handcuffs.

"So," I remarked, as we walked home, "your casts of the stick and the footprints were not wanted after all."

"On the contrary," he replied, "they are wanted very much. If the seal should fail to hang Mr. Lyon, the casts will assuredly fit the rope round his neck." (This, by the way, actually happened. The defence that Lyon received the seal from some unknown person was countered by the unexpected production in court of the casts of Lyon's feet and the stick, which proved that the prisoner had been at Pinwell, and in the company of the deceased at or about the date of the murder, and secured his conviction.)

"By the way," said I, "how did you fix this crime on Lyon? It began, I think, with those stick impressions in the wood. What was there peculiar about those impressions?"

"Their peculiarity was that they were the impressions of a stick which apparently did not belong to the person who was carrying it."

"Good Lord, Thorndyke!" I exclaimed, "is that possible? How could an impression on the ground suggest ownership?"

"It is a curious point," he replied, "though essentially simple, which turns on the way in which the ferrule of a stick becomes worn. In a plain, symmetrical stick with out a handle, the ferrule wears evenly all round; but in a stick with a crook or other definite handle, which is grasped in a particular way and always put down in the same position, the ferrule becomes worn on one side—the side opposite the handle, or the front of the stick. But the important point is that the bevel of wear is not exactly opposite the handle. It is slightly to one side, for this reason. A man puts his stick down with the handle fore and aft; but as he steps forward, his hand swings away from his body, rotating the stick slightly outward.

"Consequently, the wear on the ferrule is slightly inward. That is to say, that in a right-handed man's stick the wear is slightly to the left and in a left-handed man's stick the wear is slightly to the right. But if a right-handed man walks with a left-handed stick, the impression on the ground will show the bevel of wear on the right side—which is the wrong side; and the right-handed rotation will throw it still farther to the right. Now in this case, the impressions showed a shallow part, corresponding to the bevel of wear, on the right side. Therefore it was a left-handed stick. But it was being carried in the right hand. Therefore it—apparently—did not belong to the person who was carrying it.

"Of course, as the person was unknown, the point was merely curious and did not concern us. But see how quickly circumstantial evidence mounts up. When we saw the feet of deceased, we knew that the footprints in the wood were his. Consequently the man with the stick was in his company; and that man at once came into the picture. Then Tom Rowlands told us that he had lost his stick and that he was left-handed; and he showed us the stick that he had got in exchange, and behold! that is a right-handed stick, as I ascertained by examining the ferrule.

"Here, then, is a left-handed man who has lost a stick and got a right-handed one in exchange; and there, in the wood, was a right-handed man who was carrying a left-handed stick and who was in company with the deceased. It was a striking coincidence. But further, the suggestion was that this unknown man was one of those who had called at Tom's office, and therefore one who wanted to get possession of the seal. This instantly suggested the question, Did he succeed in getting possession of the seal? We went to the safe and at once it became obvious that he did."

"The seal in the safe was a forgery, of course?"

"Yes; and a bad forgery, though skilfully done. It was an electrotype; it was unsymmetrical; it did not agree with the keeper's measurements; and the perforation, though soiled at the ends, was bright in the middle from the boring tool."

"But how did you know that Lyon had made it?"

"I didn't. But he was by far the most probable person. He had a seal-rolling, from which an electro could be made, and he had the great skill that was necessary to turn a flat electro into a cylinder. He was an experienced faker of antiques, and he was a dealer who would have facilities for getting rid of the stolen seal. But it was only a probability, though, as time pressed, we had to act on it. Of course, when we saw him with the stick in his hand, it became virtually a certainty."

"And how did you guess that the seal was in the bust?"

"I had expected to find it enclosed in some plaster object, that being the safest way to hide it and smuggle it out of this country and into the United States. When I saw the bust, it was obvious. It was a hastily-made copy of one of Brucciani's busts. The plaster was damp—Brucciani's bake theirs dry—and had evidently been made only a few hours. So I broke it. If I had been mistaken I could have replaced it for five shillings, but the whole circumstances made it practically a certainty."

"Have you any idea as to how Lyon administered the poison?"

"We can only surmise," he replied. "Probably he took with him some solution of cyanide—if that was what was used—and poured it into Rowlands' whisky when his attention was otherwise occupied. It would be quite easy; and a single gulp of a quick-acting poison like that would finish the business in a minute or two. But we are not likely ever to know the details."

The evidence at the inquest showed that Thorndyke was probably right, and his evidence at the trial clinched the case against Lyon. As to the other man—who proved to be an American dealer well known to the New York Customs officials—the case against him broke down from lack of evidence that he was privy either to the murder or the theft. And so ended the case of Nebuchadnezzar's seal: a case that left Mr. Brodribb more than ever convinced that Thorndyke was either gifted with a sixth sense which enabled him to smell out evidence or was in league with some familiar demon who did it for him.

The Naturalist at Law

A hush had fallen on the court as the coroner concluded his brief introductory statement and the first witness took up his position by the long table. The usual preliminary questions elicited that Simon Moffet, the witness aforesaid, was fifty-eight years of age, that he followed the calling of a shepherd and that he was engaged in supervising the flocks that fed upon the low-lying meadows adjoining the little town of Bantree in Buckinghamshire.

"Tell us how you came to discover the body," said the coroner.

"'Twas on Wednesday morning, about half-past five," Moffet began. "I was getting the sheep through the gate into the big meadow by Reed's farm, when I happened to look down the dyke, and then I noticed a boot sticking up out of the water. Seemed to me as if there was a foot in it by the way it stuck up, so as soon as all the sheep was in, I shut the gate and walked down the dyke to have a look at un. When I got close I see the toe of another boot just alongside. Looks a bit queer, I thinks, but I couldn't see anything more, 'cause the duckweed is that thick as it looks as if you could walk on it.

"Howsever, I clears away the weed with my stick, and then I see 'twas a dead man. Give me a rare turn, it did. He was a-layin' at the bottom of the ditch with his head near the middle and his feet up close to the bank. Just then young Harry Walker comes along the cart-track on his way to work, so I shows him the body and sends him back to the town for to give notice at the police station."

"And is that all you know about the affair?"

"Ay. Later on I see the sergeant come along with a man wheelin' the stretcher, and I showed him where the body was and helped to pull it out and load it on the stretcher. And that's all I know about it."

On this the witness was dismissed and his place taken by a shrewd-looking, business-like police sergeant, who deposed as follows:

"Last Wednesday, the 8th of May, at 6.15 a.m., I received information from Henry Walker that a dead body was lying in the ditch by the cart-track leading from Ponder's Road to Reed's farm. I proceeded there forthwith, accompanied by Police-Constable Ketchum, and taking with us a wheeled stretcher. On the track I was met by the last witness, who conducted me to the place where the body was lying and where I found it in the position that he has described; but we had to clear away the duck-weed before we could see it distinctly. I examined the bank carefully, but could see no trace of footprints, as the grass grows thickly right down to the water's edge.

"There were no signs of a struggle or any disturbance on the bank. With the aid of Moffet and Ketchum, I drew the body out and placed it on the stretcher. I could not see any injuries or marks of violence on the body or anything unusual about it. I conveyed it to the mortuary, and with Constable Ketchum's assistance removed the clothing and emptied the pockets, putting the contents of each pocket in a separate envelope and writing the description on each. In a letter-case from the coat pocket were some visiting cards bearing the name and address of Mr. Cyrus Pedley, of 21 Hawtrey Mansions, Kensington, and a letter signed Wilfred Pedley, apparently from deceased's brother. Acting on instructions, I communicated with him and served a summons to attend this inquest."

"With regard to the ditch in which you found the body," said the coroner, "can you tell us how deep it is?"

"Yes; I measured it with Moffet's crook and a tape measure. In the deepest part, where the body was lying, it is four feet two inches deep. From there it slopes up pretty sharply to the bank."

"So far as you can judge, if a grown man fell into the ditch by accident, would he have any difficulty in getting out?"

"None at all, I should say, if he were sober and in ordinary health. A man of medium height, standing in the middle at the deepest part, would have his head and shoulders out of water; and the sides are not too steep to climb up easily, especially with the grass and rushes on the bank to lay hold of."

"You say there were no signs of disturbance on the bank. Were there any in the ditch itself?"

"None that I could see. But, of course, signs of disturbance soon disappear in water. The duck-weed drifts about as the wind drives it, and there are creatures moving about on the bottom. I noticed that deceased had some weed grasped in one hand."

This concluded the sergeant's evidence, and as he retired, the name of Dr. Albert Parton was called. The new witness was a young man of grave and professional aspect, who gave his evidence with an extreme regard for clearness and accuracy.

"I have made an examination of the body of the deceased," he began, after the usual preliminaries. "It is that of a healthy man of about forty-five. I first saw it about two hours after it was found. It had then been dead from twelve to fifteen hours. Later I made a complete examination. I found no injuries, marks of violence or any definite bruises, and no signs of disease."

"Did you ascertain the cause of death?" the coroner asked.

"Yes. The cause of death was drowning."

"You are quite sure of that?"

"Quite sure. The lungs contained a quantity of water and duckweed, and there was more than a quart of water mixed with duckweed and water-weed in the stomach. That is a clear proof of death by drowning. The water in the lungs was the immediate cause of death, by making breathing impossible, and as the water and weed in the stomach must have been swallowed, they furnish conclusive evidence that deceased was alive when he fell into the water."

"The water and weed could not have got into the stomach after death?

"No, that is quite impossible. They must have been swallowed when the head of the deceased was just below the surface; and the water must have been drawn into the lungs by spasmodic efforts to breathe when the mouth was under water."

"Did you find any signs indicating that deceased might have been intoxicated?"

"No. I examined the water from the stomach very carefully with that question in view, but there was no trace of alcohol—or, indeed, of anything else. It was simple ditch-water. As the point is important I have preserved it, and—" here the witness produced a paper parcel which he unfastened, revealing a large glass jar containing about a quart of water plentifully sprinkled with duck-weed. This he presented to the coroner, who waved it away hastily and indicated the jury; to whom it was then offered and summarily rejected with emphatic head-shakes.

"Finally it came to rest on the table by the place where I was sitting with my colleague, Dr. Thorndyke, and our client, Mr. Wilfred Pedley. I glanced at it with faint interest, noting how the duck-weed plants had risen to the surface and floated, each with its tassel of roots hanging down into the water, and how a couple of tiny, flat shells, like miniature ammonites, had sunk and lay on the bottom of the jar. Thorndyke also glanced at it; indeed, he did more than glance, for he drew the jar towards him and examined its contents in the systematic way in which it was his habit to examine everything. Meanwhile the coroner asked: "Did you find anything abnormal or unusual, or anything that could throw light on how deceased came to be in the water?"

"Nothing whatever," was the reply. "I found simply that deceased met his death by drowning."

Here, as the witness seemed to have finished his evidence, Thorndyke interposed.

"The witness states, sir, there were no definite bruises. Does he mean that there were any marks that might have been bruises?"

The coroner glanced at Dr. Parton, who replied: "There was a faint mark on the outside of the right arm, just above the elbow, which had somewhat the appearance of a bruise, as if the deceased had been struck with a stick. But it was very indistinct. I shouldn't like to swear that it was a bruise at all."

This concluded the doctor's evidence, and when he had retired, the name of our client, Wilfred Pedley, was called. He rose, and having taken the oath and given his name and address, deposed: "I have viewed the body of deceased. It is that of my brother, Cyrus Pedley, who is forty-three years of age. The last time I saw deceased alive was on Tuesday morning, the day before the body was found."

"Did you notice anything unusual in his manner or state of mind?"

The witness hesitated but at length replied: "Yes. He seemed anxious and depressed. He had been in low spirits for some time past, but on this occasion he seemed more so than usual."

"Had you any reason to suspect that he might contemplate taking his life?"

"No," the witness replied, emphatically, "and I do not believe that he would, under any circumstances, have contemplated suicide."

"Have you any special reason for that belief?"

"Yes. Deceased was a highly conscientious man and he was in my debt. He had occasion to borrow two thousand pounds from me, and the debt was secured by an insurance on his life. If he had committed suicide that insurance would be invalidated and the debt would remain unpaid. From my knowledge of him, I feel certain that he would not have done such a thing."

The coroner nodded gravely, and then asked: "What was deceased's occupation?"

"He was employed in some way by the Foreign Office, I don't know in what capacity. I know very little about his affairs."

"Do you know if he had any money worries or any troubles or embarrassments of any kind?"

"I have never heard of any; but deceased was a very reticent man. He lived alone in his flat, taking his meals at his club, and no one knew—at least, I did not—how he spent his time or what was the state of his finances. He was not married, and I am his only near relative."

"And as to deceased's habits. Was he ever addicted to taking more stimulants than was good for him?"

"Never," the witness replied emphatically. "He was a most temperate and abstemious man."

"Was he subject to fits of any kind, or fainting attacks?"

"I have never heard that he was."

"Can you account for his being in this solitary place at this time—apparently about eight o'clock at night?"

"I cannot. It is a complete mystery to me. I know of no one with whom either of us was acquainted in this district. I had never heard of the place until I got the summons to the inquest."

This was the sum of our client's evidence, and, so far, things did not look very favourable from our point of view—we were retained on the insurance question, to rebut, if possible, the suggestion of suicide. However, the coroner was a discreet man, and having regard to the obscurity of the case—and perhaps to the interests involved—summed up in favour of an open verdict; and the jury, taking a similar view, found that deceased met his death by drowning, but under what circumstances there was no evidence to show.

"Well," I said, as the court rose, "that leaves it to the insurance people to make out a case of suicide if they can. I think you are fairly safe, Mr. Pedley. There is no positive evidence."

"No," our client replied. "But it isn't only the money I am thinking of. It would be some consolation to me for the loss of my poor brother if I had some idea how he met with his death, and could feel sure that it was an unavoidable misadventure. And for my own satisfaction—leaving the insurance out of the question—I should like to have definite proof that it was not suicide."

He looked half-questioningly at Thorndyke, who nodded gravely. "Yes," the latter agreed, "the suggestion of suicide ought to be disposed of if possible, both for legal and sentimental reasons. How far away is the mortuary?"

"A couple of minutes' walk," replied Mr. Pedley. "Did you wish to inspect the body?"

"If it is permissible," replied Thorndyke; "and then I propose to have a look at the place where the body was found."

"In that case," our client said, "I will go down to the Station Hotel and wait for you. We may as well travel up to town together, and you can then tell me if you have seen any further light on the mystery."

As soon as he was gone, Dr. Parton advanced, tying the string of the parcel which once more enclosed the jar of ditch-water.

"I heard you say, sir, that you would like to inspect the body," said he. "If you like, I will show you the way to the mortuary. The sergeant will let us in, won't you, sergeant? This gentleman is a doctor as well as a lawyer."

"Bless you, sir," said the sergeant, "I know who Dr. Thorndyke is, and I shall feel it an honour to show him anything he wishes to see."

Accordingly we set forth together, Dr. Parton and Thorndyke leading the way.

"The coroner and the jury didn't seem to appreciate my exhibit," the former remarked with a faint grin, tapping the parcel as he spoke.

"No," Thorndyke agreed; "and it is hardly reason able to expect a layman to share our own matter-of-fact outlook. But you were quite right to produce the specimen. That ditch-water furnishes conclusive evidence on a vitally material question. Further, I would advise you to preserve that jar for the present, well covered and under lock and key."

Parton looked surprised. "Why?" he asked. "The inquest is over and the verdict pronounced."

"Yes, but it was an open verdict, and an open verdict leaves the case in the air. The inquest has thrown no light on the question as to how Cyrus Pedley came by his death."

"There doesn't seem to me much mystery about it," said the doctor. "Here is a man found drowned in a shallow ditch which he could easily have got out of if he had fallen in by accident. He was not drunk. Apparently he was not in a fit of any kind. There are no marks of violence and no signs of a struggle, and the man is known to have been in an extremely depressed state of mind. It looks like a clear case of suicide, though I admit that the jury were quite right, in the absence of direct evidence."

"Well," said Thorndyke, "it will be my duty to contest that view if the insurance company dispute the claim on those grounds."

"I can't think what you will have to offer in answer to the suggestion of suicide," said Parton.

"Neither can I, at present," replied Thorndyke. "But the case doesn't look to me quite so simple as it does to you."

"You think it possible that an analysis of the contents of this jar may be called for?"

"That is a possibility," replied Thorndyke. "But I mean that the case is obscure, and that some further inquiry into the circumstances of this man's death is by no means unlikely."

"Then," said Parton, "I will certainly follow your advice and lock up this precious jar. But here we are at the mortuary. Is there anything in particular that you want to see?"

"I want to see all that there is to see," Thorndyke replied. "The evidence has been vague enough so far. Shall we begin with that bruise or mark that you mentioned?"

Dr. Parton advanced to the grim, shrouded figure that lay on the slate-topped table, like some solemn effigy on an altar tomb, and drew back the sheet that covered it. We all approached, stepping softly, and stood beside the table, looking down with a certain awesome curiosity at the still, waxen figure that, but a few hours since, had been a living man like ourselves. The body was that of a good-looking, middle-aged man with a refined, intelligent face—slightly disfigured by a scar on the cheek—now set in the calm, reposeful expression that one so usually finds on the faces of the drowned; with drowsy, half-closed eyes and slightly parted lips that revealed a considerable gap in the upper front teeth.

Thorndyke stood awhile looking down on the dead man with a curious questioning expression. Then his eye travelled over the body, from the placid face to the marble-like torso and the hand which, though now relaxed, still lightly grasped a tuft of water-weed. The latter Thorndyke gently disengaged from the limp hand, and, after a glance at the dark green, feathery fronds, laid it down and stooped to examine the right arm at the spot above the elbow that Parton had spoken of.

"Yes," he said, "I think I should call it a bruise, though it is very faint. As you say, it might have been produced by a blow with a stick or rod. I notice that there are some teeth missing. Presumably he wore a plate?"

"Yes," replied Parton; "a smallish gold plate with four teeth on it—at least, so his brother told me. Of course, it fell out when he was in the water, but it hasn't been found; in fact, it hasn't been looked for."

Thorndyke nodded and then turned to the sergeant. "Could I see what you found in the pockets?" he asked.

The sergeant complied readily, and my colleague watched his orderly procedure with evident approval. The collection of envelopes was produced from an *attaché*-case and conveyed to a side table, where the sergeant emptied out the contents of each into a little heap, opposite which he placed the appropriate envelope with its written description. Thorndyke ran his eye over the collection—which was commonplace enough—until he came to the tobacco pouch, from which protruded the corner of a scrap of crumpled paper. This he drew forth and smoothed out the creases, when it was seen to be a railway receipt for an excess fare.

"Seems to have lost his ticket or travelled without one," the sergeant remarked. "But not on this line."

"No," agreed Thorndyke. "It is the Tilbury and Southend line. But you notice the date. It is the 18th; and the body was found on the morning of Wednesday, the 19th. So it would appear that he must have come into this neighbourhood in the evening; and that he must have come either by way of London or by a very complicated cross-country route. I wonder what brought him here."

He produced his notebook and was beginning to copy the receipt when the sergeant said: "You had better take the paper, sir. It is of no use to us now, and it isn't very easy to make out."

Thorndyke thanked the officer, and, handing me the paper, asked: "What do you make of it, Jervis?"

I scrutinised the little crumpled scrap and deciphered with difficulty the hurried scrawl, scribbled with a hard, ill-sharpened pencil.

"It seems to read 'Ldn to C.B'. or 'S.B', 'Hlt'—that is some 'Halt,' I presume. But the amount, 4/9, is clear enough, and that will give us a clue if we want one." I returned the paper to Thorndyke, who bestowed it in his pocket-book and then remarked: "I don't see any keys."

"No, sir," replied the sergeant, "there aren't any. Rather queer, that, for he must have had at least a latch key. They must have fallen out into the water."

"That is possible," said Thorndyke, "but it would be worth while to make sure. Is there anyone who could show us the place where the body was found?"

"I will walk up there with you myself, sir, with pleasure," said the sergeant, hastily repacking the envelopes. "It is only a quarter of an hour's walk from here."

"That is very good of you, sergeant," my colleague responded; "and as we seem to have seen everything here, I propose that we start at once. You are not coming with us, Parton?"

"No," the doctor replied. "I have finished with the case and I have got my work to do." He shook hands with us heartily and watched us—with some curiosity, I think—as we set forth in company with the sergeant.

His curiosity did not seem to me to be unjustified. In fact, I shared it. The presence of the police officer precluded discussion, but as we took our way out of the town I found myself speculating curiously on my colleague's proceedings. To me, suicide was written plainly on every detail of the case. Of course, we did not wish to take that view, but what other was possible? Had Thorndyke some alternative theory? Or was he merely, according to his invariable custom, making an impartial survey of everything, no matter how apparently trivial, in the hope of lighting on some new and informative fact?

The temporary absence of the sergeant, who had stopped to speak to a constable on duty, enabled me to put the question: "Is this expedition intended to clear up anything in particular?"

"No," he replied, "excepting the keys, which ought to be found. But you must see for yourself that this is not a straightforward case. That man did not come all this way merely to drown himself in a ditch. I am quite in the dark at present, so there is nothing for it but to examine everything with our own eyes and see if there is anything that has been overlooked that may throw some light on either the motive or the circumstances. It is always desirable to examine the scene of a crime or a tragedy."

Here the return of the sergeant put a stop to the discussion and we proceeded on our way in silence. Already we had passed out of the town, and we now turned out of the main road into a lane or by-road, bordered by meadows and orchards and enclosed by rather high hedgerows.

"This is Ponder's Road," said the sergeant. "It leads to Renham, a couple of miles farther on, where it joins the Aylesbury Road. The cart track is on the left a little way along."

A few minutes later we came to our turning, a narrow and rather muddy lane, the entrance to which was shaded by a grove of tall elms. Passing through this shady avenue, we came out on a grass-covered track, broken by deep wagon-ruts and bordered on each side by a ditch, beyond which was a wide expanse of marshy meadows.

"This is the place," said the sergeant, halting by the side of the right-hand ditch and indicating a spot where the rushes had been flattened down. "It was just as you see it now, only the feet were just visible sticking out of the duck-weed, which had drifted back after Moffet had disturbed it."

We stood awhile looking at the ditch, with its thick mantle of bright green, spotted with innumerable small dark objects and showing here and there a faint track where a water-vole had swum across.

"Those little dark objects are water-snails, I suppose," said I, by way of making some kind of remark.

"Yes," replied Thorndyke; "the common Amber shell, I think— *Succinea putris*." He reached out his stick and fished up a sample of the duck-weed, on which one or two of the snails were crawling. "Yes," he repeated. "*Succinea putris* it is; a queer little left handed shell, with the spire, as you see, all lop-sided. They have a habit of swarming in this extraordinary way. You notice that the ditch is covered with them."

I had already observed this, but it hardly seemed to be worth commenting on under the present circumstances—which was apparently the sergeant's view also, for he looked at Thorndyke with some surprise, which developed into impatience when my colleague proceeded further to expand on the subject of natural history.

"These water-weeds," he observed, "are very remarkable plants in their various ways. Look at this duck-weed, for instance. Just a little green oval disc with a single root hanging down into the water, like a tiny umbrella with a long handle; and yet it is a complete plant, and a flowering plant, too." He picked a specimen off the end of his stick and held it up by its root to exhibit its umbrella-like form; and as he did so, he looked in my face with an expression that I felt to be somehow significant; but of which I could not extract the meaning. But there was no difficulty in interpreting the expression on the sergeant's face. He had come here on business and be wanted to "cut the cackle and get to the hosses."

"Well, sergeant," said Thorndyke, "there isn't much to see, but I think we ought to have a look for those keys. He must have had keys of some kind, if only a latchkey; and they must be in this ditch."

The sergeant was not enthusiastic. "I've no doubt you are right, sir," said he; "but I don't see that we should be much forrader if we found them. However, we may as well have a look, only I can't stay more than a few minutes. I've got my work to do at the station."

"Then," said Thorndyke, "let us get to work at once. We had better hook out the weed and look it over; and if the keys are not in that, we must try to expose the bottom where the body was lying. You must tell us if we are working in the right place."

With this he began, with the crooked handle of his stick, to rake up the tangle of weed that covered the bottom of the ditch and drag the detached masses ashore, piling them on the bank and carefully looking them through to see if the keys should chance to be entangled in their meshes. In this work I took my part under the sergeant's direction, raking in load after load of the delicate, stringy weed, on the pale green ribbon-like leaves of which multitudes of the water-snails were creeping; and sorting over each batch in hopeless and fruitless search for the missing keys.

In about ten minutes we had removed the entire weedy covering from the bottom of the ditch over an area of from eight to nine feet—the place which, according to the sergeant, the body had occupied; and as the duck-weed had been caught by the tangled masses of water-weed that we had dragged ashore, we now had an uninterrupted view of the cleared space save for the clouds of mud that we had stirred up.

"We must give the mud a few minutes to settle," said Thorndyke.

"Yes," the sergeant agreed, "it will take some time; and as it doesn't really concern me now that the inquest is over, I think I will get back to the station if you will excuse me."

Thorndyke excused him very willingly, I think, though politely and with many thanks for his help. When he had gone I remarked, "I am inclined to agree with the sergeant. If we find the keys we shan't be much forrader."

"We shall know that he had them with him," he replied. "Though, of course, if we don't find them, that will not prove that they are not here. Still, I think we should try to settle the question."

His answer left me quite unconvinced; but the care with which he searched the ditch and sorted out the weed left me in no doubt that, to him, the matter seemed to be of some importance. However, nothing came of the search. If the keys were there they were buried in the mud, and eventually we had to give up the search and make our way back towards the station.

As we passed out of the lane into Ponder's Road, Thorndyke stopped at the entrance, under the trees, by a little triangle of turf which marked the beginning of the lane, and looked down at the muddy ground.

"Here is quite an interesting thing, Jervis," he remarked, "which shows us how standardised objects tend to develop an individual character. These are the tracks of a car, or more probably a tradesman's van, which was fitted with Barlow tyres. Now there must be thousands of vans fitted with these tyres; they are the favourite type for light covered vans, and when new they are all alike and indistinguishable. Yet this tyre—of the off hind wheel—has acquired a character which would enable one to pick it out with certainty from ten thousand others.

"First, you see, there is a deep cut in the tyre at an angle of forty-five, then a kidney-shaped 'Blakey' has stuck in the outer tyre without puncturing the inner; and finally some adhesive object—perhaps a lump of pitch from a newly-mended road—has become fixed on just behind the 'Blakey.' Now, if we make a rough sketch of those three marks and indicate their distance apart, thus"—here he made a rapid sketch in his notebook, and wrote in the intervals in inches—"we have the means of swearing to the identity of a vehicle which we have never seen."

"And which," I added, "had for some reason swerved over to the wrong side of the road. Yes, I should say that tyre is certainly unique. But surely most tyres are identifiable when they have been in use for some time."

"Exactly," he replied. "That was my point. The standardised thing is devoid of character only when it is new."

It was not a very subtle point, and as it was fairly obvious I made no comment, but presently reverted to the case of Pedley deceased.

"I don't quite see why you are taking all this trouble. The insurance claim is not likely to be contested. No one can prove that it was a case of suicide, though I should think no one will feel any doubt that it was, at least that is my own feeling."

Thorndyke looked at me with an expression of reproach.

"I am afraid that my learned friend has not been making very good use of his eyes," said he. "He has allowed his attention to be distracted by superficial appearances."

"You don't think that it was suicide, then?" I asked, considerably taken aback.

"It isn't a question of thinking," he replied. "It was certainly not suicide. There are the plainest indications of homicide; and, of course, in the particular circumstances, homicide means murder."

I was thunderstruck. In my own mind I had dismissed the case somewhat contemptuously as a mere commonplace suicide. As my friend had truly said, I had accepted the obvious appearances and let them mislead me, whereas Thorndyke had followed his golden rule of accepting nothing and observing everything. But what was it that he had observed? I knew that it was useless to ask, but still I ventured on a tentative question.

"When did you come to the conclusion that it was a case of homicide?"

"As soon as I had had a good look at the place where the body was found," he replied promptly.

This did not help me much, for I had given very little attention to anything but the search for the keys. The absence of those keys was, of course, a suspicious fact, if it was a fact. But we had not proved their absence; we had only failed to find them.

"What do you propose to do next?" I asked.

"Evidently," he answered, "there are two things to be done. One is to test the murder theory—to look for more evidence for or against it; the other is to identify the murderer, if possible. But really the two problems are one, since they involve the questions Who had a motive for killing Cyrus Pedley? and Who had the opportunity and the means?"

Our discussion brought us to the station, where, outside the hotel, we found Mr. Pedley waiting for us.

"I am glad you have come," said he. "I was beginning to fear that we should lose this train. I suppose there is no new light on this mysterious affair?"

"No," Thorndyke replied. "Rather there is a new problem. No keys were found in your brother's pockets, and we have failed to find them in the ditch; though, of course, they may be there."

"They must be," said Pedley. "They must have fallen out of his pocket and got buried in the mud, unless he lost them previously, which is most unlikely. It is a pity, though. We shall have to break open his cabinets and drawers, which he would have hated. He was very fastidious about his furniture."

"You will have to break into his flat, too," said I.

"No," he replied, "I shan't have to do that. I have a duplicate of his latchkey. He had a spare bedroom which he let me use if I wanted to stay in town." As he spoke, he produced his key-bunch and exhibited a small Chubb latchkey. "I wish we had the others, though," he added.

Here the up-train was heard approaching and we hurried on to the platform, selecting an empty first-class compartment as it drew up. As soon as the train had started, Thorndyke began his inquiries, to which I listened attentively.

"You said that your brother had been anxious and depressed lately. Was there anything more than this? Any nervousness or foreboding?"

"Well yes," replied Pedley. "Looking back, I seem to see that the possibility of death was in his mind. A week or two ago he brought his will to me to see if it was quite satisfactory to me as the principal beneficiary and he handed to me his last receipt for the insurance premium. That looks a little suggestive."

"It does," Thorndyke agreed. "And as to his occupation and his associates, what do you know about them?"

"His private friends are mostly my own, but of his official associates I know nothing. He was connected with the Foreign Office; but in what capacity I don't know at all. He was extremely reticent on the subject. I only know that he travelled about a good deal, presumably on official business."

This was not very illuminating, but it was all our client had to tell; and the conversation languished somewhat until the train drew up at Marylebone, when Thorndyke said, as if by an after-thought: "You have your brother's latchkey. How would it be if we just took a glance at the flat? Have you time now?"

"I will make time," was the reply, "if you want to see the flat. I don't see what you could learn from inspecting it; but that is your affair. I am in your hands."

"I should like to look round the rooms," Thorndyke answered; and as our client assented, we approached a taxi-cab and entered while Pedley gave the driver the necessary directions. A quarter of an hour later we drew up opposite a tall block of buildings, and Mr. Pedley, having paid off the cab, led the way to the lift.

The dead man's flat was on the third floor, and, like the others, was distinguished only by the number on the door. Mr. Pedley inserted the key into the latch, and having opened the door, preceded us across the small lobby into the sitting-room.

"Ha!" he exclaimed, as he entered, "this solves your problem." As he spoke, he pointed to the table, on which lay a small bunch of keys, including a latch key similar to the one that he had shown us. "But," he continued, "it is rather extraordinary. It just shows what a very disturbed state his mind must have been in."

"Yes," Thorndyke agreed, looking critically about the room; "and as the latchkey is there, it raises the question whether the keys may have been out of his possession. Do you know what the various locked receptacles contain?"

"I know pretty well what is in the bureau; but as to the cupboard above it, I have never seen it open and don't know what he kept in it. I always assumed that he reserved it for his official papers. I will just see if anything seems to have been disturbed."

He unlocked and opened the flap of the old-fashioned bureau and pulled out the small drawers one after the other, examining the contents of each. Then he opened each of the larger drawers and turned over the various articles in them. As he closed the last one, he reported "Everything seems to be in order—cheque-book, insurance policy, a few share certificates, and so on. Nothing seems to have been touched. Now we will try the cupboard, though I don't suppose its contents would be of much interest to anyone but himself. I wonder which is the key."

He looked at the keyhole and made a selection from the bunch, but it was evidently the wrong key. He tried another and yet another with a like result, until he had exhausted the resources of the bunch.

"It is very remarkable," he said. "None of these keys seems to fit. I wonder if he kept this particular key locked up or hidden. It wasn't in the bureau. Will you try what you can do?"

He handed the bunch to Thorndyke, who tried all the keys in succession with the same result. None of them was the key belonging to the lock. At length, having tried them all, he inserted one and turned it as far as it would go. Then he gave a sharp pull; and immediately the door came open.

"Why, it was unlocked after all!" exclaimed Mr. Pedley. "And there is nothing in it. That is why there was no key on the bunch. Apparently he didn't use the cupboard."

Thorndyke looked critically at the single vacant shelf, drawing his finger along it in two places and inspecting his finger-tips. Then he turned his attention to the lock, which was of the kind that is screwed on the inside of the door, leaving the bolt partly exposed. He took the bolt in his fingers and pushed it out and then in again; and by the way it moved I could see that the spring was broken. On this he made no comment, but remarked, "The cupboard has been in use pretty lately. You can see the trace of a largish volume—possibly a box-file—on the shelf. There is hardly any dust there whereas the rest of the shelf is fairly thickly coated However, that does not carry us very far; and the appearance of the rooms is otherwise quite normal."

"Quite," agreed Pedley. "But why shouldn't it be? You didn't suspect—"

"I was merely testing the suggestion offered by the absence of the keys," said Thorndyke. "By the way, have you communicated with the Foreign Office?"

"No," was the reply, "but I suppose I ought to. What had I better say to them?"

"I should merely state the facts in the first instance. But you can, if you like, say that I definitely reject the idea of suicide."

"I am glad to hear you say that," said Pedley. "Can I give any reasons for your opinion?"

"Not in the first place," replied Thorndyke. "I will consider the case and let you have a reasoned report in a day or two, which you can show to the Foreign Office and also to the insurance company."

Mr. Pedley looked as if he would have liked to ask some further questions, but as Thorndyke now made his way to the door, he followed in silence, pocketing the keys as we went out. He accompanied us down to the entry and there we left him, setting forth in the direction of South Kensington Station.

"It looked to me," said I, as soon as we were out of ear-shot, "as if that lock had been forced. What do you think?"

"Well," he answered, "locks get broken in ordinary use, but taking all the facts together, I think you are right. There are too many coincidences for reasonable probability. First, this man leaves his keys, including his latchkey, on the table, which is an extraordinary thing to do. On that very occasion, he is found dead under inexplicable circumstances. Then, of all the locks in his rooms, the one which happens to be broken is the one of which the key is not on the bunch. That is a very suspicious group of facts."

"It is," I agreed. "And if there is, as you say—though I can't imagine on what grounds—evidence of foul play, that makes it still more suspicious. But what is the next move? Have you anything in view?"

"The next move," he replied, "is to clear up the mystery of the dead man's movements on the day of his death. The railway receipt shows that on that day be travelled down somewhere into Essex. From that place, he took a long, cross-country journey of which the destination was a ditch by a lonely meadow in Buckinghamshire. The questions that we have to answer are, What was he doing in Essex? Why did he make that strange journey? Did he make it alone? and, if not, Who accompanied him?

"Now, obviously, the first thing to do is to locate that place in Essex; and when we have done that, to go down there and see if we can pick up any traces of the dead man."

"That sounds like a pretty vague quest," said I; "but if we fail, the police may be able to find out something. By the way, we want a new Bradshaw."

"An excellent suggestion, Jervis," said he. "I will get one as we go into the station."

A few minutes later, as we sat on a bench waiting for our train, he passed to me the open copy of Bradshaw, with the crumpled railway receipt.

"You see," said he, "it was apparently 'G.B.Hlt.,' and the fare from London was four and ninepence. Here is Great Buntingfield Halt, the fare to which is four and ninepence. That must be the place. At any rate, we will give it a trial. May I take it that you are coming to lend a hand? I shall start in good time tomorrow morning."

I assented emphatically. Never had I been more completely in the dark than I was in this case, and seldom had I known Thorndyke to be more positive and confident. Obviously, he had something up his sleeve; and I was racked with curiosity as to what that something was.

On the following morning we made a fairly early start, and half-past ten found us seated in the train, looking out across a dreary waste of marshes, with the estuary of the Thames a mile or so distant. For the first time in my recollection Thorndyke had come unprovided with his inevitable "research case," but I noted that he had furnished himself with a botanist's vasculum—or tin collecting-case—and that his pocket bulged as if he had some other appliances concealed about his person. Also that he carried a walking-stick that was strange to me.

"This will be our destination, I think," he said, as the train slowed down; and sure enough it presently came to rest beside a little makeshift platform on which was displayed the name "Great Buntingfield Halt." We were the only passengers to alight, and the guard, having noted the fact, blew his whistle and dismissed the little station with a contemptuous wave of his flag.

Thorndyke lingered on the platform after the train had gone, taking a general survey of the country. Half a mile away to the north a small village was visible; while to the south the marshes stretched away to the river, their bare expanse unbroken save by a solitary building whose unredeemed hideousness proclaimed it a factory of some kind. Presently the station-master approached deferentially, and as we proffered our tickets, Thorndyke remarked: "You don't seem overburdened with traffic here."

"No, sir. You're right," was the emphatic reply. "'Tis a dead-alive place. Excepting the people at the Golomite Works and one now and then from the village, no one uses the halt. You're the first strangers I've seen for more than a month."

"Indeed," said Thorndyke. "But I think you are forgetting one. An acquaintance of mine came here last Tuesday—and by the same token, he hadn't got a ticket and had to pay his fare."

"Oh, I remember," the station-master replied. "You mean a gentleman with a scar on his cheek. But I don't count him as a stranger. He has been here before; I think he is connected with the works, as he always goes up their road."

"Do you happen to remember what time he came back?" Thorndyke asked.

"He didn't come back at all," was the reply. "I am sure of that, because I work the halt and level crossing by myself. I remember thinking it queer that he didn't come back, because the ticket that he had lost was a return. He must have gone back in the van belonging to the works—that one that you see coming towards the crossing."

As he spoke, he pointed to a van that was approaching down the factory road—a small covered van with the name "Golomite Works" painted, not on the cover, but on a board that was attached to it. The station-master walked towards the crossing to open the gates, and we followed; and when the van had passed, Thorndyke wished our friend "Good morning," and led the way along the road, looking about him with lively interest and rather with the air of one looking for something in particular.

We had covered about two-thirds of the distance to the factory when the road approached a wide ditch; and from the attention with which my friend regarded it, I suspected that this was the something for which he had been looking. It was, however, quite unapproachable, for it was bordered by a wide expanse of soft mud thickly covered with rushes and trodden deeply by cattle. Nevertheless, Thorndyke followed its margin, still looking about him keenly, until, about a couple of hundred yards from the factory, I observed a small decayed wooden staging or quay, apparently the remains of a vanished footbridge. Here Thorndyke halted and unbuttoning his coat, began to empty out his pockets, producing first the vasculum, then a small case containing three wide-mouthed bottles—both of which he deposited on the ground—and finally a sort of miniature landing-net, which he proceeded to screw on to the ferrule of his stick.

"I take it," said I, "that these proceedings are a blind to cover some sort of observations."

"Not at all," he replied. "We are engaged in the study of pond and ditch natural history, and a most fascinating and instructive study it is. The variety of forms is endless. This ditch, you observe, like the one at Bantree, is covered with a dense growth of duck-weed: but whereas that ditch was swarming with *succinea* here there is not a single *succinea* to be seen."

I grunted a sulky assent, and watched suspiciously as he filled the bottles with water from the ditch and then made a preliminary sweep with his net.

"Here is a trial sample," said he, holding the loaded net towards me. "Duck-weed, horn-weed, *Planorbis nautileus*, but no *succinea*. What do you think of it, Jervis?"

I looked distastefully at the repulsive mess, but yet with attention, for I realised that there was a meaning in his question. And then, suddenly, my attention sharpened. I picked out of the net a strand of dark green, plumy weed and examined it. "So this is horn-weed," I said. "Then it was a piece of horn-weed that Cyrus Pedley held grasped in his hand; and now I come to think of it, I don't remember seeing any horn-weed in the ditch at Bantree."

He nodded approvingly. "There wasn't any," said he.

"And these little ammonite-like shells are just like those that I noticed at the bottom of Dr. Parton's jar. But I don't remember seeing any in the Bantree ditch."

"There were none there," said he. "And the duck-weed?"

"Oh, well," I replied, "duck-weed is duck-weed, and there's an end of it."

He chuckled aloud at my answer, and quoting: "*A primrose by the river's brim A yellow primrose was to him*," bestowed a part of the catch in the vasculum, then turned once more to the ditch and began to ply his net vigorously, emptying out each netful on the grass, looking it over quickly and then making a fresh sweep, dragging the net each time through the mud at the bottom. I watched him now with a new and very lively interest; for enlightenment was dawning, mingled with some self-contempt and much speculation as to how Thorndyke had got his start in this case.

But I was not the only interested watcher. At one of the windows of the factory I presently observed a man who seemed to be looking our way. After a few seconds' inspection he disappeared, to reappear almost immediately with a pair of field-glasses, through which he took a long look at us. Then he disappeared again, but in less than a minute I saw him emerge from a side door and advance hurriedly towards us.

"We are going to have a notice of ejectment served on us, I fancy," said I.

Thorndyke glanced quickly at the approaching stranger but continued to ply his net, working, as I noticed, methodically from left to right. When the man came within fifty yards he hailed us with a brusque inquiry as to what our business was. I went forward to meet him and, if possible, to detain him in conversation; but this plan failed, for he ignored me and bore straight down on Thorndyke.

"Now, then," said he, "what's the game? What are you doing here?"

Thorndyke was in the act of raising his net from the water, but he now suddenly let it fall to the bottom of the ditch while he turned to confront the stranger.

"I take it that you have some reason for asking," said he.

"Yes, I have," the other replied angrily and with a slight foreign accent that agreed with his appearance—he looked like a Slav of some sort. "This is private land. It belongs to the factory. I am the manager."

"The land is not enclosed," Thorndyke remarked.

"I tell you the land is private land," the fellow retorted excitedly. "You have no business here. I want to know what you are doing."

"My good sir," said Thorndyke, "there is no need to excite yourself. My friend and I are just collecting botanical and other specimens."

"How do I know that?" the manager demanded. He looked round suspiciously and his eye lighted on the vasculum. "What have you got in that thing?" he asked.

"Let him see what is in it," said Thorndyke, with a significant look at me.

Interpreting this as an instruction to occupy the man's attention for a few moments, I picked up the vasculum and placed myself so that he must turn his back to Thorndyke to look into it. I fumbled awhile with the catch, but at length opened the case and began to pick out the weed strand by strand. As soon as the stranger's back was turned Thorndyke raised his net and quickly picked out of it something which he slipped into his pocket. Then he advanced towards us, sorting out the contents of his net as he came.

"Well," he said, "you see we are just harmless naturalists. By the way, what did you think we were looking for?"

"Never mind what I thought," the other replied fiercely. "This is private land. You have no business here, and you have got to clear out."

"Very well," said Thorndyke. "As you please. There are plenty of other ditches." He took the vasculum and the case of bottles, and having put them in his pocket, unscrewed his net, wished the stranger "Good-morning," and turned back towards the station. The man stood watching us until we were near the level crossing, when he, too, turned back and retired to the factory.

"I saw you take something out of the net," said I. "What was it?"

He glanced back to make sure that the manager was out of sight. Then he put his hand in his pocket, drew it out closed, and suddenly opened it. In his palm lay a small gold dental plate with four teeth on it.

"My word!" I exclaimed; "this clenches the matter with a vengeance. That is certainly Cyrus Pedley's plate. It corresponds exactly to the description."

"Yes," he replied, "it is practically a certainty. Of course, it will have to be identified by the dentist who made it. But it is a foregone conclusion."

I reflected as we walked towards the station on the singular sureness with which Thorndyke had followed what was to me an invisible trail. Presently I said, "What is puzzling me is how you got your start in this case. What gave you the first hint that it was homicide and not suicide or misadventure?"

"It was the old story, Jervis," he replied; "just a matter of observing and remembering apparently trivial details. Here, by the way, is a case in point."

He stopped and looked down at a set of tracks in the soft, earth road—apparently those of the van which we had seen cross the line. I followed the direction of his glance and saw the clear impression of a Blakey's protector, preceded by that of a gash in the tyre and followed by that of a projecting lump.

"But this is astounding!" I exclaimed. "It is almost certainly the same track that we saw in Ponder's Road."

"Yes," he agreed. "I noticed it as we came along." He brought out his spring-tape and notebook, and handing the latter to me, stooped and measured the distances between the three impressions. I wrote them down as he called them out, and then we compared them with the note made in Ponder's Road. The measurements were identical, as were the relative positions of the impressions.

"This is an important piece of evidence," said he. "I wish we were able to take casts, but the notes will be pretty conclusive. And now," he continued as we resumed our progress towards the station, "to return to your question. Parton's evidence at the inquest proved that Cyrus Pedley was drowned in water which contained duck-weed. He produced a specimen and we both saw it. We saw the duck-weed in it and also two *Planorbis* shells. The presence of those two shells proved that the water in which he was drowned must have swarmed with them. We saw the body, and observed that one hand grasped a wisp of horn-weed. Then we went to view the ditch and we examined it. That was when I got, not a mere hint, but a crucial and conclusive fact. The ditch was covered with duck-weed, as we expected. But it was the wrong duck-weed."

"The wrong duck-weed!" I exclaimed. "Why, how many kinds of duck-weed are there?"

"There are four British species," he replied. "The Greater Duck-weed, the Lesser Duck-weed, the Thick Duck-weed, and the Ivy-leaved Duckweed. Now the specimens in Parton's jar I noticed were the Greater Duck-weed, which is easily distinguished by its roots, which are multiple and form a sort of tassel. But the duck-weed on the Bantree ditch was the Lesser Duck weed, which is smaller than the other, but is especially distinguished by having only a single root. It is impossible to mistake one for the other.

"Here, then, was practically conclusive evidence of murder. Cyrus Pedley had been drowned in a pond or ditch. But not in the ditch in which his body was found. Therefore his dead body had been conveyed from some other place and put into this ditch. Such a proceeding furnishes *prima facie* evidence of murder. But as soon as the question was raised, there was an abundance of confirmatory evidence. There was no horn-weed or *Planorbis* shells in the ditch, but there were swarms of *succinea*, some of which would inevitably have been swallowed with the water. There was an obscure linear pressure mark on the arm of the dead man, just above the elbow: such a mark as might be made by a cord if a man were pinioned to render him helpless.

"Then the body would have had to be conveyed to this place in some kind of vehicle; and we found the traces of what appeared to be a motor-van, which had approached the cart-track on the wrong side of the road, as if to pull up there. It was a very conclusive mass of evidence; but it would have been useless but for the extraordinarily lucky chance that poor Pedley had lost his railway ticket and preserved the receipt; by which we were able to ascertain where he was on the day of his death and in what locality the murder was probably committed. But that is not the only way in which

"Fortune has favoured us. The station-master's information was, and will be, invaluable. Then it was most fortunate for us that there was only one ditch on the factory land; and that that ditch was accessible at only one point, which must have been the place where Pedley was drowned."

"The duck-weed in this ditch is, of course, the Greater Duck-weed?"

"Yes. I have taken some specimens as well as the horn-weed and shells."

He opened the vasculum and picked out one of the tiny plants, exhibiting the characteristic tassel of roots.

"I shall write to Parton and tell him to preserve the jar and the horn-weed if it has not been thrown away. But the duck-weed alone, produced in evidence, would be proof enough that Pedley was not drowned in the Bantree ditch; and the dental plate will show where he was drowned."

"Are you going to pursue the case any farther?" I asked.

"No," he replied. "I shall call at Scotland Yard on my way home and report what I have learned and what I can prove in court. Then I shall have finished with the case. The rest is for the police, and I imagine they won't have much difficulty. The circumstances seem to tell their own story. Pedley was employed by the Foreign Office, probably on some kind of secret service. I imagine that he discovered the existence of a gang of evil-doers—probably foreign revolutionaries, of whom we may assume that our friend the manager of the factory is one; that he contrived to associate himself with them and to visit the factory occasionally to ascertain what was made there besides Golomite—if Golomite is not itself an illicit product.

"Then I assume that he was discovered to be a spy, that he was lured down here; that he was pinioned and drowned some time on

Tuesday night and his body put into the van and conveyed to a place miles away from the scene of his death, where it was deposited in a ditch apparently identical in character with that in which he was drowned. It was an extremely ingenious and well-thought-out plan. It seemed to have provided for every kind of inquiry, and it very narrowly missed being successful."

"Yes," I agreed. "But it didn't provide for Dr. John Thorndyke."

"It didn't provide for a searching examination of all the details," he replied; "and no criminal plan that I have ever met has done so. The completeness of the scheme is limited by the knowledge of the schemers, and, in practice, there is always something overlooked. In this case, the criminals were unlearned in the natural history of ditches."

Thorndyke's theory of the crime turned out to be substantially correct. The Golomite Works proved to be a factory where high explosives were made by a gang of cosmopolitan revolutionaries who were all known to the police. But the work of the latter was simplified by a detailed report which the dead man had deposited at his bank and which was discovered in time to enable the police to raid the factory and secure the whole gang. When once they were under lock and key, further information was forthcoming; for a charge of murder against them jointly soon produced King's Evidence sufficient to procure a conviction of the three actual perpetrators of the murder.

The Mysterious Visitor

"So," said Thorndyke, looking at me reflectively, "you are a full-blown medical practitioner with a practice of your own. How the years slip by! It seems but the other day that you were a student, gaping at me from the front bench of the lecture theatre."

"Did I gape?" I asked incredulously.

"I use the word metaphorically," said he, "to denote ostentatious attention. You always took my lecture very seriously. May I ask if you have ever found them of use in your practice?"

"I can't say that I have ever had any very thrilling medico-legal experiences since that extraordinary cremation case that you investigated—the case of Septimus Maddock, you know. But that reminds me that there is a little matter that I meant to speak to you about. It is of no interest, but I just wanted your advice, though it isn't even my business, strictly speaking. It concerns a patient of mine, a man named Crofton, who has disappeared rather unaccountably."

"And do you call that a case of no medico-legal interest?" demanded Thorndyke.

"Oh, there's nothing in it. He just went away for a holiday and he hasn't communicated with his friends very recently. That is all. What makes me a little uneasy is that there is a departure from his usual habits—he is generally a fairly regular correspondent—that seems a little significant in view of his personality. He is markedly neurotic and his family history is by no means what one would wish."

"That is an admirable thumb-nail sketch, Jardine," said Thorndyke "but it lacks detail. Let us have a full-size picture."

"Very well," said I, "but you mustn't let me bore you. To begin with Crofton: he is a nervous, anxious, worrying sort of fellow, everlastingly fussing about money affairs, and latterly this tendency has been getting worse. He fairly got the jumps about his financial position; felt that he was steadily drifting into bankruptcy and couldn't get that out of his mind. It was all bunkum. I am more or less a friend of the family, and I know that there was nothing to worry about. Mrs. Crofton assured me that, although they were a trifle hard up, they could rub along quite safely.

"As he seemed to be getting the hump worse and worse, I advised him to go away for a change and stay in a boarding-house where he would see some fresh faces. Instead of that, he elected to go down to a bungalow that he has at Seasalter, near Whitstable, and lets out in the season. He proposed to stay by himself and spend his time in sea-bathing and country walks. I wasn't very keen on this, for solitude was the last thing that he wanted. There was a strong family history of *melancholia* and some unpleasant rumours of suicide. I didn't like his being alone at all.

"However, another friend of the family, Mrs. Crofton's brother in fact, a chap named Ambrose, offered to go down and spend a weekend with him to give him a start, and afterwards to run down for an afternoon whenever he was able. So off he went with Ambrose on Friday, the sixteenth of June, and for a time all went well. He seemed to be improving in health and spirits and wrote to his wife regularly two or three times a week. Ambrose went down as often as he could to cheer him up, and the last time brought back the news that Crofton thought of moving on to Margate for a further change. So, of course, he didn't go down to the bungalow again.

"Well, in due course, a letter came from Margate; it had been written at the bungalow, but the postmark was Margate and bore the same date—the sixteenth of July—as the letter itself. I have it with me. Mrs. Crofton sent it for me to see and I haven't returned it yet. But there is nothing of interest in it beyond the statement that he was going on to Margate by the next train and would write again when he had found rooms there. That was the last that was heard of him. He never wrote and nothing is known of his movements excepting that he left Seasalter and arrived at Margate. This is the letter."

I handed it to Thorndyke, who glanced at the mark and then laid it on the table for examination later. "Have any inquiries been made?" he asked.

"Yes. His photograph has been sent to the Margate police, but, of course—well, you know what Margate like in July. Thousands of strangers coming and going every day. It is hopeless to look for him in that crowd and it is quite possible that he isn't there now. But his disappearance is most inopportune, for a big legacy has just fallen in, and, naturally, Mrs. Crofton is frantically anxious to let him know. It is a matter of about thirty thousand pounds."

"Was this legacy expected?" asked Thorndyke.

"No. The Croftons knew nothing about it. They didn't know that the old lady—Miss Shuler—had made a will or that she had very much to leave; and they didn't know that she was likely to die, or even that she was ill. Which is rather odd; for she was ill for a month or two and, as she suffered from a malignant abdominal tumour, it was known that she couldn't recover."

"When did she die?"

"On the thirteenth of July."

Thorndyke raised his eyebrows. "Just three days before the date of this letter," he remarked; "so that if he should never reappear, this letter will be the sole evidence that he survived her. It is an important document. It may come to represent a value of a thousand pounds."

"It isn't so important as it looks," said I. "Miss Shuler's will provides that if Crofton should die before the *estatrix*, the legacy should go to his wife. So whether he is alive or not, the legacy is quite safe. But we must hope that he is alive, though I must confess to some little anxiety on his account."

Thorndyke reflected a while on this statement. Presently he asked: "Do you know if Crofton has made a will?"

"Yes, he has," I replied; "quite recently. I was one of the witnesses and I read it through at Crofton's request. It was full of the usual legal verbiage, but it might have been stated in a dozen words. He leaves practically everything to his wife, but instead of saying so it enumerates the property item by item."

"It was drafted, I suppose, by the solicitor?"

"Yes; another friend of the family named Jobson, and he is the executor and residuary legatee."

Thorndyke nodded and again became deeply reflective. Still meditating, he took up the letter, and as he inspected it, I watched him curiously and not without a certain secret amusement. First he looked over the envelope, back and front. Then he took from his pocket a powerful Coddington lens and with this examined the flap and the postmark. Next, he drew out the letter, held it up to the light, then read it through and finally examined various parts of the writing through his lens. "Well," I asked, with an irreverent grin, "I should think you have extracted the last grain of meaning from it."

He smiled as he put away his lens and handed the letter back to me.

"As this may have to be produced in proof of survival," said he, "it had better be put in a place of safety. I notice that he speaks of returning later to the bungalow. I take it that it has been ascertained that he did not return there?"

"I don't think so. You see, they have been waiting for him to write. You think that someone ought—"

I paused; for it began to be borne in on me that Thorndyke was taking a somewhat gloomy view of the case.

"My dear Jardine," said he, "I am merely following your own suggestion. Here is a man with an inherited tendency to melancholia and suicide who has suddenly disappeared. He went away from an empty house and announced his intention of returning to it later. As that house is the only known locality in which he could be sought, it is obvious that it ought to have been examined. And even if he never came back there, the house might contain some clues to his present whereabouts."

This last sentence put an idea into my mind which I was a little shy of broaching. What was a clue to Thorndyke might be perfectly meaningless to an ordinary person. I recalled his amazing interpretations of most commonplace facts in the mysterious Maddock case and the idea took fuller possession. At length I said tentatively: "I would go down myself if I felt competent. Tomorrow is Saturday, and I could get a colleague to look after my practice; there isn't much doing just now. But when you speak of clues, and when I remember what duffer I was last time—I wish it were possible for you to have a look at the place."

To my surprise, he assented almost with enthusiasm.

"Why not?" said he. "It is a week-end. We can put up at the bungalow, I suppose, and have a little gipsy holiday. And there are undoubtedly points of interest in the case. Let us go down tomorrow. We can lunch in the train and have the afternoon before us. You had better get a key from Mrs. Crofton, or, if she hasn't got one, an authority to visit the house. We may want that if we have to enter without a key. And we go alone, of course."

I assented joyfully. Not that I had any expectations as to what we might learn from our inspection. But something in Thorndyke's manner gave me the impression that he had extracted from my account of the case some significance that was not apparent to me.

The bungalow stood on a space of rough ground a little way behind the sea-wall, along which we walked towards it from Whitstable, passing on our way a ship-builder's yard and a slipway, on which a collier brigantine was hauled up for repairs. There were one or two other bungalows adjacent, but a considerable distance apart, and we looked at them as we approached to make out the names painted on the gates.

"That will probably be the one," said Thorndyke, indicating a small building enclosed within a wooden fence and provided, like the others, with a bathing hut just above high-water mark. Its solitary, deserted aspect and lowered blinds supported his opinion, and when we reached the gate, the name "Middlewick" painted on it settled the matter.

"The next question is," said I, "how the deuce we are going to get in? The gate is locked, and there is no bell. Is it worth while to hammer at the fence?"

"I wouldn't do that," replied Thorndyke. "The place is pretty certainly empty or the gate wouldn't be locked. We shall have to climb over unless there is a back gate unlocked, so the less noise we make the better."

We walked round the enclosure, but there was no other gate, nor was there any tree or other cover to disguise our rather suspicious proceedings.

"There's no help for it, Jardine," said Thorndyke, "so here goes."

He put his green canvas suit-case on the ground, grasped the top of the fence with both hands and went over like a harlequin. I picked up the case and handed it over to him, and, having taken a quick glance round, followed my leader.

"Well," I said, "here we are. And now, how are we to get into the house?"

"We shall have to pick a lock if there is no door open, or else go in by a window. Let us take a look round."—We walked round the house to the back door, but found it not only locked, but bolted top and bottom, as Thorndyke ascertained with his knife-blade. The windows were all casements and all fastened with their catches.

"The front door will be the best," said Thorndyke. "It can't be bolted unless he got out by the chimney and I think my 'smoker's companion' will be able to cope with an ordinary door-lock. It looked like a common builder's fitting."

As he spoke, we returned to the front of the house and he produced the 'smoker's companion' from his pocket (I don't know what kind of smoker it was designed to accompany). The lock was apparently a simple affair, for the second trial with the 'companion' shot back the bolt, and when I turned the handle, the door opened. As a precaution, I called out to inquire if there was anybody within, and then, as there was no answer, we entered, walking straight into the living-room, as there was no hall or lobby.

A couple of paces from the threshold we halted to look round the room, and on me the aspect of the place produced a vague sense of discomfort. Though it was early in a bright afternoon, the room was almost completely dark, for not only were the blinds lowered, but the curtains were drawn as well.

"It looks," said I, peering about the dim and gloomy apartment with sun-dazzled eyes, "as if he had gone away at night. He wouldn't have drawn the curtains in the daytime."

"One would think not," Thorndyke agreed; "but it doesn't follow."

He stepped to the front window and drawing back the curtains pulled up the blind, revealing a half-curtain of green serge over the lower part of the window. As the bright daylight flooded the room, he stood with his back to the window looking about with deep attention, letting his eyes travel slowly over the walls, the furniture, and especially the floor. Presently he stooped to pick up a short match-end which lay just under the table opposite the door, and as he looked at it thoughtfully, he pointed to a couple of spots of candle grease on the linoleum near the table. Then he glanced at the mantelpiece and from that to an ash-bowl on the table.

"These are only trifling discrepancies," said he, "but they are worth noting. You see," he continued in response to my look of inquiry, "that this room is severely trim and orderly. Everything seems to be in place. The match-box, for instance, has its fixed receptacle above the mantelpiece, and there is a bowl for the burnt matches, regularly used, as its contents show. Yet there is a burnt match thrown on the floor, although the bowl is on the table quite handy. And the match, you notice, is not of the same kind as those in the box over the mantelpiece, which is a large Bryant and May, or as the burnt matches in the bowl which have evidently come from it. But if you look in the bowl," he continued, picking it up, "you will see two burnt matches of this same kind—apparently the small size Bryant and May—one burnt quite short and one only half burnt. The suggestion is fairly obvious, but, as I say, there is a slight discrepancy."

"I don't know," said I, "that either the suggestion or the discrepancy is very obvious to me."

He walked over to the mantelpiece and took the match box from its case.

"You see," said he, opening it, "that this box is nearly full. It has an appointed place and it was in that place. We find a small match, burnt right out, under the table opposite the door, and two more in the bowl under the hanging lamp. A reasonable inference is that someone came in in the dark and struck a match as he entered. That match must have come from a box that he brought with him in his pocket. It burned out and he struck another, which also burned out while he was raising the chimney of the lamp, and he struck a third to light the lamp. But if that person was Crofton, why did he need to strike a match to light the room when the match-box was in its usual place; and why did he throw the match-end on the floor?"

"You mean that the suggestion is that the person was not Crofton; and I think you are right. Crofton doesn't carry matches in his pocket. He uses wax vestas and carries them in a silver case."

"It might possibly have been Ambrose," Thorndyke suggested.

"I don't think so," said I. "Ambrose uses a petrol lighter."

Thorndyke nodded. "There may be nothing in it," said he, "but it offers a suggestion. Shall we look over the rest of the premises?"

He paused for a moment to glance at a small key board on the wall on which one or two keys were hanging, each distinguished by a little ivory label and by the name written underneath the peg; then he opened a door in the corner of the room. As this led into the kitchen, I closed it and opened an adjoining one which gave access to a bedroom.

"This is probably the extra bedroom," he remarked as we entered. "The blinds have not been drawn down, and there is a general air of trimness that suggests the tidy up of an unoccupied room. And the bed looks if it had been out of use."

After an attentive look round, he returned to the living room and crossed to the remaining door. As he opened it, we looked into a nearly dark room, both the windows being covered by thick serge curtains.

"Well," he observed, when he had drawn back the curtains and raised the blinds, "there is nothing painfully tidy here. That is a very roughly-made bed, and the blanket is outside the counterpane."

He looked critically about the room and especially the bedside table.

"Here are some more discrepancies," said he. "There are two candlesticks, in one of which the candle has burned itself right out, leaving a fragment of wick. There are five burnt matches in it, two large ones from the box by its side and three small ones, of which two are mere stumps. The second candle is very much guttered, and I think"—he lifted it out of the socket—"yes, it has been used out of the candlestick. You see that the grease has run down right to the bottom and there is a distinct impression of a thumb—apparently a left thumb—made while the grease was warm. Then you notice the mark on the table of a tumbler which had contained some liquid that was not water, but there is no tumbler. However, it may be an old mark, though it looks fresh."

"It is hardly like Crofton to leave an old mark on the table," said I. "He is a regular old maid. We had better see if the tumbler is in the kitchen."

"Yes," agreed Thorndyke. "But I wonder what he was doing with that candle. Apparently he took it out-of-doors, as there is a spot on the floor of the living-room; and you see that there are one or two spots on the floor here." He walked over to a chest of drawers near the door and was looking into a drawer which he had pulled out, and which I could see was full of clothes, when I observed a faint smile spreading over his face. "Come round here, Jardine," he said in a low voice, "and take a peep through the crack of the door."

I walked round, and, applying my eye to the crack, looked across the living-room at the end window. Above the half-curtain I could distinguish the unmistakable top of a constabulary helmet.

"Listen," said Thorndyke. "They are in force."

As he spoke, there came from the neighbourhood of the kitchen a furtive scraping sound, suggestive of a pocket knife persuading a window-catch. It was followed by the sound of an opening window and then of a stealthy entry. Finally, the kitchen door opened softly, someone tip-toed across the living-room and a burly police-sergeant appeared, framed in the bedroom doorway.

"Good afternoon, sergeant," said Thorndyke, with a genial smile.

"Yes, that's all very well," was the response, "but the question is, who might you be, and what might you be doing in this house?"

Thorndyke briefly explained our business, and, when, we had presented our cards and Mrs. Crofton's written authority, the sergeant's professional stiffness vanished like magic.

"It's all right, Tomkins," he sang out to an invisible myrmidon. "You had better shut the window and go out by the front door. You must excuse me, gentlemen," he added; "but the tenant of the next bungalow cycled down and gave us the tip. He watched you through his glasses and saw you pick the front-door lock. It did look a bit queer, you must admit."

Thorndyke admitted it freely with a faint chuckle, and we walked across the living-room to the kitchen. Here, the sergeant's presence seemed to inhibit comments, but I noticed that my colleague cast a significant glance at a frying-pan that rested on a Primus stove. The congealed fat in it presented another "discrepancy;" for I could hardly imagine the fastidious Crofton going away and leaving it in that condition.

Noting that there was no unwashed tumbler in evidence, I followed my friend back to the living-room, where he paused with his eye on the key-board.

"Well," remarked the sergeant, "if he ever did come back here, it's pretty clear that he isn't here now. You've been all over the premises, I think?"

"All excepting the bathing-hut," replied Thorndyke; and, as he spoke, he lifted the key so labelled from its hook.

The sergeant laughed softly. "He's not very likely to have taken up quarters there," said he. "Still, there nothing like being thorough. But you notice that the key of the front door and that of the gate have both been taken away, so we can assume that he has taken himself away too."

"That is a reasonable inference," Thorndyke admitted; "but we may as well make our survey complete."

With this he led the way out into the garden and to the gate, where he unblushingly produced the 'smoker's companion' and insinuated its prongs into the keyhole.

"Well, I'm sure!" exclaimed the sergeant as the lock clicked and the gate opened. "That's a funny sort of tool; and you seem quite handy with it, too. Might I have a look at it?"

He looked at it so very long and attentively, when Thorndyke handed it to him, that I suspected him of an intention to infringe the patent. By the time he had finished his inspection we were at the bottom of the bank below the sea-wall and Thorndyke had inserted the key into the lock of the bathing-hut. As the sergeant returned the 'companion' Thorndyke took it and pocketed it then he turned the key and pushed the door open; and the officer started back with a shout of amazement.

It was certainly a grim spectacle that we looked in on. The hut was a small building about six feet square, devoid of any furniture or fittings, excepting one or two pegs high up the wall. The single, unglazed window was closely shuttered, and on the bare floor in the farther corner a man was sitting, leaning back into the corner, with his head dropped forward on his breast. The man was undoubtedly Arthur Crofton. That much I could say with certainty, notwithstanding the horrible changes wrought by death and the lapse of time. "But," I added when I had identified the body, "I should have said that he had been dead more than a fortnight. He must have come straight back from Margate and done this. And that will probably be the missing tumbler," I concluded, pointing to one that stood on the floor close to the right hand of the corpse.

"No doubt," replied Thorndyke, somewhat abstractedly. He had been looking critically about the interior of the hut, and now remarked: "I wonder why he did not shoot the bolt instead of locking himself in; and what has become of the key? He must have taken it out of the lock and put it in his pocket."

He looked interrogatively at the sergeant, who having no option but to take the hint, advanced with an expression of horrified disgust and proceeded very gingerly to explore the dead man's clothing.

"Ah!" he exclaimed at length, "here we are." He drew from the waistcoat pocket a key with a small ivory label attached to it. "Yes, this is the one. You see, it is marked 'Bathing-hut.'"

He handed it to Thorndyke, who looked at it attentively, and even with an appearance of surprise, and then, producing an indelible pencil from his pocket, wrote on the label, "Found on body."

"The first thing," said he, "is to ascertain it fits the lock."

"Why, it must," said the sergeant, "if he locked himself in with it."

"Undoubtedly," Thorndyke agreed, "but that is the point. It doesn't look quite similar to the other one."

He drew out the key which we had brought from the house and gave it to me to hold. Then he tried the key from the dead man's pocket; but it not only did not fit, it would not even enter the keyhole.

The sceptical indifference faded suddenly from the sergeant's face. He took the key from Thorndyke, having tried it with the same result, stood up and stared, round-eyed, at my colleague.

"Well!" he exclaimed. "This is a facer! It's the wrong key!"

"There may be another key on the body," said Thorndyke. "It isn't likely, but, you had better make sure."

The sergeant showed no reluctance this time. He searched the dead man's pockets thoroughly and produced a bunch of keys. But they were all quite small keys, none of them in the least resembling that of the hut door. Nor, I noticed, did they include those of the bungalow door or the garden gate. Once more the officer drew himself up and stared at Thorndyke.

"There's something rather fishy about this affair," said he.

"There is," Thorndyke agreed. "The door was certainly locked; and as it was not locked from within, it must have been locked from without. Then that key—the wrong key—was presumably placed in the dead man's pocket by some other person. And there are some other suspicious facts. A tumbler has disappeared from the bedside table, and there is a tumbler here. You notice one or two spots of candle-grease on the floor here, and it looks as if a candle had been stood in that corner near the door. There is no candle here now; but in the bedroom there is a candle which has been carried without a candle stick and which, by the way, bears an excellent impression of a thumb. The first thing to do will be to take the deceased's finger-prints. Would you mind fetching my case from the bedroom, Jardine?"

I ran back to the house (not unobserved by the gentleman in the next bungalow) and, catching up the case, carried it down to the hut. When I arrived there I found Thorndyke holding the tumbler delicately in his gloved left hand while he examined it against the light with the aid of his lens. He handed the latter to me and observed.

"If you look at this carefully, Jardine, you will see a very interesting thing. There are the prints of two different thumbs—both left hands, and therefore of different persons. You will remember that the tumbler stood by the right hand of the body and that the table, which bore the mark of a tumbler, was at the left-hand side of the bed."

When I had examined the thumb-prints he placed the tumbler carefully on the floor and opened his "research-case," which was fitted as a sort of portable laboratory. From this he took a little brass box containing an ink-tube, a tiny roller and some small cards, and, using the box-lid as an inking plate, he proceeded methodically to take the dead man's finger-prints, writing the particulars on each card.

"I don't quite see what you want with Crofton's finger-prints," said I. "The other man's would be more to the point."

"Undoubtedly," Thorndyke replied. "But we have to prove that they are another man's—that they are not Crofton's. And there is that print on the candle. That is a very important point to settle; and as we have finished here, we had better go and settle it at once."

He closed his case, and, taking up the tumbler with his gloved hand, led the way back to the house, the sergeant following when he had locked the door. We proceeded directly to the bedroom, where Thorndyke took the candle from its socket and, with the aid of his lens, compared it carefully with the two thumb-prints on the card, and then with the tumbler.

"It is perfectly clear," said he. "This is a mark of a left thumb. It is totally unlike Crofton's and it appears to be identical with the strange thumb-print on the tumbler. From which it seems to follow that the stranger took the candle from this room to the hut and brought it back. But he probably blew it out before leaving the house and lit it again in the hut."

The sergeant and I examined the cards, the candle and the tumbler, and then the former asked: "I suppose you have no idea whose thumb-print that might be? You don't know, for instance, of anyone who might have had any motive for making away with Mr. Crofton?"

"That," replied Thorndyke, "is rather a question for the coroner's jury."

"So it is," the sergeant agreed. "But there won't be much question about their verdict. It is a pretty clear case of wilful murder."

To this Thorndyke made no reply excepting to give some directions as to the safe-keeping of the candle and tumbler; and our proposed "gipsy holiday" being now evidently impossible, we took our leave of the sergeant—who already had our cards—and wended back to the station.

"I suppose," said I, "we shall have to break the news to Mrs. Crofton."

"That is hardly our business," he replied. "We can leave that to the solicitor or to Ambrose. If you know the lawyer's address, you might send him a telegram, arranging a meeting at eight o'clock tonight. Give no particulars. Just say "Crofton found," but mark the telegram "urgent" so that he will keep the appointment."

On reaching the station, I sent off the telegram, and very soon afterwards the London train was signalled. It turned out to be a slow train, which gave us ample time to discuss the case and me ample time for reflection. And, in fact, I reflected a good deal; for there was a rather uncomfortable question in my mind—the very question that the sergeant had raised and that Thorndyke had obviously evaded. Was there anyone who might have had a motive for making away with Crofton? It was an awkward question when one remembered the great legacy that had just fallen in and the terms of Miss Shuler's will; which expressly provided that, if Crofton died before his wife, the legacy should go to her. Now, Ambrose was the wife's brother; and Ambrose had been in the bungalow alone with Crofton, and nobody else was known to have been there at all. I meditated on these facts uncomfortably and would have liked to put the case to Thorndyke; but his reticence, his evasion of the sergeant's question and his decision to communicate with the solicitor rather than with the family showed pretty clearly what was in his mind and that he did not wish to discuss the matter.

Promptly at eight o'clock, having dined at a restaurant, we presented ourselves at the solicitor's house and were shown into the study, where we found Mr. Jobson seated at a writing-table. He looked at Thorndyke with some surprise, and when the introductions had been made, said somewhat dryly: "We may take it that Dr. Thorndyke is in some way connected with our rather confidential business?"

"Certainly," I replied. "That is why he is here."

Jobson nodded. "And how is Crofton?" he asked, "and where did you dig him up?"

"I am sorry to say," I replied, "that he is dead. It is a dreadful affair. We found his body locked in the bathing-hut. He was sitting in a corner with a tumbler on the floor by his side."

"Horrible! horrible!" exclaimed the solicitor. "He ought never to have gone there alone. I said so at the time. And it is most unfortunate on account of the insurance, though that is not a large amount. Still the suicide clause, you know—"

"I doubt whether the insurance will be affected," said Thorndyke. "The coroner's finding will almost certainly be wilful murder."

Jobson was thunderstruck. In a moment his face grew livid and he gazed at Thorndyke with an expression of horrified amazement.

"Murder!" he repeated incredulously. "But you said he was locked in the hut. Surely that is clear proof of suicide."

"He hadn't locked himself in, you know. There was no key inside."

"Ah!" The solicitor spoke almost in a tone relief. "But, perhaps—did you examine his pockets?"

"Yes; and we found a key labelled 'Bathing hut.' But it was the wrong key. It wouldn't go into the lock. There is no doubt whatever that the door was locked from the outside."

"Good God!" exclaimed Jobson, in a faint voice. "It does look suspicious. But still, I can't believe—It seems quite incredible."

"That may be," said Thorndyke, "but it is all perfectly clear. There is evidence that a stranger entered the bungalow at night and that the affair took place in the bedroom. From thence the stranger carried the body down to the hut and he also took a tumbler and a candle from the bedside table. By the light of the candle—which was stood on the floor of the hut in a corner—he arranged the body, having put into its pocket a key from the board in the living-room. Then he locked the hut, went back to the house, put the key on its peg and the candle in its candlestick. Then he locked up the house and the garden gate and took the keys away with him."

The solicitor listened to this recital in speechless amazement. At length he asked: "How long ago do you suppose this happened?"

"Apparently on the night of the fifteenth of this month," was the reply.

"But," objected Jobson, "he wrote home on the sixteenth."

"He wrote," said Thorndyke, "on the sixth. Somebody put a one in front of the six and posted the letter at Margate on the sixteenth. I shall give evidence to that effect at the inquest."

I was becoming somewhat mystified. Thorndyke's dry, stern manner—so different from his usual suavity—and the solicitor's uncalled-for agitation, seemed to hint at something more than met the eye. I watched Jobson as he lit a cigarette—with a small Bryant and May match, which he threw on the floor—and listened expectantly for his next question. At length he asked: "Was there any sort of—er—clue as to who this stranger might be?"

"The man who will be charged with the murder? Oh, yes. The police have the means of identifying him with absolute certainty."

"That is, if they can find him," said Jobson.

"Naturally. But when all the very remarkable facts have transpired at the inquest, that individual will probably come pretty clearly into view."

Jobson continued to smoke furiously with his eyes fixed on the floor, as if he were thinking hard. Presently he asked, without looking up: "Supposing they do find this man. What then? What evidence is there that he murdered Crofton?"

"You mean direct evidence?" said Thorndyke. "I can't say, as I did not examine the body; but the circumstantial evidence that I have given you would be enough to convict unless there were some convincing explanation other than murder. And I may say," he added, "that if the suspected person has a plausible explanation to offer, he would be well advised to produce it before he is charged. A voluntary statement has a good deal more weight than the same statement made by a prisoner in answer to a charge."

There was an interval of silence, in which I looked bewilderment from Thorndyke's stern visage to the pale face of the solicitor. At length the latter rose abruptly and, after one or two quick strides up and down the room, halted by the fireplace, and, still avoiding Thorndyke's eye, said, somewhat brusquely, though in a low, husky voice: "I will tell you how it happened. I went down to Seasalter, as you said, on the night of the fifteenth, on the chance of finding Crofton at the bungalow. I wanted to tell him of Miss Shuler's death and of the provisions her will."

"You had some private information on that subject, I presume?" said Thorndyke.

"Yes. My cousin was her solicitor and he kept me informed about the will."

"And about the state of her health?"

"Yes. Well, when I arrived at the bungalow, it was in darkness. The gate and the front door were unlocked, so I entered, calling out Crofton's name. As no one answered, I struck a match and lit the lamp. Then I went into the bedroom and struck a match there; and by its light I could see Crofton lying on the bed, quite still. I spoke to him, but he did not answer or move. Then I lighted a candle on his table; and now I could see what I had already guessed, that he was dead, and that he had been dead some time—probably more than a week.

"It was an awful shock to find a dead man in this solitary house, and my first impulse was to rush out and give the alarm. But when I went into the living-room, I happened to see a letter lying on writing-table and noticed that it was in his own hand and addressed to his wife. Unfortunately, I had the curiosity to take it out of the unsealed envelope and read it. It was dated the sixth and stated his intention of going to Margate for a time and then coming back to the bungalow.

"Now, the reading of that letter exposed me to an enormous temptation. By simply putting a one in front of the six and thus altering the date from the sixth to the sixteenth and posting the letter at Margate, I stood to gain thirty thousand pounds. I saw that at a glance. But I did not decide immediately to do it. I pulled down the blinds, drew the curtains and locked up the house while I thought it over. There seemed to be practically no risk, unless someone should come to the bungalow and notice that the state of the body did not agree with the altered date on the letter. I went back and looked at the dead man.

There was a burnt-out candle by his side and a tumbler containing the dried-up remains of some brown liquid. He had evidently poisoned himself. Then it occurred to me that, if I put the body and the tumbler in some place where they were not likely to be found for some time, the discrepancy between the condition of the body and the date of the letter would not be noticed.

"For some time I could think of no suitable place, but at last I remembered the bathing-hut. No one would look there for him. If they came to the bungalow and didn't find him there, they would merely conclude that he had not come back from Margate. I took the candle and the key from the key-board and went down to the hut; but there was a key in the door already, so I brought the other key back and put it in Crofton's pocket, never dreaming that it might not be the duplicate. Of course, I ought to have tried it in the door.

"Well, you know the rest. I took the body down about two in the morning, locked up the hut, brought away the key and hung it on the board, took the counterpane off the bed, as it had some marks on it, and re-made the bed with the blanket outside. In the morning I took the train to Margate, posted the letter, after altering the date, and threw the gate-key and that of the front door into the sea.

"That is what really happened. You may not believe me; but I think you will as you have seen the body and will realise that I had no motive for killing Crofton before the fifteenth, whereas Crofton evidently died before that date."

"I would not say 'evidently,'" said Thorndyke; "but, as the date of his death is the vital point in your defence, you would be wise to notify the coroner of the importance of the issue."

✦✦✦✦✦✦✦✦

"I don't understand this case," I said, as we walked homewards (I was spending the evening with Thorndyke). "You seemed to smell a rat from the very first. And I don't see how you spotted Jobson. It is a mystery to me."

"It wouldn't be if you were a lawyer," he replied. "The case against Jobson was contained in what you told me at our first interview. You yourself commented on the peculiarity of the will that he drafted for Crofton. The intention of the latter was to leave all his property to his wife. But instead of saying so, the will specified each item of property, and appointed a residuary legatee, which was Jobson himself. This might have appeared like mere legal verbiage; but when Miss Shuler's legacy was announced, the transaction took on a rather different aspect. For this legacy was not among the items specified in the will. Therefore it did not go to Mrs. Crofton. It would be included in the residue of the estate and would go to the residuary legatee."

"The deuce it would!" I exclaimed.

"Certainly; until Crofton revoked his will or made a fresh one. This was rather suspicious. It suggested that Jobson had private information as to Miss Shuler's will and had drafted Crofton's will in accordance with it; and as she died of malignant disease, her doctor must have known for some time that she was dying and it looked as if Jobson had information on that point, too. Now the position of affairs that you described to me was this:

"Crofton, a possible suicide, had disappeared, and had made no fresh will.

"Miss Shuler died on the thirteenth, leaving thirty thousand pounds to Crofton, if he survived her, or if he did not, then to Mrs. Crofton. The important question then was whether Crofton was alive or dead; and if he was dead, whether he had died before or after the thirteenth. For if he died before the thirteenth the legacy went to Mrs. Crofton, but if he died after that date the legacy went to Jobson.

"Then you showed me that extraordinarily opportune letter dated the sixteenth. Now, seeing that that date was worth thirty thousand pounds to Jobson, I naturally scrutinised it narrowly. The letter was written with ordinary blue-black ink. But this ink, even in the open, takes about a fortnight to blacken completely. In a closed envelope it takes considerably longer. On examining this date through a lens, the one was very perceptibly bluer than the six. It had therefore been added later. But for what reason? And by whom?

"The only possible reason was that Crofton was dead and had died before the thirteenth. The only person who had any motive for making the alteration was Jobson. Therefore, when we started for Seasalter I already felt sure that Crofton was dead and that the letter had been posted at Margate by Jobson. I had further no doubt that Crofton's body was concealed somewhere on the premises of the bungalow. All that I had to do was to verify those conclusions."

"Then you believe that Jobson has told us the truth?"

"Yes. But I suspect that he went down there with the deliberate intention of making away with Crofton before he could make a fresh will. The finding of Crofton's body must have been a fearful disappointment, but I must admit that he showed considerable resource in dealing with the situation; and he failed only by the merest chance. I think his defence against the murder charge will be admitted; but, of course, it will involve plea of guilty to the charge of fraud in connection with the legacy."

Thorndyke's forecast turned out to be correct. Jobson was acquitted of the murder of Arthur Crofton, but is at present "doing time" in respect of the forged letter and the rest of his too-ingenious scheme.

The Man with the Nailed Shoes

There are, I suppose, few places even on the East Coast of England more lonely and remote than the village of Little Sundersley and the country that surrounds it. Far from any railway, and some miles distant from any considerable town, it remains an outpost of civilization, in which primitive manners and customs and old-world tradition linger on into an age that has elsewhere forgotten them. In the summer, it is true, a small contingent of visitors, adventurous in spirit, though mostly of sedate and solitary habits, make their appearance to swell its meagre population, and impart to the wide stretches of smooth sand that fringe its shores a fleeting air of life and sober gaiety; but in late September—the season of the year in which I made its acquaintance—its pasture-lands lie desolate, the rugged paths along the cliffs are seldom trodden by human foot, and the sands are a desert waste on which, for days together, no footprint appears save that left by some passing sea-bird.

I had been assured by my medical agent, Mr. Turcival, that I should find the practice of which I was now taking charge 'an exceedingly soft billet, and suitable for a studious man;' and certainly he had not misled me, for the patients were, in fact, so few that I was quite concerned for my principal, and rather dull for want of work. Hence, when my friend John Thorndyke, the well-known medico-legal expert, proposed to come down and stay with me for a weekend and perhaps a few days beyond, I hailed the proposal with delight, and welcomed him with open arms.

"You certainly don't seem to be overworked, Jervis," he remarked, as we turned out of the gate after tea, on the day of his arrival, for a stroll on the shore. "Is this a new practice, or an old one in a state of senile decay?"

"Why, the fact is," I answered, "there is virtually no practice. Cooper—my principal—has been here about six years, and as he has private means he has never made any serious effort to build one up; and the other man, Dr. Burrows, being uncommonly keen, and the people very conservative, Cooper has never really got his foot in. However, it doesn't seem to trouble him."

"Well, if he is satisfied, I suppose you are," said Thorndyke, with a smile. "You are getting a seaside holiday, and being paid for it. But I didn't know you were as near to the sea as this."

We were entering, as he spoke, an artificial gap-way cut through the low cliff, forming a steep cart-track down to the shore. It was locally known as Sundersley Gap, and was used principally, when used at all, by the farmers' carts which came down to gather seaweed after a gale.

"What a magnificent stretch of sand!" continued Thorndyke, as we reached the bottom, and stood looking out seaward across the deserted beach. "There is something very majestic and solemn in a great expanse of sandy shore when the tide is out, and I know of nothing which is capable of conveying the impression of solitude so completely. The smooth, unbroken surface not only displays itself untenanted for the moment, but it offers convincing testimony that it has lain thus undisturbed through a considerable lapse of time. Here, for instance, we have clear evidence that for several days only two pairs of feet besides our own have trodden this gap."

"How do you arrive at the 'several days'?" I asked.

"In the simplest manner possible," he replied. "The moon is now in the third quarter, and the tides are consequently neap-tides. You can see quite plainly the two lines of seaweed and jetsam which indicate the high-water marks of the spring-tides and the neap-tides respectively. The strip of comparatively dry sand between them, over which the water has not risen for several days, is, as you see, marked by only two sets of footprints, and those footprints will not be completely obliterated by the sea until the next spring-tide—nearly a week from today."

"Yes, I see now, and the thing appears obvious enough when one has heard the explanation. But it is really rather odd that no one should have passed through this gap for days, and then that four persons should have come here within quite a short interval of one another."

"What makes you think they have done so?" Thorndyke asked.

"Well," I replied, "both of these sets of footprints appear to be quite fresh, and to have been made about the same time."

"Not at the same time, Jervis," rejoined Thorndyke. "There is certainly an interval of several hours between them, though precisely how many hours we cannot judge, since there has been so little wind lately to disturb them; but the fisherman unquestionably passed here not more than three hours ago, and I should say probably within an hour; whereas the other man—who seems to have come up from a boat to fetch something of considerable weight—returned through the gap certainly not less, and probably more, than four hours ago."

I gazed at my friend in blank astonishment, for these events befell in the days before I had joined him as his assistant, and his special knowledge and powers of inference were not then fully appreciated by me.

"It is clear, Thorndyke," I said, "that footprints have a very different meaning to you from what they have for me. I don't see in the least how you have reached any of these conclusions."

"I suppose not," was the reply; "but, you see, special knowledge of this kind is the stock-in-trade of the medical jurist, and has to be acquired by special study, though the present example is one of the greatest simplicity. But let us consider it point by point; and first we will take this set of footprints which I have inferred to be a fisherman's. Note their enormous size. They should be the footprints of a giant. But the length of the stride shows that they were made by a rather short man. Then observe the massiveness of the soles, and the fact that there are no nails in them. Note also the peculiar clumsy tread—the deep toe and heel marks, as if the walker had wooden legs, or fixed ankles and knees. From that character we can safely infer high boots of thick, rigid leather, so that we can diagnose high boots, massive and stiff, with nailless soles, and many sizes too large for the wearer.

"But the only boot that answers this description is the fisherman's thigh-boot—made of enormous size to enable him to wear in the winter two or three pairs of thick knitted stockings, one over the other. Now look at the other footprints; there is a double track, you see, one set coming from the sea and one going towards it. As the man (who was bow-legged and turned his toes in) has trodden in his own footprints, it is obvious that he came from the sea, and returned to it. But observe the difference in the two sets of prints; the returning ones are much deeper than the others, and the stride much shorter. Evidently he was carrying something when he returned, and that something was very heavy. Moreover, we can see, by the greater depth of the toe impressions, that he was stooping forward as he walked, and so probably carried the weight on his back. Is that quite clear?"

"Perfectly," I replied. "But how do you arrive at the interval of time between the visits of the two men?"

"That also is quite simple. The tide is now about halfway out; it is thus about three hours since high water. Now, the fisherman walked just about the neap-tide, high-water mark, sometimes above it and sometimes below. But none of his footprints have been obliterated; therefore he passed after high water—that is, less than three hours ago; and since his footprints are all equally distinct, he could not have passed when the sand was very wet. Therefore he probably passed less than an hour ago. The other man's footprints, on the other hand, reach only to the neap-tide, high-water mark, where they end abruptly. The sea has washed over the remainder of the tracks and obliterated them. Therefore he passed not less than three hours and not more than four days ago—probably within twenty-four hours."

As Thorndyke concluded his demonstration the sound of voices was borne to us from above, mingled with the tramping of feet, and immediately afterwards a very singular party appeared at the head of the gap descending towards the shore. First came a short burly fisherman clad in oilskins and sou'-wester, clumping along awkwardly in his great sea-boots, then the local police-sergeant in company with my professional rival Dr. Burrows, while the rear of the procession was brought up by two constables carrying a stretcher. As he reached the bottom of the gap the fisherman, who was evidently acting as guide, turned along the shore, retracing his own tracks, and the procession followed in his wake.

"A surgeon, a stretcher, two constables, and a police-sergeant," observed Thorndyke. "What does that suggest to your mind, Jervis?"

"A fall from the cliff," I replied, "or a body washed up on the shore."

"Probably," he rejoined; "but we may as well walk in that direction."

We turned to follow the retreating procession, and as we strode along the smooth surface left by the retiring tide Thorndyke resumed: "The subject of footprints has always interested me deeply for two reasons. First, the evidence furnished by footprints is constantly being brought forward, and is often of cardinal importance; and, secondly, the whole subject is capable of really systematic and scientific treatment. In the main the data are anatomical, but age, sex, occupation, health, and disease all give their various indications. Clearly, for instance, the footprints of an old man will differ from those of a young man of the same height, and I need not point out to you that those of a person suffering from *locomotor ataxia* or *paralysis agitans* would be quite unmistakable."

"Yes, I see that plainly enough," I said.

"Here, now," he continued, "is a case in point." He halted to point with his stick at a row of footprints that appeared suddenly above high-water mark, and having proceeded a short distance, crossed the line again, and vanished where the waves had washed over them. They were easily distinguished from any of the others by the clear impressions of circular rubber heels.

"Do you see anything remarkable about them?" he asked.

"I notice that they are considerably deeper than our own," I answered.

"Yes, and the boots are about the same size as ours, whereas the stride is considerably shorter—quite a short stride, in fact. Now there is a pretty constant ratio between the length of the foot and the length of the leg, between the length of leg and the height of the person, and between the stature and the length of stride. A long foot means a long leg, a tall man, and a long stride. But here we have a long foot and a short stride. What do you make of that?" He laid down his stick—a smooth partridge cane, one side of which was marked by small lines into inches and feet—beside the footprints to demonstrate the discrepancy.

"The depth of the footprints shows that he was a much heavier man than either of us," I suggested; "perhaps he was unusually fat."

"Yes," said Thorndyke, "that seems to be the explanation. The carrying of a dead weight shortens the stride, and fat is practically a dead weight. The conclusion is that he was about five feet ten inches high, and excessively fat." He picked up his cane, and we resumed our walk, keeping an eye on the procession ahead until it had disappeared round a curve in the coast-line, when we mended our pace somewhat. Presently we reached a small headland, and, turning the shoulder of cliff, came full upon the party which had preceded us. The men had halted in a narrow bay, and now stood looking down at a prostrate figure beside which the surgeon was kneeling.

"We were wrong, you see," observed Thorndyke. "He has not fallen over the cliff, nor has he been washed up by the sea. He is lying above high-water mark, and those footprints that we have been examining appear to be his."

As we approached, the sergeant turned and held up his hand.

"I'll ask you not to walk round the body just now, gentlemen," he said. "There seems to have been foul play here, and I want to be clear about the tracks before anyone crosses them."

Acknowledging this caution, we advanced to where the constables were standing, and looked down with some curiosity at the dead man. He was a tall, frail-looking man, thin to the point of emaciation, and appeared to be about thirty-five years of age. He lay in an easy posture, with half-closed eyes and a placid expression that contrasted strangely enough with the tragic circumstances of his death.

"It is a clear case of murder," said Dr. Burrows, dusting the sand from his knees as he stood up. "There is a deep knife-wound above the heart, which must have caused death almost instantaneously."

"How long should you say he has been dead, Doctor?" asked the sergeant.

"Twelve hours at least," was the reply. "He is quite cold and stiff."

"Twelve hours, eh?" repeated the officer. "That would bring it to about six o'clock this morning."

"I won't commit myself to a definite time," said Dr. Burrows hastily. "I only say not less than twelve hours. It might have been considerably more."

"Ah!" said the sergeant. "Well, he made a pretty good fight for his life, to all appearances." He nodded at the sand, which for some feet around the body bore the deeply indented marks of feet, as though a furious struggle had taken place. "It's a mighty queer affair," pursued the sergeant, addressing Dr. Burrows. "There seems to have been only one man in it—there is only one set of footprints besides those of the deceased—and we've got to find out who he is; and I reckon there won't be much trouble about that, seeing the kind of trade-marks he has left behind him."

"No," agreed the surgeon; "there ought not to be much trouble in identifying those boots. He would seem to be a labourer, judging by the hob-nails."

"No, sir; not a labourer," dissented the sergeant. "The foot is too small, for one thing; and then the nails are not regular hob-nails. They're a good deal smaller; and a labourer's boots would have the nails all round the edges, and there would be iron tips on the heels, and probably on the toes too. Now these have got no tips, and the nails are arranged in a pattern on the soles and heels. They are probably shooting-boots or sporting shoes of some kind."

He strode to and fro with his notebook in his hand, writing down hasty memoranda, and stooping to scrutinize the impressions in the sand. The surgeon also busied himself in noting down the facts concerning which he would have to give evidence, while Thorndyke regarded in silence and with an air of intense preoccupation the footprints around the body which remained to testify to the circumstances of the crime.

"It is pretty clear, up to a certain point," the sergeant observed, as he concluded his investigations, "how the affair happened, and it is pretty clear, too, that the murder was premeditated. You see, Doctor, the deceased gentleman, Mr. Hearn, was apparently walking home from Port Marston; we saw his footprints along the shore—those rubber heels make them easy to identify—and he didn't go down Sundersley Gap. He probably meant to climb up the cliff by that little track that you see there, which the people about here call the Shepherd's Path. Now the murderer must have known that he was coming, and waited upon the cliff to keep a lookout. When he saw Mr. Hearn enter the bay, he came down the path and attacked him, and, after a tough struggle, succeeded in stabbing him. Then he turned and went back up the path. You can see the double track between the path and the place where the struggle took place, and the footprints going to the path are on top of those coming from it."

"If you follow the tracks," said Dr. Burrows, "you ought to be able to see where the murderer went to."

"I'm afraid not," replied the sergeant. "There are no marks on the path itself—the rock is too hard, and so is the ground above, I fear. But I'll go over it carefully all the same."

The investigations being so far concluded, the body was lifted on to the stretcher, and the cortege, consisting of the bearers, the Doctor, and the fisherman, moved off towards the Gap, while the sergeant, having civilly wished us "Good-evening," scrambled up the Shepherd's Path, and vanished above.

"A very smart officer that," said Thorndyke. "I should like to know what he wrote in his notebook."

"His account of the circumstances of the murder seemed a very reasonable one," I said.

"Very. He noted the plain and essential facts, and drew the natural conclusions from them. But there are some very singular features in this case; so singular that I am disposed to make a few notes for my own information."

He stooped over the place where the body had lain, and having narrowly examined the sand there and in the place where the dead man's feet had rested, drew out his notebook and made a memorandum. He next made a rapid sketch-plan of the bay, marking the position of the body and the various impressions in the sand, and then, following the double track leading from and to the Shepherd's Path, scrutinized the footprints with the deepest attention, making copious notes and sketches in his book.

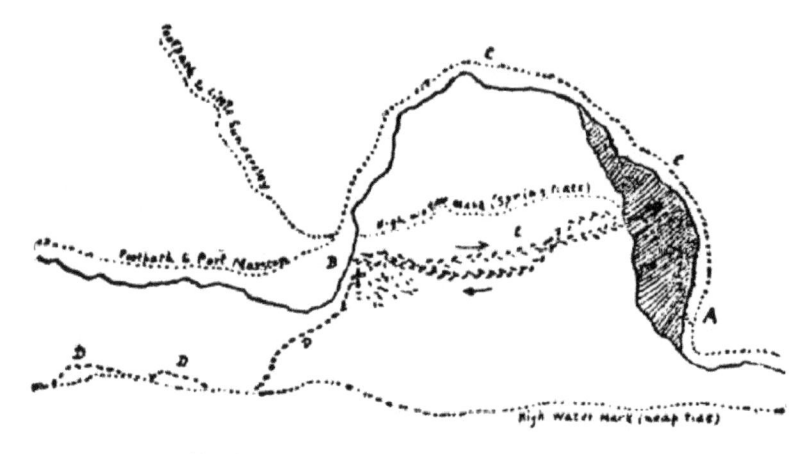

[sketch-plan of the bay]

+ Position of body. A, Top of Shepherd's Path
B, Overhanging cliff. C, Footpath along edge of cliff.
D D D, Tracks of Hearn's shoes. E, Tracks of the nailed shoes.
F, Shepherd's Path ascending shelving cliff.

"We may as well go up by the Shepherd's Path," said Thorndyke. "I think we are equal to the climb, and there may be visible traces of the murderer after all. The rock is only a sandstone, and not a very hard one either."

We approached the foot of the little rugged track which zigzagged up the face of the cliff, and, stooping down among the stiff, dry herbage, examined the surface. Here, at the bottom of the path, where the rock was softened by the weather, there were several distinct impressions on the crumbling surface of the murderer's nailed boots, though they were somewhat confused by the tracks of the sergeant, whose boots were heavily nailed. But as we ascended the marks became rather less distinct, and at quite a short distance from the foot of the cliff we lost them altogether, though we had no difficulty in following the more recent traces of the sergeant's passage up the path.

When we reached the top of the cliff we paused to scan the path that ran along its edge, but here, too, although the sergeant's heavy boots had left quite visible impressions on the ground, there were no signs of any other feet. At a little distance the sagacious officer himself was pursuing his investigations, walking backwards and forwards with his body bent double, and his eyes fixed on the ground.

"Not a trace of him anywhere," said he, straightening himself up as we approached. "I was afraid there wouldn't be after all this dry weather. I shall have to try a different tack. This is a small place, and if those boots belong to anyone living here they'll be sure to be known."

"The deceased gentleman—Mr. Hearn, I think you called him," said Thorndyke as we turned towards the village—"is he a native of the locality?"

"Oh no, sir," replied the officer. "He is almost a stranger. He has only been here about three weeks; but, you know, in a little place like this a man soon gets to be known—and his business, too, for that matter," he added, with a smile.

"What was his business, then?" asked Thorndyke.

"Pleasure, I believe. He was down here for a holiday, though it's a good way past the season; but, then, he had a friend living here, and that makes a difference. Mr. Draper up at the Poplars was an old friend of his, I understand. I am going to call on him now."

We walked on along the footpath that led towards the village, but had only proceeded two or three hundred yards when a loud hail drew our attention to a man running across a field towards us from the direction of the cliff.

"Why, here is Mr. Draper himself," exclaimed the sergeant, stopping short and waving his hand. "I expect he has heard the news already."

Thorndyke and I also halted, and with some curiosity watched the approach of this new party to the tragedy. As the stranger drew near we saw that he was a tall, athletic-looking man of about forty, dressed in a Norfolk knickerbocker suit, and having the appearance of an ordinary country gentleman, excepting that he carried in his hand, in place of a walking-stick, the staff of a butterfly-net, the folding ring and bag of which partly projected from his pocket.

"Is it true, Sergeant?" he exclaimed as he came up to us, panting from his exertions. "About Mr. Hearn, I mean. There is a rumour that he has been found dead on the beach."

"It's quite true, sir, I am sorry to say; and, what is worse, he has been murdered."

"My God! you don't say so!"

He turned towards us a face that must ordinarily have been jovial enough, but was now white and scared and, after a brief pause, he exclaimed:

"Murdered! Good God! Poor old Hearn! How did it happen, Sergeant? and when? and is there any clue to the murderer?"

"We can't say for certain when it happened," replied the sergeant, "and as to the question of clues, I was just coming up to call on you."

"On me!" exclaimed Draper, with a startled glance at the officer. "What for?"

"Well, we should like to know something about Mr. Hearn—who he was, and whether he had any enemies, and so forth; anything, in fact, that would give as a hint where to look for the murderer. And you are the only person in the place who knew him at all intimately."

Mr Draper's pallid face turned a shade paler, and he glanced about him with an obviously embarrassed air.

"I'm afraid." he began in a hesitating manner, "I'm afraid I shan't be able to help you much. I didn't know much about his affairs. You see he was—well—only a casual acquaintance—"

"Well," interrupted the sergeant, "you can tell us who and what he was, and where he lived, and so forth. We'll find out the rest if you give us the start."

"I see," said Draper. "Yes, I expect you will." His eyes glanced restlessly to and fro, and he added presently: "You must come up to-morrow, and have a talk with me about him, and I'll see what I can remember."

"I'd rather come this evening," said the sergeant firmly.

"Not this evening," pleaded Draper. "I'm feeling rather—this affair, you know, has upset me. I couldn't give proper attention—"

His sentence petered out into a hesitating mumble, and the officer looked at him in evident surprise at his nervous, embarrassed manner. His own attitude, however, was perfectly firm, though polite.

"I don't like pressing you, sir," said he, "but time is precious—we'll have to go single file here; this pond is a public nuisance. They ought to bank it up at this end. After you, sir."

The pond to which the sergeant alluded had evidently extended at one time right across the path, but now, thanks to the dry weather, a narrow isthmus of half-dried mud traversed the morass, and along this Mr. Draper proceeded to pick his way. The sergeant was about to follow, when suddenly he stopped short with his eyes riveted upon the muddy track. A single glance showed me the cause of his surprise, for on the stiff, putty-like surface, standing out with the sharp distinctness of a wax mould, were the fresh footprints of the man who had just passed, each footprint displaying on its sole the impression of stud-nails arranged in a diamond-shaped pattern, and on its heel a group of similar nails arranged in a cross.

The sergeant hesitated for only a moment, in which he turned a quick startled glance upon us; then he followed, walking gingerly along the edge of the path as if to avoid treading in his predecessor's footprints. Instinctively we did the same, following closely, and anxiously awaiting the next development of the tragedy. For a minute or two we all proceeded in silence, the sergeant being evidently at a loss how to act, and Mr. Draper busy with his own thoughts. At length the former spoke.

"You think, Mr. Draper, you would rather that I looked in on you tomorrow about this affair?"

"Much rather, if you wouldn't mind," was the eager reply.

"Then, in that case," said the sergeant, looking at his watch, "as I've got a good deal to see to this evening, I'll leave you here, and make my way to the station."

With a farewell flourish of his hand he climbed over a stile, and when, a few moments later, I caught a glimpse of him through an opening in the hedge, he was running across the meadow like a hare.

The departure of the police-officer was apparently a great relief to Mr. Draper, who at once fell back and began to talk with us.

"You are Dr. Jervis, I think," said he. "I saw you coming out of Dr. Cooper's house yesterday. We know everything that is happening in the village, you see." He laughed nervously, and added: "But I don't know your friend."

I introduced Thorndyke, at the mention of whose name our new acquaintance knitted his brows, and glanced inquisitively at my friend.

"Thorndyke," he repeated; "the name seems familiar to me. Are you in the Law, sir?"

Thorndyke admitted the impeachment, and our companion, having again bestowed on him a look full of curiosity, continued: "This horrible affair will interest you, no doubt, from a professional point of view. You were present when my poor friend's body was found, I think?"

"No," replied Thorndyke; "we came up afterwards, when they were removing it."

Our companion then proceeded to question as about the murder, but received from Thorndyke only the most general and ambiguous replies. Nor was there time to go into the matter at length, for the footpath presently emerged on to the road close to Mr. Draper's house.

"You will excuse my not asking you in tonight," said he, "but you will understand that I am not in much form for visitors just now."

We assured him that we fully understood, and, having wished him "Good-evening," pursued our way towards the village.

"The sergeant is off to get a warrant, I suppose," I observed.

"Yes; and mighty anxious lest his man should be off before he can execute it. But he is fishing in deeper waters than he thinks, Jervis. This is a very singular and complicated case; one of the strangest, in fact, that I have ever met. I shall follow its development with deep interest."

"The sergeant seems pretty cocksure, all the same," I said.

"He is not to blame for that," replied Thorndyke. "He is acting on the obvious appearances, which is the proper thing to do in the first place. Perhaps his notebook contains more than I think it does. But we shall see."

When we entered the village I stopped to settle some business with the chemist, who acted as Dr. Cooper's dispenser, suggesting to Thorndyke that he should walk on to the house; but when I emerged from the shop some ten minutes later he was waiting outside, with a smallish brown-paper parcel under each arm. Of one of these parcels I insisted on relieving him, in spite of his protests, but when he at length handed it to me its weight completely took me by surprise.

"I should have let them send this home on a barrow," I remarked.

"So I should have done," he replied, "only I did not wish to draw attention to my purchase, or give my address."

Accepting this hint I refrained from making any inquiries as to the nature of the contents (although I must confess to considerable curiosity on the subject), and on arriving home I assisted him to deposit the two mysterious parcels in his room.

When I came downstairs a disagreeable surprise awaited me. Hitherto the long evenings had been spent by me in solitary and undisturbed enjoyment of Dr. Cooper's excellent library, but tonight a perverse fate decreed that I must wander abroad, because, forsooth, a preposterous farmer, who resided in a hamlet five miles distant, had chosen the evening of my guest's arrival to dislocate his bucolic elbow. I half hoped that Thorndyke would offer to accompany me, but he made no such suggestion, and in fact seemed by no means afflicted at the prospect of my absence.

"I have plenty to occupy me while you are away," he said cheerfully; and with this assurance to comfort me I mounted my bicycle and rode off somewhat sulkily along the dark road.

My visit occupied in all a trifle under two hours, and when I reached home, ravenously hungry and heated by my ride, half-past nine had struck, and the village had begun to settle down for the night.

"Sergeant Payne is a-waiting in the surgery, sir," the housemaid announced as I entered the hall.

"Confound Sergeant Payne!" I exclaimed. "Is Dr. Thorndyke with him?"

"No, sir," replied the grinning damsel. "Dr. Thorndyke is hout."

"Hout!" I repeated (my surprise leading to unintentional mimicry).

"Yes, sir. He went hout soon after you, sir, on his bicycle. He had a basket strapped on to it—leastways a hamper—and he borrowed a basin and a kitchen-spoon from the cook."

I stared at the girl in astonishment. The ways of John Thorndyke were, indeed, beyond all understanding.

"Well, let me have some dinner or supper at once," I said, "and I will see what the sergeant wants."

The officer rose as I entered the surgery, and, laying his helmet on the table, approached me with an air of secrecy and importance.

"Well, sir," said he, "the fat's in the fire. I've arrested Mr. Draper, and I've got him locked up in the court-house. But I wish it had been someone else."

"So does he, I expect," I remarked.

"You see, sir," continued the sergeant, "we all like Mr. Draper. He's been among us a matter of seven years, and he's like one of ourselves. However, what I've come about is this; it seems the gentleman who was with you this evening is Dr. Thorndyke, the great expert. Now Mr. Draper seems to have heard about him, as most of us have, and he is very anxious for him to take up the defence. Do you think he would consent?"

"I expect so," I answered, remembering Thorndyke's keen interest in the case; "but I will ask him when he comes in."

"Thank you, sir," said the sergeant. "And perhaps you wouldn't mind stepping round to the court-house presently yourself. He looks uncommon queer, does Mr. Draper, and no wonder, so I'd like you to take a look at him, and if you could bring Dr. Thorndyke with you, he'd like it, and so should I, for, I assure you, sir, that although a conviction would mean a step up the ladder for me, I'd be glad enough to find that I'd made a mistake."

I was just showing my visitor out when a bicycle swept in through the open gate, and Thorndyke dismounted at the door, revealing a square hamper—evidently abstracted from the surgery—strapped on to a carrier at the back. I conveyed the sergeant's request to him at once, and asked if he was willing to take up the case.

"As to taking up the defence," he replied, "I will consider the matter; but in any case I will come up and see the prisoner."

With this the sergeant departed, and Thorndyke, having unstrapped the hamper with as much care as if it contained a collection of priceless porcelain, bore it tenderly up to his bedroom; whence he appeared, after a considerable interval, smilingly apologetic for the delay.

"I thought you were dressing for dinner," I grumbled as he took his seat at the table.

"No," he replied. "I have been considering this murder. Really it is a most singular case, and promises to be uncommonly complicated, too."

"Then I assume that you will undertake the defence?"

"I shall if Draper gives a reasonably straightforward account of himself."

It appeared that this condition was likely to be fulfilled, for when we arrived at the court-house (where the prisoner was accommodated in a spare office, under rather free-and-easy conditions considering the nature of the charge) we found Mr. Draper in an eminently communicative frame of mind.

"I want you, Dr. Thorndyke, to undertake my defence in this terrible affair, because I feel confident that you will be able to clear me. And I promise you that there shall be no reservation or concealment on my part of anything that you ought to know."

"Very well," said Thorndyke. "By the way, I see you have changed your shoes."

"Yes, the sergeant took possession of those I was wearing. He said something about comparing them with some footprints, but there can't be any footprints like those shoes here in Sundersley. The nails are fixed in the soles in quite a peculiar pattern. I had them made in Edinburgh."

"Have you more than one pair?"

"No. I have no other nailed boots."

"That is important," said Thorndyke. "And now I judge that you have something to tell us that bears on this crime. Am I right?"

"Yes. There is something that I am afraid it is necessary for you to know, although it is very painful to me to revive memories of my past that I had hoped were buried for ever. But perhaps, after all, it may not be necessary for these confidences to be revealed to anyone but yourself."

"I hope not," said Thorndyke; "and if it is not necessary you may rely upon me not to allow any of your secrets to leak out. But you are wise to tell me everything that may in any way bear upon the case."

At this juncture, seeing that confidential matters were about to be discussed, I rose and prepared to withdraw; but Draper waved me back into my chair.

"You need not go away, Dr. Jervis," he said. "It is through you that I have the benefit of Dr. Thorndyke's help, and I know that you doctors can be trusted to keep your own counsel and your clients' secrets. And now for some confessions of mine. In the first place, it is my painful duty to tell you that I am a discharged convict—an 'old lag,' as the cant phrase has it."

He coloured a dusky red as he made this statement, and glanced furtively at Thorndyke to observe its effect. But he might as well have looked at a wooden figure-head or a stone mask as at my friend's immovable visage; and when his communication had been acknowledged by a slight nod, he proceeded:

"The history of my wrong-doing is the history of hundreds of others. I was a clerk in a bank, and getting on as well as I could expect in that not very progressive avocation, when I had the misfortune to make four very undesirable acquaintances. They were all young men, though rather older than myself, and were close friends, forming a sort of little community or club. They were not what is usually described as 'fast.' They were quite sober and decently-behaved young follows, but they were very decidedly addicted to gambling in a small way, and they soon infected me.

"Before long I was the keenest gambler of them all. Cards, billiards, pool, and various forms of betting began to be the chief pleasures of my life, and not only was the bulk of my scanty salary often consumed in the inevitable losses, but presently I found myself considerably in debt, without any visible means of discharging my liabilities. It is true that my four friends were my chief—in fact, almost my only—creditors, but still, the debts existed, and had to be paid.

"Now these four friends of mine—named respectively Leach, Pitford, Hearn, and Jezzard—were uncommonly clever men, though the full extent of their cleverness was not appreciated by me until too late. And I, too, was clever in my way, and a most undesirable way it was, for I possessed the fatal gift of imitating handwriting and signatures with the most remarkable accuracy. So perfect were my copies that the writers themselves were frequently unable to distinguish their own signatures from my imitations, and many a time was my skill invoked by some of my companions to play off practical jokes upon the others. But these jests were strictly confined to our own little set, for my four friends were most careful and anxious that my dangerous accomplishment should not become known to outsiders.

"And now follows the consequence which you have no doubt foreseen. My debts, though small, were accumulating, and I saw no prospect of being able to pay them. Then, one night, Jezzard made a proposition. We had been playing bridge at his rooms, and once more my ill luck had caused me to increase my debt. I scribbled out an IOU, and pushed it across the table to Jezzard, who picked it up with a very wry face, and pocketed it.

"'Look here, Ted,' he said presently, 'this paper is all very well, but, you know, I can't pay my debts with it. My creditors demand hard cash.'

"'I'm very sorry,' I replied, 'but I can't help it.'

"'Yes, you can,' said he, 'and I'll tell you how.' He then propounded a scheme which I at first rejected with indignation, but which, when the others backed him up, I at last allowed myself to be talked into, and actually put into execution. I contrived, by taking advantage of the carelessness of some of my superiors at the bank, to get possession of some blank cheque forms, which I filled up with small amounts—not more than two or three pounds—and signed with careful imitations of the signatures of some of our clients. Jezzard got some stamps made for stamping on the account numbers, and when this had been done I handed over to him the whole collection of forged cheques in settlement of my debts to all of my four companions.

"The cheques were duly presented—by whom I do not know; and although, to my dismay, the modest sums for which I had drawn them had been skilfully altered into quite considerable amounts, they were all paid without demur excepting one. That one, which had been altered from three pounds to thirty-nine, was drawn upon an account which was already slightly overdrawn. The cashier became suspicious; the cheque was impounded, and the client communicated with. Then, of course, the mine exploded. Not only was this particular forgery detected, but inquiries were set afoot which soon brought to light the others. Presently circumstances, which I need not describe, threw some suspicion on me. I at once lost my nerve, and finally made a full confession.

"The inevitable prosecution followed. It was not conducted vindictively. Still, I had actually committed the forgeries, and though I endeavoured to cast a part of the blame on to the shoulders of my treacherous confederates, I did not succeed. Jezzard, it is true, was arrested, but was discharged for lack of evidence, and, consequently, the whole burden of the forgery fell upon me. The jury, of course, convicted me, and I was sentenced to seven years' penal servitude.

"During the time that I was in prison an uncle of mine died in Canada, and by the provisions of his will I inherited the whole of his very considerable property, so that when the time arrived for my release, I came out of prison, not only free, but comparatively rich. I at once dropped my own name, and, assuming that of Alfred Draper, began to look about for some quiet spot in which I might spend the rest of my days in peace, and with little chance of my identity being discovered. Such a place I found in Sundersley, and here I have lived for the last seven years, liked and respected, I think, by my neighbours, who have little suspected that they were harbouring in their midst a convicted felon.

"All this time I had neither seen nor heard anything of my four confederates, and I hoped and believed that they had passed completely out of my life. But they had not. Only a month ago I met them once more, to my sorrow, and from the day of that meeting all the peace and security of my quiet existence at Sundersley have vanished. Like evil spirits they have stolen into my life, changing my happiness into bitter misery, filling my days with dark forebodings and my nights with terror."

Here Mr. Draper paused, and seemed to sink into a gloomy reverie.

"Under what circumstances did you meet these men?" Thorndyke asked.

"Ah!" exclaimed Draper, arousing with sudden excitement, "the circumstances were very singular and suspicious. I had gone over to Eastwich for the day to do some shopping. About eleven o'clock in the forenoon I was making some purchases in a shop when I noticed two men looking in the window, or rather pretending to do so, whilst they conversed earnestly. They were smartly dressed, in a horsy fashion, and looked like well-to-do farmers, as they might very naturally have been since it was market-day.

"But it seemed to me that their faces were familiar to me. I looked at them more attentively, and then it suddenly dawned upon me, most unpleasantly, that they resembled Leach and Jezzard. And yet they were not quite like. The resemblance was there, but the differences were greater than the lapse of time would account for. Moreover, the man who resembled Jezzard had a rather large mole on the left cheek just under the eye, while the other man had an eyeglass stuck in one eye, and wore a waxed moustache, whereas Leach had always been clean-shaven, and had never used an eyeglass.

"As I was speculating upon the resemblance they looked up, and caught my intent and inquisitive eye, whereupon they moved away from the window; and when, having completed my purchases, I came out into the street, they were nowhere to be seen.

"That evening, as I was walking by the river outside the town before returning to the station, I overtook a yacht which was being towed down-stream. Three men were walking ahead on the bank with a long tow-line, and one man stood in the cockpit steering. As I approached, and was reading the name *Otter* on the stern, the man at the helm looked round, and with a start of surprise I recognised my old acquaintance Hearn.

"The recognition, however, was not mutual, for I had grown a beard in the interval, and I passed on without appearing to notice him; but when I overtook the other three men, and recognised, as I had feared, the other three members of the gang, I must have looked rather hard at Jezzard, for he suddenly halted, and exclaimed: 'Why, it's our old friend Ted! Our long-lost and lamented brother!' He held out his hand with effusive cordiality, and began to make inquiries as to my welfare; but I cut him short with the remark that I was not proposing to renew the acquaintance, and, turning off on to a footpath that led away from the river, strode off without looking back.

"Naturally this meeting exercised my mind a good deal, and when I thought of the two men whom I had seen in the town, I could hardly believe that their likeness to my quondam friends was a mere coincidence. And yet when I had met Leach and Jezzard by the river, I had found them little altered, and had particularly noticed that Jezzard had no mole on his face, and that Leach was clean-shaven as of old.

"But a day or two later all my doubts were resolved by a paragraph in the local paper. It appeared that on the day of my visit to Eastwich a number of forged cheques had been cashed at the three banks. They had been presented by three well-dressed, horsy-looking men who looked like well-to-do farmers. One of them had a mole on the left cheek, another was distinguished by a waxed moustache and a single eyeglass, while the description of the third I did not recognise.

"None of the cheques had been drawn for large amounts, though the total sum obtained by the forgers was nearly four hundred pounds; but the most interesting point was that the cheque-forms had been manufactured by photographic process, and the water-mark skilfully, though not quite perfectly, imitated. Evidently the swindlers were clever and careful men, and willing to take a good deal of trouble for the sake of security, and the result of their precautions was that the police could make no guess as to their identity.

"The very next day, happening to walk over to Port Marston, I came upon the Otter lying moored alongside the quay in the harbour. As soon as I recognised the yacht, I turned quickly and walked away, but a minute later I ran into Leach and Jezzard, who were returning to their craft. Jezzard greeted me with an air of surprise. 'What! Still hanging about here, Ted—' he exclaimed. 'That is not discreet of you, dear boy. I should earnestly advise you to clear out.'

"'What do you mean—' I asked.

"'Tut, tut!' said he. 'We read the papers like other people, and we know now what business took you to Eastwich. But it's foolish of you to hang about the neighbourhood where you might be spotted at any moment.'

"The implied accusation took me aback so completely that I stood staring at him in speechless astonishment, and at that unlucky moment a tradesman, from whom I had ordered some house-linen, passed along the quay. Seeing me, he stopped and touched his hat.

"'Beg pardon, Mr. Draper,' said he, 'but I shall be sending my cart up to Sundersley tomorrow morning if that will do for you.'

"I said that it would, and as the man turned away, Jezzard's face broke out into a cunning smile.

"So you are Mr. Draper, of Sundersley, now, are you—' said he. 'Well, I hope you won't be too proud to come and look in on your old friends. We shall be staying here for some time.'

"That same night Hearn made his appearance at my house. He had come as an emissary from the gang, to ask me to do some work for them—to execute some forgeries, in fact. Of course I refused, and pretty bluntly, too, whereupon Hearn began to throw out vague hints as to what might happen if I made enemies of the gang, and to utter veiled, but quite intelligible, threats. You will say that I was an idiot not to send him packing, and threaten to hand over the whole gang to the police; but I was never a man of strong nerve, and I don't mind admitting that I was mortally afraid of that cunning devil, Jezzard.

"The next thing that happened was that Hearn came and took lodgings in Sundersley, and, in spite of my efforts to avoid him, he haunted me continually. The yacht, too, had evidently settled down for some time at a berth in the harbour, for I heard that a local smack-boy had been engaged as a deck-hand; and I frequently encountered Jezzard and the other members of the gang, who all professed to believe that I had committed the Eastwich forgeries.

"One day I was foolish enough to allow myself to be lured on to the yacht for a few minutes, and when I would have gone ashore, I found that the shore ropes had been cast off, and that the vessel was already moving out of the harbour. At first I was furious, but the three scoundrels were so jovial and good-natured, and so delighted with the joke of taking me for a sail against my will, that I presently cooled down, and having changed into a pair of rubber-soled shoes (so that I should not make dents in the smooth deck with my hobnails), bore a hand at sailing the yacht, and spent quite a pleasant day.

"From that time I found myself gradually drifting back into a state of intimacy with these agreeable scoundrels, and daily becoming more and more afraid of them. In a moment of imbecility I mentioned what I had seen from the shop-window at Eastwich, and, though they passed the matter off with a joke, I could see that they were mightily disturbed by it. Their efforts to induce me to join them were redoubled, and Hearn took to calling almost daily at my house—usually with documents and signatures which he tried to persuade me to copy.

"A few evenings ago he made a new and startling proposition. We were walking in my garden, and he had been urging me once more to rejoin the gang—unsuccessfully, I need not say. Presently he sat down on a seat against a yew-hedge at the bottom of the garden, and, after an interval of silence, said suddenly:

"'Then you absolutely refuse to go in with us—'

"'Of course I do,' I replied. 'Why should I mix myself up with a gang of crooks when I have ample means and a decent position—'

"'Of course,' he agreed, 'you'd be a fool if you did. But, you see, you know all about this Eastwich job, to say nothing of our other little exploits, and you gave us away once before. Consequently, you can take it from me that, now Jezzard has run you to earth, he won't leave you in peace until you have given us some kind of a hold on you. You know too much, you see, and as long as you have a clean sheet you are a standing menace to us. That is the position. You know it, and Jezzard knows it, and he is a desperate man, and as cunning as the devil.'

"'I know that,' I said gloomily.

"'Very well,' continued Hearn. 'Now I'm going to make you an offer. Promise me a small annuity—you can easily afford it—or pay me a substantial sum down, and I will set you free for ever from Jezzard and the others.'

"'How will you do that—' I asked.

"'Very simply,' he replied. 'I am sick of them all, and sick of this risky, uncertain mode of life. Now I am ready to clean off my own slate and set you free at the same time; but I must have some means of livelihood in view.'

"'You mean that you will turn King's evidence—' I asked.

"'Yes, if you will pay me a couple of hundred a year, or, say, two thousand down on the conviction of the gang.'

"I was so taken aback that for some time I made no reply, and as I sat considering this amazing proposition, the silence was suddenly broken by a suppressed sneeze from the other side of the hedge.

"Hearn and I started to our feet. Immediately hurried footsteps were heard in the lane outside the hedge. We raced up the garden to the gate and out through a side alley, but when we reached the lane there was not a soul in sight. We made a brief and fruitless search in the immediate neighbourhood, and then turned back to the house. Hearn was deathly pale and very agitated, and I must confess that I was a good deal upset by the incident.

"'This is devilish awkward,' said Hearn.

"'It is rather,' I admitted; 'but I expect it was only some inquisitive yokel.'

"'I don't feel so sure of that,' said he. 'At any rate, we were stark lunatics to sit up against a hedge to talk secrets.'

"He paced the garden with me for some time in gloomy silence, and presently, after a brief request that I would think over his proposal, took himself off.

"I did not see him again until I met him last night on the yacht. Pitford called on me in the morning, and invited me to come and dine with them. I at first declined, for my housekeeper was going to spend the evening with her sister at Eastwich, and stay there for the night, and I did not much like leaving the house empty. However, I agreed eventually, stipulating that I should be allowed to come home early, and I accordingly went. Hearn and Pitford were waiting in the boat by the steps—for the yacht had been moved out to a buoy—and we went on board and spent a very pleasant and lively evening. Pitford put me ashore at ten o'clock, and I walked straight home, and went to bed. Hearn would have come with me, but the others insisted on his remaining, saying that they had some matters of business to discuss."

"Which way did you walk home?" asked Thorndyke.

"I came through the town, and along the main road."

"And that is all you know about this affair?"

"Absolutely all," replied Draper. "I have now admitted you to secrets of my past life that I had hoped never to have to reveal to any human creature, and I still have some faint hope that it may not be necessary for you to divulge what I have told you."

"Your secrets shall not be revealed unless it is absolutely indispensable that they should be," said Thorndyke; "but you are placing your life in my hands, and you must leave me perfectly free to act as I think best."

With this he gathered his notes together, and we took our departure.

"A very singular history, this, Jervis," he said, when, having wished the sergeant "Good-night," we stepped out on to the dark road. "What do you think of it?"

"I hardly know what to think," I answered, "but, on the whole, it seems rather against Draper than otherwise. He admits that he is an old criminal, and it appears that he was being persecuted and blackmailed by the man Hearn. It is true that he represents Jezzard as being the leading spirit and prime mover in the persecution, but we have only his word for that. Hearn was in lodgings near him, and was undoubtedly taking the most active part in the business, and it is quite possible, and indeed probable, that Hearn was the actual *deus ex machina*."

Thorndyke nodded. "Yes," he said, "that is certainly the line the prosecution will take if we allow the story to become known. Ha!

what is this? We are going to have some rain."

"Yes, and wind too. We are in for an autumn gale, I think."

"And that," said Thorndyke, "may turn out to be an important factor in our case."

"How can the weather affect your case?" I asked in some surprise. But, as the rain suddenly descended in a pelting shower, my companion broke into a run, leaving my question unanswered.

On the following morning, which was fair and sunny after the stormy night, Dr. Burrows called for my friend. He was on his way to the extemporized mortuary to make the post-mortem examination of the murdered man's body. Thorndyke, having notified the coroner that he was watching the case on behalf of the accused, had been authorized to be present at the autopsy; but the authorization did not include me, and, as Dr. Burrows did not issue any invitation, I was not able to be present. I met them, however, as they were returning, and it seemed to me that Dr. Burrows appeared a little huffy.

"Your friend," said he, in a rather injured tone, "is really the most outrageous stickler for forms and ceremonies that I have ever met."

Thorndyke looked at him with an amused twinkle, and chuckled indulgently.

"Here was a body," Dr. Burrows continued irritably, "found under circumstances clearly indicative of murder, and bearing a knife-wound that nearly divided the arch of the aorta; in spite of which, I assure you that Dr. Thorndyke insisted on weighing the body, and examining every organ—lungs, liver, stomach, and brain—yes, actually the brain!—as if there had been no clue whatever to the cause of death. And then, as a climax, he insisted on sending the contents of the stomach in a jar, sealed with our respective seals, in charge of a special messenger, to Professor Copland, for analysis and report. I thought he was going to demand an examination for the *tubercle bacillus*, but he didn't; which," concluded Dr. Burrows, suddenly becoming sourly facetious, "was an oversight, for, after all, the fellow may have died of consumption."

Thorndyke chuckled again, and I murmured that the precautions appeared to have been somewhat excessive.

"Not at all," was the smiling response. "You are losing sight of our function. We are the expert and impartial umpires, and it is our business to ascertain, with scientific accuracy, the cause of death. The prima facie appearances in this case suggest that the deceased was murdered by Draper, and that is the hypothesis advanced. But that is no concern of ours. It is not our function to confirm an hypothesis suggested by outside circumstances, but rather, on the contrary, to make certain that no other explanation is possible. And that is my invariable practice. No matter how glaringly obvious the appearances may be, I refuse to take anything for granted."

Dr. Burrows received this statement with a grunt of dissent, but the arrival of his dogcart put a stop to further discussion.

Thorndyke was not subpoenaed for the inquest. Dr. Burrows and the sergeant having been present immediately after the finding of the body, his evidence was not considered necessary, and, moreover, he was known to be watching the case in the interests of the accused. Like myself, therefore, he was present as a spectator, but as a highly interested one, for he took very complete shorthand notes of the whole of the evidence and the coroner's comments.

I shall not describe the proceedings in detail. The jury, having been taken to view the body, trooped into the room on tiptoe, looking pale and awe-stricken, and took their seats; and thereafter, from time to time, directed glances of furtive curiosity at Draper as he stood, pallid and haggard, confronting the court, with a burly rural constable on either side.

The medical evidence was taken first. Dr. Burrows, having been sworn, began, with sarcastic emphasis, to describe the condition of the lungs and liver, until he was interrupted by the coroner.

"Is all this necessary?" the latter inquired. "I mean, is it material to the subject of the inquiry?"

"I should say not," replied Dr. Burrows. "It appears to me to be quite irrelevant, but Dr. Thorndyke, who is watching the case for the defence, thought it necessary."

"I think," said the coroner, "you had better give us only the facts that are material. The jury want you to tell them what you consider to have been the cause of death. They don't want a lecture on pathology."

"The cause of death," said Dr. Burrows, "was a penetrating wound of the chest, apparently inflicted with a large knife. The weapon entered between the second and third ribs on the left side close to the sternum or breast-bone. It wounded the left lung, and partially divided both the pulmonary artery and the aorta—the two principal arteries of the body."

"Was this injury alone sufficient to cause death?" the coroner asked.

"Yes," was the reply; "and death from injury to these great vessels would be practically instantaneous."

"Could the injury have been self-inflicted?"

"So far as the position and nature of the wound are concerned," replied the witness, "self-infliction would be quite possible. But since death would follow in a few seconds at the most, the weapon would be found either in the wound, or grasped in the hand, or, at least, quite close to the body. But in this case no weapon was found at all, and the wound must therefore certainly have been homicidal."

"Did you see the body before it was moved?"

"Yes. It was lying on its back, with the arms extended and the legs nearly straight; and the sand in the neighbourhood of the body was trampled as if a furious struggle had taken place."

"Did you notice anything remarkable about the footprints in the sand?"

"I did," replied Dr. Burrows. "They were the footprints of two persons only. One of these was evidently the deceased, whose footmarks could be easily identified by the circular rubber heels. The other footprints were those of a person—apparently a man—who wore shoes, or boots, the soles of which were studded with nails; and these nails were arranged in a very peculiar and unusual manner, for those on the soles formed a lozenge or diamond shape, and those on the heel were set out in the form of a cross."

"Have you ever seen shoes or boots with the nails arranged in this manner?"

"Yes. I have seen a pair of shoes which I am informed belong to the accused; the nails in them are arranged as I have described."

"Would you say that the footprints of which you have spoken were made by those shoes?"

"No; I could not say that. I can only say that, to the best of my belief, the pattern on the shoes is similar to that in the footprints."

This was the sum of Dr. Burrows' evidence, and to all of it Thorndyke listened with an immovable countenance, though with the closest attention. Equally attentive was the accused man, though not equally impassive; indeed, so great was his agitation that presently one of the constables asked permission to get him a chair.

The next witness was Arthur Jezzard. He testified that he had viewed the body, and identified it as that of Charles Hearn; that he had been acquainted with deceased for some years, but knew practically nothing of his affairs. At the time of his death deceased was lodging in the village.

"Why did he leave the yacht?" the coroner inquired. "Was there any kind of disagreement!"

"Not in the least," replied Jezzard. "He grew tired of the confinement of the yacht, and came to live ashore for a change. But we were the best of friends, and he intended to come with us when we sailed."

"When did you see him last?"

"On the night before the body was found—that is, last Monday. He had been dining on the yacht, and we put him ashore about midnight. He said as we were rowing him ashore that he intended to walk home along the sands us the tide was out. He went up the stone steps by the watch-house, and turned at the top to wish us good-night. That was the last time I saw him alive."

"Do you know anything of the relations between the accused and the deceased?" the coroner asked.

"Very little," replied Jezzard. "Mr. Draper was introduced to us by the deceased about a month ago. I believe they had been acquainted some years, and they appeared to be on excellent terms. There was no indication of any quarrel or disagreement between them."

"What time did the accused leave the yacht on the night of the murder?"

"About ten o'clock. He said that he wanted to get home early, as his housekeeper was away and he did not like the house to be left with no one in it."

This was the whole of Jezzard's evidence, and was confirmed by that of Leach and Pitford. Then, when the fisherman had deposed to the discovery of the body, the sergeant was called, and stepped forward, grasping a carpet-bag, and looking as uncomfortable as if he had been the accused instead of a witness. He described the circumstances under which he saw the body, giving the exact time and place with official precision.

"You have heard Dr. Burrows' description of the footprints?" the coroner inquired.

"Yes. There were two sets. One set were evidently made by deceased. They showed that he entered St. Bridget's Bay from the direction of Port Marston. He had been walking along the shore just about high-water mark, sometimes above and sometimes below. Where he had walked below high-water mark the footprints had of course been washed away by the sea."

"How far back did you trace the footprints of deceased?"

"About two-thirds of the way to Sundersley Gap. Then they disappeared below high-water mark. Later in the evening I walked from the Gap into Port Marston, but could not find any further traces of deceased. He must have walked between the tide-marks all the way from Port Marston to beyond Sundersley. When these footprints entered St. Bridget's Bay they became mixed up with the footprints of another man, and the shore was trampled for a space of a dozen yards as if a furious struggle had taken place. The strange man's tracks came down from the Shepherd's Path, and went up it again; but, owing to the hardness of the ground from the dry weather, the tracks disappeared a short distance up the path, and I could not find them again."

"What were these strange footprints like?" inquired the coroner.

"They were very peculiar," replied the sergeant. "They were made by shoes armed with smallish hob-nails, which were arranged in a diamond-shaped pattern on the holes and in a cross on the heels. I measured the footprints carefully, and made a drawing of each foot at the time." Here the sergeant produced a long notebook of funereal aspect, and, having opened it at a marked place, handed it to the coroner, who examined it attentively, and then passed it on to the jury. From the jury it was presently transferred to Thorndyke, and, looking over his shoulder, I saw a very workmanlike sketch of a pair of footprints with the principal dimensions inserted.

Thorndyke surveyed the drawing critically, jotted down a few brief notes, and returned the sergeant's notebook to the coroner, who, as he took it, turned once more to the officer.

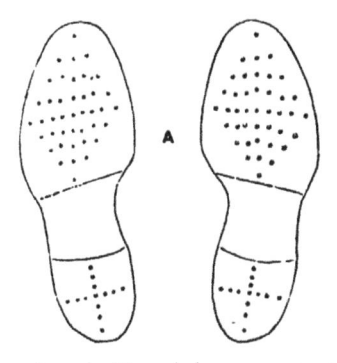

Extreme length, 11 and three-quarter inches.
Width at A, 4 and a half inches.
Length of heel, 3 and one quarter inches
Width of heel at cross, 3 inches.

"Have you any clue, sergeant, to the person who made these footprints?" he asked.

By way of reply the sergeant opened his carpet-bag, and, extracting therefrom a pair of smart but stoutly made shoes, laid them on the table.

"Those shoes," he said, "are the property of the accused; he was wearing them when I arrested him. They appear to correspond exactly to the footprints of the murderer. The measurements are the same, and the nails with which they are studded are arranged in a similar pattern."

"Would you swear that the footprints were made with these shoes?" asked the coroner.

"No, sir, I would not," was the decided answer. "I would only swear to the similarity of size and pattern."

"Had you ever seen these shoes before you made the drawing?"

"No, sir," replied the sergeant; and he then related the incident of the footprints in the soft earth by the pond which led him to make the arrest.

The coroner gazed reflectively at the shoes which he held in his hand, and from them to the drawing; then, passing them to the foreman of the jury, he remarked:

"Well, gentlemen, it is not for me to tell you whether these shoes answer to the description given by Dr. Burrows and the sergeant, or whether they resemble the drawing which, as you have heard, was made by the officer on the spot and before he had seen the shoes; that is a matter for you to decide. Meanwhile, there is another question that we must consider." He turned to the sergeant and asked: "Have you made any inquiries as to the movements of the accused on the night of the murder?"

"I have," replied the sergeant, "and I find that, on that night, the accused was alone in the house, his housekeeper having gone over to Eastwich. Two men saw him in the town about ten o'clock, apparently walking in the direction of Sundersley."

This concluded the sergeant's evidence, and when one or two more witnesses had been examined without eliciting any fresh facts, the coroner briefly recapitulated the evidence, and requested the jury to consider their verdict. Thereupon a solemn hush fell upon the court, broken only by the whispers of the jurymen, as they consulted together; and the spectators gazed in awed expectancy from the accused to the whispering jury. I glanced at Draper, sitting huddled in his chair, his clammy face as pale as that of the corpse in the mortuary hard by, his hands tremulous and restless; and, scoundrel as I believed him to be, I could not but pity the abject misery that was written large all over him, from his damp hair to his incessantly shifting feet.

The jury took but a short time to consider their verdict. At the end of five minutes the foreman announced that they were agreed, and, in answer to the coroner's formal inquiry, stood up and replied:

"We find that the deceased met his death by being stabbed in the chest by the accused man, Alfred Draper."

"That is a verdict of wilful murder," said the coroner, and he entered it accordingly in his notes. The Court now rose. The spectators reluctantly trooped out, the jurymen stood up and stretched themselves, and the two constables, under the guidance of the sergeant, carried the wretched Draper in a fainting condition to a closed fly that was waiting outside.

"I was not greatly impressed by the activity of the defence," I remarked maliciously as we walked home.

Thorndyke smiled. "You surely did not expect me to cast my pearls of forensic learning before a coroner's jury," said he.

"I expected that you would have something to say on behalf of your client," I replied. "As it was, his accusers had it all their own way."

"And why not?" he asked. "Of what concern to us is the verdict of the coroner's jury?"

"It would have seemed more decent to make some sort of defence," I replied.

"My dear Jervis," he rejoined, "you do not seem to appreciate the great virtue of what Lord Beaconsfield so felicitously called 'a policy of masterly inactivity'; and yet that is one of the great lessons that a medical training impresses on the student."

"That may be so," said I. "But the result, up to the present, of your masterly policy is that a verdict of wilful murder stands against your client, and I don't see what other verdict the jury could have found."

"Neither do I," said Thorndyke.

I had written to my principal, Dr. Cooper, describing the stirring events that were taking place in the village, and had received a reply from him instructing me to place the house at Thorndyke's disposal, and to give him every facility for his work. In accordance with which edict my colleague took possession of a well-lighted, disused stable-loft, and announced his intention of moving his things into it. Now, as these "things" included the mysterious contents of the hamper that the housemaid had seen, I was possessed with a consuming desire to be present at the "flitting," and I do not mind confessing that I purposely lurked about the stairs in the hopes of thus picking up a few crumbs of information.

But Thorndyke was one too many for me. A misbegotten infant in the village having been seized with inopportune convulsions, I was compelled, most reluctantly, to hasten to its relief; and I returned only in time to find Thorndyke in the act of locking the door of the loft.

"A nice light, roomy place to work in," he remarked, as he descended the steps, slipping the key into his pocket.

"Yes," I replied, and added boldly: "What do you intend to do up there?"

"Work up the case for the defence," he replied, "and, as I have now heard all that the prosecution have to say, I shall be able to forge ahead."

This was vague enough, but I consoled myself with the reflection that in a very few days I should, in common with the rest of the world, be in possession of the results of his mysterious proceedings. For, in view of the approaching assizes, preparations were being made to push the case through the magistrate's court as quickly as possible in order to obtain a committal in time for the ensuing sessions. Draper had, of course, been already charged before a justice of the peace and evidence of arrest taken, and it was expected that the adjourned hearing would commence before the local magistrates on the fifth day after the inquest.

The events of these five days kept me in a positive ferment of curiosity. In the first place an inspector of the Criminal Investigation Department came down and browsed about the place in company with the sergeant. Then Mr. Bashfield, who was to conduct the prosecution, came and took up his abode at the "Cat and Chicken." But the most surprising visitor was Thorndyke's laboratory assistant, Polton, who appeared one evening with a large trunk and a sailor's hammock, and announced that he was going to take up his quarters in the loft.

As to Thorndyke himself, his proceedings were beyond speculation. From time to time he made mysterious appearances at the windows of the loft, usually arrayed in what looked suspiciously like a nightshirt. Sometimes I would see him holding a negative up to the light, at others manipulating a photographic printing-frame; and once I observed him with a paintbrush and a large galipot; on which I turned away in despair, and nearly collided with the inspector.

"Dr. Thorndyke is staying with you, I hear," said the latter, gazing earnestly at my colleague's back, which was presented for his inspection at the window."

"Yes," I answered. "Those are his temporary premises."

"That is where he does his bedevilments, I suppose?" the officer suggested.

"He conducts his experiments there," I corrected haughtily.

"That's what I mean," said the inspector; and, as Thorndyke at this moment turned and opened the window, our visitor began to ascend the steps.

"I've just called to ask if I could have a few words with you, Doctor," said the inspector, as he reached the door.

"Certainly," Thorndyke replied blandly. "If you will go down and wait with Dr. Jervis, I will be with you in five minutes."

The officer came down the steps grinning, and I thought I heard him murmur "Sold!" But this may have been an illusion. However, Thorndyke presently emerged, and he and the officer strode away into the shrubbery. What the inspector's business was, or whether he had any business at all, I never learned; but the incident seemed to throw some light on the presence of Polton and the sailor's hammock. And this reference to Polton reminds me of a very singular change that took place about this time in the habits of this usually staid and sedate little man; who, abandoning the somewhat clerical style of dress that he ordinarily affected, broke out into a semi-nautical costume, in which he would sally forth every morning in the direction of Port Marston. And there, on more than one occasion, I saw him leaning against a post by the harbour, or lounging outside a waterside tavern in earnest and amicable conversation with sundry nautical characters.

On the afternoon of the day before the opening of the proceedings we had two new visitors. One of them, a grey-haired spectacled man, was a stranger to me, and for some reason I failed to recall his name, Copland, though I was sure I had heard it before. The other was Anstey, the barrister who usually worked with Thorndyke in cases that went into Court. I saw very little of either of them, however, for they retired almost immediately to the loft, where, with short intervals for meals, they remained for the rest of the day, and, I believe, far into the night. Thorndyke requested me not to mention the names of his visitors to anyone, and at the same time apologized for the secrecy of his proceedings.

"But you are a doctor, Jervis," he concluded, "and you know what professional confidences are; and you will understand how greatly it is in our favour that we know exactly what the prosecution can do, while they are absolutely in the dark as to our line of defence."

I assured him that I fully understood his position, and with this assurance he retired, evidently relieved, to the council chamber.

The proceedings, which opened on the following day, and at which I was present throughout, need not be described in detail. The evidence for the prosecution was, of course, mainly a repetition of that given at the inquest. Mr. Bashfield's opening statement, however, I shall give at length, inasmuch as it summarized very clearly the whole of the case against the prisoner.

"The case that is now before the Court," said the counsel, "involves a charge of wilful murder against the prisoner Alfred Draper, and the facts, in so far as they are known, are briefly these: On the night of Monday, the 27th of September, the deceased, Charles Hearn, dined with some friends on board the yacht Otter. About midnight he came ashore, and proceeded to walk towards Sundersley along the beach. As he entered St. Bridget's Bay, a man, who appears to have been lying in wait, and who came down the Shepherd's Path, met him, and a deadly struggle seems to have taken place. The deceased received a wound of a kind calculated to cause almost instantaneous death, and apparently fell down dead.

"And now, what was the motive of this terrible crime? It was not robbery, for nothing appears to have been taken from the corpse. Money and valuables were found, as far as is known, intact. Nor, clearly, was it a case of a casual affray. We are, consequently, driven to the conclusion that the motive was a personal one, a motive of interest or revenge, and with this view the time, the place, and the evident deliberateness of the murder are in full agreement.

"So much for the motive. The next question is, Who was the perpetrator of this shocking crime? And the answer to that question is given in a very singular and dramatic circumstance, a circumstance that illustrates once more the amazing lack of precaution shown by persons who commit such crimes. The murderer was wearing a very remarkable pair of shoes, and those shoes left very remarkable footprints in the smooth sand, and those footprints were seen and examined by a very acute and painstaking police-officer, Sergeant Payne, whose evidence you will hear presently. The sergeant not only examined the footprints, he made careful drawings of them on the spot—on the spot, mind you, not from memory—and he made very exact measurements of them, which he duly noted down. And from those drawings and those measurements, those tell-tale shoes have been identified, and are here for your inspection.

"And now, who is the owner of those very singular, those almost unique shoes? I have said that the motive of this murder must have been a personal one, and, behold! the owner of those shoes happens to be the one person in the whole of this district who could have had a motive for compassing the murdered man's death. Those shoes belong to, and were taken from the foot of, the prisoner, Alfred Draper, and the prisoner, Alfred Draper, is the only person living in this neighbourhood who was acquainted with the deceased.

"It has been stated in evidence at the inquest that the relations of these two men, the prisoner and the deceased, were entirely friendly; but I shall prove to you that they were not so friendly as has been supposed. I shall prove to you, by the evidence of the prisoner's housekeeper, that the deceased was often an unwelcome visitor at the house, that the prisoner often denied himself when he was really at home and disengaged, and, in short, that he appeared constantly to shun and avoid the deceased.

"One more question and I have finished. Where was the prisoner on the night of the murder? The answer is that he was in a house little more than half a mile from the scene of the crime. And who was with him in that house? Who was there to observe and testify to his going forth and his coming home? No one. He was alone in the house. On that night, of all nights, he was alone. Not a soul was there to rouse at the creak of a door or the tread of a shoe—to tell as whether he slept or whether he stole forth in the dead of the night.

"Such are the facts of this case. I believe that they are not disputed, and I assert that, taken together, they are susceptible of only one explanation, which is that the prisoner, Alfred Draper, is the man who murdered the deceased, Charles Hearn."

Immediately on the conclusion of this address, the witnesses were called, and the evidence given was identical with that at the inquest. The only new witness for the prosecution was Draper's housekeeper, and her evidence fully bore out Mr. Bashfield's statement. The sergeant's account of the footprints was listened to with breathless interest, and at its conclusion the presiding magistrate—a retired solicitor, once well known in criminal practice—put a question which interested me as showing how clearly Thorndyke had foreseen the course of events, recalling, as it did, his remark on the night when we were caught in the rain.

"Did you," the magistrate asked, "take these shoes down to the beach and compare them with the actual footprints?"

"I obtained the shoes at night," replied the sergeant, "and I took them down to the shore at daybreak the next morning. But, unfortunately, there had been a storm in the night, and the footprints were almost obliterated by the wind and rain."

When the sergeant had stepped down, Mr. Bashfield announced that that was the case for the prosecution. He then resumed his seat, turning an inquisitive eye on Anstey and Thorndyke.

The former immediately rose and opened the case for the defence with a brief statement.

"The learned counsel for the prosecution," said he, "has told us that the facts now in the possession of the Court admit of but one explanation—that of the guilt of the accused. That may or may not be; but I shall now proceed to lay before the Court certain fresh facts—facts, I may say, of the most singular and startling character, which will, I think, lead to a very different conclusion. I shall say no more, but call the witnesses forthwith, and let the evidence speak for itself."

The first witness for the defence was Thorndyke; and as he entered the box I observed Polton take up a position close behind him with a large wicker trunk. Having been sworn, and requested by Anstey to tell the Court what he knew about the case, he commenced without preamble:

"About half-past four in the afternoon of the 28th of September I walked down Sundersley Gap with Dr. Jervis. Our attention was attracted by certain footprints in the sand, particularly those of a man who had landed from a boat, had walked up the Gap, and presently returned, apparently to the boat.

"As we were standing there Sergeant Payne and Dr. Burrows passed down the Gap with two constables carrying a stretcher. We followed at a distance, and as we walked along the shore we encountered another set of footprints—those which the sergeant has described as the footprints of the deceased. We examined these carefully, and endeavoured to frame a description of the person by whom they had been made."

"And did your description agree with the characters of the deceased?" the magistrate asked.

"Not in the least," replied Thorndyke, whereupon the magistrate, the inspector, and Mr. Bashfield laughed long and heartily.

"When we turned into St. Bridget's Bay, I saw the body of deceased lying on the sand close to the cliff. The sand all round was covered with footprints, as if a prolonged, fierce struggle had taken place. There were two sets of footprints, one set being apparently those of the deceased and the other those of a man with nailed shoes of a very peculiar and conspicuous pattern. The incredible folly that the wearing of such shoes indicated caused me to look more closely at the footprints, and then I made the surprising discovery that there had in reality been no struggle; that, in fact, the two sets of footprints had been made at different times."

"At different times!" the magistrate exclaimed in astonishment.

"Yes. The interval between them may have been one of hours or one only of seconds, but the undoubted fact is that the two sets of footprints were made, not simultaneously, but in succession."

"But how did you arrive at that fact?" the magistrate asked.

"It was very obvious when one looked," said Thorndyke. "The marks of the deceased man's shoes showed that he repeatedly trod in his own footprints; but never in a single instance did he tread in the footprints of the other man, although they covered the same area. The man with the nailed shoes, on the contrary, not only trod in his own footprints, but with equal frequency in those of the deceased. Moreover, when the body was removed, I observed that the footprints in the sand on which it was lying were exclusively those of the deceased. There was not a sign of any nail-marked footprint under the corpse, although there were many close around it. It was evident, therefore, that the footprints of the deceased were made first and those of the nailed shoes afterwards."

As Thorndyke paused the magistrate rubbed his nose thoughtfully, and the inspector gazed at the witness with a puzzled frown.

"The singularity of this fact," my colleague resumed, "made me look at the footprints yet more critically, and then I made another discovery. There was a double track of the nailed shoes, leading apparently from and back to the Shepherd's Path. But on examining these tracks more closely, I was astonished to find that the man who had made them had been walking backwards; that, in fact, he had walked backwards from the body to the Shepherd's Path, had ascended it for a short distance, had turned round, and returned, still walking backwards, to the face of the cliff near the corpse, and there the tracks vanished altogether.

"On the sand at this spot were some small, inconspicuous marks which might have been made by the end of a rope, and there were also a few small fragments which had fallen from the cliff above. Observing these, I examined the surface of the cliff, and at one spot, about six feet above the beach, I found a freshly rubbed spot on which were parallel scratches such as might have been made by the nailed sole of a boot. I then ascended the Shepherd's Path, and examined the cliff from above, and here I found on the extreme edge a rather deep indentation, such as would be made by a taut rope, and, on lying down and looking over, I could see, some five feet from the top, another rubbed spot with very distinct parallel scratches."

"You appear to infer," said the chairman, "that this man performed these astonishing evolutions and was then hauled up the cliff?"

"That is what the appearances suggested," replied Thorndyke.

The chairman pursed up his lips, raised his eyebrows, and glanced doubtfully at his brother magistrates. Then, with a resigned air, he bowed to the witness to indicate that he was listening.

"That same night," Thorndyke resumed, "I cycled down to the shore, through the Gap, with a supply of plaster of Paris, and proceeded to take plaster moulds of the more important of the footprints." (Here the magistrates, the inspector, and Mr. Bashfield with one accord sat up at attention; Sergeant Payne swore quite audibly; and I experienced a sudden illumination respecting a certain basin and kitchen spoon which had so puzzled me on the night of Thorndyke's arrival.) "As I thought that liquid plaster might confuse or even obliterate the prints in sand, I filled up the respective footprints with dry plaster, pressed it down lightly, and then cautiously poured water on to it. The moulds, which are excellent impressions, of course show the appearance of the boots which made the footprints, and from these moulds I have prepared casts which reproduce the footprints themselves.

"The first mould that I made was that of one of the tracks from the boat up to the Gap, and of this I shall speak presently. I next made a mould of one of the footprints which have been described as those of the deceased."

"Have been described!" exclaimed the chairman. "The deceased was certainly there, and there were no other footprints, so, if they were not his, he must have flown to where he was found."

"I will call them the footprints of the deceased," replied Thorndyke imperturbably. "I took a mould of one of them, and with it, on the same mould, one of my own footprints. Here is the mould, and here is a cast from it." (He turned and took them from the triumphant Polton, who had tenderly lifted them out of the trunk in readiness.) "On looking at the cast, it will be seen that the appearances are not such as would be expected. The deceased was five feet nine inches high, but was very thin and light, weighing only nine stone six pounds, as I ascertained by weighing the body, whereas I am five feet eleven and weigh nearly thirteen stone. But yet the footprint of the deceased is nearly twice as deep as mine—that is to say, the lighter man has sunk into the sand nearly twice as deeply as the heavier man."

The magistrates were now deeply attentive. They were no longer simply listening to the despised utterances of a mere scientific expert. The cast lay before them with the two footprints side by side; the evidence appealed to their own senses and was proportionately convincing.

"This is very singular," said the chairman; "but perhaps you can explain the discrepancy?"

"I think I can," replied Thorndyke; "but I should prefer to place all the facts before you first."

"Undoubtedly that would be better," the chairman agreed. "Pray proceed."

"There was another remarkable peculiarity about these footprints," Thorndyke continued, "and that was their distance apart—the length of the stride, in fact. I measured the steps carefully from heel to heel, and found them only nineteen and a half inches. But a man of Hearn's height would have an ordinary stride of about thirty-six inches—more if he was walking fast. Walking with a stride of nineteen and a half inches he would look as if his legs were tied together.

"I next proceeded to the Bay, and took two moulds from the footprints of the man with the nailed shoes, a right and a left. Here is a cast from the mould, and it shows very clearly that the man was walking backwards."

"How does it show that?" asked the magistrate.

"There are several distinctive points. For instance, the absence of the usual 'kick off' at the toe, the slight drag behind the heel, showing the direction in which the foot was lifted, and the undisturbed impression of the sole."

"You have spoken of moulds and casts. What is the difference between them?"

"A mould is a direct, and therefore reversed, impression. A cast is the impression of a mould, and therefore a facsimile of the object. If I pour liquid plaster on a coin, when it sets I have a mould, a sunk impression, of the coin. If I pour melted wax into the mould I obtain a cast, a facsimile of the coin. A footprint is a mould of the foot. A mould of the footprint is a cast of the foot, and a cast from the mould reproduces the footprint."

"Thank you," said the magistrate. "Then your moulds from these two footprints are really facsimiles of the murderer's shoes, and can be compared with these shoes which have been put in evidence?"

"Yes, and when we compare them they demonstrate a very important fact."

"What is that?"

"It is that the prisoner's shoes were not the shoes that made those footprints." A buzz of astonishment ran through the court, but Thorndyke continued stolidly: "The prisoner's shoes were not in my possession, so I went on to Barker's pond, on the clay margin of which I had seen footprints actually made by the prisoner. I took moulds of those footprints, and compared them with these from the sand. There are several important differences, which you will see if you compare them. To facilitate the comparison I have made transparent photographs of both sets of moulds to the same scale. Now, if we put the photograph of the mould of the prisoner's right shoe over that of the murderer's right shoe, and hold the two superposed photographs up to the light, we cannot make the two pictures coincide. They are exactly of the same length, but the shoes are of different shape.

"Moreover, if we put one of the nails in one photograph over the corresponding nail in the other photograph, we cannot make the rest of the nails coincide. But the most conclusive fact of all—from which there is no possible escape—is that the number of nails in the two shoes is not the same. In the sole of the prisoner's right shoe there are forty nails; in that of the murderer there are forty-one. The murderer has one nail too many."

There was a deathly silence in the court as the magistrates and Mr. Bashfield pored over the moulds and the prisoner's shoes, and examined the photographs against the light. Then the chairman asked: "Are these all the facts, or have you something more to tell us?" He was evidently anxious to get the key to this riddle.

"There is more evidence, your Worship," said Anstey. "The witness examined the body of deceased." Then, turning to Thorndyke, he asked:

"You were present at the post-mortem examination?"

"I was."

"Did you form any opinion as to the cause of death?"

"Yes. I came to the conclusion that death was occasioned by an overdose of *morphia*."

A universal gasp of amazement greeted this statement. Then the presiding magistrate protested breathlessly:

"But there was a wound, which we have been told was capable of causing instantaneous death. Was that not the case?"

"There was undoubtedly such a wound," replied Thorndyke. "But when that wound was inflicted the deceased had already been dead from a quarter to half an hour."

"This is incredible!" exclaimed the magistrate. "But, no doubt, you can give us your reasons for this amazing conclusion?"

"My opinion," said Thorndyke, "was based on several facts. In the first place, a wound inflicted on a living body gapes rather widely, owing to the retraction of the living skin. The skin of a dead body does not retract, and the wound, consequently, does not gape. This wound gaped very slightly, showing that death was recent, I should say, within half an hour. Then a wound on the living body becomes filled with blood, and blood is shed freely on the clothing. But the wound on the deceased contained only a little blood-clot. There was hardly any blood on the clothing, and I had already noticed that there was none on the sand where the body had lain."

"And you consider this quite conclusive?" the magistrate asked doubtfully.

"I do," answered Thorndyke. "But there was other evidence which was beyond all question. The weapon had partially divided both the aorta and the pulmonary artery—the main arteries of the body. Now, during life, these great vessels are full of blood at a high internal pressure, whereas after death they become almost empty. It follows that, if this wound had been inflicted during life, the cavity in which those vessels lie would have become filled with blood. As a matter of fact, it contained practically no blood, only the merest oozing from some small veins, so that it is certain that the wound was inflicted after death. The presence and nature of the poison I ascertained by analyzing certain secretions from the body, and the analysis enabled me to judge that the quantity of the poison was large; but the contents of the stomach were sent to Professor Copland for more exact examination."

"Is the result of Professor Copland's analysis known?" the magistrate asked Anstey.

"The professor is here, your Worship," replied Anstey, "and is prepared to swear to having obtained over one grain of *morphia* from the contents of the stomach; and as this, which is in itself a poisonous dose, is only the unabsorbed residue of what was actually swallowed, the total quantity taken must have been very large indeed."

"Thank you," said the magistrate. "And now, Dr. Thorndyke, if you have given us all the facts, perhaps you will tell us what conclusions you have drawn from them."

"The facts which I have stated," said Thorndyke, "appear to me to indicate the following sequence of events. The deceased died about midnight on September 27, from the effects of a poisonous dose of *morphia*, how or by whom administered I offer no opinion. I think that his body was conveyed in a boat to Sundersley Gap. The boat probably contained three men, of whom one remained in charge of it, one walked up the Gap and along the cliff towards St. Bridget's Bay, and the third, having put on the shoes of the deceased, carried the body along the shore to the Bay. This would account for the great depth and short stride of the tracks that have been spoken of as those of the deceased. Having reached the Bay, I believe that this man laid the corpse down on his tracks, and then trampled the sand in the neighbourhood.

"He next took off deceased's shoes and put them on the corpse; then he put on a pair of boots or shoes which he had been carrying—perhaps hung round his neck—and which had been prepared with nails to imitate Draper's shoes. In these shoes he again trampled over the area near the corpse. Then he walked backwards to the Shepherd's Path, and from it again, still backwards, to the face of the cliff. Here his accomplice had lowered a rope, by which he climbed up to the top. At the top he took off the nailed shoes, and the two men walked back to the Gap, where the man who had carried the rope took his confederate on his back, and carried him down to the boat to avoid leaving the tracks of stockinged feet. The tracks that I saw at the Gap certainly indicated that the man was carrying something very heavy when he returned to the boat."

"But why should the man have climbed a rope up the cliff when he could have walked up the Shepherd's Path?" the magistrate asked.

"Because," replied Thorndyke, "there would then have been a set of tracks leading out of the Bay without a corresponding set leading into it; and this would have instantly suggested to a smart police-officer—such as Sergeant Payne—a landing from a boat."

"Your explanation is highly ingenious," said the magistrate, "and appears to cover all the very remarkable facts. Have you anything more to tell us?"

"No, your Worship," was the reply, "excepting" (here he took from Polton the last pair of moulds and passed them up to the magistrate) "that you will probably find these moulds of importance presently."

As Thorndyke stepped from the box—for there was no cross-examination—the magistrates scrutinised the moulds with an air of perplexity; but they were too discreet to make any remark.

When the evidence of Professor Copland (which showed that an unquestionably lethal dose of *morphia* must have been swallowed) had been taken, the clerk called out the—to me—unfamiliar name of Jacob Gummer. Thereupon an enormous pair of brown dreadnought trousers, from the upper end of which a smack-boy's head and shoulders protruded, walked into the witness-box.

Jacob admitted at the outset that he was a smack-master's apprentice, and that he had been "hired out" by his master to one Mr. Jezzard as deck-hand and cabin-boy of the yacht Otter.

"Now, Gummer," said Anstey, "do you remember the prisoner coming on board the yacht?"

"Yes. He has been on board twice. The first time was about a month ago. He went for a sail with us then. The second time was on the night when Mr. Hearn was murdered."

"Do you remember what sort of boots the prisoner was wearing the first time he came?"

"Yes. They were shoes with a lot of nails in the soles. I remember them because Mr. Jezzard made him take them off and put on a canvas pair."

"What was done with the nailed shoes?"

"Mr. Jezzard took 'em below to the cabin."

"And did Mr. Jezzard come up on deck again directly?"

"No. He stayed down in the cabin about ten minutes."

"Do you remember a parcel being delivered on board from a London boot-maker?"

"Yes. The postman brought it about four or five days after Mr. Draper had been on board. It was labelled 'Walker Bros., Boot and Shoe Makers, London.' Mr. Jezzard took a pair of shoes from it, for I saw them on the locker in the cabin the same day."

"Did you ever see him wear them?"

"No. I never see 'em again."

"Have you ever heard sounds of hammering on the yacht?"

"Yes. The night after the parcel came I was on the quay alongside, and I heard someone a-hammering in the cabin."

"What did the hammering sound like?"

"It sounded like a cobbler a-hammering in nails."

"Have you over seen any boot-nails on the yacht?"

"Yes. When I was a-clearin' up the cabin the next mornin', I found a hobnail on the floor in a corner by the locker."

"Were you on board on the night when Mr. Hearn died?"

"Yes. I'd been ashore, but I came aboard about half-past nine."

"Did you see Mr. Hearn go ashore?"

"I see him leave the yacht. I had turned into my bunk and gone to sleep, when Mr. Jezzard calls down to me: 'We're putting Mr. Hearn ashore,' says he; 'and then,' he says, 'we're a-going for an hour's fishing. You needn't sit up,' he says, and with that he shuts the scuttle. Then I got up and slid back the scuttle and put my head out, and I see Mr. Jezzard and Mr. Leach a-helpin' Mr. Hearn acrost the deck. Mr. Hearn he looked as if he was drunk. They got him into the boat—and a rare job they had—and Mr. Pitford, what was in the boat already, he pushed off. And then I popped my head in again, 'cause I didn't want them to see me."

"Did they row to the steps?"

"No. I put my head out again when they were gone, and I heard 'em row round the yacht, and then pull out towards the mouth of the harbour. I couldn't see the boat, 'cause it was a very dark night."

"Very well. Now I am going to ask you about another matter. Do you know anyone of the name of Polton?"

"Yes," replied Gummer, turning a dusky red. "I've just found out his real name. I thought he was called Simmons."

"Tell us what you know about him," said Anstey, with a mischievous smile.

"Well," said the boy, with a ferocious scowl at the bland and smiling Polton, "one day he come down to the yacht when the gentlemen had gone ashore. I believe he'd seen 'em go. And he offers me ten shillin' to let him see all the boots and shoes we'd got on board. I didn't see no harm, so I turns out the whole lot in the cabin for him to look at. While he was lookin' at 'em he asks me to fetch a pair of mine from the fo'c'sle, so I fetches 'em. When I come back he was pitchin' the boots and shoes back into the locker. Then, presently, he nips off, and when he was gone I looked over the shoes, and then I found there was a pair missing. They was an old pair of Mr. Jezzard's, and what made him nick 'em is more than I can understand."

"Would you know those shoes if you saw them!"

"Yes, I should," replied the lad.

"Are these the pair?" Anstey handed the boy a pair of dilapidated canvas shoes, which he seized eagerly.

"Yes, these is the ones what he stole!" he exclaimed.

Anstey took them back from the boy's reluctant hands, and passed them up to the magistrate's desk. "I think," said he, "that if your Worship will compare these shoes with the last pair of moulds, you will have no doubt that these are the shoes which made the footprints from the sea to Sundersley Gap and back again."

The magistrates together compared the shoes and the moulds amidst a breathless silence. At length the chairman laid them down on the desk.

"It is impossible to doubt it," said he. "The broken heel and the tear in the rubber sole, with the remains of the chequered pattern, make the identity practically certain."

As the chairman made this statement I involuntarily glanced round to the place where Jezzard was sitting. But he was not there; neither he, nor Pitford, nor Leach. Taking advantage of the preoccupation of the Court, they had quietly slipped out of the door. But I was not the only person who had noted their absence. The inspector and the sergeant were already in earnest consultation, and a minute later they, too, hurriedly departed.

The proceedings now speedily came to an end. After a brief discussion with his brother-magistrates, the chairman addressed the Court.

"The remarkable and I may say startling evidence, which has been heard in this court today, if it has not fixed the guilt of this crime on any individual, has, at any rate, made it clear to our satisfaction that the prisoner is not the guilty person, and he is accordingly discharged. Mr. Draper, I have great pleasure in informing you that you are at liberty to leave the court, and that you do so entirely clear of all suspicion; and I congratulate you very heartily on the skill and ingenuity of your legal advisers, but for which the decision of the Court would, I am afraid, have been very different."

That evening, lawyers, witnesses, and the jubilant and grateful client gathered round a truly festive board to dine, and fight over again the battle of the day. But we were scarcely halfway through our meal when, to the indignation of the servants, Sergeant Payne burst breathlessly into the room.

"They've gone, sir!" he exclaimed, addressing Thorndyke. "They've given us the slip for good."

"Why, how can that be?" asked Thorndyke.

"They're dead, sir! All three of them!"

"Dead!" we all exclaimed.

"Yes. They made a burst for the yacht when they left the court, and they got on board and put out to sea at once, hoping, no doubt, to get clear as the light was just failing. But they were in such a hurry that they did not see a steam trawler that was entering, and was hidden by the pier. Then, just at the entrance, as the yacht was creeping out, the trawler hit her amidships, and fairly cut her in two. The three men were in the water in an instant, and were swept away in the eddy behind the north pier; and before any boat could put out to them they had all gone under. Jezzard's body came up on the beach just as I was coming away."

We were all silent and a little awed, but if any of us felt regret at the catastrophe, it was at the thought that three such cold-blooded villains should have made so easy an exit; and to one of us, at least, the news came as a blessed relief.

The Case of the White Footprints

"Well," said my friend Foxton, pursuing a familiar and apparently inexhaustible topic, "I'd sooner have your job than my own."

"I've no doubt you would," was my unsympathetic reply. "I never met a man who wouldn't. We all tend to consider other men's jobs in terms of their advantages and our own in terms of their drawbacks. It is human nature."

"Oh, it's all very well for you to be so beastly philosophical," retorted Foxton. "You wouldn't be if you were in my place. Here, in Margate, it's measles, chickenpox and scarlatina all the summer, and bronchitis, colds and rheumatism an the winter. A deadly monotony. Whereas you and Thorndyke sit there in your chambers and let your clients feed you up with the raw material of romance. Why, your life is a sort of everlasting Adelphi drama."

"You exaggerate, Foxton," said I. "We, like you, have our routine work, only it is never heard of outside the Law Courts; and you, like every other doctor, must run up against mystery and romance from time to time."

Foxton shook his head as he held out his hand for my cup. "I don't," said be. "My practice yields nothing but an endless round of dull routine."

And then, as if in commentary on this last statement, the housemaid burst into the room and, with hardly dissembled agitation, exclaimed:

"If you please, sir, the page from Beddingfield's Boarding-house says that a lady has been found dead in her bed and would you go round there immediately."

"Very well, Jane," said Foxton, and as the maid retired, he deliberately helped himself to another fried egg and, looking across the table at me, exclaimed: "Isn't that always the way? Come immediately—now—this very instant, although the patient may have been considering for a day or two whether he'll send for you or not. But directly he decides you must spring out of bed, or jump up from your breakfast, and run."

"That's quite true," I agreed; "but this really does seem to be an urgent case."

"What's the urgency?" demanded Foxton. "The woman is already dead. Anyone would think she was in imminent danger of coming to life again and that my instant arrival the only thing that could prevent such a catastrophe."

"You've only a third-hand statement that she is dead," said I. "It is just possible that she isn't; and even if she is, as you will have to give evidence at the inquest, you do not want the police to get there first and turn out the room before you've made your inspection."

"Gad!" exclaimed Foxton. "I hadn't thought of that. Yes. You're right. I'll hop round at once."

He swallowed the remainder of the egg at a single gulp rose from the table. Then he paused and stood for a few moments looking down at me irresolutely.

"I wonder, Jervis," he said, "if you would mind coming round with me. You know all the medico-legal ropes, and I don't. What do you say?"

I agreed instantly, having, in fact, been restrained only by delicacy from making the suggestion myself; and when I had fetched from my room my pocket camera and telescopic tripod, we set forth together without further delay.

Beddingfield's Boarding-house was but a few minutes walk from Foxton's residence being situated near the middle of Ethelred Road, Cliftonville, a quiet, suburban street which abounded in similar establishments, many of which, I noticed, were undergoing a spring-cleaning and renovation to prepare them for the approaching season.

"That's the house," said Foxton, "where that woman is standing at the front door. Look at the boarders, collected at the dining-room window. There's a rare commotion in that house, I'll warrant."

Here, arriving at the house, he ran up the steps and accosted in sympathetic tones the elderly woman who stood by the open street door.

"What a dreadful thing this is, Mrs. Beddingfield! Terrible! Most distressing for you!"

"Ah, you're right, Dr. Foxton," she replied. "It's an awful affair.

Shocking. So bad for business, too. I do hope, and trust there won't be any scandal."

"I'm sure I hope not," said Foxton. "There shan't be if I can help it. And as my friend Dr. Jervis, who is staying with me for a few days, is a lawyer as well as a doctor, we shall have the best advice. When was the affair discovered?"

"Just before I sent for you, Dr. Foxton. The maid, noticed that Mrs. Toussaint—that is the poor creature's name—had not taken in her hot water, so she knocked at the door. As she couldn't get any answer, she tried the door and found it bolted on the inside, and then she came and told me. I went up and knocked loudly, and then, as I couldn't get any reply, I told our boy, James, to force the door open with a case-opener, which he did quite easily as the bolt was only a small one. Then I went in, all of a tremble, for I had a presentiment that there was something wrong; and there she was lying stone dead, with a most 'orrible stare on her face and an empty bottle in her hand."

"A bottle, eh!" said Foxton.

"Yes. She'd made away with herself, poor thing; and all on account of some silly love affair—and it was hardly even that."

"Ah," said Foxton. "The usual thing. You must tell us about that later. Now we'd better go up and see the patient—at least the—er—perhaps you'll show us the room, Mrs. Beddingfield."

The landlady turned and preceded us up the stairs to the first-floor back, where she paused, and softly opening a door, peered nervously into the room. As we stepped past her and entered, she seemed inclined to follow, but, at a significant glance from me, Foxton persuasively ejected her and closed the door. Then we stood silent for a while and looked about us.

In the aspect of the room there was something strangely incongruous with the tragedy that had been enacted within its walls; a mingling of the commonplace and the terrible that almost amounted to anticlimax. Through the wide-open window the bright spring sunshine streamed in on the garish wallpaper and cheap furniture; from the street below, the periodic shouts of a man selling "sole and mack-ro!" broke into the brisk *staccato* of a barrel-organ and both sounds mingled with a raucous voice close at hand, cheerfully trolling a popular song, and accounted for by a linen-clad elbow that bobbed in front of the window and evidently appertained to a house-painter on an adjacent ladder.

It was all very commonplace and familiar and discordantly out of character with the stark figure that lay on the bed like a waxen effigy symbolic of tragedy. Here was none of that gracious somnolence in which death often presents itself with a suggestion of eternal repose. This woman was dead; horribly, aggressively dead. The thin, sallow face was rigid as stone, the dark eyes stared into infinite space with a horrid fixity that was quite disturbing to look on. And yet the posture of the corpse was not uneasy, being, in fact, rather curiously symmetrical, with both arms outside the bedclothes and both hands closed, the right grasping, as Mrs. Beddingfield had said, an empty bottle.

"Well," said Foxton, as he stood looking down on the dead woman, "it seems a pretty clear case. She appears to have laid herself out and kept hold of the bottle so that there should be no mistake. How long do you suppose this woman has been dead, Jervis?"

I felt the rigid limbs and tested the temperature of the body surface.

"Not less than six hours," I replied. "Probably more. I should say that she died about two o'clock this morning."

"And that is about all we can say," said Foxton, "until the post-mortem has been made. Everything looks quite straightforward. No signs of a struggle or marks of violence. That blood on the mouth is probably due to her biting her lip when she drank from the bottle. Yes; here's a little cut on the inside of the lip, corresponding to the upper incisors. By the way, I wonder if there is anything left in the bottle."

As he spoke, he drew the small, unlabelled, green glass phial from the closed hand—out of which it slipped quite easily—and held it up to the light.

"Yes," he exclaimed, "there's more than a *drachm* left; quite enough for an analysis. But I don't recognise the smell. Do you?"

I sniffed at the bottle and was aware of a faint unfamiliar vegetable odour.

"No," I answered. "It appears to be a watery solution of some kind, but I can't give it a name. Where is the cork?"

"I haven't seen it," he replied. "Probably it is on the floor somewhere."

We both stooped to look for the missing cork and presently found it in the shadow, under the little bedside table. But, in the course of that brief search, I found something else, which had indeed been lying in full view all the time—a wax match. Now a wax match is a perfectly innocent and very commonplace object, but yet the presence of this one gave me pause. In the first place, women do not, as a rule, use wax matches, though there was not much in that. What was more to the point was that the candlestick by the bedside contained a box of safety matches, and that, as the burnt remains of one lay in the tray, it appeared to have been used to light the candle. Then why the wax match?

While I was turning over this problem Foxton had corked the bottle, wrapped it carefully in a piece of paper which he took from the dressing-table and bestowed it in his pocket.

"Well, Jervis," said he, "I think we've seen everything. The analysis and the post-mortem will complete the case. Shall we go down and hear what Mrs. Beddingfield has to say?"

But that wax match, slight as was its significance, taken alone, had presented itself to me as the last of a succession of phenomena each of which was susceptible of a sinister interpretation; and the cumulative effect of these slight suggestions began to impress me somewhat strongly.

"One moment, Foxton," said I. "Don't let us take anything for granted. We are here to collect evidence, and we must go warily. There is such a thing as homicidal poisoning, you know."

"Yes, of course," he replied, "but there is nothing to suggest it in this case; at least, I see nothing. Do you?"

"Nothing very positive," said I; "but there are some facts that seem to call for consideration. Let us go over what we have seen. In the first place, there is a distinct discrepancy in the appearance of the body. The general easy, symmetrical posture, like that of a figure on a tomb, suggests the effect of a slow, painless poison. But look at the face. There is nothing reposeful about that. It is very strongly suggestive of pain or terror or both."

"Yes," said Foxton, "that is so. But you can't draw any satisfactory conclusions from the facial expression of dead bodies. Why, men who have been hanged, or even, stabbed, often look as peaceful as babes."

"Still," I urged, "it is a fact to be noted. Then there is that cut on the lip. It may have been produced in the way you suggest; but it may equally well be the result of pressure on the mouth."

Foxton made no comment on this beyond a slight shrug of the shoulders, and I continued: "Then there is the state of the hand. It was closed, but, it did not really grasp the object it contained. You drew the bottle out without any resistance. It simply lay in the closed hand. But that is not a normal state of affairs. As you know, when a person dies grasping any object, either the hand relaxes and lets it drop, or the muscular action passes into cadaveric spasm and grasps the object firmly. And lastly, there is this wax match. Where did it come from? The dead woman apparently lit her candle with a safety match from the box. It is a small matter, but it wants explaining."

Foxton raised his eyebrows protestingly. "You're like all specialists, Jervis," said he. "You see your speciality in everything. And while you are straining these flimsy suggestions to turn a simple suicide into murder, you ignore the really conclusive fact that the door was bolted and had to be broken open before anyone could get in."

"You are not forgetting, I suppose," said I, "that the window was wide open and that there were house-painters about and possibly a ladder left standing against the house."

"As to the ladder," said Foxton, "that is a pure assumption; but we can easily settle the question by asking that fellow out there if it was or was not left standing last night."

Simultaneously we moved towards the window; but halfway we both stopped short. For the question of the ladder had in a moment became negligible. Staring up at us from the dull red linoleum which covered the floor were the impressions of a pair of bare feet, imprinted in white paint with the distinctness of a woodcut. There was no need to ask if they had been made by the dead woman: they were unmistakably the feet of a man, and large feet at that.

Nor could there be any doubt as to whence those feet had come. Beginning with startling distinctness under the window, the tracks shed rapidly in intensity until they reached the carpeted portion of the room, where they vanished abruptly; and only by the closest scrutiny was it possible to detect the faint traces of the retiring tracks.

Foxton and I stood for some moments gazing in, silence at the sinister white shapes; then we looked at one another.

"You've saved me from a most horrible blunder, Jervis," said Foxton. "Ladder or no ladder, that fellow came in at the window; and he came in last night, for I saw them painting these window-sills yesterday afternoon. Which side did he come from, I wonder?"

We moved to the window and looked out on the sill. A set of distinct, though smeared impressions on the new paint gave unneeded confirmation and showed that the intruder had approached from the left side, close to which was a cast-iron stack-pipe, now covered with fresh green paint.

"So," said Foxton, "the presence or absence of the ladder is of no significance. The man got into the window somehow, and that's all that matters."

"On the contrary," said I, "the point may be of considerable importance in identification. It isn't everyone who could climb up a stack-pipe, whereas most people could make shift to climb a ladder, even if it were guarded by a plank. But the fact that the man took off his boots and socks suggests that he came up by the pipe. If he had merely aimed at silencing his footfalls, he would probably have removed his boots only."

From the window we turned to examine more closely the footprints on the floor, and while I took a series of measurements with my spring tape Foxton entered them in my notebook.

"Doesn't it strike you as rather odd, Jervis," said he, "that neither of the little toes has made any mark?"

"It does indeed," I replied. "The appearances suggest that the little toes were absent, but I have never met with such a condition. Have you?"

"Never. Of course one is acquainted with the supernumerary toe deformity, but I have never heard of congenitally deficient little toes."

Once more we scrutinized the footprints, and even examined those on the window-sill, obscurely marked on the fresh paint; but, exquisitely distinct as were those on the linoleum, showing every wrinkle and minute skin-marking, not the faintest hint of a little toe was to be seen on either foot.

"It's very extraordinary," said Foxton. "He has certainly lost his little toes, if he ever had any. They couldn't have failed to make some mark. But it's a queer affair. Quite a windfall for the police, by the way; I mean for purposes of identification."

"Yes," I agreed, "and having regard to the importance of the footprints, I think it would be wise to get a photograph of them."

"Oh, the police will see to that," said Foxton. "Besides, we haven't got a camera, unless you thought of using that little toy snapshotter of yours."

As Foxton was no photographer I did not trouble to explain that my camera, though small, had been specially made for scientific purposes.

"Any photograph is better than none," I said, and with this I opened the tripod and set it over one of the most distinct of the footprints, screwed the camera to the goose-neck, carefully framed the footprint in the finder and adjusted the focus, finally making the exposure by means of an Antinous release. This process I repeated four times, twice on a right footprint and twice on a left.

"Well," Foxton remarked, "with all those photographs the police ought to be able to pick up the scent."

"Yes, they've got something to go on; but they'll have to catch their hare before they can cook him. He won't be walking about barefooted, you know."

"No. It's a poor clue in that respect. And now we may as well be off as we've seen all there is to see. I think we won't have much to say to Mrs. Beddingfield. This is a police case, and the less I'm mixed up in it the better it will be for my practice."

I was faintly amused at Foxton's caution when considered by the light of his utterances at the breakfast-table. Apparently his appetite for mystery and romance was easily satisfied. But that was no affair of mine. I waited on the doorstep while he said a few—probably evasive—words to the landlady and then, as we started off together in the direction of the police station, I began to turn over in my mind the salient features of the case. For some time we walked on in silence, and must have been pursuing a parallel train of thought for, when he at length spoke, he almost put my reflections into words.

"You know, Jervis," said he, "there ought to be a clue in those footprints. I realise that you can't tell how many toes a man has by looking at his booted feet. But those unusual footprints ought to give an expert a hint as to what sort of man to look for. Don't they convey any hint to you?"

I felt that Foxton was right; that if my brilliant colleague, Thorndyke, had been in my place he would have extracted from those footprints some leading fact that would have given the police a start along some definite line of inquiry; and that belief, coupled with Foxton's challenge, put me on my mettle.

"They offer no particular suggestions to me at this moment," said I, "but I think that, if we consider them systematically, we may be able to draw some useful deductions."

"Very well," said Foxton, "then let us consider them systematically. Fire away. I should like to hear how you work these things out."

Foxton's frankly spectatorial attitude was a little disconcerting, especially as it seemed to commit me to a result that I was by no means confident of attaining. I therefore began a little diffidently.

"We are assuming that both the feet that made those prints were from some cause devoid of little toes. That assumption—which is almost certainly correct—we treat as a fact, and, taking it as our starting point, the first step in the inquiry is to find some explanation of it. Now there are three possibilities, and only three: deformity, injury, and disease. The toes may have been absent from birth, they may have been lost as a result of mechanical injury, or they may have been lost by disease. Let us take those possibilities in order.

"Deformity we exclude since such a malformation is unknown to us.

"Mechanical injury seems to be excluded by the fact that the two little toes are on opposite sides of the body and could not conceivably be affected by any violence which left the intervening feet uninjured. This seems to narrow the possibilities down to disease; and the question that arises is, What diseases are there which might result in the loss of both little toes?"

I looked inquiringly at Foxton, but he merely nodded encouragingly. His role was that of listener.

"Well," I pursued, "the loss of both toes seems to exclude local disease, just as it excluded local injury; and as to general diseases, I can think only of three which might produce this condition—Raynaud's disease, ergotism, and frost-bite."

"You don't call frost-bite a general disease, do you?" objected Foxton.

"For our present purpose, I do. The effects are local, but the cause—low external temperature—affects the whole body and is a general cause. Well, now, taking the diseases in order. I think we can exclude Raynaud's disease. It does, it is true, occasionally cause the fingers or toes to die and drop off, and the little toes would be especially liable to be affected as being most remote from the heart. But in such a severe case the other toes would be affected. They would be shrivelled and tapered, whereas, if you remember, the toes of these feet were quite plump and full, to judge by the large impressions they made. So I think we may safely reject Raynaud's disease. There remain ergotism and frost-bite; and the choice between them is just a question of relative frequency. Frost-bite is more common; therefore frost-bite is more probable."

"Do they tend equally to affect the little toes?" asked Foxton.

"As a matter of probability, yes. The poison of ergot acting from within, and intense cold acting from without, contract the small blood-vessels and arrest, the circulation. The feet, being the most distant parts of the body from the heart, are the first to feel the effects; and the little toes, which are the most distant parts of the feet, are the most susceptible of all."

Foxton reflected awhile, and then remarked:

"This is all very well, Jervis, but I don't see that you are much forrarder. This man has lost both his little toes and on your showing, the probabilities are that the loss was due either to chronic ergot poisoning or to frost-bite, with a balance of probability in favour of frost-bite. That's all. No proof, no verification, just the law of probability applied to a particular case, which is always unsatisfactory. He may have lost his toes in some totally different way. But even if the probabilities work out correctly, I don't see what use your conclusions would be to the police. They wouldn't tell them what sort of man to look for."

There was a good deal of truth in Foxton's objection. A man who has suffered from ergotism or frost-bite is not externally different from any other man. Still, we had not exhausted the case, as I ventured to point out.

"Don't be premature, Foxton," said I. "Let us pursue our argument a little farther. We have established a probability that this unknown man has suffered either from ergotism or frost-bite. That, as you say, is of no use by itself; but supposing we can show that these conditions tend to affect a particular class of persons, we shall have established a fact that will indicate a line of investigation. And I think we can. Let us take the case of ergotism first.

"Now how is chronic ergot poisoning caused? Not by the medicinal use of the drug, but, by the consumption of the diseased rye in which ergot occurs. It is therefore peculiar to countries in which rye is used extensively as food. Those countries, broadly speaking, are the countries of North-Eastern Europe, and especially Russia and Poland.

"Then take the case of frost-bite. Obviously, the most likely person to get frost-bitten is the inhabitant of a country with a cold climate. The most rigorous climates inhabited by white people are North America and North-Eastern Europe, especially Russia and Poland. So you see, the areas associated with ergotism and frost-bite overlap to some extent. In fact they do more than overlap; for a person even slightly affected by ergot would be specially liable to frost-bite, owing to the impaired circulation. The conclusion is that, racially, in both ergotism and frost-bite, the balance of probability is in favour of a Russian, a Pole, or a Scandinavian.

"Then in the case of frost-bite there is the occupation factor. What class of men tend most to become frost-bitten? Well, beyond all doubt, the greatest sufferers from frost-bite are sailors, especially those on sailing ships, and, naturally, on ships trading to Arctic and sub-Arctic countries. But the bulk of such sailing ships are those engaged in the Baltic and Archangel trade; and the crews of those ships are almost exclusively Scandinavians, Finns, Russians and Poles. So that, again, the probabilities point to a native of North-Eastern Europe, and, taken as a whole, by the over-lapping of factors, to a Russian, a Pole, or a Scandinavian."

Foxton smiled sardonically. "Very ingenious, Jervis," said he. "Most ingenious. As an academic statement of probabilities, quite excellent. But for practical purposes absolutely useless. However, here we are at the police-station. I'll just run in and give them the facts and then go on to the coroner's office."

"I suppose I'd better not come in with you?" I said.

"Well, no," he replied. "You see, you have no official connection with the case, and they mightn't like it. You'd better go and amuse yourself while I get the morning's visits done. We can talk things over at lunch."

With this he disappeared into the police-station, and I turned away with a smile of grim amusement. Experience is apt to make us a trifle uncharitable, and experience had taught me that those who are the most scornful of academic reasoning are often not above retailing it with some reticence as to its original authorship. I had a shrewd suspicion that Foxton was at this very moment disgorging my despised "academic statement of probabilities" to an admiring police-inspector.

My way towards the sea lay through Ethelred Road, and I had traversed about half its length and was approaching the house of the tragedy when I observed Mrs. Beddingfield at the bay window. Evidently she recognised me, for a few moments later she appeared in outdoor clothes on the doorstep and advanced to meet me.

"Have you seen the police?" she asked, as we met.

I replied that Dr. Foxton was even now at the police-station.

"Ah!" she said, "it's a dreadful affair; most unfortunate, too, just at the beginning of the season. A scandal is absolute ruin to a boarding-house. What do you think of the case? Will it be possible to hush it up? Dr. Foxton said you were a lawyer, I think, Dr. Jervis?"

"Yes, I am a lawyer, but really I know nothing of the circumstances of this case. Did I understand that there had been something in the nature of a love affair?"

"Yes—at least—well, perhaps I oughtn't to have said that. But hadn't I better tell you the whole story?—that is, if I am not taking up too much of your time."

"I should be interested to hear what led to the disaster," said I.

"Then," she said, "I will tell you all about it. Will you come indoors, or shall I walk a little way with you?"

As I suspected that the police were at that moment on their way to the house, I chose the latter alternative and led her away seawards at a pretty brisk pace.

"Was this poor lady a widow?" I asked, as we started up the street.

"No, she wasn't," replied Mrs. Beddingfield, "and that was the trouble. Her husband was abroad—at least, he had been, and he was just coming home. A pretty home-coming it will be for him, poor man. He is an officer in the Civil Police at Sierra Leone, but he hasn't been there long. He went there for his health."

"What! To Sierra Leone!" I exclaimed, for the "White Man's Grave" seemed a queer health resort.

"Yes. You see, Mr. Toussaint is a French Canadian, and it seems that he has always been somewhat of a rolling stone. For some time he was in the Klondyke, but he suffered so much from the cold that he had to come away. It injured his health very severely; I don't quite know in what way, but I do know that he was quite a cripple for a time. When he got better he looked out for a post in a warm climate and eventually obtained the appointment of Inspector of Civil Police at Sierra Leone. That was about ten months ago, and when he sailed for Africa his wife came to stay with me, and has been here ever since."

"And this love affair that you spoke of?"

"Yes, but I oughtn't to have called it that. Let me explain what happened. About three months ago a Swedish gentleman—a Mr. Bergson—came to stay here, and he seemed to be very much smitten with Mrs. Toussaint."

"And she?"

"Oh, she liked him well enough. He is a tall, good-looking man—though for that matter he is no taller than her husband, nor any better-looking. Both men are over six feet. But there was no harm so far as she was concerned, excepting that she didn't see the position quite soon enough. She wasn't very discreet, in fact I thought it necessary to give her a little advice. However, Mr. Bergson left here and went to live at Ramsgate to superintend the unloading of the ice-ships (he came from Sweden in one), and I thought the trouble was at an end. But it wasn't, for he took to coming over to see Mrs. Toussaint, and of course I couldn't have that. So at last I had to tell him that he mustn't come to the house again.

"It was very unfortunate, for on that occasion I think he had been 'tasting', as they say in Scotland. He wasn't drunk, but he was excitable and noisy, and when I told him he mustn't come again he made such a disturbance that two of the gentlemen boarders—Mr. Wardale and Mr. Macauley—had to interfere. And then he was most insulting to them, especially to Mr. Macauley, who is a coloured gentleman; called him a 'buck n—r' and all sorts of offensive names."

"And how did the coloured gentleman take it?"

"Not very well, I am sorry to say, considering that he is a gentleman—a law student with chambers in the Temple. In fact, his language was so objectionable that Mr. Wardale insisted on my giving him notice on the spot. But I managed to get him taken in next door but one; you see, Mr. Wardale had been a Commissioner at, Sierra Leone—it was through him that Mr. Toussaint got his appointment—so I suppose he was rather on his dignity with coloured people."

"And was that the last you heard of Mr. Bergson?"

"He never came here again, but he wrote several times to Mrs. Toussaint, asking her to meet him. At last, only a few days ago, she wrote to him and told him that the acquaintance must cease."

"And has it ceased?"

"As far as I know, it has."

"Then, Mrs. Beddingfield," said I, "what makes you connect the affair with—with what has happened?"

"Well, you see," she explained, "there is the husband. He was coming home, and is probably in England already."

"Indeed!" said I.

"Yes," she continued. "He went up into the bush to arrest some natives belonging to one of these gangs of murderers—Leopard Societies, I think they are called—and he got seriously wounded. He wrote to his wife from hospital saying that he would be sent home as soon as he was fit to travel, and about ten days ago she got a letter from him saying that he was coming by the next ship.

"I noticed that she seemed very nervous and upset when she got the letters from hospital, and still more so when the last letter came. Of course, I don't know what he said to her in those letters. It may be that he had heard something about Mr. Bergson, and threatened to take some action. Of course, I can't say. I only know that she was very nervous and restless, and when we saw in the paper four days ago that the ship he would be coming by had arrived in Liverpool she seemed dreadfully upset. And she got worse and worse until—well, until last night."

"Has anything been heard of the husband since the ship arrived?" I asked.

"Nothing whatever," replied Mrs. Beddingfield, with a meaning look at me which I had no difficulty in interpreting. "No letter, no telegram, not a word. And you see, if he hadn't come by that ship he would almost certainly have sent a letter to her. He must have arrived in England, but why hasn't he turned up, or at least sent a wire? What is he doing? Why is he staying away? Can he have heard something? And what does he mean to do? That's what kept the poor thing on wires, and that, I feel certain, is what drove her to make away with herself."

It was not my business to contest Mrs. Beddingfield's erroneous deductions. I was seeking information—it seemed that I had nearly exhausted the present source. But one point required amplifying.

"To return to Mr. Bergson, Mrs. Beddingfield," said I. "Do I understand that he is a seafaring man?"

"He was," she replied. "At present he is settled at Ramsgate as manager of a company in the ice trade, but formerly he was a sailor. I have heard him say that he was one of the crew of an exploring ship that went in search of the North Pole and that he was locked up in the ice for months and months. I should have thought he would have had enough of ice after that."

With this view I expressed warm agreement, and having now obtained all the information that appeared to be available I proceeded to bring the interview to an end.

"Well, Mrs. Beddingfield," I said, "it is a rather mysterious affair. Perhaps more light may be thrown on it at the inquest. Meanwhile, I should think that it will be wise of you to keep your own counsel as far as outsiders are concerned."

The remainder of the morning I spent pacing the smooth stretch of sand that lies to the east of the jetty, and reflecting on the evidence that I had acquired in respect of this singular crime. Evidently there was no lack of clues in this case. On the contrary, there were two quite obvious lines of inquiry, for both the Swede and the missing husband presented the characters of the hypothetical murderer. Both had been exposed to the conditions which tend to produce frost-bite; one of them had probably been a consumer of rye meal, and both might be said to have a motive—though, to be sure, it was a very insufficient one—for committing the crime. Still in both cases the evidence was merely speculative; it suggested a line of investigation but it did nothing more.

When I met Foxton at lunch I was sensible of a curious change in his manner. His previous expansiveness had given place to marked reticence and a certain official secretiveness.

"I don't think, you know, Jervis," he said, when I opened the subject, "that we had better discuss this affair. You see, I am the principal witness, and while the case is *sub judice*—well, in fact the police don't want the case talked about."

"But surely I am a witness, too, and an expert witness, moreover—"

"That isn't the view of the police. They look on you as more or less of an amateur, and as you have no official connection with the case, I don't think they propose to *subpœna* you. Superintendent Platt, who is in charge of the case, wasn't very pleased at my having taken you to the house. Said it was quite irregular. Oh, and by the way, he says you must hand over those photographs."

"But isn't Platt going to have the footprints photographed on his own account?" I objected.

"Of course he is. He is going to have a set of proper photographs taken by an expert photographer—he was mightily amused when he heard about your little snapshot affair. Oh, you can trust Platt. He is a great man. He has had a course of instruction at the Fingerprint Department in London."

"I don't see how that is going to help him, as there aren't any fingerprints in this case."

This was a mere fly-cast on my part, but Foxton rose at once at the rather clumsy bait.

"Oh, aren't there?" he exclaimed. "You didn't happen to spot them, but they were there. Platt has got the prints of a complete right hand. This is in strict confidence, you know," he added, with somewhat belated caution.

Foxton's sudden reticence restrained me from uttering the obvious comment on the superintendent's achievement. I returned to the subject of the photographs.

"Supposing I decline to hand over my film?" said I.

"But I hope you won't—and in fact you mustn't. I am officially connected with the case, and I've got to live with these people. As the police-surgeon, I am responsible for the medical evidence, and Platt expects me to get those photographs from you. Obviously you can't keep them. It would be most irregular."

It was useless to argue. Evidently the police did not want me to be introduced into the case, and after all the superintendent was within his rights, if he chose to regard me, as a private individual and to demand the surrender of the film.

Nevertheless I was loath to give up the photographs, at least until I had carefully studied them. The case was within my own speciality of practice, and was a strange and interesting one. Moreover, it appeared to be in unskilful hands, judging from the fingerprint episode, and then experience had taught me to treasure up small scraps of chance evidence, since one never knew when one might be drawn into a case in a professional capacity. In effect, I decided not to give up the photographs, though that decision committed me to a ruse that I was not very willing to adopt. I would rather have acted quite straightforwardly.

"Well if you insist, Foxton," I said, "I will hand over the film or, if you like, I will destroy it in your presence."

"I think Platt would rather have the film uninjured," said Foxton. "Then he'll know, you know," he added, with a sly grin.

In my heart, I thanked Foxton for that grin. It made my own guileful proceedings so much easier; for a suspicious man invites you to get the better of him if you can.

After lunch I went up to my room, locked the door and took the little camera from my pocket. Having fully wound up the film, I extracted it, wrapped it up carefully and bestowed it in my inside breast-pocket. Then I inserted a fresh film, and going to the open window, took four successive snapshots of the sky. This done, I closed the camera, slipped it into my pocket and went downstairs. Foxton was in the hall, brushing his hat, as I descended, and at once renewed his demand.

"About those photographs, Jervis," said he; "I shall be looking in at the police-station presently, so if you wouldn't mind—"

"To be sure," said I. "I will give you the film now if you like."

Taking the camera from my pocket, I solemnly wound up the remainder of the film, extracted it, stuck down the loose end with ostentatious care, and handed it to him.

"Better not expose it to the light," I said, going the whole hog of deception, "or you may fog the exposures."

Foxton took the spool from me as if it were hot—he was not a photographer—and thrust it into his handbag. He was still thanking me quite profusely when the front-door bell rang.

The visitor who stood revealed when Foxton opened the door was a small, spare gentleman with a complexion of peculiar brown-papery quality that suggests long residence the tropics. He stepped in briskly and introduced himself and his business without preamble.

"My name is Wardale—boarder at Beddingfield's. I called with reference to the tragic event which—"

Here Foxton interposed in his frostiest official tone. "I am afraid, Mr. Wardale, I can't give you any information about the case at present."

"I saw you two gentlemen at the house this morning—" Mr. Wardale continued, but Foxton again cut him short.

"You did. We were there—or at least, I was—as representative of the Law, and while the case is *sub judice*—"

"It isn't yet," interrupted Wardale.

"Well, I can't enter into any discussion of it—"

"I am not asking you to," said Wardale a little impatiently. "But I understand that one of you is Dr. Jervis."

"I am," said I.

"I must really warn you—" Foxton began again; but Mr. Wardale interrupted testily:

"My dear sir, I am a lawyer and a magistrate and understand perfectly well what is and what is not permissible. I have come simply to make a professional engagement with Dr. Jervis."

"In what way can I be of service to you?" I asked.

"I will tell you," said Mr. Wardale. "This poor lady, whose death has occurred in so mysterious a manner, was the wife of a man who was, like myself a servant of the Government of Sierra Leone. I was the friend of both of them, and in the absence of the husband I should like to have the inquiry into the circumstances of this lady's death watched by a competent lawyer with the necessary special knowledge of medical evidence. Will you or your colleague, Dr. Thorndyke, undertake to watch the case for me?"

Of course I was willing to undertake the case and said so.

"Then," said Mr. Wardale, "I will instruct my solicitor to write to you and formally retain you in the case. Here is my card. You will find my name in the Colonial Office List, and you know my address here."

He handed me his card, wished us both good afternoon, and then, with a stiff little bow, turned and took his departure.

"I think I had better run up to town and confer with Thorndyke," said I. "How do the trains run?"

"There is a good train in about three-quarters of an hour," replied Foxton.

"Then I will go by it, but I shall come down again tomorrow or the next day, and probably Thorndyke will come down with me."

"Very well," said Foxton. "Bring him in to lunch or dinner, but I can't put him up, I am afraid."

"It would be better not," said I. "Your friend Platt wouldn't like it. He won't want Thorndyke—or me either for that matter. And what about those photographs? Thorndyke will want them, you know."

"He can't have them," said Foxton doggedly, "unless Platt is willing to hand them back; which I don't suppose he will be."

I had private reasons for thinking otherwise, but I kept them to myself; and as Foxton went forth on his afternoon round, I returned upstairs to pack my suitcase and write the telegram to Thorndyke informing him of my movements.

It was only a quarter past five when I let myself into our chambers in King's Bench Walk. To my relief I found my colleague at home and our laboratory assistant, Polton, in the act of laying tea, for two.

"I gather," said Thorndyke, as we shook hands, "that my learned brother brings grist to the mill?"

"Yes," I replied. "Nominally a watching brief, but I think you will agree with me that it is a case for independent investigation."

"Will there be anything in my line, sir?" inquired Polton, who was always agog at the word 'investigation'.

"There is a film to be developed. Four exposures of white footprints on a dark ground."

"Ah!" said Polton, "you'll want good strong negatives, and they ought to be enlarged if they are, from the little camera. Can you give me the dimensions?"

I wrote out the measurements from my notebook and handed him the paper together with the spool of film, with which he retired gleefully to the laboratory.

"And now, Jervis," said Thorndyke, "while Polton is operating on the film and we are discussing our tea, let us have a sketch of the case."

I gave him more than a sketch, for the events were recent and I had carefully sorted out the facts during my journey to town, making rough notes, which I now consulted. To my rather lengthy recital he listened in his usual attentive manner, without any comment, excepting in regard to my manœuvre to retain possession of the exposed film.

"It's almost a pity you didn't refuse," said he. "They could hardly have enforced their demand, and my feeling is that it is more convenient as well as more dignified to avoid direct deception unless one is driven to it. But perhaps you considered that you were."

As a matter of fact I had at the time, but I had since come to Thorndyke's opinion. My little manoeuvre was going to be a source of inconvenience presently.

"Well," said Thorndyke, when I had finished my recital, "I think we may take it that the police theory is, in the main, your own theory derived from Foxton."

"I think so, excepting that I learned from Foxton that Superintendent Platt has obtained the complete fingerprints of a right hand."

Thorndyke raised his eyebrows. "Fingerprints!" he exclaimed. "Why, the fellow must be a mere simpleton. But there," he added, "everybody—police, lawyers, judges, even Galton himself—seems to lose every vestige of common sense as soon as the subject of fingerprints is raised. But it would be interesting to know how he got them and what they are like. We must try to find that out. However, to return to your case, since your theory and the police theory are probably the same, we may as well consider the value of your inferences.

"At present we are dealing with the case in the abstract. Our data are largely assumptions, and our inferences are largely derived from an application of the mathematical laws of probability. Thus we assume that a murder has been committed, whereas it may turn out to have been suicide. We assume the murder to have been committed by the person, who made the footprints, and we assume that that person has no little toes, whereas he may have retracted little toes which do not touch the ground and so leave no impression. Assuming the little toes to be absent, we account for their absence by considering known causes in the order of their probability. Excluding—quite properly, I think—Raynaud's disease, we arrive at frost-bite and ergotism.

"But two persons, both of whom are of a stature corresponding to the size of the footprints, may have had a motive—though a very inadequate one—for committing the crime, and both have been exposed to the conditions which tend to produce frost-bite, while one of them has, probably, been exposed to the conditions which tend to produce ergotism. The laws of probability point to both of these two men; and the chances in favour of the Swede being the murderer rather than the Canadian would be represented by the common factor—frost-bite—multiplied by the additional factor, ergotism. But this is purely speculative at present.

"There is no evidence that either man has ever been frost-bitten or has ever eaten spurred rye. Nevertheless, it is a perfectly sound method at this stage. It indicates a line of investigation. If it should transpire that either man has suffered from frost-bite or ergotism, a definite advance would have been made. But here is Polton with a couple of finished prints. How on earth did you manage it in the time, Polton?"

"Why, you see, sir, I just dried the film with spirit," replied Polton. "It saved a lot of time. I will let you have a pair of enlargements in about a quarter of an hour."

Handing us the two wet prints, each stuck on a glass plate, he retired to the laboratory, and Thorndyke and I proceeded to scrutinise the photographs with the aid of our pocket lenses. The promised enlargements were really hardly necessary excepting for the purpose of comparative measurements, for the image of the white footprint, fully two inches long, was so microscopically sharp that, with the assistance of the lens, the minutest detail could be clearly seen.

"There is certainly not a vestige of little toe," remarked Thorndyke, "and the plump appearance of the other toes supports your rejection of Raynaud's disease. Does the character of the footprint convey any other suggestion to you, Jervis?"

"It gives me the impression that the man had been accustomed to go bare-footed in early life and had only taken to boots comparatively recently. The position of the great toe suggests this, and the presence of a number of small scars on the toes and ball of the foot seems to confirm it. A person walking bare-foot would sustain innumerable small wounds from treading on small, sharp objects."

Thorndyke looked dissatisfied. "I agree with you," he said, "as to the suggestion offered by the undeformed state of the great toes; but those little pits do not convey to me the impression of scars produced as you suggest. Still, you may be right."

Here our conversation was interrupted by a knock on the outer oak. Thorndyke stepped out through the lobby and I heard him open the door. A moment or two later he re-entered, accompanied by a short, brown-faced gentleman whom I instantly recognised as Mr. Wardale.

"I must have come up by the same train as you," he remarked, as we shook hands, "and to a certain extent, I suspect, on the same errand. I thought I would like to put our arrangement on a business footing, as I am a stranger to both of you."

"What do you want us to do?" asked Thorndyke.

"I want you to watch the case, and, if necessary, to look into the facts independently."

"Can you give us any information that may help us?"

Mr. Wardale reflected. "I don't think I can," he said at length. "I have no facts that you have not, and any surmises of mine might be misleading. I had rather you kept an open mind. But perhaps we might go into the question of costs."

This, of course, was somewhat difficult, but Thorndyke contrived to indicate the probable liabilities involved, to Mr. Wardale's satisfaction.

"There is one other little matter," said Wardale, as he rose to depart. "I have got a suitcase here which Mrs. Beddingfield lent me to bring some things up to town. It is one that Mr. Macauley left behind when he went away from the boarding-house. Mrs. Beddingfield suggested that I might leave it at his chambers when I had finished with it; but I don't know his address, excepting that it is somewhere in the Temple, and I don't want to meet the fellow if he should happen to have come up to town."

"Is it empty?" asked Thorndyke.

"Excepting for a suit of pyjamas and a pair of shocking old slippers." He opened the suitcase as he spoke and exhibited its contents with a grin.

"Characteristic of a negro, isn't it? Pink silk pyjamas and slippers about three sizes too small."

"Very well," said Thorndyke. "I will get my man to find out the address and leave it there."

As Mr. Wardale went out, Polton entered with the enlarged photographs, which showed the footprints the natural size. Thorndyke handed them to me, and as I sat down to examine them he followed his assistant to the laboratory. He returned in a few minutes, and after a brief inspection of the photographs, remarked:

"They show us nothing more than we have seen, though they may be useful later. So your stock of facts is all we have to go on at present. Are you going home tonight?"

"Yes, I shall go back to Margate tomorrow."

"Then, as I have to call at Scotland Yard, we may as well walk to Charing Cross together."

As we walked down the Strand we gossiped on general topics, but before we separated at Charing Cross, Thorndyke reverted to the case.

"Let me know the date of the inquest," said he, "and try to find out what the poison was—if it was really a poison."

"The liquid that was left in the bottle seemed to be a watery solution of some kind," said I, "as I think I mentioned."

"Yes," said Thorndyke. "Possibly a watery infusion of *strophanthus*."

"Why *strophanthus*?" I asked.

"Why not?" demanded Thorndyke. And with this and an inscrutable smile, he turned and walked down Whitehall.

Three days later I found myself at Margate—sitting beside Thorndyke in a room adjoining the Town Hall, in which the inquest on the death of Mrs. Toussaint was to be held. Already the coroner was in his chair, the jury were in their seats and the witnesses assembled in a group of chairs apart. These included Foxton, a stranger who sat by him—presumably the other medical witness—Mrs. Beddingfield, Mr. Wardale, the police superintendent and a well-dressed coloured man, whom I correctly assumed to be Mr. Macauley.

As I sat by my rather sphinx-like colleague my mind recurred for the hundredth time to his extraordinary powers of mental synthesis. That parting remark of his as to the possible nature of the poison had brought home to me in a flash the fact that he already had a definite theory of this crime, and that his theory was not mine nor that of the police. True, the poison might not be *strophanthus*, after all, but that would not alter the position. He had a theory of the crime, but yet he was in possession of no facts excepting those with which I had supplied him. Therefore those facts contained the material for a theory, whereas I had deduced from them nothing but the bald, ambiguous mathematical probabilities.

The first witness called was naturally Dr. Foxton, who described the circumstances already known to me. He further stated that he had been present at the autopsy, that he had found on the throat and limbs of the deceased bruises that suggested a struggle and violent restraint. The immediate cause of death was heart failure, but whether that failure was due to shock, terror, or the action of a poison he could not positively say.

The next witness was a Dr. Prescott, an expert pathologist and toxicologist. He had made the autopsy and agreed with Dr. Foxton as to the cause of death. He had examined the liquid contained in the bottle taken from the hand of the deceased and found it to be a watery infusion or decoction of *strophanthus* seeds. He had analysed the fluid contained in the stomach and found it to consist largely of the same infusion.

"Is infusion of *strophanthus* seeds used in medicine?" the coroner asked.

"No," was the reply. "The tincture is the form in which *strophanthus* is administered unless it is given in the form of *strophanthine*."

"Do you consider that the *strophanthus* caused or contributed to death?"

"It is difficult to say," replied Dr. Prescott. "*Strophanthus* is a heart poison, and there was a very large poisonous dose. But very little had been absorbed, and the appearances were not inconsistent with death from shock."

"Could death have been self-produced by the voluntary taking of the poison?" asked the coroner.

"I should say, decidedly not. Dr. Foxton's evidence shows that the bottle was almost certainly placed in the hands of the deceased after death, and this is in complete agreement with the enormous dose and small absorption."

"Would you say that appearances point to suicidal or homicidal poisoning?"

"I should say that they point to homicidal poisoning, but that death was probably due mainly to shock."

This concluded the expert's evidence. It was followed by that of Mrs. Beddingfield, which brought out nothing new to me but the fact that a trunk had been broken open and a small *attaché*-case belonging to the deceased abstracted and taken away.

"Do you know what the deceased kept in that case?" the coroner asked.

"I have seen her put her husband's letters into it. She had quite a number of them. I don't know what else she kept in it except, of course, her cheque-book."

"Had she any considerable balance at the bank?"

"I believe she had. Her husband used to send most of his pay home and she used to pay it in and leave it with the bank. She might have two or three hundred pounds to her credit."

As Mrs. Beddingfield concluded Mr. Wardale was called, and he was followed by Mr. Macauley. The evidence of both was quite brief and concerned entirely with the disturbance made by Bergson, whose absence from the court I had already noted.

The last witness was the police superintendent, and he, as I had expected, was decidedly reticent. He did refer to the footprints, but, like Foxton—who presumably had his instructions—he abstained from describing their peculiarities. Nor did he say anything about fingerprints. As to the identity of the criminal, that had to be further inquired into. Suspicion had at first fastened upon Bergson, but it had since transpired that the Swede sailed from Ramsgate on an ice-ship two days before the occurrence of the tragedy.

Then suspicion had pointed to the husband, who was known to have landed at Liverpool four days before the death of his wife and who had mysteriously disappeared. But he (the superintendent) had only that morning received a telegram from the Liverpool police informing him that the body of Toussaint had been found floating in the Mersey, and that it bore a number of wounds of an apparently homicidal character. Apparently he had been murdered and his corpse thrown into the river.

"This is very terrible," said the coroner. "Does this second murder throw any light on the case which we are investigating?"

"I think it does," replied the officer, without any great conviction, however; "but it is not advisable to go into details."

"Quite so," agreed the coroner. "Most inexpedient. But are we to understand that you have a clue to the perpetrator of this crime—assuming a crime to have been committed?"

"Yes," replied Platt. "We have several important clues."

"And do they point to any particular individual?"

The superintendent hesitated. "Well. . ." he began with some embarrassment, but the coroner interrupted him:

"Perhaps the question is indiscreet. We mustn't hamper the police, gentlemen, and the point is not really material to our inquiry. You would rather we waived that question, Superintendent?"

"If you please, sir," was the emphatic reply.

"Have any cheques from the deceased woman's cheque book been presented at the bank?"

"Not since her death. I inquired at the bank only this morning."

This concluded the evidence, and after a brief but capable summing-up by the coroner, the jury returned a verdict of "Wilful murder against some person unknown".

As the proceedings terminated, Thorndyke rose and turned round, and then to my surprise I perceived Superintendent Miller, of the Criminal Investigation Department, who had come in unperceived by me and was sitting immediately behind us.

"I have followed your instructions, sir," said he, addressing Thorndyke, "but before we take any definite action I should like to have a few words with you."

He led the way to an adjoining room and, as we entered we were followed by Superintendent Platt and Dr. Foxton.

"Now, doctor," said Miller, carefully closing the door, "I have carried out your suggestions. Mr. Macauley is being detained, but before we commit ourselves to an arrest we must have something to go upon. I shall want you to make out a *prima facie* case."

"Very well," said Thorndyke, laying upon the table the small green suitcase that was his almost invariable companion.

"I've seen that *prima facie* case before," Miller remarked with a grin, as Thorndyke unlocked it and drew out a large envelope. "Now, what have you got there?"

As Thorndyke extracted from the envelope Polton's enlargements of my small photographs, Platt's eyes appeared to bulge, while Foxton gave me a quick glance of reproach.

"These," said Thorndyke "are the full-sized photographs of the footprints of the suspected murderer. Superintendent Platt can probably verify them."

Rather reluctantly Platt produced from his pocket a pair of whole-plate photographs, which he laid beside the enlargements.

"Yes," said Miller, after comparing them, "they are the same footprints. But you say, doctor, that they are Macauley's footprints. Now, what evidence have you?"

Thorndyke again had recourse to the green case, from which he produced two copper plates mounted on wood and coated with printing ink.

"I propose," said he, lifting the plates out of their protecting frame, "that we take prints of Macauley's feet and compare them with the photographs."

"Yes," said Platt. "And then there are the fingerprints that we've got. We can test those, too."

"You don't want fingerprints if you've got a set of toeprints," objected Miller.

"With regard to those fingerprints," said Thorndyke. "May I ask if they were obtained from the bottle?"

"They were," Platt admitted.

"And were there any other fingerprints?"

"No," replied Platt. "These were the only ones."

As he spoke he laid on the table a photograph showing the prints of the thumb and fingers of a right hand.

Thorndyke glanced at the photograph and, turning to Miller, said: "I suggest that those are Dr. Foxton's fingerprints."

"Impossible!" exclaimed Platt, and then suddenly fell silent.

"We can soon see," said Thorndyke, producing from the case a pad of white paper. "If Dr. Foxton will lay the fingertips of his right hand first on this inked plate and then on the paper, we can compare the prints with the photograph."

Foxton placed his fingers on the blackened plate and then pressed them on the paper pad, leaving on the latter four beautifully clear, black fingerprints. These Superintendent Platt scrutinized eagerly, and as his glance travelled from the prints to the photographs he broke into a sheepish grin.

"Sold again!" he muttered. "They are the same prints."

"Well," said Miller, in a tone of disgust, "you must have been a mug not to have thought of that when you knew that Dr. Foxton had handled the bottle."

"The fact, however, is important," said Thorndyke. "The absence of any fingerprints but Dr. Foxton's not only suggests that the murderer took the precaution to wear gloves, but especially it proves that the bottle was not handled by the deceased during life. A suicide's hands will usually be pretty moist and would leave conspicuous, if not very clear, impressions."

"Yes," agreed Miller, "that is quite true. But with regard to these footprints. We can't compel this man to let us examine his feet without arresting him. Don't think, Dr. Thorndyke, that I suspect you of guessing. I've known you too long for that. You've got your facts all right, I don't doubt, but you must let us have enough to justify our arrest."

Thorndyke's answer was to plunge once more into the inexhaustible green case, from which he now produced two objects wrapped in tissue-paper. The paper being removed, there was revealed what looked like a model of an excessively shabby pair of brown shoes.

"These," said Thorndyke, exhibiting the "models" to Superintendent Miller—who viewed them with an undisguised grin—"are plaster casts of the interiors of a pair of slippers—very old and much too tight—belonging to Mr. Macauley. His name was written inside them. The casts have been waxed and painted with raw umber, which has been lightly rubbed off, thus accentuating the prominences and depressions. You will notice that the impressions of the toes on the soles and of the "knuckles" on the uppers appear as prominences; in fact we have in these casts a sketchy reproduction of the actual feet.

"Now, first as to dimensions. Dr. Jervis's measurements of the footprints give us ten inches and three-quarters as, the extreme length and four inches and five-eighths as the extreme width at the heads of the *metatarsus*. On these casts, as you see, the extreme length is ten inches and five-eighths—the loss of one-eighth being accounted for by the curve of the sole—and the extreme width is four inches and a quarter—three-eighths being accounted for by the lateral compression of a tight slipper. The agreement of the dimensions is remarkable, considering the unusual size. And now as to the peculiarities of the feet.

"You notice that each toe has made a perfectly distinct impression on the sole, excepting the little toe; of which there is no trace in either cast. And, turning to the uppers, you notice that the knuckles of the toes appear quite distinct and prominent—again excepting the little toes, which have made no impression at all. Thus it is not a case of retracted little toes, for they would appear as an extra prominence. Then, looking at the feet as a whole, it is evident that the little toes are absent; there is a distinct hollow, where there should be a prominence."

"M'yes," said Miller dubiously, "it's all very neat. But isn't it just a bit speculative?"

"Oh, come, Miller," protested Thorndyke; "just consider the facts. Here is a suspected murderer known to have feet of an unusual size and presenting a very rare deformity; and they are the feet of a man who had actually lived in the same house as the murdered woman and who, at the date of the crime, was living only two doors away. What more would you have?"

"Well, there is the question of motive," objected Miller.

"That hardly belongs to a prima facie case," said Thorndyke. "But even if it did, is there not ample matter for suspicion? Remember who the murdered woman was, what her husband was, and who this Sierra Leone gentleman is."

"Yes, yes; that's true," said Miller somewhat hastily, either perceiving the drift of Thorndyke's argument (which I did not), or being unwilling to admit that he was still in the dark. "Yes, we'll have the fellow in and get his actual footprints."

He went to the door and, putting his head out, made some sign, which was almost immediately followed by a trampling of feet, and Macauley entered the room, followed by two large plain-clothes policemen. The man was evidently alarmed, for he looked about him with the wild expression of a hunted animal. But his manner was aggressive and truculent.

"Why am I being interfered with in this impertinent manner?" he demanded in the deep buzzing voice characteristic of the male negro.

"We want to have a look at your feet, Mr. Macauley," said Miller. "Will you kindly take off your shoes and socks?"

"No," roared Macauley. "I'll see you damned first!"

"Then," said Miller, "I arrest you on a charge of having murdered—"

The rest of the sentence was drowned in a sudden uproar. The tall, powerful man, bellowing like an angry bull, had whipped out a large, strangely-shaped knife and charged furiously at the Superintendent. But the two plain-clothes men had been watching him from behind and now sprang upon him, each seizing an arm. Two sharp, metallic clicks in quick succession, a thunderous crash and an ear-splitting yell, and he lay prostrate on the floor with one massive constable sitting astride his chest and the other seated on his knees.

"Now's your chance, doctor," said Miller. "I'll get his shoes and socks off."

As Thorndyke re-inked his plates, Miller and the local superintendent expertly removed the smart patent shoes and the green silk socks from the feet of the writhing, bellowing man. Then Thorndyke rapidly and skilfully applied the inked plates to the soles of the feet—which I steadied for the purpose—and followed up with a dexterous pressure of the paper pad, first to one foot and then—having torn off the printed sheet—to the other. In spite of the difficulties occasioned by Macauley's struggles, each sheet presented a perfectly clear and sharp print of the sole of the foot, even the ridge-patterns of the toes and ball of the foot being quite distinct. Thorndyke laid each of the new prints on the table beside the corresponding large photograph, and invited the two superintendents to compare them.

"Yes," said Miller—and Superintendent Platt nodded his acquiescence—"there can't be a shadow of a doubt. The ink-prints and the photographs are identical, to every line and skin-marking. You've made out your case, doctor, as you always do."

"So you see," said Thorndyke, as we smoked our evening pipes on the old stone pier, "your method was a perfectly sound one, only you didn't apply it properly. Like too many mathematicians, you started on your calculations before you had secured your data. If you had applied the simple laws of probability to the real data, they would have pointed straight to Macauley."

"How do you suppose he lost his little toes?" I asked.

"I don't suppose at all. Obviously it was a clear case of double *ainhum*."

"*Ainhum!*" I exclaimed with a sudden flash of recollection.

"Yes; that was what you overlooked, you compared the probabilities of three diseases either of which only very rarely causes the loss of even one little toe and infinitely rarely causes the loss of both, and none of which conditions is confined to any definite class of persons; and you ignored *ainhum*, a disease which attacks almost exclusively the little toe, causing it to drop off, and quite commonly destroys both little toes—a disease, moreover, which is confined to the black-skinned races. In European practice *ainhum* is unknown, but in Africa, and to a less extent in India, it is quite common.

"If you were to assemble all the men in the world who have lost both little toes more than nine-tenths of them would be suffering from *ainhum*; so that, by the laws of probability, your footprints were, by nine chances to one, those of a man who had suffered from *ainhum*, and therefore a black-skinned man. But as soon as you had established a black man as the probable criminal, you opened up a new field of corroborative evidence. There was a black man on the spot.

"That man was a native of Sierra Leone and almost certainly a man of importance there. But the victim's husband had deadly enemies in the native secret societies of Sierra Leone. The letters of the husband to the wife probably contained matter incriminating certain natives of Sierra Leone. The evidence became cumulative, you see. Taken as a whole, it pointed plainly to Macauley, apart from the new fact of the murder of Toussaint in Liverpool, a city with a considerable floating population of West Africans."

"And I gather from your reference to the African poison, *strophanthus*, that you fixed on Macauley at once when I gave you my sketch of the case?"

"Yes; especially when I saw your photographs of the footprints with the absent little toes and those characteristic chigger-scars on the toes that remained. But it was sheer luck that enabled me to fit the keystone into its place and turn mere probability into virtual certainty. I could have embraced the magician Wardale when he brought us the magic slippers. Still, it isn't an absolute certainty, even now, though I expect it will be by tomorrow."

And Thorndyke was right. That very evening the police entered Macauley's chambers in Tanfield Court, where they discovered the dead woman's *attaché*-case. It still contained Toussaint's letters to his wife, and one of those letters mentioned by name, as members of a dangerous secret society, several prominent Sierra Leone men, including the accused, David Macauley.

The Aluminium Dagger

The "urgent call"—the instant, peremptory summons to professional duty—is an experience that appertains to the medical rather than the legal practitioner, and I had supposed, when I abandoned the clinical side of my profession in favour of the forensic, that henceforth I should know it no more; that the interrupted meal, the broken leisure, and the jangle of the night-bell, were things of the past; but in practice it was otherwise. The medical jurist is, so to speak, on the borderland of the two professions, and exposed to the vicissitudes of each calling, and so it happened from time to time that the professional services of my colleague or myself were demanded at a moment's notice. And thus it was in the case that I am about to relate.

The sacred rite of the "tub" had been duly performed, and the freshly-dried person of the present narrator was about to be insinuated into the first instalment of clothing, when a hurried step was heard upon the stair, and the voice of our laboratory assistant, Polton, arose at my colleague's door.

"There's a gentleman downstairs, sir, who says he must see you instantly on most urgent business. He seems to be in a rare twitter, sir—"

Polton was proceeding to descriptive particulars, when a second and more hurried step became audible, and a strange voice addressed Thorndyke.

"I have come to beg your immediate assistance, sir; a most dreadful thing has happened. A horrible murder has been committed. Can you come with me now?"

"I will be with you almost immediately," said Thorndyke. "Is the victim quite dead?"

"Quite. Cold and stiff. The police think—"

"Do the police know that you have come for me?" interrupted Thorndyke.

"Yes. Nothing is to be done until you arrive."

"Very well. I will be ready in a few minutes."

"And if you would wait downstairs, sir," Polton added persuasively, "I could help the doctor to get ready."

With this crafty appeal, he lured the intruder back to the sitting-room, and shortly after stole softly up the stairs with a small breakfast tray, the contents of which he deposited firmly in our respective rooms, with a few timely words on the folly of "undertaking murders on an empty stomach." Thorndyke and I had meanwhile clothed ourselves with a celerity known only to medical practitioners and quick-change artists, and in a few minutes descended the stairs together, calling in at the laboratory for a few appliances that Thorndyke usually took with him on a visit of investigation.

As we entered the sitting-room, our visitor, who was feverishly pacing up and down, seized his hat with a gasp of relief. "You are ready to come?" he asked. "My carriage is at the door;" and, without waiting for an answer, he hurried out, and rapidly preceded us down the stairs.

The carriage was a roomy brougham, which fortunately accommodated the three of us, and as soon as we had entered and shut the door, the coachman whipped up his horse and drove off at a smart trot.

"I had better give you some account of the circumstances, as we go," said our agitated friend. "In the first place, my name is Curtis, Henry Curtis; here is my card. Ah! and here is another card, which I should have given you before. My solicitor, Mr. Marchmont, was with me when I made this dreadful discovery, and he sent me to you. He remained in the rooms to see that nothing is disturbed until you arrive."

"That was wise of him," said Thorndyke. "But now tell us exactly what has occurred."

"I will," said Mr. Curtis. "The murdered man was my brother-in-law, Alfred Hartridge, and I am sorry to say he was—well, he was a bad man. It grieves me to speak of him thus—*de mortuis,* you know—but, still, we must deal with the facts, even though they be painful."

"Undoubtedly," agreed Thorndyke.

"I have had a great deal of very unpleasant correspondence with him—Marchmont will tell you about that—and yesterday I left a note for him, asking for an interview, to settle the business, naming eight o'clock this morning as the hour, because I had to leave town before noon. He replied, in a very singular letter, that he would see me at that hour, and Mr. Marchmont very kindly consented to accompany me. Accordingly, we went to his chambers together this morning, arriving punctually at eight o'clock. We rang the bell several times, and knocked loudly at the door, but as there was no response, we went down and spoke to the hall-porter. This man, it seems, had already noticed, from the courtyard, that the electric lights were full on in Mr. Hartridge's sitting-room, as they had been all night, according to the statement of the night-porter; so now, suspecting that something was wrong, he came up with us, and rang the bell and battered at the door.

"Then, as there was still no sign of life within, he inserted his duplicate key and tried to open the door—unsuccessfully, however, as it proved to be bolted on the inside. Thereupon the porter fetched a constable, and, after a consultation, we decided that we were justified in breaking open the door; the porter produced a crowbar, and by our unified efforts the door was eventually burst open. We entered, and—my God! Dr. Thorndyke, what a terrible sight it was that met our eyes! My brother-in-law was lying dead on the floor of the sitting-room. He had been stabbed—stabbed to death; and the dagger had not even been withdrawn. It was still sticking out of his back."

He mopped his face with his handkerchief, and was about to continue his account of the catastrophe when the carriage entered a quiet side-street between Westminster and Victoria, and drew up before a block of tall, new, red-brick buildings. A flurried hall-porter ran out to open the door, and we alighted opposite the main entrance.

"My brother-in-law's chambers are on the second-floor," said Mr. Curtis. "We can go up in the lift."

The porter had hurried before us, and already stood with his hand upon the rope. We entered the lift, and in a few seconds were discharged on to the second floor, the porter, with furtive curiosity, following us down the corridor. At the end of the passage was a half-open door, considerably battered and bruised. Above the door, painted in white lettering, was the inscription, "Mr. Hartridge;" and through the doorway protruded the rather foxy countenance of Inspector Badger.

"I am glad you have come, sir," said he, as he recognised my colleague. "Mr. Marchmont is sitting inside like a watch-dog, and he growls if any of us even walks across the room."

The words formed a complaint, but there was a certain geniality in the speaker's manner which made me suspect that Inspector Badger was already navigating his craft on a lee shore.

We entered a small lobby or hall, and from thence passed into the sitting-room, where we found Mr. Marchmont keeping his vigil, in company with a constable and a uniformed inspector. The three rose softly as we entered, and greeted us in a whisper; and then, with one accord, we all looked towards the other end of the room, and so remained for a time without speaking.

There was, in the entire aspect of the room, something very grim and dreadful. An atmosphere of tragic mystery enveloped the most commonplace objects; and sinister suggestions lurked in the most familiar appearances. Especially impressive was the air of suspense—of ordinary, every-day life suddenly arrested—cut short in the twinkling of an eye. The electric lamps, still burning dim and red, though the summer sunshine streamed in through the windows; the half-emptied tumbler and open book by the empty chair, had each its whispered message of swift and sudden disaster, as had the hushed voices and stealthy movements of the waiting men, and, above all, an awesome shape that was but a few hours since a living man, and that now sprawled, prone and motionless, on the floor.

"This is a mysterious affair," observed Inspector Badger, breaking the silence at length, "though it is clear enough up to a certain point. The body tells its own story."

We stepped across and looked down at the corpse. It was that of a somewhat elderly man, and lay, on an open space of floor before the fireplace, face downwards, with the arms extended. The slender hilt of a dagger projected from the back below the left shoulder, and, with the exception of a trace of blood upon the lips, this was the only indication of the mode of death. A little way from the body a clock-key lay on the carpet, and, glancing up at the clock on the mantelpiece, I perceived that the glass front was open.

"You see," pursued the inspector, noting my glance, "he was standing in front of the fireplace, winding the clock. Then the murderer stole up behind him—the noise of the turning key must have covered his movements—and stabbed him. And you see, from the position of the dagger on the left side of the back, that the murderer must have been left-handed. That is all clear enough. What is not clear is how he got in, and how he got out again."

"The body has not been moved, I suppose," said Thorndyke.

"No. We sent for Dr. Egerton, the police-surgeon, and he certified that the man was dead. He will be back presently to see you and arrange about the post-mortem."

"Then," said Thorndyke, "we will not disturb the body till he comes, except to take the temperature and dust the dagger-hilt."

He took from his bag a long, registering chemical thermometer and an insufflator or powder-blower. The former he introduced under the dead man's clothing against the abdomen, and with the latter blew a stream of fine yellow powder on to the black leather handle of the dagger. Inspector Badger stooped eagerly to examine the handle, as Thorndyke blew away the powder that had settled evenly on the surface.

THE ALUMINIUM DAGGER.

"No fingerprints," said he, in a disappointed tone. "He must have worn gloves. But that inscription gives a pretty broad hint."

He pointed, as he spoke, to the metal guard of the dagger, on which was engraved, in clumsy lettering, the single word, "*TRADITORE.*"

"That's the Italian for 'traitor,'" continued the inspector, "and I got some information from the porter that fits in with that suggestion. We'll have him in presently, and you shall hear."

"Meanwhile," said Thorndyke, "as the position of the body may be of importance in the inquiry, I will take one or two photographs and make a rough plan to scale. Nothing has been moved, you say? Who opened the windows?"

"They were open when we came in," said Mr. Marchmont. "Last night was very hot, you remember. Nothing whatever has been moved."

Thorndyke produced from his bag a small folding camera, a telescopic tripod, a surveyor's measuring-tape, a boxwood scale, and a sketch-block. He set up the camera in a corner, and exposed a plate, taking a general view of the room, and including the corpse. Then he moved to the door and made a second exposure.

"Will you stand in front of the clock, Jervis," he said, "and raise your hand as if winding it? Thanks; keep like that while I expose a plate."

I remained thus, in the position that the dead man was assumed to have occupied at the moment of the murder, while the plate was exposed, and then, before I moved, Thorndyke marked the position of my feet with a blackboard chalk. He next set up the tripod over the chalk marks, and took two photographs from that position, and finally photographed the body itself.

The photographic operations being concluded, he next proceeded, with remarkable skill and rapidity, to lay out on the sketch-block a ground-plan of the room, showing the exact position of the various objects, on a scale of a quarter of an inch to the foot—a process that the inspector was inclined to view with some impatience.

"You don't spare trouble, Doctor," he remarked; "nor time either," he added, with a significant glance at his watch.

"No," answered Thorndyke, as he detached the finished sketch from the block; "I try to collect all the facts that may bear on a case. They may prove worthless, or they may turn out of vital importance; one never knows beforehand, so I collect them all. But here, I think, is Dr. Egerton."

The police-surgeon greeted Thorndyke with respectful cordiality, and we proceeded at once to the examination of the body. Drawing out the thermometer, my colleague noted the reading, and passed the instrument to Dr. Egerton.

"Dead about ten hours," remarked the latter, after a glance at it. "This was a very determined and mysterious murder."

"Very," said Thorndyke. "Feel that dagger, Jervis."

I touched the hilt, and felt the characteristic grating of bone.

"It is through the edge of a rib!" I exclaimed.

"Yes; it must have been used with extraordinary force. And you notice that the clothing is screwed up slightly, as if the blade had been rotated as it was driven in. That is a very peculiar feature, especially when taken together with the violence of the blow."

"It is singular, certainly," said Dr. Egerton, "though I don't know that it helps us much. Shall we withdraw the dagger before moving the body?"

"Certainly," replied Thorndyke, "or the movement may produce fresh injuries. But wait." He took a piece of string from his pocket, and, having drawn the dagger out a couple of inches, stretched the string in a line parallel to the flat of the blade. Then, giving me the ends to hold, he drew the weapon out completely. As the blade emerged, the twist in the clothing disappeared. "Observe," said he, "that the string gives the direction of the wound, and that the cut in the clothing no longer coincides with it. There is quite a considerable angle, which is the measure of the rotation of the blade."

"Yes, it is odd," said Dr. Egerton, "though, as I said, I doubt that it helps us."

"At present," Thorndyke rejoined dryly, "we are noting the facts."

"Quite so," agreed the other, reddening slightly; "and perhaps we had better move the body to the bedroom, and make a preliminary inspection of the wound."

We carried the corpse into the bedroom, and, having examined the wound without eliciting anything new, covered the remains with a sheet, and returned to the sitting-room.

"Well, gentlemen," said the inspector, "you have examined the body and the wound, and you have measured the floor and the furniture, and taken photographs, and made a plan, but we don't seem much more forward. Here's a man murdered in his rooms. There is only one entrance to the flat, and that was bolted on the inside at the time of the murder. The windows are some forty feet from the ground; there is no rain-pipe near any of them; they are set flush in the wall, and there isn't a foothold for a fly on any part of that wall. The grates are modern, and there isn't room for a good-sized cat to crawl up any of the chimneys. Now, the question is, How did the murderer get in, and how did he get out again?"

"Still," said Mr. Marchmont, "the fact is that he did get in, and that he is not here now; and therefore he must have got out; and therefore it must have been possible for him to get out. And, further, it must be possible to discover how he got out."

The inspector smiled sourly, but made no reply.

"The circumstances," said Thorndyke, "appear to have been these: The deceased seems to have been alone; there is no trace of a second occupant of the room, and only one half-emptied tumbler on the table. He was sitting reading when apparently he noticed that the clock had stopped—at ten minutes to twelve; he laid his book, face downwards, on the table, and rose to wind the clock, and as he was winding it he met his death."

"By a stab dealt by a left-handed man, who crept up behind him on tiptoe," added the inspector.

Thorndyke nodded. "That would seem to be so," he said. "But now let us call in the porter, and hear what he has to tell us."

The custodian was not difficult to find, being, in fact, engaged at that moment in a survey of the premises through the slit of the letter-box.

"Do you know what persons visited these rooms last night?" Thorndyke asked him, when he entered looking somewhat sheepish.

"A good many were in and out of the building," was the answer, "but I can't say if any of them came to this flat. I saw Miss Curtis pass in about nine."

"My daughter!" exclaimed Mr. Curtis, with a start. "I didn't know that."

"She left about nine-thirty," the porter added.

"Do you know what she came about?" asked the inspector.

"I can guess," replied Mr. Curtis.

"Then don't say," interrupted Mr. Marchmont. "Answer no questions."

"You're very close, Mr. Marchmont," said the inspector; "we are not suspecting the young lady. We don't ask, for instance, if she is left-handed."

He glanced craftily at Mr. Curtis as he made this remark, and I noticed that our client suddenly turned deathly pale, whereupon the inspector looked away again quickly, as though he had not observed the change.

"Tell us about those Italians again," he said, addressing the porter. "When did the first of them come here?"

"About a week ago," was the reply. "He was a common-looking man—looked like an organ-grinder—and he brought a note to my lodge. It was in a dirty envelope, and was addressed 'Mr. Hartridge, Esq., Brackenhurst Mansions,' in a very bad handwriting. The man gave me the note and asked me to give it to Mr. Hartridge; then he went away, and I took the note up and dropped it into the letter-box."

"What happened next?"

"Why, the very next day an old hag of an Italian woman—one of them fortune-telling swines with a cage of birds on a stand—came and set up just by the main doorway. I soon sent her packing, but, bless you! she was back again in ten minutes, birds and all. I sent her off again—I kept on sending her off, and she kept on coming back, until I was reg'lar wore to a thread."

"You seem to have picked up a bit since then," remarked the inspector with a grin and a glance at the sufferer's very pronounced bow-window.

"Perhaps I have," the custodian replied haughtily. "Well, the next day there was a ice-cream man—a reg'lar waster, he was. Stuck outside as if he was froze to the pavement. Kept giving the errand-boys tasters, and when I tried to move him on, he told me not to obstruct his business. Business, indeed! Well, there them boys stuck, one after the other, wiping their tongues round the bottoms of them glasses, until I was fit to bust with aggravation. And he kept me going all day.

"Then, the day after that there was a barrel-organ, with a mangy-looking monkey on it. He was the worst of all. Profane, too, he was. Kept mixing up sacred tunes and comic songs: '*Rock of Ages,*' '*Bill Bailey,*' '*Cujus Animal,*' and '*Over the Garden Wall.*' And when I tried to move him on, that little blighter of a monkey made a run at my leg; and then the man grinned and started playing, '*Wait till the Clouds roll by.*' I tell you, it was fair sickening."

He wiped his brow at the recollection, and the inspector smiled appreciatively.

"And that was the last of them?" said the latter; and as the porter nodded sulkily, he asked: "Should you recognise the note that the Italian gave you?"

"I should," answered the porter with frosty dignity.

The inspector bustled out of the room, and returned a minute later with a letter-case in his hand. "This was in his breast-pocket," said he, laying the bulging case on the table, and drawing up a chair. "Now, here are three letters tied together. Ah! this will be the one." He untied the tape, and held out a dirty envelope addressed in a sprawling, illiterate hand to 'Mr. Hartridge, Esq.' "Is that the note the Italian gave you?"

The porter examined it critically. "Yes," said he; "that is the one."

The inspector drew the letter out of the envelope, and, as he opened it, his eyebrows went up.

"What do you make of that, Doctor?" he said, handing the sheet to Thorndyke.

Thorndyke regarded it for a while in silence, with deep attention. Then he carried it to the window, and, taking his lens from his pocket, examined the paper closely, first with the low power, and then with the highly magnifying Coddington attachment.

"I should have thought you could see that with the naked eye," said the inspector, with a sly grin at me. "It's a pretty bold design."

"Yes," replied Thorndyke; "a very interesting production. What do you say, Mr. Marchmont?"

The solicitor took the note, and I looked over his shoulder. It was certainly a curious production. Written in red ink, on the commonest notepaper, and in the same sprawling hand as the address, was the following message: "You are given six days to do what is just. By the sign above, know what to expect if you fail." The sign referred to was a skull and crossbones, very neatly, but rather unskilfully, drawn at the top of the paper.

"This," said Mr. Marchmont, handing the document to Mr. Curtis, "explains the singular letter that he wrote yesterday. You have it with you, I think?"

"Yes," replied Mr. Curtis; "here it is."

He produced a letter from his pocket, and read aloud:

> Yes: come if you like, though it is an ungodly hour. Your threatening letters have caused me great amusement. They are worthy of Sadler's Wells in its prime.
>
> Alfred Hartridge.

"Was Mr. Hartridge ever in Italy?" asked Inspector Badger.

"Oh yes," replied Mr. Curtis. "He stayed at Capri nearly the whole of last year."

"Why, then, that gives us our clue. Look here. Here are these two other letters; E.C. postmark—Saffron Hill is E.C. And just look at that!"

He spread out the last of the mysterious letters, and we saw that, besides the *memento mori,* it contained only three words: "Beware! Remember Capri!"

"If you have finished, Doctor, I'll be off and have a look round Little Italy. Those four Italians oughtn't to be difficult to find, and we've got the porter here to identify them."

"Before you go," said Thorndyke, "there are two little matters that I should like to settle. One is the dagger: it is in your pocket, I think. May I have a look at it?"

The inspector rather reluctantly produced the dagger and handed it to my colleague.

"A very singular weapon, this," said Thorndyke, regarding the dagger thoughtfully, and turning it about to view its different parts. "Singular both in shape and material. I have never seen an aluminium hilt before, and bookbinder's morocco is a little unusual."

"The aluminium was for lightness," explained the inspector, "and it was made narrow to carry up the sleeve, I expect."

"Perhaps so," said Thorndyke.

He continued his examination, and presently, to the inspector's delight, brought forth his pocket lens.

"I never saw such a man!" exclaimed the jocose detective. "His motto ought to be, 'We magnify thee.' I suppose he'll measure it next."

The inspector was not mistaken. Having made a rough sketch of the weapon on his block, Thorndyke produced from his bag a folding rule and a delicate calliper-gauge. With these instruments he proceeded, with extraordinary care and precision, to take the dimensions of the various parts of the dagger, entering each measurement in its place on the sketch, with a few brief, descriptive details.

"The other matter," said he at length, handing the dagger back to the inspector, "refers to the houses opposite."

He walked to the window, and looked out at the backs of a row of tall buildings similar to the one we were in. They were about thirty yards distant, and were separated from us by a piece of ground, planted with shrubs and intersected by gravel paths.

"If any of those rooms were occupied last night," continued Thorndyke, "we might obtain an actual eyewitness of the crime. This room was brilliantly lighted, and all the blinds were up, so that an observer at any of those windows could see right into the room, and very distinctly, too. It might be worth inquiring into."

"Yes, that's true," said the inspector; "though I expect, if any of them have seen anything, they will come forward quick enough when they read the report in the papers. But I must be off now, and I shall have to lock you out of the rooms."

As we went down the stairs, Mr. Marchmont announced his intention of calling on us in the evening, "unless," he added, "you want any information from me now."

"I do," said Thorndyke. "I want to know who is interested in this man's death."

"That," replied Marchmont, "is rather a queer story. Let us take a turn in that garden that we saw from the window. We shall be quite private there."

He beckoned to Mr. Curtis, and, when the inspector had departed with the police-surgeon, we induced the porter to let us into the garden.

"The question that you asked," Mr. Marchmont began, looking up curiously at the tall houses opposite, "is very simply answered. The only person immediately interested in the death of Alfred Hartridge is his executor and sole legatee, a man named Leonard Wolfe. He is no relation of the deceased, merely a friend, but he inherits the entire estate—about twenty thousand pounds. The circumstances are these: Alfred Hartridge was the elder of two brothers, of whom the younger, Charles, died before his father, leaving a widow and three children. Fifteen years ago the father died, leaving the whole of his property to Alfred, with the understanding that he should support his brother's family and make the children his heirs."

"Was there no will?" asked Thorndyke.

"Under great pressure from the friends of his son's widow, the old man made a will shortly before he died; but he was then very old and rather childish, so the will was contested by Alfred, on the grounds of undue influence, and was ultimately set aside. Since then Alfred Hartridge has not paid a penny towards the support of his brother's family. If it had not been for my client, Mr. Curtis, they might have starved; the whole burden of the support of the widow and the education of the children has fallen upon him.

"Well, just lately the matter has assumed an acute form, for two reasons. The first is that Charles's eldest son, Edmund, has come of age. Mr. Curtis had him articled to a solicitor, and, as he is now fully qualified, and a most advantageous proposal for a partnership has been made, we have been putting pressure on Alfred to supply the necessary capital in accordance with his father's wishes. This he had refused to do, and it was with reference to this matter that we were calling on him this morning. The second reason involves a curious and disgraceful story.

"There is a certain Leonard Wolfe, who has been an intimate friend of the deceased. He is, I may say, a man of bad character, and their association has been of a kind creditable to neither. There is also a certain woman named Hester Greene, who had certain claims upon the deceased, which we need not go into at present. Now, Leonard Wolfe and the deceased, Alfred Hartridge, entered into an agreement, the terms of which were these:

"(1) Wolfe was to marry Hester Greene, and in consideration of this service

"(2) Alfred Hartridge was to assign to Wolfe the whole of his property, absolutely, the actual transfer to take place on the death of Hartridge."

"And has this transaction been completed?" asked Thorndyke.

"Yes, it has, unfortunately. But we wished to see if anything could be done for the widow and the children during Hartridge's lifetime. No doubt, my client's daughter, Miss Curtis, called last night on a similar mission—very indiscreetly, since the matter was in our hands; but, you know, she is engaged to Edmund Hartridge—and I expect the interview was a pretty stormy one."

Thorndyke remained silent for a while, pacing slowly along the gravel path, with his eyes bent on the ground: not abstractedly, however, but with a searching, attentive glance that roved amongst the shrubs and bushes, as though he were looking for something.

"What sort of man," he asked presently, "is this Leonard Wolfe? Obviously he is a low scoundrel, but what is he like in other respects? Is he a fool, for instance?"

"Not at all, I should say," said Mr. Curtis. "He was formerly an engineer, and, I believe, a very capable mechanician. Latterly he has lived on some property that came to him, and has spent both his time and his money in gambling and dissipation. Consequently, I expect he is pretty short of funds at present."

"And in appearance?"

"I only saw him once," replied Mr. Curtis, "and all I can remember of him is that he is rather short, fair, thin, and clean-shaven, and that he has lost the middle finger of his left hand."

"And he lives at?"

"Eltham, in Kent. Morton Grange, Eltham," said Mr. Marchmont. "And now, if you have all the information that you require, I must really be off, and so must Mr. Curtis."

The two men shook our hands and hurried away, leaving Thorndyke gazing meditatively at the dingy flower-beds.

"A strange and interesting case, this, Jervis," said he, stooping to peer under a laurel-bush. "The inspector is on a hot scent—a most palpable red herring on a most obvious string; but that is his business. Ah, here comes the porter, intent, no doubt, on pumping us, whereas—" He smiled genially at the approaching custodian, and asked: "Where did you say those houses fronted?"

"Cotman Street, sir," answered the porter. "They are nearly all offices."

"And the numbers? That open second-floor window, for instance?"

"That is number six; but the house opposite Mr. Hartridge's rooms is number eight."

"Thank you."

Thorndyke was moving away, but suddenly turned again to the porter.

"By the way," said he, "I dropped something out of the window just now—a small flat piece of metal, like this." He made on the back of his visiting card a neat sketch of a circular disc, with a hexagonal hole through it, and handed the card to the porter. "I can't say where it fell," he continued; "these flat things scale about so; but you might ask the gardener to look for it. I will give him a sovereign if he brings it to my chambers, for, although it is of no value to anyone else, it is of considerable value to me."

The porter touched his hat briskly, and as we turned out at the gate, I looked back and saw him already wading among the shrubs.

The object of the porter's quest gave me considerable mental occupation. I had not seen Thorndyke drop anything, and it was not his way to finger carelessly any object of value. I was about to question him on the subject, when, turning sharply round into Cotman Street, he drew up at the doorway of number six, and began attentively to read the names of the occupants.

"'Third-floor,'" he read out, "'Mr. Thomas Barlow, Commission Agent.' Hum! I think we will look in on Mr. Barlow."

He stepped quickly up the stone stairs, and I followed, until we arrived, somewhat out of breath, on the third-floor. Outside the Commission Agent's door he paused for a moment, and we both listened curiously to an irregular sound of shuffling feet from within. Then he softly opened the door and looked into the room. After remaining thus for nearly a minute, he looked round at me with a broad smile, and noiselessly set the door wide open.

Inside, a lanky youth of fourteen was practising, with no mean skill, the manipulation of an appliance known by the appropriate name of *diabolo*; and so absorbed was he in his occupation that we entered and shut the door without being observed. At length the shuttle missed the string and flew into a large waste-paper basket; the boy turned and confronted us, and was instantly covered with confusion.

"Allow me," said Thorndyke, rooting rather unnecessarily in the waste-paper basket, and handing the toy to its owner. "I need not ask if Mr. Barlow is in," he added, "nor if he is likely to return shortly."

"He won't be back today," said the boy, perspiring with embarrassment; "he left before I came. I was rather late."

"I see," said Thorndyke. "The early bird catches the worm, but the late bird catches the *diabolo*. How did you know he would not be back?"

"He left a note. Here it is."

He exhibited the document, which was neatly written in red ink. Thorndyke examined it attentively, and then asked:

"Did you break the inkstand yesterday?"

The boy stared at him in amazement. "Yes, I did," he answered. "How did you know?"

"I didn't, or I should not have asked. But I see that he has used his stylo to write this note."

The boy regarded Thorndyke distrustfully, as he continued:

"I really called to see if your Mr. Barlow was a gentleman whom I used to know; but I expect you can tell me. My friend was tall and thin, dark, and clean-shaved."

"This ain't him, then," said the boy. "He's thin, but he ain't tall or dark. He's got a sandy beard, and he wears spectacles and a wig. I know a wig when I see one," he added cunningly, "'cause my father wears one. He puts it on a peg to comb it, and he swears at me when I larf."

"My friend had injured his left hand," pursued Thorndyke.

"I dunno about that," said the youth. "Mr. Barlow nearly always wears gloves; he always wears one on his left hand, anyhow."

"Ah well! I'll just write him a note on the chance, if you will give me a piece of notepaper. Have you any ink?"

"There's some in the bottle. I'll dip the pen in for you."

He produced, from the cupboard, an opened packet of cheap notepaper and a packet of similar envelopes, and, having dipped the pen to the bottom of the ink-bottle, handed it to Thorndyke, who sat down and hastily scribbled a short note. He had folded the paper, and was about to address the envelope, when he appeared suddenly to alter his mind.

"I don't think I will leave it, after all," he said, slipping the folded paper into his pocket. "No. Tell him I called—Mr. Horace Budge—and say I will look in again in a day or two."

The youth watched our exit with an air of perplexity, and he even came out on to the landing, the better to observe us over the balusters; until, unexpectedly catching Thorndyke's eye, he withdrew his head with remarkable suddenness, and retired in disorder.

To tell the truth, I was now little less perplexed than the office-boy by Thorndyke's proceedings; in which I could discover no relevancy to the investigation that I presumed he was engaged upon: and the last straw was laid upon the burden of my curiosity when he stopped at a staircase window, drew the note out of his pocket, examined it with his lens, held it up to the light, and chuckled aloud.

"Luck," he observed, "though no substitute for care and intelligence, is a very pleasant addition. Really, my learned brother, we are doing uncommonly well."

When we reached the hall, Thorndyke stopped at the housekeeper's box, and looked in with a genial nod.

"I have just been up to see Mr. Barlow," said he. "He seems to have left quite early."

"Yes, sir," the man replied. "He went away about half-past eight."

"That was very early; and presumably he came earlier still?"

"I suppose so," the man assented, with a grin; "but I had only just come on when he left."

"Had he any luggage with him?"

"Yes, sir. There was two cases, a square one and a long, narrow one, about five foot long. I helped him to carry them down to the cab."

"Which was a four-wheeler, I suppose?"

"Yes, sir."

"Mr. Barlow hasn't been here very long, has he?" Thorndyke inquired.

"No. He only came in last quarter-day—about six weeks ago."

"Ah well! I must call another day. Good-morning;" and Thorndyke strode out of the building, and made directly for the cab-rank in the adjoining street. Here he stopped for a minute or two to parley with the driver of a four-wheeled cab, whom he finally commissioned to convey us to a shop in New Oxford Street. Having dismissed the cabman with his blessing and a half-sovereign, he vanished into the shop, leaving me to gaze at the lathes, drills, and bars of metal displayed in the window. Presently he emerged with a small parcel, and explained, in answer to my inquiring look: "A strip of tool steel and a block of metal for Polton."

His next purchase was rather more eccentric. We were proceeding along Holborn when his attention was suddenly arrested by the window of a furniture shop, in which was displayed a collection of obsolete French small-arms—relics of the tragedy of 1870—which were being sold for decorative purposes. After a brief inspection, he entered the shop, and shortly reappeared carrying a long sword-bayonet and an old Chassepot rifle.

"What may be the meaning of this martial display?" I asked, as we turned down Fetter Lane.

"House protection," he replied promptly. "You will agree that a discharge of musketry, followed by a bayonet charge, would disconcert the boldest of burglars."

I laughed at the absurd picture thus drawn of the strenuous house-protector, but nevertheless continued to speculate on the meaning of my friend's eccentric proceedings, which I felt sure were in some way related to the murder in Brackenhurst Chambers, though I could not trace the connection.

After a late lunch, I hurried out to transact such of my business as had been interrupted by the stirring events of the morning, leaving Thorndyke busy with a drawing-board, squares, scale, and compasses, making accurate, scaled drawings from his rough sketches; while Polton, with the brown-paper parcel in his hand, looked on at him with an air of anxious expectation.

As I was returning homeward in the evening by way of Mitre Court, I overtook Mr. Marchmont, who was also bound for our chambers, and we walked on together.

"I had a note from Thorndyke," he explained, "asking for a specimen of handwriting, so I thought I would bring it along myself, and hear if he has any news."

When we entered the chambers, we found Thorndyke in earnest consultation with Polton, and on the table before them I observed, to my great surprise, the dagger with which the murder had been committed.

"I have got you the specimen that you asked for," said Marchmont. "I didn't think I should be able to, but, by a lucky chance, Curtis kept the only letter he ever received from the party in question."

He drew the letter from his wallet, and handed it to Thorndyke, who looked at it attentively and with evident satisfaction.

"By the way," said Marchmont, taking up the dagger, "I thought the inspector took this away with him."

"He took the original," replied Thorndyke. "This is a duplicate, which Polton has made, for experimental purposes, from my drawings."

"Really!" exclaimed Marchmont, with a glance of respectful admiration at Polton; "it is a perfect replica—and you have made it so quickly, too."

"It was quite easy to make," said Polton, "to a man accustomed to work in metal."

"Which," added Thorndyke, "is a fact of some evidential value."

At this moment a hansom drew up outside. A moment later flying footsteps were heard on the stairs. There was a furious battering at the door, and, as Polton threw it open, Mr. Curtis burst wildly into the room.

"Here is a frightful thing, Marchmont!" he gasped. "Edith—my daughter—arrested for the murder. Inspector Badger came to our house and took her. My God! I shall go mad!"

Thorndyke laid his hand on the excited man's shoulder. "Don't distress yourself, Mr. Curtis," said he. "There is no occasion, I assure you. I suppose," he added, "your daughter is left-handed?"

"Yes, she is, by a most disastrous coincidence. But what are we to do? Good God! Dr. Thorndyke, they have taken her to prison—to prison—think of it! My poor Edith!"

"We'll soon have her out," said Thorndyke. "But listen; there is someone at the door."

A brisk rat-tat confirmed his statement; and when I rose to open the door, I found myself confronted by Inspector Badger. There was a moment of extreme awkwardness, and then both the detective and Mr. Curtis proposed to retire in favour of the other.

"Don't go, inspector," said Thorndyke; "I want to have a word with you. Perhaps Mr. Curtis would look in again, say, in an hour. Will you? We shall have news for you by then, I hope."

Mr. Curtis agreed hastily, and dashed out of the room with his characteristic impetuosity. When he had gone, Thorndyke turned to the detective, and remarked dryly:

"You seem to have been busy, inspector?"

"Yes," replied Badger; "I haven't let the grass grow under my feet; and I've got a pretty strong case against Miss Curtis already. You see, she was the last person seen in the company of the deceased; she had a grievance against him; she is left-handed, and you remember that the murder was committed by a left-handed person."

"Anything else?"

"Yes. I have seen those Italians, and the whole thing was a put-up job. A woman, in a widow's dress and veil, paid them to go and play the fool outside the building, and she gave them the letter that was left with the porter. They haven't identified her yet, but she seems to agree in size with Miss Curtis."

"And how did she get out of the chambers, with the door bolted on the inside?"

"Ah, there you are! That's a mystery at present—unless you can give us an explanation." The inspector made this qualification with a faint grin, and added: "As there was no one in the place when we broke into it, the murderer must have got out somehow. You can't deny that."

"I do deny it, nevertheless," said Thorndyke. "You look surprised," he continued (which was undoubtedly true), "but yet the whole thing is exceedingly obvious. The explanation struck me directly I looked at the body. There was evidently no practicable exit from the flat, and there was certainly no one in it when you entered. Clearly, then, the murderer had never been in the place at all."

"I don't follow you in the least," said the inspector.

"Well," said Thorndyke, "as I have finished with the case, and am handing it over to you, I will put the evidence before you *seriatim*. Now, I think we are agreed that, at the moment when the blow was struck, the deceased was standing before the fireplace, winding the clock. The dagger entered obliquely from the left, and, if you recall its position, you will remember that its hilt pointed directly towards an open window."

"Which was forty feet from the ground."

"Yes. And now we will consider the very peculiar character of the weapon with which the crime was committed."

He had placed his hand upon the knob of a drawer, when we were interrupted by a knock at the door. I sprang up, and, opening it, admitted no less a person than the porter of Brackenhurst Chambers. The man looked somewhat surprised on recognising our visitors, but advanced to Thorndyke, drawing a folded paper from his pocket.

"I've found the article you were looking for, sir," said he, "and a rare hunt I had for it. It had stuck in the leaves of one of them shrubs."

Thorndyke opened the packet, and, having glanced inside, laid it on the table.

"Thank you," said he, pushing a sovereign across to the gratified official. "The inspector has your name, I think?"

"He have, sir," replied the porter; and, pocketing his fee, he departed, beaming.

"To return to the dagger," said Thorndyke, opening the drawer. "It was a very peculiar one, as I have said, and as you will see from this model, which is an exact duplicate." Here he exhibited Polton's production to the astonished detective. "You see that it is extraordinarily slender, and free from projections, and of unusual materials. You also see that it was obviously not made by an ordinary dagger-maker; that, in spite of the Italian word scrawled on it, there is plainly written all over it 'British mechanic.' The blade is made from a strip of common three-quarter-inch tool steel; the hilt is turned from an aluminium rod; and there is not a line of engraving on it that could not be produced in a lathe by any engineer's apprentice.

"Even the boss at the top is mechanical, for it is just like an ordinary hexagon nut. Then, notice the dimensions, as shown on my drawing. The parts A and B, which just project beyond the blade, are exactly similar in diameter—and such exactness could hardly be accidental. They are each parts of a circle having a diameter of 10.9 millimetres—a dimension which happens, by a singular coincidence, to be exactly the calibre of the old Chassepot rifle, specimens of which are now on sale at several shops in London. Here is one, for instance."

He fetched the rifle that he had bought, from the corner in which it was standing, and, lifting the dagger by its point, slipped the hilt into the muzzle. When he let go, the dagger slid quietly down the barrel, until its hilt appeared in the open breech.

"Good God!" exclaimed Marchmont. "You don't suggest that the dagger was shot from a gun?"

"I do, indeed; and you now see the reason for the aluminium hilt—to diminish the weight of the already heavy projectile—and also for this hexagonal boss on the end?"

"No, I do not," said the inspector; "but I say that you are suggesting an impossibility."

"Then," replied Thorndyke, "I must explain and demonstrate. To begin with, this projectile had to travel point foremost; therefore it had to be made to spin—and it certainly was spinning when it entered the body, as the clothing and the wound showed us. Now, to make it spin, it had to be fired from a rifled barrel; but as the hilt would not engage in the rifling, it had to be fitted with something that would. That something was evidently a soft metal washer, which fitted on to this hexagon, and which would be pressed into the grooves of the rifling, and so spin the dagger, but would drop off as soon as the weapon left the barrel. Here is such a washer, which Polton has made for us."

He laid on the table a metal disc, with a hexagonal hole through it.

"This is all very ingenious," said the inspector, "but I say it is impossible and fantastic."

"It certainly sounds rather improbable," Marchmont agreed.

"We will see," said Thorndyke. "Here is a makeshift cartridge of Polton's manufacture, containing an eighth charge of smokeless powder for a 20-bore gun."

He fitted the washer on to the boss of the dagger in the open breech of the rifle, pushed it into the barrel, inserted the cartridge, and closed the breech. Then, opening the office-door, he displayed a target of padded strawboard against the wall.

"The length of the two rooms," said he, "gives us a distance of thirty-two feet. Will you shut the windows, Jervis?"

I complied, and he then pointed the rifle at the target. There was a dull report—much less loud than I had expected—and when we looked at the target, we saw the dagger driven in up to its hilt at the margin of the bull's-eye.

"You see," said Thorndyke, laying down the rifle, "that the thing is practicable. Now for the evidence as to the actual occurrence. First, on the original dagger there are linear scratches which exactly correspond with the grooves of the rifling. Then there is the fact that the dagger was certainly spinning from left to right—in the direction of the rifling, that is—when it entered the body. And then there is this, which, as you heard, the porter found in the garden."

He opened the paper packet. In it lay a metal disc, perforated by a hexagonal hole. Stepping into the office, he picked up from the floor the washer that he had put on the dagger, and laid it on the paper beside the other. The two discs were identical in size, and the margin of each was indented with identical markings, corresponding to the rifling of the barrel.

The inspector gazed at the two discs in silence for a while; then, looking up at Thorndyke, he said:

"I give in, Doctor. You're right, beyond all doubt; but how you came to think of it beats me into fits. The only question now is, Who fired the gun, and why wasn't the report heard?"

"As to the latter," said Thorndyke, "it is probable that he used a compressed-air attachment, not only to diminish the noise, but also to prevent any traces of the explosive from being left on the dagger. As to the former, I think I can give you the murderer's name; but we had better take the evidence in order. You may remember," he continued, "that when Dr. Jervis stood as if winding the clock, I chalked a mark on the floor where he stood. Now, standing on that marked spot, and looking out of the open window, I could see two of the windows of a house nearly opposite. They were the second-and third-floor windows of No. 6, Cotman Street. The second-floor is occupied by a firm of architects; the third-floor by a commission agent named Thomas Barlow. I called on Mr. Barlow, but before describing my visit, I will refer to another matter. You haven't those threatening letters about you, I suppose?"

"Yes, I have," said the inspector; and he drew forth a wallet from his breast-pocket.

"Let us take the first one, then," said Thorndyke. "You see that the paper and envelope are of the very commonest, and the writing illiterate. But the ink does not agree with this. Illiterate people usually buy their ink in penny bottles. Now, this envelope is addressed with

Draper's dichroic ink—a superior office ink, sold only in large bottles—and the red ink in which the note is written is an unfixed, scarlet ink, such as is used by draughtsmen, and has been used, as you can see, in a stylographic pen. But the most interesting thing about this letter is the design drawn at the top. In an artistic sense, the man could not draw, and the anatomical details of the skull are ridiculous. Yet the drawing is very neat. It has the clean, wiry line of a machine drawing, and is done with a steady, practised hand.

"It is also perfectly symmetrical; the skull, for instance, is exactly in the centre, and, when we examine it through a lens, we see why it is so, for we discover traces of a pencilled centre-line and ruled cross-lines. Moreover, the lens reveals a tiny particle of draughtsman's soft, red, rubber, with which the pencil lines were taken out; and all these facts, taken together, suggest that the drawing was made by someone accustomed to making accurate mechanical drawings. And now we will return to Mr. Barlow. He was out when I called, but I took the liberty of glancing round the office, and this is what I saw. On the mantelshelf was a twelve-inch flat boxwood rule, such as engineers use, a piece of soft, red rubber, and a stone bottle of Draper's dichroic ink.

"I obtained, by a simple ruse, a specimen of the office notepaper and the ink. We will examine it presently. I found that Mr. Barlow is a new tenant, that he is rather short, wears a wig and spectacles, and always wears a glove on his left hand. He left the office at 8.30 this morning, and no one saw him arrive. He had with him a square case, and a narrow, oblong one about five feet in length; and he took a cab to Victoria, and apparently caught the 8.51 train to Chatham."

"Ah!" exclaimed the inspector.

"But," continued Thorndyke, "now examine those three letters, and compare them with this note that I wrote in Mr. Barlow's office. You see that the paper is of the same make, with the same water-mark, but that is of no great significance. What is of crucial importance is this: You see, in each of these letters, two tiny indentations near the bottom corner. Somebody has used compasses or drawing-pins over the packet of notepaper, and the points have made little indentations, which have marked several of the sheets.

"Now, notepaper is cut to its size after it is folded, and if you stick a pin into the top sheet of a section, the indentations on all the underlying sheets will be at exactly similar distances from the edges and corners of the sheet. But you see that these little dents are all at the same distance from the edges and the corner." He demonstrated the fact with a pair of compasses. "And now look at this sheet, which I obtained at Mr. Barlow's office. There are two little indentations—rather faint, but quite visible—near the bottom corner, and when we measure them with the compasses, we find that they are exactly the same distance apart as the others, and the same distance from the edges and the bottom corner. The irresistible conclusion is that these four sheets came from the same packet."

The inspector started up from his chair, and faced Thorndyke. "Who is this Mr. Barlow?" he asked.

"That," replied Thorndyke, "is for you to determine; but I can give you a useful hint. There is only one person who benefits by the death of Alfred Hartridge, but he benefits to the extent of twenty thousand pounds. His name is Leonard Wolfe, and I learn from Mr. Marchmont that he is a man of indifferent character—a gambler and a spendthrift. By profession he is an engineer, and he is a capable mechanician. In appearance he is thin, short, fair, and clean-shaven, and he has lost the middle finger of his left hand. Mr. Barlow is also short, thin, and fair, but wears a wig, a board, and spectacles, and always wears a glove on his left hand. I have seen the handwriting of both these gentlemen, and should say that it would be difficult to distinguish one from the other."

"That's good enough for me," said the inspector. "Give me his address, and I'll have Miss Curtis released at once."

****

The same night Leonard Wolfe was arrested at Eltham, in the very act of burying in his garden a large and powerful compressed-air rifle. He was never brought to trial, however, for he had in his pocket a more portable weapon—a large-bore Derringer pistol—with which he managed to terminate an exceedingly ill-spent life.

"And, after all," was Thorndyke's comment, when he heard of the event, "he had his uses. He has relieved society of two very bad men, and he has given us a most instructive case. He has shown us how a clever and ingenious criminal may take endless pains to mislead and delude the police, and yet, by inattention to trivial details, may scatter clues broadcast. We can only say to the criminal class generally, in both respects, '*Go thou and do likewise.*'"

The Mandarin's Pearl

Mr. Brodribb stretched out his toes on the kerb before the blazing fire with the air of a man who is by no means insensible to physical comfort.

"You are really an extraordinarily polite fellow, Thorndyke," said he.

He was an elderly man, rosy-gilled, portly, and convivial, to whom a mass of bushy, white hair, an expansive double chin, and a certain prim sumptuousness of dress imparted an air of old-world distinction. Indeed, as he dipped an amethystine nose into his wine-glass, and gazed thoughtfully at the glowing end of his cigar, he looked the very type of the well-to-do lawyer of an older generation.

"You are really an extraordinarily polite fellow, Thorndyke," said Mr. Brodribb.

"I know," replied Thorndyke. "But why this reference to an admitted fact?"

"The truth has just dawned on me," said the solicitor. "Here am I, dropping in on you, uninvited and unannounced, sitting in your own armchair before your fire, smoking your cigars, drinking your Burgundy—and deuced good Burgundy, too, let me add—and you have not dropped a single hint of curiosity as to what has brought me here."

"I take the gifts of the gods, you see, and ask no questions," said Thorndyke.

"Devilish handsome of you, Thorndyke—unsociable beggar like you, too," rejoined Mr. Brodribb, a fan of wrinkles spreading out genially from the corners of his eyes; "but the fact is I have come, in a sense, on business—always glad of a pretext to look you up, as you know—but I want to take your opinion on a rather queer case. It is about young Calverley. You remember Horace Calverley? Well, this is his son. Horace and I were schoolmates, you know, and after his death the boy, Fred, hung on to me rather. We're near neighbours down at Weybridge, and very good friends. I like Fred. He's a good fellow, though cranky, like all his people."

"What has happened to Fred Calverley?" Thorndyke asked, as the solicitor paused.

"Why, the fact is," said Mr. Brodribb, "just lately he seems to be going a bit queer—not mad, mind you—at least, I think not—but undoubtedly queer. Now, there is a good deal of property, and a good many highly interested relatives, and, as a natural consequence, there is some talk of getting him certified. They're afraid he may do something involving the estate or develop homicidal tendencies, and they talk of possible suicide—you remember his father's death—but I say that's all bunkum. The fellow is just a bit cranky, and nothing more."

"What are his symptoms?" asked Thorndyke.

"Oh, he thinks he is being followed about and watched, and he has delusions; sees himself in the glass with the wrong face, and that sort of thing, you know."

"You are not highly circumstantial," Thorndyke remarked.

Mr. Brodribb looked at me with a genial smile.

"What a glutton for facts this fellow is, Jervis. But you're right, Thorndyke; I'm vague. However, Fred will be here presently. We travel down together, and I took the liberty of asking him to call for me. We'll get him to tell you about his delusions, if you don't mind. He's not shy about them. And meanwhile I'll give you a few preliminary facts. The trouble began about a year ago. He was in a railway accident, and that knocked him all to pieces. Then he went for a voyage to recruit, and the ship broke her propeller-shaft in a storm and became helpless. That didn't improve the state of his nerves. Then he went down the Mediterranean, and after a month or two, back he came, no better than when he started. But here he is, I expect."

He went over to the door and admitted a tall, frail young man whom Thorndyke welcomed with quiet geniality, and settled in a chair by the fire. I looked curiously at our visitor. He was a typical neurotic—slender, fragile, eager. Wide-open blue eyes with broad pupils, in which I could plainly see the characteristic "*hippus*"—that incessant change of size that marks the unstable nervous equilibrium—parted lips, and wandering taper fingers, were as the *stigmata* of his disorder. He was of the stuff out of which prophets and devotees, martyrs, reformers, and third-rate poets are made.

"I have been telling Dr. Thorndyke about these nervous troubles of yours," said Mr. Brodribb presently. "I hope you don't mind. He is an old friend, you know, and he is very much interested."

"It is very good of him," said Calverley. Then he flushed deeply, and added: "But they are not really nervous, you know. They can't be merely subjective."

"You think they can't be?" said Thorndyke.

"No, I am sure they are not." He flushed again like a girl, and looked earnestly at Thorndyke with his big, dreamy eyes. "But you doctors," he said, "are so dreadfully sceptical of all spiritual phenomena. You are such materialists."

"Yes," said Mr. Brodribb; "the doctors are not hot on the supernatural, and that's the fact."

"Supposing you tell us about your experiences," said Thorndyke persuasively. "Give us a chance to believe, if we can't explain away."

Calverley reflected for a few moments; then, looking earnestly at Thorndyke, he said: "Very well; if it won't bore you, I will. It is a curious story."

"I have told Dr. Thorndyke about your voyage and your trip down the Mediterranean," said Mr. Brodribb.

"Then," said Calverley, "I will begin with the events that are actually connected with these strange visitations. The first of these occurred in Marseilles. I was in a curio-shop there, looking over some Algerian and Moorish tilings, when my attention was attracted by a sort of charm or pendant that hung in a glass case. It was not particularly beautiful, but its appearance was quaint and curious, and took my fancy. It consisted of an oblong block of ebony in which was set a single pear-shaped pearl more than three-quarters of an inch long. The sides of the ebony block were lacquered—probably to conceal a joint—and bore a number of Chinese characters, and at the top was a little gold image with a hole through it, presumably for a string to suspend it by. Excepting for the pearl, the whole thing was uncommonly like one of those ornamental tablets of Chinese ink.

"Now, I had taken a fancy to the thing, and I can afford to indulge my fancies in moderation. The man wanted five pounds for it; he assured me that the pearl was a genuine one of fine quality, and obviously did not believe it himself. To me, however, it looked like a real pearl, and I determined to take the risk; so I paid the money, and he bowed me out with a smile—I may almost say a grin—of satisfaction. He would not have been so well pleased if he had followed me to a jeweller's to whom I took it for an expert opinion; for the jeweller pronounced the pearl to be undoubtedly genuine, and worth anything up to a thousand pounds.

"A day or two later, I happened to show my new purchase to some men whom I knew, who had dropped in at Marseilles in their yacht. They were highly amused at my having bought the thing, and when I told them what I had paid for it, they positively howled with derision.

"'Why, you silly guffin,' said one of them, a man named Halliwell, 'I could have had it ten days ago for half a sovereign, or probably five shillings. I wish now I had bought it; then I could have sold it to you.'

"It seemed that a sailor had been hawking the pendant round the harbour, and had been on board the yacht with it.

"'Deuced anxious the beggar was to get rid of it, too,' said Halliwell, grinning at the recollection. 'Swore it was a genuine pearl of priceless value, and was willing to deprive himself of it for the trifling sum of half a jimmy. But we'd heard that sort of thing before. However, the curio-man seems to have speculated on the chance of meeting with a greenhorn, and he seems to have pulled it off. Lucky curio man!'

"I listened patiently to their gibes, and when they had talked themselves out I told them about the jeweller. They were most frightfully sick; and when we had taken the pendant to a dealer in gems who happened to be staying in the town, and he had offered me five hundred pounds for it, their language wasn't fit for a divinity students' debating club. Naturally the story got noised abroad, and when I left, it was the talk of the place. The general opinion was that the sailor, who was traced to a tea-ship that had put into the harbour, had stolen it from some Chinese passenger; and no less than seventeen different Chinamen came forward to claim it as their stolen property.

"Soon after this I returned to England, and, as my nerves were still in a very shaky state, I came to live with my cousin Alfred, who has a large house at Weybridge. At this time he had a friend staying with him, a certain Captain Raggerton, and the two men appeared to be on very intimate terms. I did not take to Raggerton at all. He was a good-looking man, pleasant in his manners, and remarkably plausible. But the fact is—I am speaking in strict confidence, of course—he was a bad egg. He had been in the Guards, and I don't quite know why he left; but I do know that he played bridge and baccarat pretty heavily at several clubs, and that he had a reputation for being a rather uncomfortably lucky player. He did a good deal at the race-meetings, too, and was in general such an obvious undesirable that I could never understand my cousin's intimacy with him, though I must say that Alfred's habits had changed somewhat for the worse since I had left England.

"The fame of my purchase seems to have preceded me, for when, one day, I produced the pendant to show them, I found that they knew all about it. Raggerton had heard the story from a naval man, and I gathered vaguely that he had heard something that I had not, and that he did not care to tell me; for when my cousin and he talked about the pearl, which they did pretty often, certain significant looks passed between them, and certain veiled references were made which I could not fail to notice.

"One day I happened to be telling them of a curious incident that occurred on my way home. I had travelled to England on one of Holt's big China boats, not liking the crowd and bustle of the regular passenger-lines. Now, one afternoon, when we had been at sea a couple of days, I took a book down to my berth, intending to have a quiet read till tea-time. Soon, however, I dropped off into a doze, and must have remained asleep for over an hour. I awoke suddenly, and as I opened my eyes, I perceived that the door of the state-room was half-open, and a well-dressed Chinaman, in native costume, was looking in at me. He closed the door immediately, and I remained for a few moments paralyzed by the start that he had given me. Then I leaped from my bunk, opened the door, and looked out. But the alley-way was empty. The Chinaman had vanished as if by magic.

"This little occurrence made me quite nervous for a day or two, which was very foolish of me; but my nerves were all on edge—and I am afraid they are still."

"Yes," said Thorndyke. "There was nothing mysterious about the affair. These boats carry a Chinese crew, and the man you saw was probably a Serang, or whatever they call the gang-captains on these vessels. Or he may have been a native passenger who had strayed into the wrong part of the ship."

"Exactly," agreed our client. "But to return to Raggerton. He listened with quite extraordinary interest as I was telling this story, and when I had finished he looked very queerly at my cousin.

"'A deuced odd thing, this, Calverley,' said he. 'Of course, it may be only a coincidence, but it really does look as if there was something, after all, in that—'

"'Shut up, Raggerton,' said my cousin. 'We don't want any of that rot.'

"'What is he talking about?' I asked.

"'Oh, it's only a rotten, silly yarn that he has picked up somewhere. You're not to tell him, Raggerton.'

"'I don't see why I am not to be told,' I said, rather sulkily. 'I'm not a baby.'

"'No,' said Alfred, 'but you're an invalid. You don't want any horrors.'

"In effect, he refused to go into the matter any further, and I was left on tenter-hooks of curiosity.

"However, the very next day I got Raggerton alone in the smoking-room, and had a little talk with him. He had just dropped a hundred pounds on a double event that hadn't come off, and I expected to find him pliable. Nor was I disappointed, for, when we had negotiated a little loan, he was entirely at my service, and willing to tell me everything, on my promising not to give him away to Alfred.

"'Now, you understand,' he said, 'that this yarn about your pearl is nothing but a damn silly fable that's been going the round in Marseilles. I don't know where it came from, or what sort of demented rotter invented it; I had it from a Johnnie in the Mediterranean Squadron, and you can have a copy of his letter if you want it.'

"I said that I did want it. Accordingly, that same evening he handed me a copy of the narrative extracted from his friend's letter, the substance of which was this:

"About four months ago there was lying in Canton Harbour a large English barque. Her name is not mentioned, but that is not material to the story. She had got her cargo stowed and her crew signed on, and was only waiting for certain official formalities to be completed before putting to sea on her homeward voyage. Just ahead of her, at the same quay, was a Danish ship that had been in collision outside, and was now laid up pending the decision of the Admiralty Court. She had been unloaded, and her crew paid off, with the exception of one elderly man, who remained on board as ship-keeper. Now, a considerable part of the cargo of the English barque was the property of a certain wealthy *mandarin*, and this person had been about the vessel a good deal while she was taking in her lading.

"One day, when the *mandarin* was on board the barque, it happened that three of the seamen were sitting in the galley smoking and chatting with the cook—an elderly Chinaman named Wo-li—and the latter, pointing out the *mandarin* to the sailors, expatiated on his enormous wealth, assuring them that he was commonly believed to carry on his person articles of sufficient value to buy up the entire lading of a ship.

"Now, unfortunately for the *mandarin*, it chanced that these three sailors were about the greatest rascals on board; which is saying a good deal when one considers the ordinary moral standard that prevails in the forecastle of a sailing-ship. Nor was Wo-li himself an angel; in fact, he was a consummate villain, and seems to have been the actual originator of the plot which was presently devised to rob the *mandarin*.

"This plot was as remarkable for its simplicity as for its cold-blooded barbarity. On the evening before the barque sailed, the three seamen, Nilsson, Foucault, and Parratt, proceeded to the Danish ship with a supply of whisky, made the ship-keeper royally drunk, and locked him up in an empty berth. Meanwhile Wo-li made a secret communication to the *mandarin* to the effect that certain stolen property, believed to be his, had been secreted in the hold of the empty ship. Thereupon the *mandarin* came down hot-foot to the quay-side, and was received on board by the three seamen, who had got the covers off the after-hatch in readiness. Parratt now ran down the iron ladder to show the way, and the *mandarin* followed; but when they reached the lower deck, and looked down the hatch into the black darkness of the lower hold, he seems to have taken fright, and begun to climb up again.

"Meanwhile Nilsson had made a running bowline in the end of a loose halyard that was rove through a block aloft, and had been used for hoisting out the cargo. As the *mandarin* came up, he leaned over the coaming of the hatch, dropped the noose over the Chinaman's head, jerked it tight, and then he and Foucault hove on the fall of the rope. The unfortunate Chinaman was dragged from the ladder, and, as he swung clear, the two rascals let go the rope, allowing him to drop through the hatches into the lower hold. Then they belayed the rope, and went down below. Parratt had already lighted a slush-lamp, by the glimmer of which they could see the *mandarin* swinging to and fro like a pendulum within a few feet of the ballast, and still quivering and twitching in his death-throes.

"They were now joined by Wo-li, who had watched the proceedings from the quay, and the four villains proceeded, without loss of time, to rifle the body as it hung. To their surprise and disgust, they found nothing of value excepting an ebony pendant set with a single large pearl; but Wo-li, though evidently disappointed at the nature of the booty, assured his comrades that this alone was well worth the hazard, pointing out the great size and exceptional beauty of the pearl.

As to this, the seamen know nothing about pearls, but the thing was done, and had to be made the best of; so they made the rope fast to the lower deck-beams, cut off the remainder and unrove it from the block, and went back to their ship.

"It was twenty-four hours before the ship-keeper was sufficiently sober to break out of the berth in which he had been locked, by which time the barque was well out to sea; and it was another three days before the body of the *mandarin* was found. An active search was then made for the murderers, but as they were strangers to the ship-keeper, no clues to their whereabouts could be discovered.

"Meanwhile, the four murderers were a good deal exercised as to the disposal of the booty. Since it could not be divided, it was evident that it must be entrusted to the keeping of one of them. The choice in the first place fell upon Wo-li, in whose chest the pendant was deposited as soon as the party came on board, it being arranged that the Chinaman should produce the jewel for inspection by his confederates whenever called upon.

"For six weeks nothing out of the common occurred; but then a very singular event befell. The four conspirators were sitting outside the galley one evening, when suddenly the cook uttered a cry of amazement and horror. The other three turned to see what it was that had so disturbed their comrade, and then they, too, were struck dumb with consternation; for, standing at the door of the companion-hatch—the barque was a flush-decked vessel—was the *mandarin* whom they had left for dead. He stood quietly regarding them for fully a minute, while they stared at him transfixed with terror. Then he beckoned to them, and went below.

"So petrified were they with astonishment and mortal fear that they remained for a long time motionless and dumb. At last they plucked up courage, and began to make furtive inquiries among the crew; but no one—not even the steward—knew anything of any passengers, or, indeed, of any Chinaman, on board the ship, excepting Wo-li.

"At daybreak the next morning, when the cook's mate went to the galley to fill the coppers, he found Wo-li hanging from a hook in the ceiling. The cook's body was stiff and cold, and had evidently been hanging several hours. The report of the tragedy quickly spread through the ship, and the three conspirators hurried off to remove the pearl from the dead man's chest before the officers should come to examine it. The cheap lock was easily picked with a bent wire, and the jewel abstracted; but now the question arose as to who should take charge of it. The eagerness to be the actual custodian of the precious bauble, which had been at first displayed, now gave place to equally strong reluctance. But someone had to take charge of it, and after a long and angry discussion Nilsson was prevailed upon to stow it in his chest.

"A fortnight passed. The three conspirators went about their duties soberly, like men burdened with some secret anxiety, and in their leisure moments they would sit and talk with bated breath of the apparition at the companion-hatch, and the mysterious death of their late comrade.

"At last the blow fell.

"It was at the end of the second dog-watch that the hands were gathered on the forecastle, preparing to make sail after a spell of bad weather. Suddenly Nilsson gave a husky shout, and rushed at Parratt, holding out the key of his chest.

"'Here you, Parratt,' he exclaimed, 'go below and take that accursed thing out of my chest.'

"'What for—' demanded Parratt; and then he and Foucault, who was standing close by, looked aft to see what Nilsson was staring at.

"Instantly they both turned white as ghosts, and fell trembling so that they could hardly stand; for there was the *mandarin*, standing calmly by the companion, returning with a steady, impassive gaze their looks of horror. And even as they looked he beckoned and went below.

"'D'ye hear, Parratt—' gasped Nilsson; 'take my key and do what I say, or else—'

"But at this moment the order was given to go aloft and set all plain sail; the three men went off to their respective posts, Nilsson going up the fore-topmast rigging, and the other two to the main-top. Having finished their work aloft, Foucault and Parratt who were both in the port watch, came down on deck, and then, it being their watch below, they went and turned in.

"When they turned out with their watch at midnight, they looked about for Nilsson, who was in the starboard watch, but he was nowhere to be seen. Thinking he might have slipped below unobserved, they made no remark, though they were very uneasy about him; but when the starboard watch came on deck at four o'clock, and Nilsson did not appear with his mates, the two men became alarmed, and made inquiries about him. It was now discovered that no one had seen him since eight o'clock on the previous evening, and, this being reported to the officer of the watch, the latter ordered all hands to be called. But still Nilsson did not appear. A thorough search was now instituted, both below and aloft, and as there was still no sign of the missing man, it was concluded that he had fallen overboard.

"But at eight o'clock two men were sent aloft to shake out the fore-royal. They reached the yard almost simultaneously, and were just stepping on to the foot-ropes when one of them gave a shout; then the pair came sliding down a backstay, with faces as white as tallow. As soon as they reached the deck, they took the officer of the watch forward, and, standing on the heel of the bowsprit, pointed aloft. Several of the hands, including Foucault and Parratt, had followed, and all looked up; and there they saw the body of Nilsson, hanging on the front of the fore-topgallant sail. He was dangling at the end of a gasket, and bouncing up and down on the taut belly of the sail as the ship rose and fell to the scend of the sea.

"The two survivors were now in some doubt about having anything further to do with the pearl. But the great value of the jewel, and the consideration that it was now to be divided between two instead of four, tempted them. They abstracted it from Nilsson's chest, and then, as they could not come to an agreement in any other way, they decided to settle who should take charge of it by tossing a coin. The coin was accordingly spun, and the pearl went to Foucault's chest.

"From this moment Foucault lived in a state of continual apprehension. When on deck, his eyes were for ever wandering towards the companion hatch, and during his watch below, when not asleep, he would sit moodily on his chest, lost in gloomy reflection. But a fortnight passed, then three weeks, and still nothing happened. Land was sighted, the Straits of Gibraltar passed, and the end of the voyage was but a matter of days. And still the dreaded *mandarin* made no sign.

"At length the ship was within twenty-four hours of Marseilles, to which port a large part of the cargo was consigned. Active preparations were being made for entering the port, and among other things the shore tackle was being overhauled. A share in this latter work fell to Foucault and Parratt, and about the middle of the second dog-watch—seven o'clock in the evening—they were sitting on the deck working an eye-splice in the end of a large rope. Suddenly Foucault, who was facing forward, saw his companion turn pale and stare aft with an expression of terror. He immediately turned and looked over his shoulder to see what Parratt was staring at. It was the *mandarin*, standing by the companion, gravely watching them; and as Foucault turned and met his gaze, the Chinaman beckoned and went below.

"For the rest of that day Parratt kept close to his terrified comrade, and during their watch below he endeavoured to remain awake, that he might keep his friend in view. Nothing happened through the night, and the following morning, when they came on deck for the forenoon watch, their port was well in sight. The two men now separated for the first time, Parratt going aft to take his trick at the wheel, and Foucault being set to help in getting ready the ground tackle.

"Half an hour later Parratt saw the mate stand on the rail and lean outboard, holding on to the mizzen-shrouds while he stared along the ship's side. Then he jumped on to the deck and shouted angrily: 'Forward, there! What the deuce is that man up to under the starboard cat-head—'

"The men on the forecastle rushed to the side and looked over; two of them leaned over the rail with the bight of a rope between them, and a third came running aft to the mate. 'It's Foucault, sir,' Parratt heard him say. 'He's hanged hisself from the cat-head.'

"As soon as he was off duty, Parratt made his way to his dead comrade's chest, and, opening it with his pick-lock, took out the pearl. It was now his sole property, and, as the ship was within an hour or two of her destination, he thought he had little to fear from its murdered owner. As soon as the vessel was alongside the wharf, he would slip ashore and get rid of the jewel, even if he sold it at a comparatively low price. The thing looked perfectly simple.

"In actual practice, however, it turned out quite otherwise. He began by accosting a well-dressed stranger and offering the pendant for fifty pounds; but the only reply that he got was a knowing smile and a shake of the head. When this experience had been repeated a dozen times or more, and he had been followed up and down the streets for nearly an hour by a suspicious *gendarme*, he began to grow anxious. He visited quite a number of ships and yachts in the harbour, and at each refusal the price of his treasure came down, until he was eager to sell it for a few *francs*.

"But still no one would have it. Everyone took it for granted that the pearl was a sham, and most of the persons whom he accosted assumed that it had been stolen. The position was getting desperate. Evening was approaching—the time of the dreaded dog-watches— and still the pearl was in his possession. Gladly would he now have given it away for nothing, but he dared not try, for this would lay him open to the strongest suspicion.

"At last, in a by-street, he came upon the shop of a curio-dealer. Putting on a careless and cheerful manner, he entered and offered the pendant for ten *francs*. The dealer looked at it, shook his head, and handed it back.

"'What will you give me for it—' demanded Parratt, breaking out into a cold sweat at the prospect of a final refusal.

"The dealer felt in his pocket, drew out a couple of *francs*, and held them out.

"'Very well,' said Parratt. He took the money as calmly as he could, and marched out of the shop, with a gasp of relief, leaving the pendant in the dealer's hand.

"The jewel was hung up in a glass case, and nothing more was thought about it until some ten days later, when an English tourist, who came into the shop, noticed it and took a liking to it. Thereupon the dealer offered it to him for five pounds, assuring him that it was a genuine pearl, a statement that, to his amazement, the stranger evidently believed. He was then deeply afflicted at not having asked a higher price, but the bargain had been struck, and the Englishman went off with his purchase.

"This was the story told by Captain Raggerton's friend, and I have given it to you in full detail, having read the manuscript over many times since it was given to me. No doubt you will regard it as a mere traveller's tale, and consider me a superstitious idiot for giving any credence to it."

"It certainly seems more remarkable for picturesqueness than for credibility," Thorndyke agreed. "May I ask," he continued, "whether Captain Raggerton's friend gave any explanation as to how this singular story came to his knowledge, or to that of anybody else?"

"Oh yes," replied Calverley; "I forgot to mention that the seaman, Parratt, very shortly after he had sold the pearl, fell down the hatch into the hold as the ship was unloading, and was very badly injured. He was taken to the hospital, where he died on the following day; and it was while he was lying there in a dying condition that he confessed to the murder, and gave this circumstantial account of it."

"I see," said Thorndyke; "and I understand that you accept the story as literally true?"

"Undoubtedly." Calverley flushed defiantly as he returned Thorndyke's look, and continued: "You see, I am not a man of science: therefore my beliefs are not limited to things that can be weighed and measured. There are things, Dr. Thorndyke, which are outside the range of our puny intellects; things that science, with its arrogant materialism, puts aside and ignores with close-shut eyes. I prefer to believe in things which obviously exist, even though I cannot explain them. It is the humbler and, I think, the wiser attitude."

"But, my dear Fred," protested Mr. Brodribb, "this is a rank fairy-tale."

Calverley turned upon the solicitor. "If you had seen what I have seen, you would not only believe: you would *know*."

"Tell us what you have seen, then," said Mr. Brodribb.

"I will, if you wish to hear it," said Calverley. "I will continue the strange history of the *Mandarin's Pearl*."

He lit a fresh cigarette and continued:

"The night I came to Beechhurst—that is my cousin's house, you know—a rather absurd thing happened, which I mention on account of its connection with what has followed. I had gone to my room early, and sat for some time writing letters before getting ready for bed. When I had finished my letters, I started on a tour of inspection of my room. I was then, you must remember, in a very nervous state, and it had become my habit to examine the room in which I was to sleep before undressing, looking under the bed, and in any cupboards and closets that there happened to be.

"Now, on looking round my new room, I perceived that there was a second door, and I at once proceeded to open it to see where it led to. As soon as I opened the door, I got a terrible start. I found myself looking into a narrow closet or passage, lined with pegs, on which the servant had hung some of my clothes; at the farther end was another door, and, as I stood looking into the closet, I observed, with startled amazement, a man standing holding the door half-open, and silently regarding me. I stood for a moment staring at him, with my heart thumping and my limbs all of a tremble; then I slammed the door and ran off to look for my cousin.

"He was in the billiard-room with Raggerton, and the pair looked up sharply as I entered.

"'Alfred,' I said, 'where does that passage lead to out of my room—'

"'Lead to—' said he. 'Why, it doesn't lead anywhere. It used to open into a cross corridor, but when the house was altered, the corridor was done away with, and this passage closed up. It is only a cupboard now.'

"'Well, there's a man in it—or there was just now.'

"'Nonsense!' he exclaimed; 'impossible! Let us go and look at the place.'

"He and Raggerton rose, and we went together to my room. As we flung open the door of the closet and looked in, we all three burst into a laugh. There were three men now looking at us from the open door at the other end, and the mystery was solved. A large mirror had been placed at the end of the closet to cover the partition which cut it off from the cross corridor.

"This incident naturally exposed me to a good deal of chaff from my cousin and Captain Raggerton; but I often wished that the mirror had not been placed there, for it happened over and over again that, going to the cupboard hurriedly, and not thinking of the mirror, I got quite a bad shock on being confronted by a figure apparently coming straight at me through an open door. In fact, it annoyed me so much, in my nervous state, that I even thought of asking my cousin to give me a different room; but, happening to refer to the matter when talking to Raggerton, I found the captain so scornful of my cowardice that my pride was touched, and I let the affair drop.

"And now I come to a very strange occurrence, which I shall relate quite frankly, although I know beforehand that you will set me down as a liar or a lunatic. I had been away from home for a fortnight, and as I returned rather late at night, I went straight to my room. Having partly undressed, I took my clothes in one hand and a candle in the other, and opened the cupboard door. I stood for a moment looking nervously at my double, standing, candle in hand, looking at me through the open door at the other end of the passage; then I entered, and, setting the candle on a shelf, proceeded to hang up my clothes.

"I had hung them up, and had just reached up for the candle, when my eye was caught by something strange in the mirror. It no longer reflected the candle in my hand, but instead of it, a large coloured paper lantern. I stood petrified with astonishment, and gazed into the mirror; and then I saw that my own reflection was changed, too; that, in place of my own figure, was that of an elderly Chinaman, who stood regarding me with stony calm.

"I must have stood for near upon a minute, unable to move and scarce able to breathe, face to face with that awful figure. At length I turned to escape, and, as I turned, he turned also, and I could see him, over my shoulder, hurrying away. As I reached the door, I halted for a moment, looking back with the door in my hand, holding the candle above my head; and even so *he* halted, looking back at me, with his hand upon the door and his lantern held above his head.

"I was so much upset that I could not go to bed for some hours, but continued to pace the room, in spite of my fatigue. Now and again I was impelled, irresistibly, to peer into the cupboard, but nothing was to be seen in the mirror save my own figure, candle in hand, peeping in at me through the half-open door. And each time that I looked into my own white, horror-stricken face, I shut the door hastily and turned away with a shudder; for the pegs, with the clothes hanging on them, seemed to call to me. I went to bed at last, and before I fell asleep I formed the resolution that, if I was spared until the next day, I would write to the British Consul at Canton, and offer to restore the pearl to the relatives of the murdered *mandarin*.

"On the following day I wrote and despatched the letter, after which I felt more composed, though I was haunted continually by the recollection of that stony, impassive figure; and from time to time I felt an irresistible impulse to go and look in at the door of the closet, at the mirror and the pegs with the clothes hanging from them. I told my cousin of the visitation that I had received, but he merely laughed, and was frankly incredulous; while the Captain bluntly advised me not to be a superstitious donkey.

"For some days after this I was left in peace, and began to hope that my letter had appeased the spirit of the murdered man; but on the fifth day, about six o'clock in the evening, happening to want some papers that I had left in the pocket of a coat which was hanging in the closet, I went in to get them. I took in no candle, as it was not yet dark, but left the door wide open to light me. The coat that I wanted was near the end of the closet, not more than four paces from the mirror, and as I went towards it I watched my reflection rather nervously as it advanced to meet me. I found my coat, and as I felt for the papers, I still kept a suspicious eye on my double.

"And, even as I looked, a most strange phenomenon appeared: the mirror seemed for an instant to darken or cloud over, and then, as it cleared again, I saw, standing dark against the light of the open door behind him, the figure of the *mandarin*. After a single glance, I ran out of the closet, shaking with agitation; but as I turned to shut the door, I noticed that it was my own figure that was reflected in the glass. The Chinaman had vanished in an instant.

"It now became evident that my letter had not served its purpose, and I was plunged in despair; the more so since, on this day, I felt again the dreadful impulse to go and look at the pegs on the walls of the closet. There was no mistaking the meaning of that impulse, and each time that I went, I dragged myself away reluctantly, though shivering with horror. One circumstance, indeed, encouraged me a little; the *mandarin* had not, on either occasion, beckoned to me as he had done to the sailors, so that perhaps some way of escape yet lay open to me.

"During the next few days I considered very earnestly what measures I could take to avert the doom that seemed to be hanging over me. The simplest plan, that of passing the pearl on to some other person, was out of the question; it would be nothing short of murder. On the other hand, I could not wait for an answer to my letter; for even if I remained alive, I felt that my reason would have given way long before the reply reached me. But while I was debating what I should do, the *mandarin* appeared to me again; and then, after an interval of only two days, he came to me once more. That was last night. I remained gazing at him, fascinated, with my flesh creeping, as he stood, lantern in hand, looking steadily in my face. At last he held out his hand to me, as if asking me to give him the pearl; then the mirror darkened, and he vanished in a flash; and in the place where he had stood there was my own reflection looking at me out of the glass.

"That last visitation decided me. When I left home this morning the pearl was in my pocket, and as I came over Waterloo Bridge, I leaned over the parapet and flung the thing into the water. After that I felt quite relieved for a time; I had shaken the accursed thing off without involving anyone in the curse that it carried. But presently I began to feel fresh misgivings, and the conviction has been growing upon me all day that I have done the wrong thing. I have only placed it for ever beyond the reach of its owner, whereas I ought to have burnt it, after the Chinese fashion, so that its non-material essence could have joined the spiritual body of him to whom it had belonged when both were clothed with material substance.

"But it can't be altered now. For good or for evil, the thing is done, and God alone knows what the end of it will be."

As he concluded, Calverley uttered a deep sigh, and covered his face with his slender, delicate hands. For a space we were all silent and, I think, deeply moved; for, grotesquely unreal as the whole thing was, there was a pathos, and even a tragedy, in it that we all felt to be very real indeed.

Suddenly Mr. Brodribb started and looked at his watch.

"Good gracious, Calverley, we shall lose our train."

The young man pulled himself together and stood up. "We shall just do it if we go at once," said he. "Goodbye," he added, shaking Thorndyke's hand and mine. "You have been very patient, and I have been rather prosy, I am afraid. Come along, Mr. Brodribb."

Thorndyke and I followed them out on to the landing, and I heard my colleague say to the solicitor in a low tone, but very earnestly: "Get him away from that house, Brodribb, and don't let him out of your sight for a moment."

I did not catch the solicitor's reply, if he made any, but when we were back in our room I noticed that Thorndyke was more agitated than I had ever seen him.

"I ought not to have let them go," he exclaimed. "Confound me! If I had had a grain of wit, I should have made them lose their train."

He lit his pipe and fell to pacing the room with long strides, his eyes bent on the floor with an expression sternly reflective. At last, finding him hopelessly taciturn, I knocked out my pipe and went to bed.

As I was dressing on the following morning, Thorndyke entered my room. His face was grave even to sternness, and he held a telegram in his hand.

"I am going to Weybridge this morning," he said shortly, holding the "flimsy" out to me. "Shall you come?"

I took the paper from him, and read:

Come, for God's sake! F. C. is dead. You will understand.—Brodribb.

I handed him back the telegram, too much shocked for a moment to speak. The whole dreadful tragedy summed up in that curt message rose before me in an instant, and a wave of deep pity swept over me at this miserable end to the sad, empty life.

"What an awful thing, Thorndyke!" I exclaimed at length. "To be killed by a mere grotesque delusion."

"Do you think so?" he asked dryly. "Well, we shall see; but you will come?"

"Yes," I replied; and as he retired, I proceeded hurriedly to finish dressing.

Half an hour later, as we rose from a rapid breakfast, Polton came into the room, carrying a small roll-up case of tools and a bunch of skeleton keys.

"Will you have them in a bag, sir?" he asked.

"No," replied Thorndyke; "in my overcoat pocket. Oh, and here is a note, Polton, which I want you to take round to Scotland Yard. It is to the Assistant Commissioner, and you are to make sure that it is in the right hands before you leave. And here is a telegram to Mr. Brodribb."

He dropped the keys and the tool-case into his pocket, and we went down together to the waiting hansom.

At Weybridge Station we found Mr. Brodribb pacing the platform in a state of extreme dejection. He brightened up somewhat when he saw us, and wrung our hands with emotional heartiness.

"It was very good of you both to come at a moment's notice," he said warmly, "and I feel your kindness very much. You understood, of course, Thorndyke?"

"Yes," Thorndyke replied. "I suppose the *mandarin* beckoned to him."

Mr. Brodribb turned with a look of surprise. "How did you guess that?" he asked; and then, without waiting for a reply, he took from his pocket a note, which he handed to my colleague. "The poor old fellow left this for me," he said. "The servant found it on his dressing-table."

Thorndyke glanced through the note and passed it to me. It consisted of but a few words, hurriedly written in a tremulous hand.

He has beckoned to me, and I must go. Goodbye, dear old friend.

"How does his cousin take the matter?" asked Thorndyke.

"He doesn't know of it yet," replied the lawyer. "Alfred and Raggerton went out after an early breakfast, to cycle over to Guildford on some business or other, and they have not returned yet. The catastrophe was discovered soon after they left. The maid went to his room with a cup of tea, and was astonished to find that his bed had not been slept in. She ran down in alarm and reported to the butler, who went up at once and searched the room; but he could find no trace of the missing one, except my note, until it occurred to him to look in the cupboard. As he opened the door he got rather a start from his own reflection in the mirror; and then he saw poor Fred hanging from one of the pegs near the end of the closet, close to the glass. It's a melancholy affair—but here is the house, and here is the butler waiting for us. Mr. Alfred is not back yet, then, Stevens?"

"No, sir." The white-faced, frightened-looking man had evidently been waiting at the gate some distance from the house, and he now walked back with manifest relief at our arrival. When we entered the house, he ushered us without remark up on to the first-floor, and, preceding us along a corridor, halted near the end. "That's the room, sir," said he; and without another word he turned and went down the stairs.

We entered the room, and Mr. Brodribb followed on tiptoe, looking about him fearfully, and casting awe-struck glances at the shrouded form on the bed. To the latter Thorndyke advanced, and gently drew back the sheet.

"You'd better not look, Brodribb," said he, as he bent over the corpse. He felt the limbs and examined the cord, which still remained round the neck, its raggedly-severed end testifying to the terror of the servants who had cut down the body. Then he replaced the sheet and looked at his watch. "It happened at about three o'clock in the morning," said he. "He must have struggled with the impulse for some time, poor fellow! Now let us look at the cupboard."

We went together to a door in the corner of the room, and, as we opened it, we were confronted by three figures, apparently looking in at us through an open door at the other end.

"It is really rather startling," said the lawyer, in a subdued voice, looking almost apprehensively at the three figures that advanced to meet us. "The poor lad ought never to have been here."

It was certainly an eerie place, and I could not but feel, as we walked down the dark, narrow passage, with those other three dimly-seen figures silently coming towards us, and mimicking our every gesture, that it was no place for a nervous, superstitious man like poor Fred Calverley. Close to the end of the long row of pegs was one from which hung an end of stout box-cord, and to this Mr. Brodribb pointed with an awe-struck gesture. But Thorndyke gave it only a brief glance, and then walked up to the mirror, which he proceeded to examine minutely. It was a very large glass, nearly seven feet high, extending the full width of the closet, and reaching to within a foot of the floor; and it seemed to have been let into the partition from behind, for, both above and below, the woodwork was in front of it.

While I was making these observations, I watched Thorndyke with no little curiosity. First he rapped his knuckles on the glass; then he lighted a wax match, and, holding it close to the mirror, carefully watched the reflection of the flame. Finally, laying his cheek on the glass, he held the match at arm's length, still close to the mirror, and looked at the reflection along the surface. Then he blew out the match and walked back into the room, shutting the cupboard door as we emerged.

"I think," said he, "that as we shall all undoubtedly be subpoenaed by the coroner, it would be well to put together a few notes of the facts. I see there is a writing-table by the window, and I would propose that you, Brodribb, just jot down a *précis* of the statement that you heard last night, while Jervis notes down the exact condition of the body. While you are doing this, I will take a look round."

"We might find a more cheerful place to write in," grumbled Mr. Brodribb; "however—"

Without finishing the sentence, he sat down at the table, and, having found some sermon paper, dipped a pen in the ink by way of encouraging his thoughts. At this moment Thorndyke quietly slipped out of the room, and I proceeded to make a detailed examination of the body: in which occupation I was interrupted at intervals by requests from the lawyer that I should refresh his memory.

We had been occupied thus for about a quarter of an hour, when a quick step was heard outside, the door was opened abruptly, and a man burst into the room. Brodribb rose and held out his hand.

"This is a sad homecoming for you, Alfred," said he.

"Yes, my God!" the newcomer exclaimed. "It's awful."

He looked askance at the corpse on the bed, and wiped his forehead with his handkerchief. Alfred Calverley was not extremely prepossessing. Like his cousin, he was obviously neurotic, but there were signs of dissipation in his face, which, just now, was pale and ghastly, and wore an expression of abject fear. Moreover, his entrance was accompanied by that of a perceptible odour of brandy.

He had walked over, without noticing me, to the writing-table, and as he stood there, talking in subdued tones with the lawyer, I suddenly found Thorndyke at my side. He had stolen in noiselessly through the door that Calverley had left open.

"Show him Brodribb's note," he whispered, "and then make him go in and look at the peg."

With this mysterious request, he slipped out of the room as silently as he had come, unperceived either by Calverley or the lawyer.

"Has Captain Raggerton returned with you?" Brodribb was inquiring.

"No, he has gone into the town," was the reply; "but he won't be long. This will be a frightful shock to him."

At this point I stepped forward. "Have you shown Mr. Calverley the extraordinary letter that the deceased left for you?" I asked.

"What letter was that?" demanded Calverley, with a start.

Mr. Brodribb drew forth the note and handed it to him. As he read it through, Calverley turned white to the lips, and the paper trembled in his hand.

"'He has beckoned to me, and I must go,'" he read. Then, with a furtive glance at the lawyer: "Who had beckoned? What did he mean?"

Mr. Brodribb briefly explained the meaning of the allusion, adding: "I thought you knew all about it."

"Yes, yes," said Calverley, with some confusion; "I remember the matter now you mention it. But it's all so dreadful and bewildering."

At this point I again interposed. "There is a question," I said, "that may be of some importance. It refers to the cord with which the poor fellow hanged himself. Can you identify that cord, Mr. Calverley?"

"I!" he exclaimed, staring at me, and wiping the sweat from his white face; "how should I? Where is the cord?"

"Part of it is still hanging from the peg in the closet. Would you mind looking at it?"

"If you would very kindly fetch it—you know I—er—naturally—have a—"

"It must not be disturbed before the inquest," said I; "but surely you are not afraid—"

"I didn't say I was afraid," he retorted angrily. "Why should I be?"

With a strange, tremulous swagger, he strode across to the closet, flung open the door, and plunged in.

A moment later we heard a shout of horror, and he rushed out, livid and gasping.

"What is it, Calverley?" exclaimed Mr. Brodribb, starting up in alarm.

But Calverley was incapable of speech. Dropping limply into a chair, he gazed at us for a while in silent terror; then he fell back uttering a wild shriek of laughter.

Mr. Brodribb looked at him in amazement. "What is it, Calverley?" he asked again.

As no answer was forthcoming, he stepped across to the open door of the closet and entered, peering curiously before him. Then he, too, uttered a startled exclamation, and backed out hurriedly, looking pale and flurried.

"Bless my soul!" he ejaculated. "Is the place bewitched?"

He sat down heavily and stared at Calverley, who was still shaking with hysteric laughter; while I, now consumed with curiosity, walked over to the closet to discover the cause of their singular behaviour. As

I flung open the door, which the lawyer had closed, I must confess to being very considerably startled; for though the reflection of the open door was plain enough in the mirror, my own reflection was replaced by that of a Chinaman. After a momentary pause of astonishment, I entered the closet and walked towards the mirror; and simultaneously the figure of the Chinaman entered and walked towards me. I had advanced more than halfway down the closet when suddenly the mirror darkened; there was a whirling flash, the Chinaman vanished in an instant, and, as I reached the glass, my own reflection faced me.

I turned back into the room pretty completely enlightened, and looked at Calverley with a new-born distaste. He still sat facing the bewildered lawyer, one moment sobbing convulsively, the next yelping with hysteric laughter. He was not an agreeable spectacle, and when, a few moments later, Thorndyke entered the room, and halted by the door with a stare of disgust, I was moved to join him. But at this juncture a man pushed past Thorndyke, and, striding up to Calverley, shook him roughly by the arm.

"Stop that row!" he exclaimed furiously. "Do you hear? Stop it!"

"I can't help it, Raggerton," gasped Calverley. "He gave me such a turn—the *mandarin*, you know."

"What!" ejaculated Raggerton.

He dashed across to the closet, looked in, and turned upon Calverley with a snarl. Then he walked out of the room.

"Brodribb," said Thorndyke, "I should like to have a word with you and Jervis outside." Then, as we followed him out on to the landing, he continued: "I have something rather interesting to show you. It is in here."

He softly opened an adjoining door, and we looked into a small unfurnished room. A projecting closet occupied one side of it, and at the door of the closet stood Captain Raggerton, with his hand upon the key. He turned upon us fiercely, though with a look of alarm, and demanded:

"What is the meaning of this intrusion? And who the deuce are you? Do you know that this is my private room?"

"I suspected that it was," Thorndyke replied quietly. "Those will be your properties in the closet, then?"

Raggerton turned pale, but continued to bluster. "Do I understand that you have dared to break into my private closet?" he demanded.

"I have inspected it," replied Thorndyke, "and I may remark that it is useless to wrench at that key, because I have hampered the lock."

"The devil you have!" shouted Raggerton.

"Yes; you see, I am expecting a police-officer with a search warrant, so I wished to keep everything intact."

Raggerton turned livid with mingled fear and rage. He stalked up to Thorndyke with a threatening air, but, suddenly altering his mind, exclaimed, "I must see to this!" and flung out of the room.

Thorndyke took a key from his pocket, and, having locked the door, turned to the closet. Having taken out the key to unhamper the lock with a stout wire, he reinserted it and unlocked the door. As we entered, we found ourselves in a narrow closet, similar to the one in the other room, but darker, owing to the absence of a mirror. A few clothes hung from the pegs, and when Thorndyke had lit a candle that stood on a shelf, we could see more of the details.

"Here are some of the properties," said Thorndyke. He pointed to a peg from which hung a long, blue silk gown of Chinese make, a *mandarin's* cap, with a pigtail attached to it, and a beautifully-made *papier-mâché* mask. "Observe," said Thorndyke, taking the latter down and exhibiting a label on the inside, marked 'Renouard à Paris,' "no trouble has been spared."

He took off his coat, slipped on the gown, the mask, and the cap, and was, in a moment, in that dim light, transformed into the perfect semblance of a Chinaman.

"By taking a little more time," he remarked, pointing to a pair of Chinese shoes and a large paper lantern, "the make-up could be rendered more complete; but this seems to have answered for our friend Alfred."

"But," said Mr. Brodribb, as Thorndyke shed the disguise, "still, I don't understand—"

"I will make it clear to you in a moment," said Thorndyke. He walked to the end of the closet, and, tapping the right-hand wall, said: "This is the back of the mirror. You see that it is hung on massive well-oiled hinges, and is supported on this large, rubber-tyred castor, which evidently has ball bearings. You observe three black cords running along the wall, and passing through those pulleys above. Now, when I pull this cord, notice what happens."

He pulled one cord firmly, and immediately the mirror swung noiselessly inwards on its great castor, until it stood diagonally across the closet, where it was stopped by a rubber buffer.

"Bless my soul!" exclaimed Mr. Brodribb. "What an extraordinary thing!"

The effect was certainly very strange, for, the mirror being now exactly diagonal to the two closets they appeared to be a single, continuous passage, with a door at either end. On going up to the mirror, we found that the opening which it had occupied was filled by a sheet of plain glass, evidently placed there as a precaution to prevent any person from walking through from one closet into the other, and so discovering the trick.

"It's all very puzzling," said Mr. Brodribb; "I don't clearly understand it now."

"Let us finish here," replied Thorndyke, "and then I will explain. Notice this black curtain. When I pull the second cord, it slides across the closet and cuts off the light. The mirror now reflects nothing into the other closet; it simply appears dark. And now I pull the third cord."

He did so, and the mirror swung noiselessly back into its place.

"There is only one other thing to observe before we go out," said Thorndyke, "and that is this other mirror standing with its face to the wall. This, of course, is the one that Fred Calverley originally saw at the end of the closet; it has since been removed, and the larger swinging glass put in its place. And now," he continued, when we came out into the room, "let me explain the mechanism in detail. It was obvious to me, when I heard poor Fred Calverley's story, that the mirror was 'faked,' and I drew a diagram of the probable arrangement, which turns out to be correct. Here it is." He took a sheet of paper from his pocket and handed it to the lawyer.

"There are two sketches. Sketch 1 shows the mirror in its ordinary position, closing the end of the closet. A person standing at A, of course, sees his reflection facing him at, apparently, A 1. Sketch 2 shows the mirror swung across. Now a person standing at A does not see his own reflection at all; but if some other person is standing in the other closet at B, A sees the reflection of B apparently at B 1—that is, in the identical position that his own reflection occupied when the mirror was straight across."

"I see now," said Brodribb; "but who set up this apparatus, and why was it done?"

"Let me ask you a question," said Thorndyke. "Is Alfred Calverley the next-of-kin?"

"No; there is Fred's younger brother. But I may say that Fred has made a will quite recently very much in Alfred's favour."

"There is the explanation, then," said Thorndyke. "These two scoundrels have conspired to drive the poor fellow to suicide, and

Raggerton was clearly the leading spirit. He was evidently concocting some story with which to work on poor Fred's superstitions when the mention of the Chinaman on the steamer gave him his cue. He then invented the very picturesque story of the murdered *mandarin* and the stolen pearl. You remember that these 'visitations' did not begin until after that story had been told, and Fred had been absent from the house on a visit.

"Evidently, during his absence, Raggerton took down the original mirror, and substituted this swinging arrangement; and at the same time procured the Chinaman's dress and mask from the theatrical property dealers. No doubt he reckoned on being able quietly to remove the swinging glass and other properties and replace the original mirror before the inquest."

"By God!" exclaimed Mr. Brodribb, "it's the most infamous, cowardly plot I have ever heard of. They shall go to gaol for it, the villains, as sure as I am alive."

But in this Mr. Brodribb was mistaken; for immediately on finding themselves detected, the two conspirators had left the house, and by nightfall were safely across the Channel; and the only satisfaction that the lawyer obtained was the setting aside of the will on facts disclosed at the inquest.

As to Thorndyke, he has never to this day forgiven himself for having allowed Fred Calverley to go home to his death.

The Blue Scarab

Medico-legal practice is largely concerned with crimes against the person, the details of which are often sordid, gruesome and unpleasant. Hence the curious and romantic case of the Blue Scarab (though really outside our speciality) came as somewhat of a relief. But to me it is of interest principally as illustrating two of the remarkable gifts which made my friend, Thorndyke, unique as an investigator: his uncanny power of picking out the one essential fact at a glance, and his capacity to produce, when required, inexhaustible stores of unexpected knowledge of the most out-of-the-way subjects.

It was late in the afternoon when Mr. James Blowgrave arrived, by appointment, at our chambers, accompanied by his daughter, a rather strikingly pretty girl of about twenty-two; and when we had mutually introduced ourselves, the consultation began without preamble.

"I didn't give any details in my letter to you," said Mr. Blowgrave. "I thought it better not to, for fear you might decline the case. It is really a matter of a robbery, but not quite an ordinary robbery. There are some unusual and rather mysterious features in the case. And as the police hold out very little hope, I have come to ask if you will give me your opinion on the case and perhaps look into it for me. But first I had better tell you how the affair happened.

"The robbery occurred just a fortnight ago, about half-past nine o'clock in the evening. I was sitting in my study with my daughter, looking over some things that I had taken from a small deed-box, when a servant rushed in to tell us that one of the outbuildings was on fire. Now, my study opens by a French window on the garden at the back, and, as the outbuilding was in a meadow at the side of the garden, I went out that way, leaving the French window open; but before going I hastily put the things back in the deed-box and locked it.

"The building—which I used partly as a lumber store and partly as a workshop—was well alight and the whole household was already on the spot, the boy working the pump and the two maids carrying the buckets and throwing water on the fire. My daughter and I joined the party and helped to carry the buckets and take out what goods we could reach from the burning building. But it was nearly half an hour before we got the fire completely extinguished, and then my daughter and I went to our rooms to wash and tidy ourselves up. We returned to the study together, and when I had shut the French window my daughter proposed that we should resume our interrupted occupation. Thereupon I took out of my pocket the key of the deed-box and turned to the cabinet on which the box always stood.

"But there was no deed-box there.

"For a moment I thought I must have moved it, and cast my eyes round the room in search of it. But it was nowhere to be seen, and a moment's reflection reminded me that I had left it in its usual place. The only possible conclusion was that during our absence at the fire, somebody must have come in by the window and taken it. And it looked as if that somebody had deliberately set fire to the outbuilding for the express purpose of luring us all out of the house."

"That is what the appearances suggest," Thorndyke agreed. "Is the study window furnished with a blind, or curtains?"

"Curtains," replied Mr. Blowgrave. "But they were not drawn. Anyone in the garden could have seen into the room; and the garden is easily accessible to an active person who could climb over a low wall."

"So far, then," said Thorndyke, "the robbery might be the work of a casual prowler who had got into the garden and watched you through the window, and assuming that the things you had taken from the box were of value, seized an easy opportunity to make off with them. Were the things of any considerable value?"

"To a thief they were of no value at all. There were a number of share certificates, a lease, one or two agreements, some family photographs and a small box containing an old letter and a scarab. Nothing worth stealing, you see, for the certificates were made out in my name and were therefore unnegotiable."

"And the scarab?"

"That may have been *lapis lazuli*, but more probably it was a blue glass imitation. In any case it was of no considerable value. It was about an inch and a half long. But before you come to any conclusion, I had better finish the story. The robbery was on Tuesday, the 7th of June. I gave information to the police, with a description of the missing property, but nothing happened until Wednesday, the 15th, when I received a registered parcel bearing the Southampton postmark. On opening it I found, to my astonishment, the entire contents of the deed-box, with the exception of the scarab, and this rather mysterious communication."

He took from his pocket and handed to Thorndyke an ordinary envelope addressed in typewritten characters, and sealed with a large, elliptical seal, the face of which was covered with minute hieroglyphics.

"This," said Thorndyke, "I take to be an impression of the scarab; and an excellent impression it is."

"Yes," replied Mr. Blowgrave, "I have no doubt that it is the scarab. It is about the same size."

Thorndyke looked quickly at our client with an expression of surprise. "But," he asked, "don't you recognise the hieroglyphics on it?"

Mr. Blowgrave smiled deprecatingly. "The fact is," said he, "I don't know anything about hieroglyphics, but I should say, as far as I can judge, these look the same. What do you think, Nellie?"

Miss Blowgrave looked at the seal vaguely and replied, "I am in the same position. Hieroglyphics are to me just funny things that don't mean anything. But these look the same to me as those on our scarab, though I expect any other hieroglyphics would, for that matter."

Thorndyke made no comment on this statement, but examined the seal attentively through his lens. Then he drew out the contents of the envelope, consisting of two letters, one typewritten and the other in a faded brown handwriting. The former he read through and then inspected the paper closely, holding it up to the light to observe the watermark.

"The paper appears to be of Belgian manufacture," he remarked, passing it to me. I confirmed this observation and then read the letter, which was headed "Southampton" and ran thus:

> Dear Old Pal,
> I am sending you back some trifles removed in error. The ancient document is enclosed with this, but the curio is at present in the custody of my respected uncle. Hope its temporary loss will not inconvenience you, and that I may be able to return it to you later. Meanwhile, believe me,
>
> Your ever affectionate,
>
> Rudolpho.

"Who is Rudolpho?" I asked.

"The Lord knows," replied Mr. Blowgrave. "A pseudonym of our absent friend, I presume. He seems to be a facetious sort of person."

"He does," agreed Thorndyke. "This letter and the seal appear to be what the schoolboys would call a leg-pull. But still, this is all quite normal. He has returned you the worthless things and has kept the one thing that has any sort of negotiable value. Are you quite clear that the scarab is not more valuable than you have assumed?"

"Well," said Mr. Blowgrave, "I have had an expert's opinion on it. I showed it to M. Fouquet, the Egyptologist, when he was over here from Brussels a few months ago, and his opinion was that it was a worthless imitation. Not only was it not a genuine scarab, but the inscription was a sham, too; just a collection of hieroglyphic characters jumbled together without sense or meaning."

"Then," said Thorndyke, taking another look at the seal through his lens, "it would seem that Rudolpho, or Rudolpho's uncle, has got a bad bargain. Which doesn't throw much light on the affair."

At this point Miss Blowgrave intervened. "I think, father," said she, "you have not given Dr. Thorndyke quite all the facts about the scarab. He ought to be told about its connection with Uncle Reuben."

As the girl spoke Thorndyke looked at her with curious expression of suddenly awakened interest. Later I understood the meaning of that look, but at the time there seemed to me nothing particularly arresting in her words.

"It is just a family tradition," Mr. Blowgrave said deprecatingly. "probably it is all nonsense."

"Well, let us have it, at any rate," said Thorndyke. "We may get some light from it."

Thus urged, Mr. Blowgrave hemmed a little shyly and began:

"The story concerns my great-grandfather Silas Blowgrave, and his doings during the war with France. It seems that he commanded a privateer of which he and his brother Reuben were the joint owners, and that in the course of their last cruise they acquired a very remarkable and valuable collection of jewels. Goodness knows how they got them; not very honestly, I suspect, for they appear to have been a pair of precious rascals. Something has been said about the loot from a South American church or cathedral, but there is really nothing known about the affair.

"There are no documents. It is mere oral tradition and very vague and sketchy. The story goes that when they had sold off the ship, they came down to live at Shawstead in Hertfordshire, Silas occupying the manor house—in which I live at present—and Reuben a farm adjoining. The bulk of the loot they shared out at the end of the cruise, but the jewels were kept apart to be dealt with later—perhaps when the circumstances under which they had been acquired had been forgotten. However, both men were inveterate gamblers and it seems—according to the testimony of a servant of Reuben's who overheard them—that on a certain night when they had been playing heavily, they decided to finish up by playing for the whole collection of jewels as a single stake. Silas, who had the jewels in his custody, was seen to go to the manor house and return to Reuben's house carrying a small, iron chest.

"Apparently they played late into the night, after everyone else but the servant had gone to bed, and the luck was with Reuben, though it seems probable that he gave luck some assistance. At any rate, when the play was finished and the chest handed over, Silas roundly accused him of cheating, and we may assume that a pretty serious quarrel took place. Exactly what happened is not clear, for when the quarrel began Reuben dismissed the servant, who retired to her bedroom in a distant part of the house.

"But in the morning it was discovered that Reuben and the chest of jewels had both disappeared, and there were distinct traces of blood in the room in which the two men had been playing. Silas professed to know nothing about the disappearance; but a strong—and probably just—suspicion arose that he had murdered his brother and made away with the jewels. The result was that Silas also disappeared, and for a long time his whereabouts was not known even by his wife.

"Later it transpired that he had taken up his abode under an assumed name, in Egypt, and that he had developed an enthusiastic interest in the then new science of Egyptology—the Rosetta Stone had been deciphered only a few years previously. After a time he resumed communication with his wife, but never made any statement as to the mystery of his brother's disappearance. A few months before his death he visited his home in disguise and he then handed to his wife a little sealed packet which was to be delivered to his only son, William, on his attaining the age of twenty-one. That packet contained the scarab and the letter which you have taken from the envelope."

"Am I to read it?" asked Thorndyke.

"Certainly, if you think it worth while," was the reply. Thorndyke opened the yellow sheet of paper and, glancing through the brown and faded writing, read aloud:

Cairo, 4 March, 1833.

My Dear Son,

I am sending you, as my last gift, a valuable scarab and a few words of counsel on which I would bid you meditate. Believe me, there is much wisdom in the lore of Old Egypt. Make it your own. Treasure the scarab as a precious inheritance. Handle it often but show it to none. Give your Uncle Reuben Christian burial. It is your duty, and you will have your reward. He robbed your father, but he shall make restitution.

Farewell!

Your affectionate father,

Silas Blowgrave.

As Thorndyke laid down the letter he looked inquiringly at our client.

"Well," he said, "here are some plain instructions. How have they been carried out?

"They haven't been carried out at all," replied Mr. Blowgrave. "As to his son William, my grandfather, he was not disposed to meddle in the matter. This seemed to be a frank admission that Silas killed his brother and concealed the body, and William didn't choose to reopen the scandal. Besides, the instructions are not so very plain. It is all very well to say, 'Give your Uncle Reuben Christian burial,' but where the deuce is Uncle Reuben?"

"It is plainly hinted," said Thorndyke, "that whoever gives the body Christian burial will stand to benefit, and the word 'restitution' seems to suggest a clue to the whereabouts of the jewels. Has no one thought it worth while to find out where the body is deposited?"

"But how could they?" demanded Blowgrave. "He doesn't give the faintest clue. He talks as if his son knew where the body was. And then, you know, even supposing Silas did not take the jewels with him, there was the question, whose property were they? To begin with, they were pretty certainly stolen property, though no one knows where they came from. Then Reuben apparently got them from Silas by fraud, and Silas got them back by robbery and murder. If William had discovered them he would have had to give them up to Reuben's sons, and yet they weren't strictly Reuben's property. No one had an undeniable claim to them, even if they could have found them."

"But that is not the case now," said Miss Blowgrave.

"No," said Mr. Blowgrave, in answer to Thorndyke's look of inquiry. "The position is quite clear now. Reuben's grandson, my cousin Arthur, has died recently, and as he had no children, he has dispersed his property. The old farmhouse and the bulk of his estate he has left to a nephew, but he made a small bequest to my daughter and named her as the residuary legatee. So that what ever rights Reuben had to the jewels are now vested in her, and on my death she will be Silas's heir, too. As a matter of fact," Mr. Blowgrave continued, "we were discussing this very question on the night of the robbery. I may as well tell you that my girl will be left pretty poorly off when I go, for there is a heavy mortgage on our property and mighty little capital. Uncle Reuben's jewels would have made the old home secure for her if we could have laid our hands on them. However, I mustn't take up your time with our domestic affairs."

"Your domestic affairs are not entirely irrelevant," said Thorndyke. "But what is it that you want me to do in the matter?"

"Well," said Blowgrave, "my house has been robbed and my premises set fire to. The police can apparently do nothing. They say there is no clue at all unless the robbery was committed by somebody in the house, which is absurd, seeing that the servants were all engaged in putting out the fire. But I want the robber traced punished, and I want to get the scarab back. It may be intrinsically valueless, as M. Fouquet said, but Silas's testamentary letter seems to indicate that it had some value. At any rate, it is an heirloom, and I am loath to lose it. It seems a presumptuous thing to ask you to investigate a trumpery robbery, but I should take it as a great kindness if you would look into the matter."

"Cases of robbery pure and simple," replied Thorndyke, "are rather alien to my ordinary practice, but in this one there are certain curious features that seem to make an investigation worth while. Yes, Mr. Blowgrave, I will look into the case, and I have some hope that we may be able to lay our hands on the robber, in spite of the apparent absence of clues. I will ask you to leave both these letters for me to examine more minutely, and I shall probably want to make an inspection of the premises—perhaps tomorrow."

"Whenever you like," said Blowgrave. "I am delighted that you are willing to undertake the inquiry. I have heard so much about you from my friend Stalker, of the Griffin Life Assurance Company, for whom you have acted on several occasions."

"Before you go," said Thorndyke, "there is one point that we must clear up. Who is there besides yourselves that knows of the existence of the scarab and this letter and the history attaching to them?"

"I really can't say," replied Blowgrave. "No one has seen them but my cousin Arthur. I once showed them to him, and he may have talked about them in the family. I didn't treat the matter as a secret."

When our visitors had gone we discussed the bearings of the case.

"It is quite a romantic story," said I, "and the robbery has its points of interest, but I am rather inclined to agree with the police—there is mighty little to go on."

"There would have been less," said Thorndyke, "if our sporting friend hadn't been so pleased with himself. That typewritten letter was a piece of gratuitous impudence. Our gentleman overrated his security and crowed too loud."

"I don't see that there is much to be gleaned from the letter, all the same," said I.

"I am sorry to hear you say that, Jervis," he exclaimed, "because I was proposing to hand the letter over to you to examine and report on."

"I was only referring to the superficial appearances," I said hastily. "No doubt a detailed examination will bring something more distinctive into view."

"I have no doubt it will," he said, "and as there are reasons for pushing on the investigation as quickly as possible, I suggest that you get to work at once. I will occupy myself with the old letter and the envelope."

On this I began my examination without delay, and as a preliminary I proceeded to take a facsimile photograph of the letter by putting it in a large printing frame with a sensitive plate and a plate of clear glass. The resulting negative showed not only the typewritten lettering, but also the watermark and wire lines of the paper, and a faint grease spot. Next I turned my attention to the lettering itself, and here I soon began to accumulate quite a number of identifiable peculiarities. The machine was apparently a Corona, fitted with the small "Elite" type, and the alignment was markedly defective. The "lower case"—or small—"a" was well below the line, although the capital "A" appeared to be correctly placed; the "u" was slightly above the line, and the small "m" was partly clogged with dirt.

Up to this point I had been careful to manipulate the letter with forceps (although it had been handled by at least three persons, to my knowledge), and I now proceeded to examine it for fingerprints. As I could detect none by mere inspection, I dusted the back of the paper with finely powdered *fuchsin*, and distributed the powder by tapping the paper lightly. This brought into view quite a number of fingerprints, especially round the edges of the letter, and though most of them were very faint and shadowy, it was possible to make out the ridge pattern well enough for our purpose. Having blown off the excess of powder, I took the letter to the room where the large copying camera was set up, to photograph it before developing the fingerprints on the front. But here I found our laboratory assistant, Polton, in possession, with the sealed envelope fixed to the copying easel. "I shan't be a minute, sir," said he. "The doctor wants an enlarged photograph of this seal. I've got the plate in."

I waited while he made his exposure and then proceeded to take the photograph of the letter, or rather of the fingerprints on the back of it. When I had developed the negative I powdered the front of the letter and brought out several more fingerprints—thumbs this time. They were a little difficult to see where they were imposed on the lettering, but, as the latter was bright blue and the *fuchsin* powder was red, this confusion disappeared in the photograph, in which the lettering was almost invisible while the fingerprints were more distinct than they had appeared to the eye.

This completed my examination, and when I had verified the make of typewriter by reference to our album of specimens of typewriting, I left the negatives for Polton to dry and print and went down to the sitting-room to draw up my little report. I had just finished this and was speculating on what had become of Thorndyke, when I heard his quick step on the stair and a few moments later he entered with a roll of paper in his hand. This he unrolled on the table, fixing it open with one or two lead paper-weights, and I came round to inspect it, when I found it to be a sheet of the Ordnance map on the scale of twenty-five inches to the mile.

"Here is the Blowgraves' place," said Thorndyke, "nearly in the middle of the sheet. This is his house—Shawstead Manor—and that will probably be the outbuilding that was on fire. I take it that the house marked Dingle Farm is the one that Uncle Reuben occupied."

"Probably," I agreed. "But I don't see why you wanted this map if you are going down to the place itself tomorrow."

"The advantage of a map," said Thorndyke, "is that you can see all over it at once and get the lie of the land well into your mind; and you can measure all distances accurately and quickly with a scale and a pair of dividers. When we go down tomorrow, we shall know our way about as well as Blowgrave himself."

"And what use will that be?" I asked. "Where does the topography come into the case?"

"Well, Jervis," he replied, "there is the robber, for instance; he came from somewhere and he went somewhere. A study of the map may give us a hint as to his movements. But here comes Polton 'with the documents,' as poor Miss Flite would say. What have you got for us, Polton?"

"They aren't quite dry, sir," said Polton, laying four large bromide prints on the table. "There's the enlargement of the seal—ten by eight, mounted—and three unmounted prints of Dr. Jervis's."

Thorndyke looked at my photographs critically. "They're excellent, Jervis," said he. "The finger prints are perfectly legible, though faint. I only hope some of them are the right ones. That is my left thumb. I don't see yours. The small one is presumably Miss Blowgrave's. We must take her fingerprints tomorrow, and her father's, too. Then we shall know if we have got any of the robber's." He ran his eye over my report and nodded approvingly. "There is plenty there to enable us to identify the typewriter if we can get hold of it, and the paper is very distinctive. What do you think of the seal?" he added, laying the enlarged photograph before me.

"It is magnificent," I replied, with a grin. "Perfectly monumental."

"What are you grinning at?" he demanded.

"I was thinking that you seem to be counting your chickens in pretty good time," said I. "You are making elaborate preparations to identify the scarab, but you are rather disregarding the classical advice of the prudent Mrs. Glasse."

"I have a presentiment that we shall get that scarab," said he. "At any rate we ought to be in a position to identify it instantly and certainly if we are able to get a sight of it."

"We are not likely to," said I. "Still, there is no harm in providing for the improbable."

This was evidently Thorndyke's view, and he certainly made ample provision for this most improbable contingency; for, having furnished himself with a drawing-board and a sheet of tracing-paper, he pinned the latter over the photograph on the board and proceeded, with a fine pen and hectograph ink, to make a careful and minute tracing of the intricate and bewildering hieroglyphic inscription on the seal. When he had finished it he transferred it to a clay duplicator and took off half-a-dozen copies, one of which he handed to me. I looked at it dubiously and remarked:

"You have said that the medical jurist must make all knowledge his province. Has he got to be an Egyptologist, too?"

"He will be the better medical jurist if he is," was the reply, of which I made a mental note for my future guidance. But meanwhile Thorndyke's proceedings were, to me, perfectly incomprehensible. What was his object in making this minute tracing? The seal itself was sufficient for identification. I lingered, awhile hoping that some fresh development might throw a light on the mystery. But his next proceeding was like to have reduced me to stupefaction. I saw him go to the book-shelves and take down a book. As he laid it on the table I glanced at the title, and when I saw that it was Raper's Navigation Tables I stole softly out into the lobby, put on my hat and went for a walk.

When I returned the investigation was apparently concluded, for Thorndyke was seated in his easy chair, placidly reading The Compleat Angler. On the table lay a large circular protractor, a straight-edge, an architect's scale and a sheet of tracing-paper on which was a tracing in hectograph ink of Shawstead Manor.

"Why did you make this tracing?" I asked. "Why not take the map itself?"

"We don't want the whole of it," he replied, "and I dislike cutting up maps."

By taking an informal lunch in the train, we arrived at Shawstead Manor by half-past two. Our approach up the drive had evidently been observed, for Blowgrave and his daughter were waiting at the porch to receive us. The former came forward with outstretched hand, but a distinctly woebegone expression, and exclaimed:

"It is most kind of you to come down; but alas! you are too late."

"Too late for what?" demanded Thorndyke.

"I will show you," replied Blowgrave, and seizing my colleague by the arm, he strode off excitedly to a little wicket at the side of the house, and, passing through it, hurried along a narrow alley that skirted the garden wall and ended in a large meadow, at one end of which stood a dilapidated windmill. Across this meadow he bustled, dragging my colleague with him, until he reached a heap of freshly-turned earth, where he halted and pointed tragically to a spot where the turf had evidently been raised and untidily replaced.

"There!" he exclaimed, stooping to pull up the loose turfs and thereby exposing what was evidently a large hole, recently and hastily filled in. "That was done last night or early this morning, for I walked over this meadow only yesterday evening and there was no sign of disturbed ground then."

Thorndyke stood looking down at the hole with a faint smile. "And what do you infer from that?" he asked.

"Infer!" shrieked Blowgrave. "Why, I infer that whoever dug this hole was searching for Uncle Reuben and the lost jewels!"

"I am inclined to agree with you," Thorndyke said calmly. "He happened to search in the wrong place, but that is his affair."

"The wrong place!" Blowgrave and his daughter exclaimed in unison. "How do you know it is the wrong place?"

"Because," replied Thorndyke, "I believe I know the right place, and this is not it. But we can put the matter to the test, and we had better do so. Can you get a couple of men with picks and shovels? Or shall we handle the tools ourselves?"

"I think that would be better," said Blowgrave, who was quivering with excitement. "We don't want to take anyone into our confidence if we can help it."

"No," Thorndyke agreed. "Then I suggest that you fetch the tools while I locate the spot."

Blowgrave assented eagerly and went off at a brisk trot, while the young lady remained with us and watched Thorndyke with intense curiosity.

"I mustn't interrupt you with questions," said she "but I can't imagine how you found out where Uncle Reuben was buried."

"We will go into that later," he replied; "but first we have got to find Uncle Reuben." He laid his research case down on the ground, and opening it, took out three sheets of paper, each bearing a duplicate of his tracing of the map; and on each was marked a spot on this meadow from which a number of lines radiated like the spokes of a wheel.

"You see, Jervis," he said, exhibiting them to me, "the advantage of a map. I have been able to rule off these sets of bearings regardless of obstructions, such as those young trees, which have arisen since Silas's day, and mark the spot in its correct place. If the recent obstructions prevent us from taking the bearings, we can still find the spot by measurements with the land-chain or tape."

"Why have you got three plans?" I asked.

"Because there are three imaginable places. No. 1 is the most likely; No. 2 less likely, but possible; No. 3 is impossible. That is the one that our friend tried last night. No. 1 is among those young trees, and we will now see if we can pick up the bearings in spite of them."

We moved on to the clump of young trees, where Thorndyke took from the research-case a tall, folding camera-tripod and a large prismatic compass with an aluminium dial. With the latter he one or two trial bearings and then, setting up the tripod, fixed the compass on it. For some minutes Miss Blowgrave and I watched him as he shifted the tripod from spot to spot, peering through the sight-vane of the compass and glancing occasionally at the map.

At length he turned to us and said: "We are in luck. None of these trees interferes with our bearings." He took from the research-case a surveyor's arrow, and sticking it in the ground under the tripod, added: "That is the spot. But we may have to dig a good way round it, for a compass is only a rough instrument."

At this moment Mr. Blowgrave staggered up, breathing hard, and flung down on the ground three picks, two shovels and a spade. "I won't hinder you, doctor, by asking for explanations," said he, "but I am utterly mystified. You must tell us what it all means when we have finished our work."

This Thorndyke promised to do, but meanwhile he took off his coat, and rolling up his shirt sleeves, seized the spade and began cutting out a large square of turf. As the soil was uncovered, Blowgrave and I attacked it with picks and Miss Blowgrave shovelled away the loose earth.

"Do you know how far down we have to go?" I asked.

"The body lies six feet below the surface," Thorndyke replied; and as he spoke he laid down his spade, and taking a telescope from the research-case, swept it round the margin of the meadow and finally pointed it at a farmhouse some six hundred yards distant, of which he made a somewhat prolonged inspection, after which he took the remaining pick and fell to work on the opposite corner of the exposed square of earth.

For nearly half-an-hour we worked on steadily, gradually eating our way downwards, plying pick and shovel alternately, while Miss Blowgrave cleared the loose earth away from the edges of the deepening pit. Then a halt was called and we came to the surface, wiping our faces.

"I think, Nellie," said Blowgrave, divesting himself of his waistcoat, "a jug of lemonade and four tumblers would be useful, unless our visitors would prefer beer."

We both gave our votes for lemonade, and Miss Nellie tripped away towards the house, while Thorndyke, taking up his telescope, once more inspected the farm house.

"You seem greatly interested in that house," I remarked.

"I am," he replied, handing me the telescope. "Just take a look at the window in the right-hand gable, but keep under the tree."

I pointed the telescope at the gable and there observed an open window at which a man was seated. He held a binocular glass to his eyes and the instrument appeared to be directed at us.

"We are being spied on, I fancy," said I, passing the telescope to Blowgrave, "but I suppose it doesn't matter. This is your land, isn't it?"

"Yes," replied Blowgrave, "but still, we didn't want any spectators. That is Harold Bowker," he added steadying the telescope against a tree, "my cousin Arthur's nephew, whom I told you about as having inherited the farm-house. He seems mighty interested in us; but small things interest one in the country."

Here the appearance of Miss Nellie, advancing across the meadow with an inviting-looking basket, diverted our attention from our inquisitive watcher. Six thirsty eyes were riveted on that basket until it drew near and presently disgorged a great glass jug and four tumblers, when we each took off a long and delicious draught and then jumped down into the pit to resume our labours.

Another half-hour passed. We had excavated in some places to nearly the full depth and were just discussing the advisability of another short rest when Blowgrave, who was working in one corner, uttered a loud cry and stood up suddenly, holding something in his fingers. A glance at the object showed it to be a bone, brown and earth-stained, but evidently a bone. Evidently, too, a human bone, as Thorndyke decided when Blowgrave handed it to him triumphantly.

"We have been very fortunate," said he, "to get so near at the first trial. This is from the right great toe, so we may assume that the skeleton lies just outside this pit, but we had better excavate carefully in your corner and see exactly how the bones lie." This he proceeded to do himself, probing cautiously with the spade and clearing the earth away from the corner. Very soon the remaining bones of the right foot came into view and then the ends of the two leg-bones and a portion of the left foot.

"We can see now," said he, "how the skeleton lies, and all we have to do is to extend the excavation in that direction. But there is only room for one to work down here. I think you and Mr. Blowgrave had better dig down from the surface."

On this, I climbed out of the pit, followed reluctantly by Blowgrave, who still held the little brown bone in his hand and was in a state of wild excitement and exultation that somewhat scandalised his daughter.

"It seems rather ghoulish," she remarked, "to be gloating over poor Uncle Reuben's body in this way."

"I know," said Blowgrave, "it isn't reverent. But I didn't kill Uncle Reuben, you know, whereas—well it was a long time ago." With this rather inconsequent conclusion he took a draught of lemonade, seized his pick and fell to work with a will. I, too, indulged in a draught and passed a full tumbler down to Thorndyke. But before resuming my labours I picked up the telescope and once more inspected the farmhouse. The window was still open, but the watcher had apparently become bored with the not very thrilling spectacle. At any rate he had disappeared.

From this time onward every few minutes brought some discovery. First, a pair of deeply rusted steel shoe buckles; then one or two buttons, and presently a fine gold watch with a fob-chain and a bunch of seals, looking uncannily new and fresh and seeming more fraught with tragedy than even the bones themselves. In his cautious digging, Thorndyke was careful not to disturb the skeleton; and looking down into the narrow trench that was growing from the corner of the pit, I could see both legs, with only the right foot missing, projecting from the miniature cliff.

Meanwhile our of the trench was deepening rapidly, so that Thorndyke presently warned us to stop digging and bade us come down and shovel away the earth as he disengaged it.

At length the whole skeleton, excepting the head, was uncovered, though it lay undisturbed as it might have lain in its coffin. And now, as Thorndyke picked away the earth around the head, we could see that the skull was propped forward as if it rested on a high pillow. A little more careful probing with the pick-point served to explain this appearance. For as the earth fell away and disclosed the grinning skull, there came into view the edge and ironbound corners of a small chest.

It was an impressive spectacle; weird, solemn and rather dreadful. There for over a century the ill-fated gambler had lain, his mouldering head pillowed on the booty of unrecorded villainy, booty that had been won by fraud, retrieved by violence, and hidden at last by the final winner with the witness of his crime.

"Here is a fine text for a moralist who would preach on the vanity of riches," said Thorndyke.

We all stood silent for a while, gazing, not without awe, at the stark figure that lay guarding the ill-gotten treasure. Miss Blowgrave—who had been helped down when we descended—crept closer to her father and murmured that it was "rather awful;" while Blowgrave himself displayed a queer mixture of exultation and shuddering distaste.

Suddenly the silence was broken by a voice from above, and we all looked up with a start. A youngish man was standing on the brink of the pit, looking down on us with very evident disapproval.

"It seems that I have come just in the nick of time," observed the new-comer. "I shall have to take possession of that chest, you know, and of the remains, too, I suppose. That is my ancestor, Reuben Blowgrave."

"Well, Harold," said Blowgrave, "you can have Uncle Reuben if you want him. But the chest belongs to Nellie."

Here Mr. Harold Bowker—I recognised him now as the watcher from the window—dropped down into the pit and advanced with something of a swagger.

"I am Reuben's heir," said he, "through my Uncle Arthur, and I take possession of this property and the remains."

"Pardon me, Harold," said Blowgrave, "but Nellie is Arthur's residuary legatee, and this is the residue of the estate."

"Rubbish!" exclaimed Bowker. "By the way, how did you find out where he was buried?"

"Oh, that was quite simple," replied Thorndyke with unexpected geniality. "I'll show you the plan." He climbed up to the surface and returned in a few moments with the three tracings and his letter-case. "This is how we located the spot." He handed the plan numbered 3 to Bowker, who took it from him and stood looking at it with a puzzled frown.

"But this isn't the place," he said at length.

"Isn't it?" queried Thorndyke. "No, of course; I've given you the wrong one. This is the plan." He handed Bowker the plan marked No. 1, and took the other from him, laying it down on a heap of earth. Then, as Bowker pored gloomily over No. 1, he took a knife and a pencil from his pocket, and with his back to our visitor; scraped the lead of the pencil, letting the black powder fall on the plan that he had just laid down.

I watched him with some curiosity; and when I observed that the black scrapings fell on two spots near the edges of the paper, a sudden suspicion flashed into my mind, which was confirmed when I saw him tap the paper lightly with his pencil, gently blow away the powder, and quickly producing my photograph of the typewritten letter from his case, hold it for a moment beside the plan.

"This is all very well," said Bowker, looking up from the plan, "but how did you find out about these bearings?"

Thorndyke swiftly replaced the letter in his case, and turning round, replied, "I am afraid I can't give you any further information."

"Can't you, indeed!" Bowker exclaimed insolently. "Perhaps I shall compel you to. But, at any rate, I forbid any of you to lay hands on my property."

Thorndyke looked at him steadily and said in an ominously quiet tone: "Now, listen to me, Mr. Bowker. Let us have an end of this nonsense. You have played a risky game and you have lost. How much you have lost I can't say until I know whether Mr. Blowgrave intends to prosecute."

"To prosecute!" shouted Bowker. "What the deuce do you mean by prosecute?"

"I mean," said Thorndyke, "that on the 7th of June, after nine o'clock at night, you entered the dwelling-house of Mr. Blowgrave and stole and carried away certain of his goods and chattels. A part of them you have restored, but you are still in possession of some of the stolen property, to wit, a scarab and a deed-box."

As Thorndyke made this statement in his calm, level tones, Bowker's face blanched to a tallowy white, and he stood staring at my colleague, the very picture of astonishment and dismay. But he fired a last shot.

"This is sheer midsummer madness," he exclaimed huskily; "and you know it."

Thorndyke turned to our host. "It is for you to settle, Mr. Blowgrave," said he. "I hold conclusive evidence that Mr. Bowker stole your deed-box. If you decide to prosecute I shall produce that evidence in court and he will certainly be convicted."

Blowgrave and his daughter looked at the accused man with an embarrassment almost equal to his own.

"I am astounded," the former said at length; "but I don't want to be vindictive. Look here, Harold, hand over the scarab and we'll say no more about it."

"You can't do that," said Thorndyke. "The law doesn't allow you to compound a robbery. He can return the property if he pleases and you can do as you think best about prosecuting. But you can't make conditions."

There was silence for some seconds; then, without another word, the crestfallen adventurer turned, and scrambling up out of the pit, took a hasty departure.

It was nearly a couple of hours later that, after a leisurely wash and a hasty, nondescript meal, we carried the little chest from the dining-room to the study. Here, when he had closed the French window and drawn the curtains, Mr. Blowgrave produced a set of tools and we fell to work on the iron fastenings of the chest. It was no light task, though a century's rust had thinned the stout bands, but at length the lid yielded to the thrust of a long case-opener and rose with a protesting creak. The chest was lined with a double thickness of canvas, apparently part of a sail, and contained a number of small leathern bags, which, as we lifted them out, one by one, felt as if they were filled with pebbles. But when we untied the thongs of one and emptied its contents into a wooden bowl,

Blowgrave heaved a sigh of ecstasy and Miss Nellie uttered a little scream of delight. They were all cut stones, and most of them of exceptional size; rubies, emeralds, sapphires and a few diamonds. As to their value, we could forn but the vaguest guess; but Thorndyke, who was a fair judge of gem-stones, gave it as his opinion that they were fine specimens of their kind, though roughly cut, and that they had probably formed the enrichment of some shrine.

"The question is," said Blowgrave, gazing gloatingly on the bowl of sparkling gems, "what are we to do with them?"

"I suggest," said Thorndyke, "that Dr. Jervis stay here tonight to help you to guard them and that in the morning you take them up to London and deposit them, at your bank."

Blowgrave fell in eagerly with this suggestion, which I seconded. "But," said he, "that chest is a queer-looking package to be carrying abroad. Now, if we only had that confounded deed-box—"

"There's a deed-box on the cabinet behind you," said Thorndyke.

Blowgrave turned round sharply. "God bless us!" he exclaimed. "It has come back the way it went. Harold must have slipped in at the window while we were at tea. Well, I'm glad he has made restitution. When I look at that bowl and think what he must have narrowly missed, I don't feel inclined to be hard on him. I suppose the scarab is inside—not that it matters much now."

The scarab was inside in an envelope; and as Thorndyke turned it over in his hand and examined the hieroglyphics on it through his lens, Miss Blowgrave asked: "Is it of any value, Dr. Thorndyke? It can't have any connection with the secret of the hiding-place, because you found the jewels without it."

"By the way, doctor, I don't know whether it is permissible for me to ask, but how on earth did you find out where the jewels were hidden? To me it looks like black magic."

Thorndyke laughed in a quiet, inward fashion. "There is nothing magical about it," said he. "It was a perfectly simple, straightforward problem. But Miss Nellie is wrong. We had the scarab; that is to say we had the wax impression of it, which is the same thing. And the scarab was the key to the riddle. You see," he continued, "Silas's letter and the scarab formed together a sort of intelligence test."

"Did they?" said Blowgrave. "Then he drew a blank every time."

Thorndyke chuckled. "His descendants were certainly a little lacking in enterprise," he admitted. "Silas's instructions were perfectly plain and explicit. Whoever would find the treasure must first acquire some knowledge of Egyptian lore and must study the scarab attentively. It was the broadest of hints, but no one—excepting Harold Bowker, who must have heard about the scarab from his Uncle Arthur—seems to have paid any attention to it.

"Now it happens that I have just enough elementary knowledge of the hieroglyphic characters to enable me to spell them out when they are used alphabetically; and as soon as I saw the seal, I could see that these hieroglyphics formed English words. My attention was first attracted by the second group of signs, which spelled the word 'Reuben,' and then I saw that the first group spelled 'Uncle.' Of course, the instant I heard Miss Nellie speak of the connection between the scarab and Uncle Reuben, the murder was out. I saw at a glance that the scarab contained all the required information. Last night I made a careful tracing of the hieroglyphics and then rendered them into our own alphabet. This is the result."

He took from his letter-case and spread out on the table a duplicate of the tracing which I had seen him make, and of which he had given me a copy. But since I had last seen it, it had received an addition; under each group of signs the equivalents in modern Roman lettering had been written, and these made the following words:

UNKL RUBN IS IN TH MILL FIELD SKS FT DOWN CHURCH SPIR NORTH TEN THIRTY EAST DINGL

THORNDYKE'S TRACING OF THE INSCRIPTION OF THE SCARAB.

UNKL	RUBN	IS	IN	TH	MILL
FIELD	SKS	FT		DOWN	
CHURCH	SPIR	NORTH	TEN	THIRTY
EAST	DINGL	SOUTH	GABL	NORTH
ATY	FORTY	FIF	WST	GOD	SAF

KING JORJ

THE TRANSLITERATION OF THE HIEROGLYPHICS

SOUTH GABL NORTH ATY FORTY FIF WEST GOD SAF KING JORJ.

Our two friends gazed at Thorndyke's transliteration in blank astonishment. At length Blowgrave remarked: "But this translation must have demanded a very profound knowledge of the Egyptian writing."

"Not at all," replied Thorndyke. "Any intelligent person could master the Egyptian alphabet in an hour. The language, of course, is quite another matter. The spelling of this is a little crude, but it is quite intelligible and does Silas great credit, considering how little was known in his time."

"How do you suppose M. Fouquet came to overlook this?" Blowgrave asked.

"Naturally enough," was the reply. "He was looking for an Egyptian inscription. But this is not an Egyptian inscription. Does he speak English?"

"Very little. Practically not at all."

"Then, as the words are English words and imperfectly spelt, the hieroglyphics must have appeared to him mere nonsense. And he was right as to the scarab being an imitation."

"There is another point," said Blowgrave. "How was it that Harold made that extraordinary mistake about the place? The directions are clear enough. All you had to do was to go out there with a compass and take the bearings just as they were given."

"But," said Thorndyke, "that is exactly what he did, and hence the mistake. He was apparently unaware of the phenomenon known as the Secular Variation of the Compass. As you know, the compass does not—usually—point to true north, but to the Magnetic North; and the Magnetic North is continually changing its position. When Reuben was buried—-about 1810—it was twenty-four degrees, twenty-six minutes west of true north; at the present time it is fourteen degrees, forty-eight minutes west of true north. So Harold's bearings would be no less than ten degrees out, which of course, gave him a totally wrong position.

"But Silas was a ship-master, a navigator, and of course knew all about the vagaries of the compass; and, as his directions were intended for use at some date unknown to him, I assumed that the bearings that he gave were true bearings—that when he said 'north' he meant true north, which is always the same; and this turned out to be the case. But I also prepared a plan with magnetic bearings corrected up to date. Here are the three plans: No. 1—the one we used—showing true bearings; No. 2, showing corrected magnetic bearings which might have given us the correct spot; and No. 3, with uncorrected magnetic bearings, giving us the spot where Harold dug, and which could not possibly have been the right spot."

On the following morning I escorted the deed-box, filled with the booty and tied up and sealed with the scarab, to Mr. Blowgrave's bank. And that ended our connection with the case; excepting that, a month or two later, we attended by request the unveiling in Shawstead churchyard of a fine monument to Reuben Blowgrave. This took the slightly inappropriate form of an obelisk, on which were cut the name and approximate dates, with the added inscription: "*Cast thy bread upon the waters and it shall return after many days;*" concerning which Thorndyke remarked dryly that he supposed the exhortation applied equally even if the bread happened to belong to someone else.

The Case of Oscar Brodski

Part 1. The Mechanism of Crime

A surprising amount of nonsense has been talked about conscience. On the one hand remorse (or the "again-bite," as certain scholars of ultra-Teutonic leanings would prefer to call it); on the other hand "an easy conscience": these have been accepted as the determining factors of happiness or the reverse.

Of course there is an element of truth in the "easy conscience" view, but it begs the whole question. A particularly hardy conscience may be quite easy under the most unfavourable conditions—conditions in which the more feeble conscience might be severely afflicted with the "again-bite." And, then, it seems to be the fact that some fortunate persons have no conscience at all; a negative gift that raises them above the mental vicissitudes of the common herd of humanity.

Now, Silas Hickler was a case in point. No one, looking into his cheerful, round face, beaming with benevolence and wreathed in perpetual smiles, would have imagined him to be a criminal. Least of all, his worthy, high-church housekeeper, who was a witness to his unvarying amiability, who constantly heard him carolling light-heartedly about the house and noted his appreciative zest at meal-times.

Yet it is a fact that Silas earned his modest, though comfortable, income by the gentle art of burglary. A precarious trade and risky withal, yet not so very hazardous if pursued with judgment and moderation. And Silas was eminently a man of judgment. He worked invariably alone. He kept his own counsel. No confederate had he to turn King's Evidence at a pinch; no one he knew would bounce off in a fit of temper to Scotland Yard. Nor was he greedy and thriftless, as most criminals are. His "scoops" were few and far between, carefully planned, secretly executed, and the proceeds judiciously invested in "weekly property."

In early life Silas had been connected with the diamond industry, and he still did a little rather irregular dealing. In the trade he was suspected of transactions with I.D.B.'s, and one or two indiscreet dealers had gone so far as to whisper the ominous word "fence." But Silas smiled a benevolent smile and went his way. He knew what he knew, and his clients in Amsterdam were not inquisitive.

Such was Silas Hickler. As he strolled round his garden in the dusk of an October evening, he seemed the very type of modest, middle-class prosperity. He was dressed in the travelling suit that he wore on his little continental trips; his bag was packed and stood in readiness on the sitting-room sofa. A parcel of diamonds (purchased honestly, though without impertinent questions, at Southampton) was in the inside pocket of his waistcoat, and another more valuable parcel was stowed in a cavity in the heel of his right boot. In an hour and a half it would be time for him to set out to catch the boat train at the junction; meanwhile there was nothing to do but to stroll round the fading garden and consider how he should invest the proceeds of the impending deal. His housekeeper had gone over to Welham for the week's shopping, and would probably not be back until eleven o'clock. He was alone in the premises and just a trifle dull.

He was about to turn into the house when his ear caught the sound of footsteps on the unmade road that passed the end of the garden. He paused and listened. There was no other dwelling near, and the road led nowhere, fading away into the waste land beyond the house. Could this be a visitor? It seemed unlikely, for visitors were few at Silas Hickler's house. Meanwhile the footsteps continued to approach, ringing out with increasing loudness on the hard, stony path.

Silas strolled down to the gate, and, leaning on it, looked out with some curiosity. Presently a glow of light showed him the face of a man, apparently lighting his pipe; then a dim figure detached itself from the enveloping gloom, advanced towards him and halted opposite the garden. The stranger removed a cigarette from his mouth and, blowing out a cloud of smoke, asked—

"Can you tell me if this road will take me to Badsham Junction?"

"No," replied Hickler, "but there is a footpath farther on that leads to the station."

"Footpath!" growled the stranger. "I've had enough of footpaths. I came down from town to Catley intending to walk across to the junction. I started along the road, and then some fool directed me to a short cut, with the result that I have been blundering about in the dark for the last half-hour. My sight isn't very good, you know," he added.

"What train do you want to catch?" asked Hickler.

"Seven fifty-eight," was the reply.

"I am going to catch that train myself," said Silas, "but I shan't be starting for another hour. The station is only three-quarters of a mile from here. If you like to come in and take a rest, we can walk down together and then you'll be sure of not missing your way."

"It's very good of you," said the stranger, peering, with spectacled eyes, at the dark house, "but—I think—?"

"Might as well wait here as at the station," said Silas in his genial way, holding the gate open, and the stranger, after a momentary hesitation, entered and, flinging away his cigarette, followed him to the door of the cottage.

The sitting-room was in darkness, save for the dull glow of the expiring fire, but, entering before his guest, Silas applied a match to the lamp that hung from the ceiling. As the flame leaped up, flooding the little interior with light, the two men regarded one another with mutual curiosity.

"Brodski, by Jingo!" was Hickler's silent commentary, as he looked at his guest. "Doesn't know me, evidently—wouldn't, of course, after all these years and with his bad eyesight. Take a seat, sir," he added aloud. "Will you join me in a little refreshment to while away the time?"

Brodski murmured an indistinct acceptance, and, as his host turned to open a cupboard, he deposited his hat (a hard, grey felt) on a chair in a corner, placed his bag on the edge of the table, resting his umbrella against it, and sat down in a small armchair.

"Have a biscuit?" said Hickler, as he placed a whisky-bottle on the table together with a couple of his best star-pattern tumblers and a siphon.

"Thanks, I think I will," said Brodski. "The railway journey and all this confounded tramping about, you know—?"

"Yes," agreed Silas. "Doesn't do to start with an empty stomach. Hope you don't mind oat-cakes; I see they're the only biscuits I have."

Brodski hastened to assure him that oat-cakes were his special and peculiar fancy, and in confirmation, having mixed himself a stiff jorum, he fell to upon the biscuits with evident gusto.

Brodski was a deliberate feeder, and at present appeared to be somewhat sharp set. His measured munching being unfavourable to conversation, most of the talking fell to Silas; and, for once, that genial transgressor found the task embarrassing. The natural thing would have been to discuss his guest's destination and perhaps the object of his journey; but this was precisely what Hickler avoided doing. For he knew both, and instinct told him to keep his knowledge to himself.

Brodski was a diamond merchant of considerable reputation, and in a large way of business. He bought stones principally in the rough, and of these he was a most excellent judge. His fancy was for stones of somewhat unusual size and value, and it was well known to be his custom, when he had accumulated a sufficient stock, to carry them himself to Amsterdam and supervise the cutting of the rough stones. Of this Hickler was aware, and he had no doubt that Brodski was now starting on one of his periodical excursions; that somewhere in the recesses of his rather shabby clothing was concealed a paper packet possibly worth several thousand pounds.

Brodski sat by the table munching monotonously and talking little. Hickler sat opposite him, talking nervously and rather wildly at times, and watching his guest with a growing fascination. Precious stones, and especially diamonds, were Hickler's specialty. "Hard stuff"—silver plate—he avoided entirely; gold, excepting in the form of specie, he seldom touched; but stones, of which he could carry off a whole consignment in the heel of his boot and dispose of with absolute safety, formed the staple of his industry.

And here was a man sitting opposite him with a parcel in his pocket containing the equivalent of a dozen of his most successful "scoops;" stones worth perhaps—? Here he pulled himself up short and began to talk rapidly, though without much coherence. For, even as he talked, other Words, formed subconsciously, seemed to insinuate themselves into the interstices of the sentences, and to carry on a parallel train of thought.

"Gets chilly in the evenings now, doesn't it?" said Hickler.

"It does indeed," Brodski agreed, and then resumed his slow munching, breathing audibly through his nose.

"Five thousand at least," the subconscious train of thought resumed; "probably six or seven, perhaps ten." Silas fidgeted in his chair and endeavoured to concentrate his ideas on some topic of interest.

He was growing disagreeably conscious of a new and unfamiliar state of mind.

"Do you take any interest in gardening?", he asked. Next to diamonds and weekly "property," his besetting weakness was fuchsias.

Brodski chuckled sourly. "Hatton Garden is the nearest approach—?" He broke off suddenly, and then added, "I am a Londoner, you know."

The abrupt break in the sentence was not unnoticed by Silas, nor had he any difficulty in interpreting it. A man who carries untold wealth upon his person must needs be wary in his speech.

"Yes," he answered absently, "it's hardly a Londoner's hobby." And then, half consciously, he began a rapid calculation. Put it at five thousand pounds. What would that represent in weekly property? His last set of houses had cost two hundred and fifty pounds apiece, and he had let them at ten shillings and sixpence a week. At that rate, five thousand pounds represented twenty houses at ten and sixpence a week—say ten pounds a week—one pound eight shillings a day—five hundred and twenty pounds a year—for life. It was a competency. Added to what he already had, it was wealth. With that income he could fling the tools of his trade into the river and live out the remainder of his life in comfort and security.

He glanced furtively at his guest across the table, and then looked away quickly as he felt stirring within him an impulse the nature of which he could not mistake. This must be put an end to. Crimes against the person he had always looked upon as sheer insanity. There was, it is true, that little affair of the Weybridge policeman, but that was unforeseen and unavoidable, and it was the constable's doing after all. And there was the old housekeeper at Epsom, too, but, of course, if the old idiot would shriek in that insane fashion—well, it was an accident, very regrettable, to be sure, and no one could be more sorry for the mishap than himself. But deliberate homicide!—robbery from the person! It was the act of a stark lunatic.

Of course, if he had happened to be that sort of person, here was the opportunity of a lifetime. The immense booty, the empty house, the solitary neighbourhood, away from the main road and from other habitations; the time, the darkness—but, of course, there was the body to be thought of; that was always the difficulty. What to do with the body? Here he caught the shriek of the up express, rounding the curve in the line that ran past the waste land at the back of the house.

The sound started a new train of thought, and, as he followed it out, his eyes fixed themselves on the unconscious and taciturn Brodski, as he sat thoughtfully sipping his whisky.

At length, averting his gaze with an effort, he rose suddenly from his chair and turned to look at the clock on the mantelpiece, spreading out his hands before the dying fire. A tumult of strange sensations warned him to leave the house. He shivered slightly, though he was rather hot than chilly, and, turning his head, looked at the door.

"Seems to be a confounded draught," he said, with another slight shiver; "did I shut the door properly, I wonder?" He strode across the room and, opening the door wide, looked out into the dark garden. A desire, sudden and urgent, had come over him to get out into the open air, to be on the road and have done with this madness that was knocking at the door of his brain.

"I wonder if it is worth while to start yet," he said, with a yearning glance at the murky, starless sky.

Brodski roused himself and looked round. "Is your clock right?" he asked.

Silas reluctantly admitted that it was.

"How long will it take us to walk to the station?" inquired Brodski.

"Oh, about twenty-five minutes to half-an-hour," replied Silas, unconsciously exaggerating the distance.

"Well," said Brodski, "we've got more than an hour yet, and it's more comfortable here than hanging about the station. I don't see the use of starting before we need."

"No; of course not," Silas agreed. A wave of strange emotion, half-regretful, half-triumphant, surged through his brain. For some moments he remained standing on the threshold, looking out dreamily into the night. Then he softly closed the door; and, seemingly without the exercise of his volition, the key turned noiselessly in the lock.

He returned to his chair and tried to open a conversation with the taciturn Brodski, but the words came faltering and disjointed. He felt his face growing hot, his brain full and intense, and there was a faint, high-pitched singing in his ears. He was conscious of watching his guest with a new and fearful interest, and, by sheer force of will, turned away his eyes; only to find them a moment later involuntarily returning to fix the unconscious man with yet more horrible intensity. And ever through his mind walked, like a dreadful procession, the thoughts of what that other man—the man of blood and violence—

would do in these circumstances. Detail by detail the hideous synthesis fitted together the parts of the imagined crime, and arranged them in due sequence until they formed a succession of events, rational, connected and coherent.

He rose uneasily from his chair, with his eyes still riveted upon his guest. He could not sit any longer opposite that man with his hidden store of precious gems. The impulse that he recognised with fear and wonder was growing more ungovernable from moment to moment. If he stayed it would presently overpower him, and then? He shrank with horror from the dreadful thought, but his fingers itched to handle the diamonds. For Silas was, after all, a criminal by nature and habit. He was a beast of prey. His livelihood had never been earned; it had been taken by stealth or, if necessary, by force.

His instincts were predacious, and the proximity of unguarded valuables suggested to him, as a logical consequence, their abstraction or seizure. His unwillingness to let these diamonds go away beyond his reach was fast becoming overwhelming.

But he would make one more effort to escape. He would keep out of Brodski's actual presence until the moment for starting came.

"If you'll excuse me," he said, "I will go and put on a thicker pair of boots. After all this dry weather we may get a change, and damp feet are very uncomfortable when you are travelling."

"Yes; dangerous too," agreed Brodski.

Silas walked through into the adjoining kitchen, where, by the light of the little lamp that was burning there, he had seen his stout, country boots placed, cleaned and in readiness, and sat down upon a chair to make the change. He did not, of course, intend to wear the country boots, for the diamonds were concealed in those he had on. But he would make the change and then alter his mind; it would all help to pass the time. He took a deep breath. It was a relief, at any rate, to be out of that room. Perhaps if he stayed away, the temptation would pass. Brodski would go on his way—he wished that he was going alone—and the danger would be over—at least—and the opportunity would have gone—the diamonds—?

He looked up as he slowly unlaced his boot. From where he sat he could see Brodski sitting by the table with his back towards the kitchen door. He had finished eating, now, and was composedly rolling a cigarette. Silas breathed heavily, and, slipping off his boot, sat for a while motionless, gazing steadily at the other man's back. Then he unlaced the other boot, still staring abstractedly at his unconscious guest, drew it off, and laid it very quietly on the floor.

Brodski calmly finished rolling his cigarette, licked the paper, put away his pouch, and, having dusted the crumbs of tobacco from his knees, began to search his pockets for a match. Suddenly, yielding to an uncontrollable impulse, Silas stood up and began stealthily to creep along the passage to the sitting-room. Not a sound came from his stockinged feet. Silently as a cat he stole forward, breathing softly with parted lips, until he stood at the threshold of the room. His face flushed duskily, his eyes, wide and staring, glittered in the lamplight, and the racing blood hummed in his ears.

Brodski struck a match—Silas noted that it was a wooden vesta—lighted his cigarette, blew out the match and flung it into the fender. Then he replaced the box in his pocket and commenced to smoke.

Slowly and without a sound Silas crept forward into the room, step by step, with catlike stealthiness, until he stood close behind Brodski's chair—so close that he had to turn his head that his breath might not stir the hair upon the other man's head. So, for half-a-minute, he stood motionless, like a symbolical statue of Murder, glaring down with horrible, glittering eyes upon the unconscious diamond merchant, while his quick breath passed without a sound through his open mouth and his fingers writhed slowly like the tentacles of a giant hydra. And then, as noiselessly as ever, he backed away to the door, turned quickly and walked back into the kitchen.

He drew a deep breath. It had been a near thing. Brodski's life had hung upon a thread For it had been so easy. Indeed, if he had happened, as he stood behind the man's chair, to have a weapon—a hammer, for instance, or even a stone?

He glanced round the kitchen and his eyes lighted on a bar that had been left by the workmen who had put up the new greenhouse. It was an odd piece cut off from a square, wrought-iron stanchion, and was about a foot long and perhaps three-quarters of an inch thick. Now, if he had had that in his hand a minute ago—

He picked the bar up, balanced it in his hand and swung it round his head. A formidable weapon this: silent, too. And it fitted the plan that had passed through his brain. Bah! He had better put the thing down.

But he did not. He stepped over to the door and looked again at Brodski, sitting, as before, meditatively smoking, with his back towards the kitchen.

Suddenly a change came over Silas. His face flushed, the veins of his neck stood out and a sullen scowl settled on his face. He drew out his watch, glanced at it earnestly and replaced it. Then he strode swiftly but silently along the passage into the sitting-room.

A pace away from his victim's chair he halted and took deliberate aim. The bar swung aloft, but not without some faint rustle of movement, for Brodski looked round quickly even as the iron whistled through the air. The movement disturbed the murderer's aim, and the bar glanced off his victim's head, making only a trifling wound. Brodski sprang up with a tremulous, bleating cry, and clutched his assailant's arms with the tenacity of mortal terror.

Then began a terrible struggle, as the two men, locked in a deadly embrace, swayed to and fro and trampled backwards and forwards. The chair was overturned, an empty glass swept from the table and, with Brodski's spectacles, crushed beneath stamping feet. And thrice that dreadful, pitiful, bleating cry rang out into the night, filling Silas, despite his murderous frenzy, with terror lest some chance wayfarer should hear it. Gathering his great strength for a final effort, he forced his victim backwards onto the table and, snatching up a corner of the tablecloth, thrust it into his face and crammed it into his mouth as it opened to utter another shriek. And thus they remained for a full two minutes, almost motionless, like some dreadful group of tragic allegory. Then, when the last faint twitchings had died away, Silas relaxed his grasp and let the limp body slip softly onto the floor.

It was over. For good or for evil, the thing was done. Silas stood up, breathing heavily, and, as he wiped the sweat from his face, he looked at the clock. The hands stood at one minute to seven. The whole thing had taken a little over three minutes. He had nearly an hour in which to finish his task The goods train that entered into his scheme came by at twenty minutes past, and it was only three hundred yards to the line. Still, he must not waste time. He was now quite composed, and only disturbed by the thought that Brodski's cries might have been heard. If no one had heard them it was all plain sailing.

He stooped, and, gently disengaging the table-cloth from the dead man's teeth, began a careful search of his pockets. He was not long finding what he sought, and, as he pinched the paper packet and felt the little hard bodies grating on one another inside, his faint regrets for what had happened were swallowed up in self-congratulations.

He now set about his task with business-like briskness and an attentive eye on the clock. A few large drops of blood had fallen on the table-cloth, and there was a small bloody smear on the carpet by the dead man's head. Silas fetched from the kitchen some water, a nail-brush and a dry cloth, and, having washed out the stains from the table-cover—not forgetting the deal table-top underneath—and cleaned away the smear from the carpet and rubbed the damp places dry, he slipped a sheet of paper under the head of the corpse to prevent further contamination. Then he set the tablecloth straight, stood the chair upright, laid the broken spectacles on the table and picked up the cigarette, which had been trodden flat in the struggle, and flung it under the grate.

Then there was the broken glass, which he swept up into a dust-pan. Part of it was the remains of the shattered tumbler, and the rest the fragments of the broken spectacles. He turned it out onto a sheet of paper and looked it over carefully, picking out the larger recognisable pieces of the spectacle-glasses and putting them aside on a separate slip of paper, together with a sprinkling of the minute fragments. The remainder he shot back into the dust-pan and, having hurriedly put on his boots, carried it out to the rubbish-heap at the back of the house.

It was now time to start. Hastily cutting off a length of string from his string-box—for Silas was an orderly man and despised the oddments of string with which many people make shift—he tied it to the dead man's bag and umbrella and slung them from his shoulder. Then he folded up the paper of broken glass, and, slipping it and the spectacles into his pocket, picked up the body and threw it over his shoulder. Brodski was a small, spare man, weighing not more than nine stone; not a very formidable burden for a big, athletic man like Silas.

The night was intensely dark, and, when Silas looked out of the back gate over the waste land that stretched from his house to the railway, he could hardly see twenty yards ahead. After listening cautiously and hearing no sound, he went out, shut the gate softly behind him and set forth at a good pace, though carefully, over the broken ground. His progress was not as silent as he could have wished for, though.

The scanty turf that covered the gravelly land was thick enough to deaden his footfalls, the swinging bag and umbrella made an irritating noise; indeed, his movements were more hampered by them than by the weightier burden.

The distance to the line was about three hundred yards. Ordinarily he would have walked it in from three to four minutes, but now, going cautiously with his burden and stopping now and again to listen, it took him just six minutes to reach the three-bar fence that separated the waste land from the railway. Arrived here he halted for a moment and once more listened attentively, peering into the darkness on all sides. Not a living creature was to be seen or heard in this desolate spot, but far away, the shriek of an engine's whistle warned him to hasten.

Lifting the corpse easily over the fence, he carried it a few yards farther to a point where the line curved sharply.

Here he laid it face downwards, with the neck over the near rail. Drawing out his pocket-knife, he cut through the knot that fastened the umbrella to the string and also secured the bag; and when he had flung the bag and umbrella on the track beside the body, he carefully pocketed the string, excepting the little loop that had fallen to the ground when the knot was cut.

The quick snort and clanking rumble of an approaching goods train began now to be clearly audible. Rapidly, Silas; drew from his pockets the battered spectacles and the packet of broken glass. The former he threw down by the dead man's head, and then, emptying the packet into his hand, sprinkled the fragments of glass around the spectacles.

He was none too soon. Already the quick, laboured puffing of the engine sounded close at hand. His impulse was to stay and watch; to witness the final catastrophe that should convert the murder into an accident or suicide. But it was hardly safe: it would be better that he should not be near lest he should not be able to get away without being seen. Hastily he climbed back over the fence and strode away across the rough fields, while the train came snorting and clattering towards the curve.

He had nearly reached his back gate when a sound from the line brought him to a sudden halt; it was a prolonged whistle accompanied by the groan of brakes and the loud clank of colliding trucks. The snorting of the engine had ceased and was replaced by the penetrating hiss of escaping steam.

The train had stopped!

For one brief moment Silas stood with bated breath and mouth agape like one petrified; then he strode forward quickly to the gate, and, letting himself in, silently slid the bolt. He was undeniably alarmed. What could have happened on the line? It was practically certain that the body had been seen; but what was happening now? and would they come to the house? He entered the kitchen, and having paused again to listen—for somebody might come and knock at the door at any moment—he walked through the sitting-room and looked round. All seemed in order there. There was the bar, though, lying where he had dropped it in the scuffle.

He picked it up and held it under the lamp. There was no blood on it; only one or two hairs. Somewhat absently he wiped it with the table-cover, and then, running out through the kitchen into the back garden, dropped it over the wall into a bed of nettles. Not that there was anything incriminating in the bar, but, since he had used it as a weapon, it had somehow acquired a sinister aspect to his eye.

He now felt that it would be well to start for the station at once. It was not time yet, for it was barely twenty-five minutes past seven; but he did not wish to be found in the house if any one should come. His soft hat was on the sofa with his bag, to which his umbrella was strapped. He put on the hat, caught up the bag and stepped over to the door; then he came back to turn down the lamp. And it was at this moment, when he stood with his hand raised to the burner, that his eyes, travelling by chance into the dim corner of the room, lighted on Brodski's grey felt hat, reposing on the chair where the dead man had placed it when he entered the house.

Silas stood for a few moments as if petrified, with the chilly sweat of mortal fear standing in beads upon his forehead. Another instant and he would have turned the lamp down and gone on his way; and then—? He strode over to the chair, snatched up the hat and looked inside it. Yes, there was the name, "Oscar Brodski," written plainly on the lining. If he had gone away, leaving it to be discovered, he would have been lost; indeed, even now, if a search-party should come to the house, it was enough to send him to the gallows.

His limbs shook with horror at the thought, but in spite of his panic he did not lose his self-possession. Darting through into the kitchen, he grabbed up a handful of the dry brush-wood that was kept for lighting fires and carried it to the sitting-room grate where he thrust it on the extinct, but still hot, embers, and crumpling up the paper that he had placed under Brodski's head—on which paper he now noticed, for the first time, a minute bloody smear—he poked it in under the wood, and striking a wax match, set light to it. As the wood flared up, he hacked at the hat with his pocket knife and threw the ragged strips into the blaze.

And all the while his heart was thumping and his hands a-tremble with the dread of discovery. The fragments of felt were far from inflammable, tending rather to fuse into cindery masses that smoked and smouldered than to burn away into actual ash. Moreover, to his dismay, they emitted a powerful resinous stench mixed with the odour of burning hair, so that he had to open the kitchen window (since he dared not unlock the front door) to disperse the reek. And still, as he fed the fire with small cut fragments, he strained his ears to catch, above the crackling of the wood, the sound of the dreaded footsteps, the knock on the door that should be as the summons of Fate.

The time, too, was speeding on. Twenty-one minutes to eight! In a few minutes more he must set out or he would miss the train. He dropped the dismembered hat-brim on the blazing wood and ran upstairs to open a window, since he must close that in the kitchen before he left. When he came back, the brim had already curled up into a black, clinkery mass that bubbled and hissed as the fat, pungent smoke rose from it sluggishly to the chimney.

Nineteen minutes to eight! It was time to start. He took up the poker and carefully beat the cinders into small particles, stirring them into the glowing embers of the wood and coal. There was nothing unusual in the appearance of the grate. It was his constant custom to burn letters and other discarded articles in the sitting-room fire: his housekeeper would notice nothing out of the common. Indeed, the cinders would probably be reduced to ashes before she returned. He had been careful to notice that there were no metallic fittings of any kind in the hat, which might have escaped burning.

Once more he picked up his bag, took a last look round, turned down the lamp and, unlocking the door, held it open for a few moments. Then he went out, locked the door, pocketed the key (of which his housekeeper had a duplicate) and set off at a brisk pace for the station.

He arrived in good time after all, and, having taken his ticket, strolled through onto the platform. The train was not yet signalled, but there seemed to be an unusual stir in the place. The passengers were collected in a group at one end of the platform, and were all looking in one direction down the line; and, even as he walked towards them, with a certain tremulous, nauseating curiosity, two men emerged from the darkness and ascended the slope to the platform, carrying a stretcher covered with a tarpaulin. The passengers parted to let the bearers pass, turning fascinated eyes upon the shape that showed faintly through the rough pall; and, when the stretcher had been borne into the lamp-room, they fixed their attention upon a porter who followed carrying a hand-bag and an umbrella.

Suddenly one of the passengers started forward with an exclamation.

"Is that his umbrella?" he demanded.

"Yes, sir," answered the porter, stopping and holding it out for the speaker's inspection.

"My God!" ejaculated the passenger; then, turning sharply to a tall man who stood close by, he said excitedly: "That's Brodski's umbrella. I could swear to it. You remember Brodski?" The tall man nodded, and the passenger, turning once more to the porter, said: "I identify that umbrella. It belongs to a gentleman named Brodski. If you look in his hat you will see his name written in it. He always writes his name in his hat."

"We haven't found his hat yet," said the porter; "but here is the station-master coming up the line." He awaited the arrival of his superior and then announced: "This gentleman, sir, has identified the umbrella."

"Oh," said the station-master, "you recognise the umbrella, sir, do you? Then perhaps you would step into the lamp-room and see if you can identify the body."

"Is it—is he—very much injured?" the passenger asked tremulously.

"Well, yes," was the reply. "You see, the engine and six of the trucks went over him before they could stop the train. Took his head clean off, in fact."

"Shocking! shocking!" gasped the passenger. "I think, if you don't mind—I'd—I'd rather not. You don't think it's necessary, doctor, do you?"

"Yes, I do," replied the tall man. "Early identification may be of the first importance."

"Then I suppose I must," said the passenger.

Very reluctantly he allowed himself to be conducted by the station-master to the lamp-room, as the clang of the bell announced the approaching train. Silas Hickler followed and took his stand with the expectant crowd outside the closed door. In a few moments the passenger burst out, pale and awe-stricken, and rushed up to his tall friend. "It is!" he exclaimed breathlessly. "It's Brodski! Poor old Brodski! Horrible! horrible! He was to have met me here and come on with me to Amsterdam."

"Had he any—merchandize about him?" the tall man asked; and Silas strained his ears to catch the reply.

"He had some stones, no doubt, but I don't know what.

His clerk will know, of course. By the way, doctor, could you watch the case for me? Just to be sure it was really an accident or—you know what. We were old friends, you know, fellow townsmen, too; we were both born in Warsaw. I'd like you to give an eye to the case."

"Very well," said the other. "I will satisfy myself that—there is nothing more than appears, and let you have a report. Will that do?"

"Thank you. It's excessively good of you, doctor. Ah! here comes the train. I hope it won't inconvenience you to stay and see to this matter."

"Not in the least," replied the doctor. "We are not due at Warmington until tomorrow afternoon, and I expect we can find out all that is necessary to know before that."

Silas looked long and curiously at the tall, imposing man who was, as it were, taking his seat at the chessboard, to play against him for his life. A formidable antagonist he looked, with his keen, thoughtful face, so resolute and calm. As Silas stepped into his carriage he thought with deep discomfort of Brodski's hat, and hoped that he had made no other oversight.

PART 2. THE MECHANISM OF DETECTION
(Related by Christopher Jervis, M.D.)

The singular circumstances that attended the death of Mr. Oscar Brodski, the well-known diamond merchant of Hatton Garden, illustrated very forcibly the importance of one or two points in medico-legal practice which Thorndyke was accustomed to insist were not sufficiently appreciated. What those points were, I shall leave my friend and teacher to state at the proper place; and meanwhile, as the case is in the highest degree instructive, I shall record the incidents in the order of their occurrence.

The dusk of an October evening was closing in as Thorndyke and

I, the sole occupants of a smoking compartment, found ourselves approaching the little station of Ludham; and, as the train slowed down, we peered out at the knot of country, people who were waiting on the platform. Suddenly Thorndyke exclaimed in a tone of surprise: "Why, that is surely Boscovitch!" and almost at the same moment a brisk, excitable little man darted at the door of our compartment and literally tumbled in.

"I hope I don't intrude on this learned conclave," he said, shaking hands genially and banging his Gladstone with impulsive violence into the rack; "but I saw your faces at the window, and naturally jumped at the chance of such pleasant companionship."

"You are very flattering," said Thorndyke; "so flattering that you leave us nothing to say. But what in the name of fortune are you doing at—what's the name of the place—Ludham?"

"My brother has a little place a mile or so from here, and I have been spending a couple of days with him," Mr. Boscovitch explained. "I shall change at Badsham Junction and catch the boat train for Amsterdam. But whither are you two bound? I see you have your mysterious little green box up on the hat-rack, so I infer that you are on some romantic quest, eh? Going to unravel some dark and intricate crime?"

"No," replied Thorndyke. "We are bound for Warmington on a quite prosaic errand. I am instructed to watch the proceedings at an inquest there tomorrow on behalf of the Griffin Life Insurance Office, and we are travelling down tonight as it is rather a cross-country journey."

"But why the box of magic?" asked Boscovitch, glancing up at the hat-rack.

"I never go away from home without it," answered Thorndyke. "One never knows what may turn up; the trouble of carrying it is small when set off against the comfort of having appliances at hand in an emergency."

Boscovitch continued to stare up at the little square case covered with Willesden canvas. Presently he remarked: "I often used to wonder what you had in it when you were down at Chelmsford in connection with that bank murder—what an amazing case that was, by the way, and didn't your methods of research astonish the police!" As he still looked up wistfully at the case, Thorndyke good-naturedly lifted it down and unlocked it. As a matter of fact he was rather proud of his "portable laboratory," and certainly it was a triumph of condensation, for, small as it was—only a foot square by four inches deep—it contained a fairly complete outfit for a preliminary investigation.

"Wonderful!" exclaimed Boscovitch, when the case lay open before him, displaying its rows of little re-agent bottles, tiny test-tubes, diminutive spirit-lamp, dwarf microscope and assorted instruments on the same Lilliputian scale; "it's like a doll's house—everything looks as if it was seen through the wrong end of a telescope. But are these tiny things really efficient? That microscope now—?"

"Perfectly efficient at low and moderate magnifications," said Thorndyke. "It looks like a toy, but it isn't one; the lenses are the best that can be had. Of course a full-sized instrument would be infinitely more convenient—but I shouldn't have it with me, and should have to make shift with a pocket-lens. And so with the rest of the under-sized appliances; they are the alternative to no appliances."

Boscovitch pored over the case and its contents, fingering the instruments delicately and asking questions innumerable about their uses; indeed, his curiosity was but half appeased when, half-an-hour later, the train began to slow down.

"By Jove!" he exclaimed, starting up and seizing his bag, "here we are at the junction already. You change here too, don't you?"

"Yes," replied Thorndyke. "We take the branch train on to Warmington."

As we stepped out onto the platform, we became aware that something unusual was happening or had happened. All the passengers and most of the porters and supernumeraries were gathered at one end of the station, and all were looking intently into the darkness down the line.

"Anything wrong?" asked Mr. Boscovitch, addressing the station-inspector.

"Yes, sir," the official replied; "a man has been run over by the goods train about a mile down the line. The station-master has gone down with a stretcher to bring him in, and I expect that is his lantern that you see coming this way."

As we stood watching the dancing light grow momentarily brighter, flashing fitful reflections from the burnished rails, a man came out of the booking-office and joined the group of onlookers. He attracted my attention, as I afterwards remembered, for two reasons: in the first place his round, jolly face was excessively pale and bore a strained and wild expression, and, in the second, though he stared into the darkness with eager curiosity he asked no questions.

The swinging lantern continued to approach, and then suddenly two men came into sight bearing a stretcher covered with a tarpaulin, through which the shape of a human figure was dimly discernible. They ascended the slope to the platform, and proceeded with their burden to the lamp-room, when the inquisitive gaze of the passengers was transferred to a porter who followed carrying a handbag and umbrella and to the station-master who brought up the rear with his lantern.

As the porter passed, Mr. Boscovitch started forward with sudden excitement.

"Is that his umbrella?" he asked.

"Yes, sir," answered the porter, stopping and holding it out for the speaker's inspection.

"My God!" ejaculated Boscovitch; then, turning sharply to Thorndyke, he exclaimed: "That's Brodski's umbrella. I could swear to it. You remember Brodski?"

Thorndyke nodded, and Boscovitch, turning once more to the porter, said: "I identify that umbrella. It belongs to a gentleman named Brodski. If you look in his hat, you will see his name written in it. He always writes his name in his hat."

"We haven't found his hat yet," said the porter; "but here is the station-master." He turned to his superior and announced: "This gentleman, sir, has identified the umbrella."

"Oh," said the station-master, "you recognise the umbrella, sir, do you? Then perhaps you would step into the lamp-room and see if you can identify the body."

Mr. Boscovitch recoiled with a look of alarm. "Is it? is he—very much injured?" he asked nervously.

"Well, yes," was the reply. "You see, the engine and six of the trucks went over him before they could stop the train. Took his head clean off, in fact."

"Shocking! shocking!" gasped Boscovitch. "I think? if you don't mind—I'd—I'd rather not. You don't think it necessary, doctor, do you?"

"Yes, I do," replied Thorndyke. "Early identification may be of the first importance."

"Then I suppose I must," said Boscovitch; and, with extreme reluctance, he followed the station-master to the lamp-room, as the loud ringing of the bell announced the approach of the boat train. His inspection must have been of the briefest, for, in a few moments, he burst out, pale and awe-stricken, and rushed up to Thorndyke.

"It is!" he exclaimed breathlessly. "It's Brodski! Poor" old Brodski! Horrible! horrible! He was to have met me here and come on with me to Amsterdam."

"Had he any—merchandise about him?" Thorndyke asked; and, as he spoke, the stranger whom I had previously noticed edged up closer as if to catch the reply.

"He had some stones, no doubt," answered Boscovitch, "but I don't know what they were. His clerk will know, of course. By the way, doctor, could you watch the case for me? Just to be sure it was really an accident or—you know what. We were old friends, you know, fellow townsmen, too; we were both born in Warsaw. I'd like you to give an eye to the case."

"Very well," said Thorndyke. "I will satisfy myself that there is nothing more than appears, and let you have a report. Will that do?"

"Thank you," said Boscovitch. "It's excessively good of you, doctor. Ah, here comes the train. I hope it won't inconvenience you to stay and see to the matter."

"Not in the least," replied Thorndyke. "We are not due at Warmington until tomorrow afternoon, and I expect we can find out all that is necessary to know and still keep our appointment."

As Thorndyke spoke, the stranger, who had kept close to us with the evident purpose of hearing what was said, bestowed on him a very curious and attentive look; and it was only when the train had actually come to rest by the platform that he hurried away to find a compartment.

No sooner had the train left the station than Thorndyke sought out the station-master and informed him of the instructions that he had received from Boscovitch. "Of course," he added, in conclusion, "we must not move in the matter until the police arrive. I suppose they have been informed?"

"Yes," replied the station-master; "I sent a message at once to the Chief Constable, and I expect him or an inspector at any moment. In fact, I think I will slip out to the approach and see if he is coming." He evidently wished to have a word in private with the police officer before committing himself to any statement.

As the official departed, Thorndyke and I began to pace the now empty platform, and my friend, as was his wont, when entering on a new inquiry, meditatively reviewed the features of the problem.

"In a case of this kind," he remarked, "we have to decide on one of three possible explanations: accident, suicide or homicide; and our decision will be determined by inferences from three sets of facts: first, the general facts of the case; second, the special data obtained by examination of the body, and, third, the special data obtained by examining the spot on which the body was found. Now the only general facts at present in our possession are that the deceased was a diamond merchant making a journey for a specific purpose and probably having on his person property of small bulk and great value.

"These facts are somewhat against the hypothesis of suicide and somewhat favourable to that of homicide. Facts relevant to the question of accident would be the existence or otherwise of a level crossing, a road or path leading to the line, an enclosing fence with or without a gate, and any other facts rendering probable or otherwise the accidental presence of the deceased at the spot where the body was found. As we do not possess these facts, it is desirable that we extend our knowledge."

"Why not put a few discreet questions to the porter who brought in the bag and umbrella?" I suggested. "He is at this moment in earnest conversation with the ticket collector and would, no doubt, be glad of a new listener."

"An excellent suggestion, Jervis," answered Thorndyke. "Let us see what he has to tell us." We approached the porter and found him, as I had anticipated, bursting to unburden himself of the tragic story.

"The way the thing happened, sir, was this," he said, in answer to Thorndyke's question: "There's a sharpish bend in the road just at that place, and the goods train was just rounding the curve when the driver suddenly caught sight of something lying across the rails. As the engine turned, the head-lights shone on it and then he saw it was a man. He shut off steam at once, blew his whistle, and put the brakes down hard, but, as you know, sir, a goods train takes some stopping; before they could bring her up, the engine and half-a-dozen trucks had gone over the poor beggar."

"Could the driver see how the man was lying?" Thorndyke asked.

"Yes, he could see him quite plain, because the headlights were full on him. He was lying on his face with his neck over the near rail on the downside. His head was in the four-foot and his body by the side of the track. It looked as if he had laid himself out a-purpose."

"Is there a level crossing thereabouts?" asked Thorndyke.

"No, sir. No crossing, no road, no path, no nothing," said the porter, ruthlessly sacrificing grammar to emphasis. "He must have come across the fields and climbed over the fence to get onto the permanent way. Deliberate suicide is what it looks like."

"How did you learn all this?" Thorndyke inquired.

"Why, the driver, you see, sir, when him and his mate had lifted the body off the track, went on to the next signal-box and sent in his report by telegram. The station-master told me all about it as we walked down the line."

Thorndyke thanked the man for his information, and, as we strolled back towards the lamp-room, discussed the bearing of these new facts.

"Our friend is unquestionably right in one respect," he said; "this was not an accident. The man might, if he were near-sighted, deaf or stupid, have climbed over the fence and got knocked down by the train. But his position, lying across the rails, can only be explained by one of two hypotheses: either it was, as the porter says, deliberate suicide, or else the man was already dead or insensible. We must leave it at that until we have seen the body, that is, if the police will allow us to see it. But here comes the station-master and an officer with him. Let us hear what they have to say."

The two officials had evidently made up their minds to decline any outside assistance. The divisional surgeon would make the necessary examination, and information could be obtained through the usual channels. The production of Thorndyke's card, however, somewhat altered the situation. The police inspector hummed and hawed irresolutely, with the card in his hand, but finally agreed to allow us to view the body, and we entered the lamp-room together, the station-master leading the way to turn up the gas.

The stretcher stood on the floor by one wall, its grim burden still hidden by the tarpaulin, and the hand-bag and umbrella lay on a large box, together with the battered frame of a pair of spectacles from which the glasses had fallen out.

"Were these spectacles found by the body?" Thorndyke inquired.

"Yes," replied the station-master. "They were close to the head and the glass was scattered about on the ballast."

Thorndyke made a note in his pocket-book, and then, as the inspector removed the tarpaulin, he glanced down on the corpse, lying limply on the stretcher and looking grotesquely horrible with its displaced head and distorted limbs. For fully a minute he remained silently stooping over the uncanny object, on which the inspector was now throwing the light of a large lantern; then he stood up and said quietly to me: "I think we can eliminate two out of the three hypotheses."

The inspector looked at him quickly, and was about to ask a question, when his attention was diverted by the travelling-case which Thorndyke had laid on a shelf and now opened to abstract a couple of pairs of dissecting forceps.

"We've no authority to make a post mortem, you know," said the inspector.

"No, of course not," said Thorndyke. "I am merely going to look into the mouth." With one pair of forceps he turned back the lip and, having scrutinized its inner surface, closely examined the teeth.

"May I trouble you for your lens, Jervis?" he said; and, as I handed him my doublet ready opened, the inspector brought the lantern close to the dead face and leaned forward eagerly. In his usual systematic fashion, Thorndyke slowly passed the lens along the whole range of sharp, uneven teeth, and then, bringing it back to the centre, examined with more minuteness the upper incisors.

At length, very delicately, he picked out with his forceps some minute object from between two of the upper front teeth and held it in the focus of the lens. Anticipating his next move, I took a labelled microscope-slide from the case and handed it to him together with a dissecting needle, and, as he transferred the object to the slide and spread it out with the needle, I set up the little microscope on the shelf.

"A drop of Farrant and a cover-glass, please, Jervis," said Thorndyke.

I handed him the bottle, and, when he had let a drop of the mounting fluid fall gently on the object and put on the cover-slip, he placed the slide on the stage of the microscope and examined it attentively.

Happening to glance at the inspector, I observed on his countenance a faint grin, which he politely strove to suppress when he caught my eye.

"I was thinking, sir," he said apologetically, "that it's a bit off the track to be finding out what he had for dinner. He didn't die of unwholesome feeding."

Thorndyke looked up with a smile. "It doesn't do, inspector, to assume that anything is off the track in an inquiry of this kind. Every fact must have some significance, you know."

"I don't see any significance in the diet of a man who has had his head cut off," the inspector rejoined defiantly.

"Don't you?" said Thorndyke. "Is there no interest attaching to the last meal of a man who has met a violent death? These crumbs, for instance, that are scattered over the dead man's waistcoat. Can we learn nothing from them?"

"I don't see what you can learn," was the dogged rejoinder.

Thorndyke picked off the crumbs, one by one, with his forceps, and having deposited them on a slide, inspected them, first with the lens and then through the microscope.

"I learn," said he, "that shortly before his death, the deceased partook of some kind of whole-meal biscuits, apparently composed partly of oatmeal."

"I call that nothing," said the inspector. "The question that we have got to settle is not what refreshments had the deceased been taking, but what was the cause of his death: did he commit suicide? was he killed by accident? or was there any foul play?"

"I beg your pardon," said Thorndyke, "the questions that remain to be settled are, who killed the deceased and with what motive? The others are already answered as far as I am, concerned."

The inspector stared in sheer amazement not unmixed with incredulity.

"You haven't been long coming to a conclusion, sir," he said.

"No, it was a pretty obvious case of murder," said Thorndyke. "As to the motive, the deceased was a diamond merchant and is believed to have had a quantity of stones about his person. I should suggest that you search the body."

The inspector gave vent to an exclamation of disgust. "I see," he said. "It was just a guess on your part. The dead man was a diamond merchant and had valuable property about him; therefore he was murdered." He drew himself up, and, regarding Thorndyke with stern reproach, added: "But you must understand, sir, that this is a judicial inquiry, not a prize competition in a penny paper. And, as to searching the body, why, that is what I principally came for." He ostentatiously turned his back on us and proceeded systematically to turn out the dead man's pockets, laying the articles, as he removed them, on the box by the side of the hand-bag and umbrella.

While he was thus occupied, Thorndyke looked over the body generally, paying special attention to the soles of the boots, which, to the inspector's undissembled amusement, he very thoroughly examined with the lens.

"I should have thought, sir, that his feet were large enough to be seen with the naked eye," was his comment; "but perhaps," he added, with a sly glance at the station-master, "you're a little near-sighted."

Thorndyke chuckled good-humouredly, and, while the officer continued his search, he looked over the articles that had already been laid on the box. The purse and pocket-book he naturally left for the inspector to open, but the reading-glasses, pocket-knife and card-case and other small pocket articles were subjected to a searching scrutiny. The inspector watched him out of the corner of his eye with furtive amusement; saw him hold up the glasses to the light to estimate their refractive power, peer into the tobacco pouch, open the cigarette book and examine the watermark of the paper, and even inspect the contents of the silver match-box.

"What might you have expected to find in his tobacco pouch?" the officer asked, laying down a bunch of keys from the dead man's pocket.

"Tobacco," Thorndyke replied stolidly; "but I did not expect to find fine-cut *Latakia*. I don't remember ever having seen pure *Latakia* smoked in cigarettes."

"You do take an interest in things, sir," said the inspector, with a side glance at the stolid station-master.

"I do," Thorndyke agreed; "and I note that there are no diamonds among this collection."

"No, and we don't know that he had any about him; but there's a gold watch and chain, a diamond scarf-pin, and a purse containing"—he opened it and tipped out its contents into his hand—"twelve pounds in gold. That doesn't look much like robbery, does it? What do you say to the murder theory now?"

"My opinion is unchanged," said Thorndyke, "and I should like to examine the spot where the body was found. Has the engine been inspected?" he added, addressing the station-master.

"I telegraphed to Bradfield to have it examined," the official answered. "The report has probably come in by now. I'd better see before we start down the line."

We emerged from the lamp-room and, at the door, found the station-inspector waiting with a telegram. He handed it to the station-master, who read it aloud.

"The engine has been carefully examined by me. I find small smear of blood on near leading wheel and smaller one on next wheel following. No other marks." He glanced questioningly at Thorndyke, who nodded and remarked: "It will be interesting to see if the line tells the same tale."

The station-master looked puzzled and was apparently about to ask for an explanation; but the inspector, who had carefully pocketed the dead man's property, was impatient to start and, accordingly, when Thorndyke had repacked his case and had, at his own request, been furnished with a lantern, we set off down the permanent way, Thorndyke carrying the light and I the indispensable green case.

"I am a little in the dark about this affair," I said, when we had allowed the two officials to draw ahead out of earshot; "you came to a conclusion remarkably quickly. What was it that so immediately determined the opinion of murder as against suicide?"

"It was a small matter but very conclusive," replied Thorndyke. "You noticed a small scalp-wound above the left temple? It was a glancing wound, and might easily have been made by the engine. But the wound had bled; and it had bled for an appreciable time. There were two streams of blood from it, and in both the blood was firmly clotted and partially dried. But the man had been decapitated; and this wound, if inflicted by the engine, must have been made after the decapitation, since it was on the side most distant from the engine as it approached. Now, a decapitated head does not bleed. Therefore, this wound was inflicted before the decapitation.

"But not only had the wound bled: the blood had trickled down in two streams at right angles to one another. First, in the order of time as shown by the appearance of the stream, it had trickled down the side of the face and dropped on the collar. The second stream ran from the wound to the back of the head. Now, you know, Jervis, there are no exceptions to the law of gravity. If the blood ran down the face towards the chin, the face must have been upright at the time; and if the blood trickled from the front to the back of the head, the head must have been horizontal and face upwards.

"But the man when he was seen by the engine-driver, was lying face downwards. The only possible inference is that when the wound was inflicted, the man was in the upright position—standing or sitting; and that subsequently, and while he was still alive, he lay on his back for a sufficiently long time for the blood to have trickled to the back of his head."

"I see. I was a duffer not to have reasoned this out for myself," I remarked contritely.

"Quick observation and rapid inference come by practice," replied Thorndyke. "What did you notice about the face?"

"I thought there was a strong suggestion of asphyxia."

"Undoubtedly," said Thorndyke. "It was the face of a suffocated man. You must have noticed, too, that the tongue was very distinctly swollen and that on the inside of the upper lip were deep indentations made by the teeth, as well as one or two slight wounds, obviously caused by heavy pressure on the mouth. And now observe how completely these facts and inferences agree with those from the scalp wound. If we knew that the deceased had received a blow on the head, had struggled with his assailant and been finally borne down and suffocated, we should look for precisely those signs which we have found."

"By the way, what was it that you found wedged between the teeth? I did not get a chance to look through the microscope."

"Ah!" said Thorndyke, "there we not only get confirmation, but we carry our inferences a stage further. The object was a little tuft of some textile fabric. Under the microscope I found it to consist of several different fibres, differently dyed. The bulk of it consisted of wool fibres dyed crimson, but there were also cotton fibres dyed blue and a few which looked like jute, dyed yellow. It was obviously a particoloured fabric and might have been part of a woman's dress, though the presence of the jute is much more suggestive of a curtain or rug of inferior quality."

"And its importance?"

"Is that, if it is not part of an article of clothing, then it must have come from an article of furniture, and furniture suggests a habitation."

"That doesn't seem very conclusive," I objected.

"It is not; but it is valuable corroboration."

"Of what?"

"Of the suggestion offered by the soles of the dead man's boots. I examined them most minutely and could find no trace of sand, gravel or earth, in spite of the fact that he must have crossed fields and rough land to reach the place where he was found. What I did find was fine tobacco ash, a charred mark as if a cigar or cigarette had been trodden on, several crumbs of biscuit, and, on a projecting brad, some coloured fibres, apparently from a carpet. The manifest suggestion is that the man was killed in a house with a carpeted floor, and carried from thence to the railway."

I was silent for some moments. Well as I knew Thorndyke, I was completely taken by surprise; a sensation, indeed, that I experienced anew every time that I accompanied him on one of his investigations. His marvellous power of co-ordinating apparently insignificant facts, of arranging them into an ordered sequence and making them tell a coherent story, was a phenomenon that I never got used to; every exhibition of it astonished me afresh.

"If your inferences are correct," I said, "the problem is practically solved. There must be abundant traces inside the house. The only question is, which house is it?"

"Quite so," replied Thorndyke; "that is the question, and a very difficult question it is. A glance at that interior would doubtless clear up the whole mystery. But how are we to get that glance? We cannot enter houses speculatively to see if they present traces of a murder. At present, our clue breaks off abruptly. The other end of it is in some unknown house, and, if we cannot join up the two ends, our problem remains unsolved. For the question is, you remember, Who killed Oscar Brodski?"

"Then what do you propose to do?" I asked.

"The next stage of the inquiry is to connect some particular house with this crime. To that end, I can only gather up all available facts and consider each in all its possible bearings. If I cannot establish any such connection, then the inquiry will have failed and we shall have to make a fresh start—say, at Amsterdam, if it turns out that Brodski really had diamonds on his person, as I have no doubt he had."

Here our conversation was interrupted by our arrival at the spot where the body had been found. The station-master had halted, and he and the inspector were now examining the near rail by the light of their lanterns.

"There's remarkably little blood about," said the former. "I've seen a good many accidents of this kind and there has always been a lot of blood, both on the engine and on the road. It's very curious."

Thorndyke glanced at the rail with but slight attention: that question had ceased to interest him. But the light of his lantern flashed onto the ground at the side of the track—a loose, gravelly soil mixed with fragments of chalk—and from thence to the soles of the inspector's boots, which were displayed as he knelt by the rail.

"You observe, Jervis?" he said in a low voice, and I nodded. The inspector's boot-soles were covered with adherent particles of gravel and conspicuously marked by the chalk on which he had trodden.

"You haven't found the hat, I suppose?" Thorndyke asked, stooping to pick up a short piece of string that lay on the ground at the side of the track.

"No," replied the inspector, "but it can't be far off. You seem to have found another clue, sir," he added, with a grin, glancing at the piece of string.

"Who knows," said Thorndyke. "A short end of white twine with a green strand in it. It may tell us something later. At any rate we'll keep it," and, taking from his pocket a small tin box containing, among other things, a number of seed envelopes, he slipped the string into one of the latter and scribbled a note in pencil on the outside. The inspector watched his proceedings with an indulgent smile, and then returned to his examination of the track, in which Thorndyke now joined.

"I suppose the poor chap was near-sighted," the officer remarked, indicating the remains of the shattered spectacles; "that might account for his having strayed onto the line."

"Possibly," said Thorndyke. He had already noticed the fragments scattered over a sleeper and the adjacent ballast, and now once more produced his "collecting-box," from which he took another seed envelope. "Would you hand me a pair of forceps, Jervis," he said; "and perhaps you wouldn't mind taking a pair yourself and helping me to gather up these fragments."

As I complied, the inspector looked up curiously.

"There isn't any doubt that these spectacles belonged to the deceased, is there?" he asked. "He certainly wore spectacles, for I saw the mark on his nose."

"Still, there is no harm in verifying the fact," said Thorndyke, and he added to me in a lower tone, "Pick up every particle you can find, Jervis. It may be most important."

"I don't quite see how," I said, groping amongst the shingle by the light of the lantern in search of the tiny splinters of glass.

"Don't you?" returned Thorndyke. "Well, look at these fragments; some of them are a fair size, but many of these on the sleeper are mere grains. And consider their number. Obviously, the condition of the glass does not agree with the circumstances in which we find it. These are thick concave spectacle-lenses broken into a great number of minute fragments. Now how were they broken? Not merely by falling, evidently: such a lens, when it is dropped, breaks into a small number of large pieces. Nor were they broken by the wheel passing over them, for they would then have been reduced to fine powder, and that powder would have been visible on the rail, which it is not. The spectacle-frames, you may remember, presented the same incongruity: they were battered and damaged more than they would have been by falling, but not nearly so much as they would have been if the wheel had passed over them."

"What do you suggest, then?" I asked.

"The appearances suggest that the spectacles had been trodden on. But, if the body was carried here the probability is that the spectacles were carried here too, and that they were then already broken; for it is more likely that they were trodden on during the struggle than that the murderer trod on them after bringing them here. Hence the importance of picking up every fragment."

"But why?" I inquired, rather foolishly, I must admit.

"Because, if, when we have picked up every fragment that we can find, there still remains missing a larger portion of the lenses than we could reasonably expect, that would tend to support our hypothesis and we might find the missing remainder elsewhere. If, on the other hand, we find as much of the lenses as we could expect to find, we must conclude that they were broken on this spot."

While we were conducting our search, the two officials were circling around with their lanterns in quest of the missing hat; and, when we had at length picked up the last fragment, and a careful search, even aided by a lens, failed to reveal any other, we could see their lanterns moving, like will-o'-the-wisps, some distance down the line.

"We may as well see what we have got before our friends come back," said Thorndyke, glancing at the twinkling lights. "Lay the case down on the grass by the fence; it will serve for a table."

I did so, and Thorndyke, taking a letter from his pocket, opened it, spread it out flat on the case, securing it with a couple of heavy stones, although the night was quite calm. Then he tipped the contents of the seed envelope out on the paper, and carefully spreading out the pieces of glass, looked at them for some moments in silence. And, as he looked, there stole over his face a very curious expression; with sudden eagerness he began picking out the large fragments and laying them on two visiting-cards which he had taken from his card-case. Rapidly and with wonderful deftness he fitted the pieces together, and, as the reconstituted lenses began gradually to take shape on their cards I looked on with growing excitement, for something in my colleague's manner told me that we were on the verge of a discovery.

At length the two ovals of glass lay on their respective cards, complete save for one or two small gaps; and the little heap that remained consisted of fragments so minute as to render further reconstruction impossible. Then Thorndyke leaned back and laughed softly.

"This is certainly an unlooked-for result," said he.

"What is?" I asked.

"Don't you see, my dear fellow? There's too much glass. We have almost completely built up the broken lenses, and the fragments that are left over are considerably more than are required to fill up the gaps."

I looked at the little heap of small fragments and saw at once that it was as he had said. There was a surplus of small pieces.

"This is very extraordinary," I said. "What do you think can be the explanation?"

"The fragments will probably tell us," he replied, "if we ask them intelligently."

He lifted the paper and the two cards carefully onto the ground, and, opening the case, took out the little microscope, to which he fitted the lowest-power objective and eye-piece—having a combined magnification of only ten diameters. Then he transferred the minute fragments of glass to a slide, and, having arranged the lantern as a microscope-lamp, commenced his examination.

"Ha!" he exclaimed presently. "The plot thickens. There is too much glass and yet too little; that is to say, there are only one or two fragments here that belong to the spectacles; not nearly enough to complete the building up of the lenses. The remainder consists of a soft, uneven, moulded glass, easily distinguished from the clear, hard optical glass. These foreign fragments are all curved, as if they had formed part of a cylinder, and are, I should say, portions of a wine-glass or tumbler." He moved the slide once or twice, and then continued:

"We are in luck, Jervis. Here is a fragment with two little diverging lines etched on it, evidently the points of an eight-rayed star—and here is another with three points—the ends of three rays. This enables us to reconstruct the vessel perfectly. It was a clear, thin glass—probably a tumbler—decorated with scattered stars; I dare say you know the pattern. Sometimes there is an ornamented band in addition, but generally the stars form the only decoration. Have a look at the specimen."

I had just applied my eye to the microscope when the station-master and the inspector came up. Our appearance, seated on the ground with the microscope between us, was too much for the police officer's gravity, and he laughed long and joyously.

"You must excuse me, gentlemen," he said apologetically, "but really, you know, to an old hand, like myself, it does look a little—well—you understand—I dare say a microscope is a very interesting and amusing thing, but it doesn't get you much forwarder in a case like this, does it?"

"Perhaps not," replied Thorndyke. "By the way, where did you find the hat, after all?"

"We haven't found it," the inspector replied.

"Then we must help you to continue the search," said Thorndyke. "If you will wait a few moments, we will come with you." He poured a few drops of xylol balsam on the cards to fix the reconstituted lenses to their supports and then, packing them and the microscope in the case, announced that he was ready to start.

"Is there any village or hamlet near?" he asked the station-master.

"None nearer than Corfield. That is about half-a-mile from here."

"And where is the nearest road?"

"There is a half-made road that runs past a house about three hundred yards from here. It belonged to a building estate that was never built. There is a footpath from it to the station."

"Are there any other houses near?"

"No. That is the only house for half-a-mile round, and there is no other road near here."

"Then the probability is that Brodski approached the railway from that direction, as he was found on that side of the permanent way."

The inspector agreeing with this view, we all set off slowly towards the house, piloted by the station-master and searching the ground as we went. The waste land over which we passed was covered with patches of docks and nettles, through each of which the inspector kicked his way, searching with feet and lantern for the missing hat. A walk of three hundred yards brought us to a low wall enclosing a garden, beyond which we could see a small house; and here we halted while the inspector waded into a large bed of nettles beside the wall and kicked vigorously. Suddenly there came a clinking sound mingled with objurgations, and the inspector hopped out holding one foot and soliloquizing profanely.

"I wonder what sort of a fool put a thing like that into a bed of nettles!" he exclaimed, stroking the injured foot. Thorndyke picked the object up and held it in the light of the lantern, displaying a piece of three-quarter inch rolled iron bar about a foot long. "It doesn't seem to have been there very long," he observed, examining it closely, "there is hardly any rust on it."

"It has been there long enough for me," growled the inspector, "and I'd like to bang it on the head of the blighter that put it there."

Callously indifferent to the inspector's sufferings, Thorndyke continued calmly to examine the bar. At length, resting his lantern on the wall, he produced his pocket-lens, with which he resumed his investigation, a proceeding that so exasperated the inspector that that afflicted official limped off in dudgeon, followed by the station-master, and we heard him, presently, rapping at the front door of the house.

"Give me a slide, Jervis, with a drop of Farrant on it," said Thorndyke. "There are some fibres sticking to this bar."

I prepared the slide, and, having handed it to him together with a cover-glass, a pair of forceps and a needle, set up the microscope on the wall.

"I'm sorry for the inspector," Thorndyke remarked, with his eye applied to the little instrument, "but that was a lucky kick for us. Just take a look at the specimen."

I did so, and, having moved the slide about until I had seen the whole of the object, I gave my opinion. "Red wool fibres, blue cotton fibres and some yellow vegetable fibres that look like jute."

"Yes," said Thorndyke; "the same combination of fibres as that which we found on the dead man's teeth and probably from the same source. This bar has probably been wiped on that very curtain or rug with which poor Brodski was stifled. We will place it on the wall for future reference, and meanwhile, by hook or by crook, we must get into that house. This is much too plain a hint to be disregarded."

Hastily repacking the case, we hurried to the front of the house, where we found the two officials looking rather vaguely up the unmade road.

"There's a light in the house," said the inspector, "but there's no one at home. I have knocked a dozen times and got no answer. And I don't see what we are hanging about here for at all. The hat is probably close to where the body was found, and we shall find it in the morning."

Thorndyke made no reply, but, entering the garden, stepped up the path, and having knocked gently at the door, stooped and listened attentively at the key-hole.

"I tell you there's no one in the house, sir," said the inspector irritably; and, as Thorndyke continued to listen, he walked away, muttering angrily. As soon as he was gone, Thorndyke flashed his lantern over the door, the threshold, the path and the small flower-beds; and, from one of the latter, I presently saw him stoop and pick something up.

"Here is a highly instructive object, Jervis," he said, coming out to the gate, and displaying a cigarette of which only half-an-inch had been smoked.

"How instructive?" I asked. "What do you learn from it?"

"Many things," he replied. "It has been lit and thrown away unsmoked; that indicates a sudden change of purpose. It was thrown away at the entrance to the house, almost certainly by someone entering it. That person was probably a stranger, or he would have taken it in with him. But he had not expected to enter the house, or he would not have lit it. These are the general suggestions; now as to the particular ones. The paper of the cigarette is of the kind known as the 'Zig-Zag' brand; the very conspicuous water-mark is quite easy to see. Now Brodski's cigarette book was a 'Zig-Zag' book—so called from the way in which the papers pull out. But let us see what the tobacco is like." With a pin from his coat, he hooked out from the unburned end a wisp of dark, dirty brown tobacco, which he held out for my inspection.

"Fine-cut *Latakia*," I pronounced, without hesitation.

"Very well," said Thorndyke. "Here is a cigarette made of an unusual tobacco similar to that in Brodski's pouch and wrapped in an unusual paper similar to those in Brodski's cigarette book. With due regard to the fourth rule of the syllogism, I suggest that this cigarette was made by Oscar Brodski. But, nevertheless, we will look for corroborative detail."

"What is that?" I asked.

"You may have noticed that Brodski's match-box contained round wooden vestas—which are also rather unusual. As he must have lighted the cigarette within a few steps of the gate, we ought to be able to find the match with which he lighted it. Let us try up the road in the direction from which he would probably have approached."

We walked very slowly up the road, searching the ground with the lantern, and we had hardly gone a dozen paces when I espied a match lying on the rough path and eagerly picked it up. It was a round wooden vesta.

Thorndyke examined it with interest and having deposited it, with the cigarette, in his "collecting-box," turned to retrace his steps. "There is now, Jervis, no reasonable doubt that Brodski was murdered in that house. We have succeeded in connecting that house with the crime, and now we have got to force an entrance and join up the other clues." We walked quickly back to the rear of the premises, where we found the inspector conversing disconsolately with the station-master.

"I think, sir," said the former, "we had better go back now; in fact, I don't see what we came here for, but—here! I say, sir, you mustn't do that!" For Thorndyke, without a word of warning, had sprung up lightly and thrown one of his long legs over the wall.

"I can't allow you to enter private premises, sir," continued the inspector; but Thorndyke quietly dropped down on the inside and turned to face the officer over the wall.

"Now, listen to me, inspector," said he. "I have good reasons for believing that the dead man, Brodski, has been in this house, in fact, I am prepared to swear an information to that effect. But time is precious; we must follow the scent while it is hot. And I am not proposing to break into the house off-hand. I merely wish to examine the dust-bin."

"The dust-bin!" gasped the inspector. "Well, you really are a most extraordinary gentleman! What do you expect to find in the dustbin?"

"I am looking for a broken tumbler or wine-glass. It is a thin glass vessel decorated with a pattern of small, eight-pointed stars. It may be in the dust-bin or it may be inside the house."

The inspector hesitated, but Thorndyke's confident manner had evidently impressed him.

"We can soon see what is in the dust-bin," he said, "though what in creation a broken tumbler has to do with the case is more than I can understand. However, here goes." He sprang up onto the wall, and, as he dropped down into the garden, the station-master and I followed.

Thorndyke lingered a few moments by the gate examining the ground, while the two officials hurried up the path. Finding nothing of interest, however, he walked towards the house, looking keenly about him as he went; but we were hardly half-way up the path when we heard the voice of the inspector calling excitedly.

"Here you are, sir, this way," he sang out, and, as we hurried forward, we suddenly came on the two officials standing over a small rubbish-heap and looking the picture of astonishment. The glare of their lanterns illuminated the heap, and showed us the scattered fragments of a thin glass, star-pattern tumbler.

"I can't imagine how you guessed it was here, sir," said the inspector, with a new-born respect in his tone, "nor what you're going to do with it now you have found it."

"It is merely another link in the chain of evidence," said Thorndyke, taking a pair of forceps from the case and stooping over the heap. "Perhaps we shall find something else." He picked up several small fragments of glass, looked at them closely and dropped them again. Suddenly his eye caught a small splinter at the base of the heap. Seizing it with the forceps, he held it close to his eye in the strong lamplight, and, taking out his lens, examined it with minute attention. "Yes," he said at length, "this is what I was looking for. Let me have those two cards, Jervis."

I produced the two visiting-cards with the reconstructed lenses stuck to them, and, laying them on the lid of the case, threw the light of the lantern on them. Thorndyke looked at them intently for some time, and from them to the fragment that he held. Then, turning to the inspector, he said: "You saw me pick up this splinter of glass?"

"Yes, sir," replied the officer.

"And you saw where we found these spectacle-glasses and know whose they were?"

"Yes, sir. They are the dead man's spectacles, and you found them where the body had been."

"Very well," said Thorndyke; "now observe;" and, as the two officials craned forward with parted lips, he laid the little splinter in a gap in one of the lenses and then gave it a gentle push forward, when it occupied the gap perfectly, joining edge to edge with the adjacent fragments and rendering that portion of the lens complete.

"My God!" exclaimed the inspector. "How on earth did you know?"

"I must explain that later," said Thorndyke. "Meanwhile we had better have a look inside the house. I expect to find there a cigarette—or possibly a cigar—which has been trodden on, some whole-meal biscuits, possibly a wooden vesta, and perhaps even the missing hat."

At the mention of the hat, the inspector stepped eagerly to the back door, but, finding it bolted, he tried the window. This also was securely fastened and, on Thorndyke's advice, we went round to the front door.

"This door is locked too," said the inspector. "I'm afraid we shall have to break in. It's a nuisance, though."

"Have a look at the window," suggested Thorndyke.

The officer did so, struggling vainly to undo the patent catch with his pocket-knife.

"It's no go," he said, coming back to the door. "We shall have to—" He broke off with an astonished stare, for the door stood open and Thorndyke was putting something in his pocket.

"Your friend doesn't waste much time—even in picking a lock," he remarked to me, as we followed Thorndyke into the house; but his reflections were soon merged in a new surprise. Thorndyke had preceded us into a small sitting-room dimly lighted by a hanging lamp turned down low.

As we entered he turned up the light and glanced about the room. A whisky-bottle was on the table, with a siphon, a tumbler and a biscuit-box. Pointing to the latter, Thorndyke said to the inspector: "See what is in that box."

The inspector raised the lid and peeped in, the station-master peered over his shoulder, and then both stared at Thorndyke.

"How in the name of goodness did you know that there were whole-meal biscuits in the house, sir?" exclaimed the station-master.

"You'd be disappointed if I told you," replied Thorndyke. "But look at this." He pointed to the hearth, where lay a flattened, half-smoked cigarette and a round wooden vesta. The inspector gazed at these objects in silent wonder, while, as to the station-master, he continued to stare at Thorndyke with what I can only describe as superstitious awe.

"You have the dead man's property with you, I believe?" said my colleague.

"Yes," replied the inspector; "I put the things in my pocket for safety."

"Then," said Thorndyke, picking up the flattened cigarette, "let us have a look at his tobacco-pouch."

As the officer produced and opened the pouch, Thorndyke neatly cut open the cigarette with his sharp pocket-knife. "Now," said he, "what kind of tobacco is in the pouch?"

The inspector took out a pinch, looked at it and smelt it distastefully. "It's one of those stinking tobaccos," he said, "that they put in mixtures—*Latakia*, I think."

"And what is this?" asked Thorndyke, pointing to the open cigarette.

"Same stuff, undoubtedly," replied the inspector.

"And now let us see his cigarette papers," said Thorndyke.

The little book, or rather packet—for it consisted of separated papers—was produced from the officer's pocket and a sample paper abstracted. Thorndyke laid the half-burnt paper beside it, and the inspector, having examined the two, held them up to the light.

"There isn't much chance of mistaking that 'Zig-Zag' watermark," he said. "This cigarette was made by the deceased; there can't be the shadow of a doubt."

"One more point," said Thorndyke, laying the burnt wooden vesta on the table. "You have his match-box?"

The inspector brought forth the little silver casket, opened it and compared the wooden vestas that it contained with the burnt end. Then he shut the box with a snap.

"You've proved it up to the hilt," said he. "If we could only find the hat, we should have a complete case."

"I'm not sure that we haven't found the hat," said Thorndyke. "You notice that something besides coal has been burned in the grate."

The inspector ran eagerly to the fireplace and began with feverish hands, to pick out the remains of the extinct fire. "The cinders are still warm," he said, "and they are certainly not all coal cinders. There has been wood burned here on top of the coal, and these little black lumps are neither coal nor wood. They may quite possibly be the remains of a burnt hat, but, lord! who can tell? You can put together the pieces of broken spectacle-glasses, but you can't build up a hat out of a few cinders." He held out a handful of little, black, spongy cinders and looked ruefully at Thorndyke, who took them from him and laid them out on a sheet of paper.

"We can't reconstitute the hat, certainly," my friend agreed, "but we may be able to ascertain the origin of these remains. They may not be cinders of a hat, after all." He lit a wax match and, taking up one of the charred fragments, applied the flame to it. The cindery mass fused at once with a crackling, seething sound, emitting a dense smoke, and instantly the air became charged with a pungent, resinous odour mingled with the smell of burning animal matter.

"Smells like varnish," the station-master remarked.

"Yes. Shellac," said Thorndyke; "so the first test gives a positive result. The next test will take more time."

He opened the green case and took from it a little flask, fitted for Marsh's arsenic test, with a safety funnel and escape tube, a small folding tripod, a spirit lamp and a disc of asbestos to serve as a sand-bath. Dropping into the flask several of the cindery masses, selected after careful inspection, he filled it up with alcohol and placed it on the disc, which he rested on the tripod. Then he lighted the spirit lamp underneath and sat down to wait for the alcohol to boil.

"There is one little point that we may as well settle," he said presently, as the bubbles began to rise in the flask. "Give me a slide with a drop of Farrant on it, Jervis."

I prepared the slide while Thorndyke, with a pair of forceps, picked out a tiny wisp from the table-cloth. "I fancy we have seen this fabric before," he remarked, as he laid the little pinch of fluff in the mounting fluid and slipped the slide onto the stage of the microscope. "Yes," he continued, looking into the eye-piece, "here are our old acquaintances, the red wool fibres, the blue cotton and the yellow jute. We must label this at once or we may confuse it with the other specimens."

"Have you any idea how the deceased met his death?" the inspector asked.

"Yes," replied Thorndyke. "I take it that the murderer enticed him into this room and gave him some refreshments. The murderer sat in the chair in which you are sitting, Brodski sat in that small arm-chair. Then I imagine the murderer attacked him with that iron bar that you found among the nettles, failed to kill him at the first stroke, struggled with him and finally suffocated him with the table-cloth. By the way, there is just one more point. You recognise this piece of string?" He took from his "collecting-box" the little end of twine that had been picked up by the line. The inspector nodded. "Look behind you, you will see where it came from."

The officer turned sharply and his eye lighted on a string-box on the mantelpiece. He lifted it down, and Thorndyke drew out from it a length of white twine with one green strand, which he compared with the piece in his hand.

"The green strand in it makes the identification fairly certain," he said. "Of course the string was used to secure the umbrella and handbag. He could not have carried them in his hand, encumbered as he was with the corpse. But I expect our other specimen is ready now." He lifted the flask off the tripod, and, giving it a vigorous shake, examined the contents through his lens. The alcohol had now become dark-brown in colour, and was noticeably thicker and more syrupy in consistence.

"I think we have enough here for a rough test," said he, selecting a pipette and a slide from the case. He dipped the former into the flask and, having sucked up a few drops of the alcohol from the bottom, held the pipette over the slide on which he allowed the contained fluid to drop.

Laying a cover-glass on the little pool of alcohol, he put the slide on the microscope stage and examined it attentively, while we watched him in expectant silence.

At length he looked up, and, addressing the inspector, asked: "Do you know what felt hats are made of?"

"I can't say that I do, sir," replied the officer.

"Well, the better quality hats are made of rabbits' and hares' wool—the soft under-fur, you know—cemented together with shellac. Now there is very little doubt that these cinders contain shellac, and with the microscope I find a number of small hairs of a rabbit. I have, therefore, little hesitation in saying that these cinders are the remains of a hard felt hat; and, as the hairs do not appear to be dyed, I should say it was a grey hat."

At this moment our conclave was interrupted by hurried footsteps on the garden path and, as we turned with one accord, an elderly woman burst into the room.

She stood for a moment in mute astonishment, and then, looking from one to the other, demanded: "Who are you? and what are you doing here?"

The inspector rose. "I am a police officer, madam," said he. "I can't give you any further information just now, but, if you will excuse me asking, who are you?"

"I am Mr. Hickler's housekeeper," she replied.

"And Mr. Hickler; are you expecting him home shortly?"

"No, I am not," was the curt reply. "Mr. Hickler is away from home just now. He left this evening by the boat train."

"For Amsterdam?" asked Thorndyke.

"I believe so, though I don't see what business it is of yours," the housekeeper answered.

"I thought he might, perhaps, be a diamond broker or merchant," said Thorndyke. "A good many of them travel by that train."

"So he is," said the woman, "at least, he has something to do with diamonds."

"Ah. Well, we must be going, Jervis," said Thorndyke, "we have finished here, and we have to find an hotel or inn. Can I have a word with you, inspector?"

The officer, now entirely humble and reverent, followed us out into the garden to receive Thorndyke's parting advice.

"You had better take possession of the house at once, and get rid of the housekeeper. Nothing must be removed. Preserve those cinders and see that the rubbish-heap is not disturbed, and, above all, don't have the room swept. An officer will be sent to relieve you."

With a friendly "goodnight" we went on our way, guided by the station-master; and here our connection with the case came to an end. Hickler (whose Christian name turned out to be Silas) was, it is true, arrested as he stepped ashore from the steamer, and a packet of diamonds, subsequently identified as the property of Oscar Brodski, found upon his person. But he was never brought to trial, for on the return voyage he contrived to elude his guards for an instant as the ship was approaching the English coast, and it was not until three days later, when a hand-cuffed body was cast up on the lonely shore by Orfordness, that the authorities knew the fate of Silas Hickler.

"An appropriate and dramatic end to a singular and yet typical case," said Thorndyke, as he put down the newspaper. "I hope it has enlarged your knowledge, Jervis, and enabled you to form one or two useful corollaries."

"I prefer to hear you sing the medico-legal doxology," I answered, turning upon him like the proverbial worm and grinning derisively (which the worm does not).

"I know you do," he retorted, with mock gravity, "and I lament your lack of mental initiative. However, the points that this case illustrates are these: First, the danger of delay; the vital importance of instant action before that frail and fleeting thing that we call a clue has time to evaporate. A delay of a few hours would have left us with hardly a single datum. Second, the necessity of pursuing the most trivial clue to an absolute finish, as illustrated by the spectacles. Third, the urgent need of a trained scientist to aid the police; and, last," he concluded, with a smile, "we learn never to go abroad without the invaluable green case."

ALSO FROM LEONAUR
AVAILABLE IN SOFTCOVER OR HARDCOVER WITH DUST JACKET

MR MUKERJI'S GHOSTS *by S. Mukerji*—Supernatural tales from the British Raj period by India's Ghost story collector.

KIPLINGS GHOSTS *by Rudyard Kipling*—Twelve stories of Ghosts, Hauntings, Curses, Werewolves & Magic.

THE COLLECTED SUPERNATURAL AND WEIRD FICTION OF WASHINGTON IRVING: VOLUME 1 *by Washington Irving*—Including one novel 'A History of New York', and nine short stories of the Strange and Unusual.

THE COLLECTED SUPERNATURAL AND WEIRD FICTION OF WASHINGTON IRVING: VOLUME 2 *by Washington Irving*—Including three novelettes 'The Legend of the Sleepy Hollow', 'Dolph Heyliger', 'The Adventure of the Black Fisherman' and thirty-two short stories of the Strange and Unusual.

THE COLLECTED SUPERNATURAL AND WEIRD FICTION OF JOHN KENDRICK BANGS: VOLUME 1 *by John Kendrick Bangs*—Including one novel 'Toppleton's Client or A Spirit in Exile', and ten short stories of the Strange and Unusual.

THE COLLECTED SUPERNATURAL AND WEIRD FICTION OF JOHN KENDRICK BANGS: VOLUME 2 *by John Kendrick Bangs*—Including four novellas 'A House-Boat on the Styx', 'The Pursuit of the House-Boat', 'The Enchanted Typewriter' and 'Mr. Munchausen' of the Strange and Unusual.

THE COLLECTED SUPERNATURAL AND WEIRD FICTION OF JOHN KENDRICK BANGS: VOLUME 3 *by John Kendrick Bangs*—Including twor novellas 'Olympian Nights', 'Roger Camerden: A Strange Story', and ten short stories of the Strange and Unusual.

THE COLLECTED SUPERNATURAL AND WEIRD FICTION OF MARY SHELLEY: VOLUME 1 *by Mary Shelley*—Including one novel 'Frankenstein or the Modern Prometheus', and fourteen short stories of the Strange and Unusual.

THE COLLECTED SUPERNATURAL AND WEIRD FICTION OF MARY SHELLEY: VOLUME 2 *by Mary Shelley*—Including one novel 'The Last Man', and three short stories of the Strange and Unusual.

THE COLLECTED SUPERNATURAL AND WEIRD FICTION OF AMELIA B. EDWARDS *by Amelia B. Edwards*—Contains two novelettes 'Monsieur Maurice', and 'The Discovery of the Treasure Isles', one ballad 'A Legend of Boisguilbert' and seventeen short stories to cill the blood.

AVAILABLE ONLINE AT **www.leonaur.com**
AND FROM ALL GOOD BOOK STORES

Milton Keynes UK
Ingram Content Group UK Ltd.
UKHW030909271124
451618UK00013B/347/J

9 781916 535923